T0304814

LAST WITNESS

LUCIE WHITEHOUSE

ORION

First published in Great Britain in 2024 by Orion Fiction
an imprint of The Orion Publishing Group Ltd
Carmelite House, 50 Victoria Embankment
London EC4Y 0DZ

An Hachette UK Company

1 3 5 7 9 10 8 6 4 2

A CIP catalogue record for this book is
available from the British Library.

ISBN (Hardback) 978 1 3987 0924 9
ISBN (Export Trade Paperback) 978 1 3987 0925 6
ISBN (Audio) 978 1 3987 0928 7
ISBN (eBook) 978 1 3987 0927 0

Typeset by Born Group
Printed and bound in Great Britain by Clays Ltd, Elcograf S.p.A.

MIX
Paper from
responsible sources
FSC
www.fsc.org   FSC® C104740

www.orionbooks.co.uk

For Charlotte Drake and
Caroline Sampson

Chapter One

In normal times, the low arch over the entrance to the little car park kept out caravans and campers, but this morning it had blocked Forensics. Forced to park on the verge outside, the CSIs in their white suits were coming and going in full view of every gawping driver on Yardley Wood Road, the terrace of houses opposite and eight or nine benighted souls waiting at the bus stop. Robin had just seen two of them scuttle out of the shelter to take pictures they'd probably posted to social media already.

The wind buffeted the car again. No point even trying to get an umbrella up – as they'd arrived, it had snatched one from a man on the pavement and sent it flying across the road; she'd braked just in time. They'd have to hope that in the wood, the trees would offer a bit of protection.

More than they had last night.

Bracing herself, she opened her door and ran to the back of the car. A second later, a hand clamped to her cap, Detective Sergeant Malia Thomas joined her under the boot's slim wedge of shelter. Robin passed her a suit, then tore open the packet of her own with her teeth, remembering too late how much Malia hated that. 'Paranoid about teeth,' she'd explained before, to Robin's surprise. She was thirty-five and very fit, especially for someone who worked sixty-hour weeks and regularly ate at the station canteen. Her teeth looked enviable, frankly, like the rest of her.

Earlier, Malia had been updating her on the domestic homicide the team was handling when Robin had seen Samir come through the incident room doors. He'd rapped a knuckle on her office door, face grim. 'Response had a call to Moseley Bog just before eight,' he'd told them. 'Man who braved this,' he'd nodded towards the window, 'to take his dog out and found a body. White male, young.'

'How young?'

'Very. Probably still teenage, they think.'

Robin's heart had dropped. Teenage. Again. Yet another life over before it really had a chance to get started. 'Stabbed?' she'd said. Knife crime was so epidemic in Birmingham now that, with young victims, the question had become a reflex.

But Samir had touched his fingertips lightly to his temple. 'No, it sounds like a head injury.'

'Any ID?'

'Not yet.'

The wind drove waves across the puddles as they hurried, heads down, towards the uniformed PC at the gate to the woods. There were uniforms at every entrance; Response had closed the whole park.

Trapped like an air pocket between central Birmingham to the north and mile upon mile of semi-suburban streets to all other points, Moseley Bog was the patch of ancient woodland that had inspired the Old Forest in *The Lord of the Rings*. Tolkien had grown up nearby and played here, a fact Robin had known since she'd traipsed behind her parents on Sunday walks during her own childhood (it was called The Dell then, though). Now, years later, she walked here again, this time with *her* teenage daughter, Lennie. They'd come the weekend before last, Robin hoping in vain that the magic of the place on a crisp autumn afternoon would lift Len's alarming new depression, if only for an hour or so.

The Lord of the Rings vibe was strong today. Within a minute, the woods had swallowed the sound of traffic and distant sirens, severing their ties to a Monday morning in 2018 and plunging them back in time. The place had always felt ancient, with its witchy self-seeded trees, their arthritic branches making tunnels over the paths. After being thrashed all night by the wind, most of them were near-naked now. The November light made everything sharp-edged, while the rain drenched it with colour: evergreen ivy and laurel, luminous moss, russet beech leaves underfoot. The air had an iron tang.

The park had open spaces, too, but at the fork in the path, the uniform's directions took them deeper into the woods instead. The tree cover grew thicker, and where the Bog earned its name and the ground grew spongy, the path was replaced by wooden boardwalks that made their footsteps echo. 'Trip trap, trip trap – the Billy Goats Gruff went over the bridge,' Lennie had intoned dully last weekend. When she'd been five and six, she'd asked for that story a lot. 'Up jumped the troll,' Robin would growl and she'd squeal in horrified delight.

After a couple of minutes, muted voices reached them through the trees, and rounding a bend in the path, they saw an electric-blue forensics tent at the edge of a clearing. Among the thousand shades of green and brown, it was like something beamed in from a different century, a poor man's Tardis. Very poor – the wind blew again and its canvas sides billowed as if to illustrate its flimsiness.

CSIs moved among the trees, just as alien. Robin and Malia gave their names for the scene log and ducked under the cordon.

As they crossed the clearing, Robin looked for evidence markers or stepping plates protecting footprints and saw none.

Another uniform unzipped the tent for them. Inside were two white-suited figures: the scene manager, Rafferty, and, kneeling, oblivious to their arrival and murmuring softly as he examined one of the victim's hands, pathologist Olly Faulkner, known as Aslan among the Homicide teams for his gentleness and leonine blond head.

The boy lay on his side, his back to them, one cheek pressed against the shoulder of the arm extended above his head. His hair was dark with rain, his baggy jeans and thin black hoodie plastered to his body so that his ribcage and his upper shoulder blade were clearly delineated. Robin's first thought – ridiculous – was that he must be freezing; they had to get him warm as quickly as possible. Her second was an image of his mother yelling at him to put a coat on as he slipped past her and out the door for the last time.

Next to her, Malia sighed and Faulkner looked up. He laid the hand slowly back down and stood to make room for them.

From the entrance, you could just about choose to imagine the boy was unconscious, conked out here after a night of underage drinking. As soon as you saw his face, however, no amount of wishful thinking would help you. Robin's first impression was of red – red and purple and grey against a bloodless deathly pallor.

Oh God, his eye.

Of all the injuries she saw, the ones to the head and face were the worst. A back was a back, a leg was a leg, but your face made you a person, your eyes showed your spirit and humour, your character. The boy's eye had burst, no longer an orb but a sinewy gelatinous mess.

She focused on detail to suppress the horror. Whatever he had been hit with – something two or so inches wide, she'd guess – had caught him diagonally from the temple that was uppermost as he lay now. The temple had been the first point of impact: the bone at the outer edge of his eye was smashed inward, the socket broken, then his nose. Blood had congealed inside his nostrils, almost black, and in the lower corner of his eye where the lid was unsupported, but, given how much blood there must have been, his face looked clean. The rain – as he'd lain here, it had washed his face.

Her own voice seemed to reach her from a distance. 'I've seen him before.'

Malia startled. 'Have you?'

'Definitely. Does he look familiar to you?'

'I don't think so, but given how badly he's hurt . . .'

Robin looked at Faulkner and Rafferty.

Faulkner shook his head, but Rafferty nodded. 'Same as you,' he said, Black Country accent making it *yow*. 'I've seen him somewhere.'

'Was it work?' Robin asked. 'Another case?'

He frowned. 'I don't know.'

'It must have been an almighty whack,' said Faulkner.

'With what, do you think?'

Rain spattered across the canvas overhead like a handful of gravel. Faulkner came closer and bent slightly to indicate the boy's temple with a gloved pinky. 'The skin here was split by the impact, not cut, so the weapon wasn't sharp. Long, though, or long-ish. I think it came in sideways, like this.' He mimed what looked like a baseball swing, double-handed.

'Could it have *been* a baseball bat?' Robin asked.

'Possible width-wise, but there are these, too.' He pointed at a scratch she'd noticed on the boy's forehead and another on his cheek. 'Could have been made by twigs on a bigger branch.'

'Did they happen at the same time?'

5

Faulkner frowned. 'That I can't tell you.'

'He was here in the dark and the wind – could a branch have swung out and caught him?'

'In theory, but Rafferty and I had a careful look outside and there's no obvious candidate – most of what's immediately around is too small and scrubby.'

'Maybe he was hurt nearby and staggered here?' suggested Malia.

Faulkner tipped his head from side to side. 'I won't know if death would have been instant or not until I've seen the brain.'

Robin said a silent prayer that it had.

'Either way, he couldn't have gone very far,' Faulkner said. 'There's also this.' He pointed at the ground near the boy's trainers. Around his left foot, the leaves were disturbed and showed a visible, though rain-flattened, arc in the mud. 'He twisted as he went down, which would be consistent with being spun round by the force of a blow.'

Robin saw it in her mind's eye, from the outside and the boy's own perspective almost simultaneously: a branch coming out of the dark, a flash of blinding light, then – in slow motion – the half-turn as his body absorbed the energy, teetered between worlds, and collapsed to the ground. She closed her eyes for a moment.

'How about time of death?' She'd imagined it in the dark, she realised, but she didn't know that yet.

'Well, the rain complicates things from a body temperature point of view,' Faulkner said, 'but it might help us, too. Look.' One hand on the boy's upper shoulder, the other on his hip, he rolled his body very gently two or three inches backwards. The leaves underneath were dry.

Robin glanced at Malia. 'What time did it start last night?' Exhausted, she'd fallen asleep on the sofa the minute she'd finished her dinner. She'd woken after midnight to find that Lennie had turned off the TV, put a blanket over her and gone to bed. When she went upstairs herself, the rain had been hammering on the landing skylight so hard, she'd been amazed the carpet underneath was still dry. Ludicrously, she'd felt a bit proud: look at her, living in a watertight house.

Malia glanced at Faulkner, she noticed. 'About ten o'clock?'

'Yes, I'd say so.'

Outside the tent, there was a distant shout. Then, a minute later, another voice, much closer by.

Rafferty picked a careful path to the opening and stepped outside. 'What is it?' They heard feet approaching across the leaves and some mumbled words. 'Thanks.'

When Rafferty reappeared, he was carrying an evidence bag, something dark inside. He held it out to her – a canvas wallet open to a short array of cards. One, a driving licence, had been pulled up from its slot to show the thumbnail photograph and, looking closer, she saw the boy now lying at their feet.

When she read the name, she frowned. It was familiar but— *Oh, shit.*

Malia and Olly Faulkner were staring at her.

'It's Ben Renshaw,' she said.

'Ben . . .?'

'One of the lads from the Heywood case.' She waited for them to make the connection and, sure enough, a second or two later, Malia's horrified expression told her she had.

'You mean, the witness? One of the ones who set up that website?'

'Oh, Jesus,' said Faulkner.

It was the first time Robin had ever heard him swear.

*

7

They trip-trapped back over the boardwalk without speaking. Robin guessed Malia was doing the same as she was, realising the extent of the situation they'd just been plunged into, trying to remember as much as she could about the earlier case. *Cases.*

Because they hadn't been homicides, her team had had nothing to do with them on a professional level, but if you'd been in Birmingham last year when the first one had gone to trial, you'd have struggled to avoid hearing about it even as a member of the public. It had been the *Birmingham Post*'s lead story for days, *Midlands Today*'s too, and Robin had heard people discussing it everywhere she went: Tesco, the pub, the mortuary. At a fundraising event at Lennie's school, three other parents had tried to shake her down for insider information, one of them with enough edge on his voice to let her know he'd heard the rumours about West Midlands' handling of the situation and believed every one of them.

Her phone buzzed in her jacket pocket as a text message arrived. As usual now, whatever else was going on, her first thought was Lennie. She unzipped the white suit and reached for it.

Hi R, Seeing pics of CSIs at M Bog on social – and looks like your car? SK

Sara Kettleborough, the *Post*'s chief crime correspondent. Already – bloody hell.

Robin swiped the message away and went to her recent calls. She'd planned to wait until they were back at the car, out of the rain, but if Sara was on it, there was no time to waste.

Samir picked up almost immediately. 'Hey.' He was alone, the word told her, and just for a moment, she let the intimacy in his voice surround her. 'How was it?'

'Well,' she said, 'we've got an ID.'

'Good.' In the case that had dominated their summer, the victim hadn't been identified for some time.

8

'No, it's not. It's really not.'

'Tell me.'

As she knew he would, he recognised Renshaw's name immediately.

'Oh God, Rob.'

'I know.'

For a few seconds, neither of them spoke. She could picture his face as he processed it, brain mapping the ramifications.

'I want to tell his family,' she said, 'I don't want to leave it to Uniform. I want them to know straight away that we're on this – Homicide in particular, I mean.' *As opposed to the part of CID that's already failed them so completely.*

'Agreed about us,' he said, 'but let me do it.'

'No, I'm SIO.' She glanced at the back of Malia's head. 'Unless this changes that?' She pressed the phone hard against her ear to try to contain his voice.

'Of course not,' he said. 'If you weren't already on it, I'd give it to you, everything being equal. It's just . . .' He paused and when he spoke again, his voice was quieter. 'Look, the only reason I'd hesitate about you leading . . . No, I wouldn't, I'm not. But be careful. Please.'

'Of course,' she said, matter-of-fact, masking her hurt from him as well as Malia. *I'm not a bull in a china shop, Samir,* she wanted to tell him, *you can trust me to be diplomatic, believe it or not. Even I can see it's going to be a political minefield.* It wasn't difficult: in the seven years she'd been leading investigations, with her old job in London at the Met and now with West Midlands, no other case had screamed 'hornets' nest' as loudly and immediately as this.

As so often, he knew what she was thinking anyway. 'I don't mean it like that, you know I don't.' His voice dropped again. 'I mean, look after *yourself.* You're so close now – just two more

9

weeks and Len'll be home and dry. So do your job but don't take any risks and don't – repeat, *don't* – stick your head over the parapet. You're vulnerable and we've already seen the rules of engagement here. If this is the same people, they're going to fight tooth and nail. Tooth and *claw*.'

Chapter Two

The Renshaws' address was just over a mile away, in a largely residential patch bordered by Alcester Road and Billesley Common. Long and wide, the street was lined with semi-detached houses with bay windows and Tudorbethan gables set back from the pavement behind small front gardens or off-road parking. In the driving rain, late Monday morning, the pavements were empty, the only visible living soul an elderly man watering houseplants in his glassed-in porch.

When she'd first moved back to Birmingham, Robin had quailed at streets like these. In London, where she'd fled at nineteen, she could lose herself in the scale of the place, the height of the buildings, the busyness, but stretching for miles in all directions, everything two storeys or three at most, these streets had made her feel exposed, as if something might come screeching out of the sky to carry her off, Daenerys Targaryen-style.

Today, though, *she* was the one swooping, intent on destruction, her black umbrella like a judge's black execution cap.

The front of the house was well cared for, if not as pimped up as some they'd passed, all herringbone parking spots and palms in terracotta planters. The silver Volvo outside the bay window was clean but nine or ten years old.

Malia rang the bell and they heard it chime inside. When it died away, all they could hear was the wind.

Robin's phone buzzed, Sara Kettleborough again but calling now. She hit *Ignore*.

A few seconds later, the inner door was opened by a man of about fifty wearing chinos, a shirt and tie – work gear, though it was past eleven and he was still at home. As he reached for the outer door, she caught his eye through the glass and saw that, despite their plain clothes, he knew what they were. How many times had he answered the door to detectives over the past year and a half?

'Roger Renshaw?'

He had to clear his throat before he could answer.

'Detective Chief Inspector Robin Lyons, and this is DS Malia Thomas. Could we come in, sir?'

He closed his eyes briefly but nodded.

From behind him, a slim woman in a navy skirt and polo neck appeared. Emma Renshaw, Ben's mother. She looked at them, eyes wide, then reached to touch his arm. 'Roger?'

He looked at her and nodded again. 'Detectives, love. Senior.'

Malia glanced at Robin. She'd heard it, too, the lack of surprise. They hadn't reported Ben missing – on the way over, Malia had called the station to check – but they'd known something wasn't right. Hence their work clothes, Robin thought: they knew he hadn't come home, but they'd been praying for a different explanation, still hoping to catch him sneaking in, read him the riot act, then head off to work. Instead, here *they* were, detectives.

Inside, the quiet seemed condensed, the air still and heavy. *Stop all the clocks.* It was also chilly: of course, because they'd usually be out during the day, the heating was off. A faint smell of yesterday's supper lingered, though – beef stew, maybe shepherd's pie, something warm and familial.

Wordlessly, the Renshaws led them through an archway on the left into a pale-blue sitting room. In normal circumstances, and ten degrees warmer, it would be nice, comfortably large enough for the two sofas that faced each other over a glass coffee table stacked with books. The built-in shelves were crammed with books, too – both the senior Renshaws were teachers, she remembered.

Emma Renshaw directed Robin and Malia towards one sofa, then took the other. When her husband sat down next to her, she squeezed his hand so hard, her knuckles whitened. Like him, she had a fine-boned face, and though she was attractive now, Robin could already see how she would look when grief had done its full number on her, when her cheekbones were exaggerated, her eye sockets grey and hollow from lack of sleep and appetite.

Robin leaned forward and spoke as gently as she could. 'Mr and Mrs Renshaw, a young man's body was discovered earlier this morning in the woods at Moseley Bog. I'm so sorry, but we have good reason to believe it's Ben.'

For a moment, Emma Renshaw seemed frozen, but then, as if the news had been a physical blow to her stomach, she hunched over, face in her hands, forehead touching her knees. Her shriek was muffled but even so, it sent a shiver down Robin's spine. The bleakness – because everything was lost.

Roger's reaction was silent. Eyes wide, he stared and then he began to shake, not just his hands but his arms and upper body, his lower lip. The movement in his body became more exaggerated, seeming to start low and rise up through his torso. When he gagged, they realised what was happening. Hand clamped over his mouth, he surged from the sofa and out of the room. Running steps in the hall and then, from the back of the house, they heard violent vomiting. Malia stood and went after him.

Whether Emma was aware he was gone or not, Robin couldn't tell. Her face was still in her hands and now her body was heaving, not like her husband's, but as if she was screaming silently, the terrible sound of the first shriek converted into great racking movements that Robin knew from experience would leave her aching as if she'd been beaten up. It was a minute, maybe two before she choked the word, 'How?'

'We'll need the post-mortem to confirm, but it looks like a head injury, a single blow. We think it would have been very quick.' The one crumb of comfort she could offer, dropped into the void.

Waves of shivers now as if she were bitterly cold, and Robin saw the image of her son as he'd lain on his carpet of leaves, the thin wet hoodie clinging to his shoulder blades.

Emma started keening, long ragged sounds of despair.

'Mrs Renshaw,' Robin said, 'my team and I will do everything in our power to find out what happened to him.'

For what felt like a long time, Emma said nothing, but then, with a sudden strangled noise, she reared upright, face streaming with tears. 'Will you?' Her eyes were wild. '*Will* you? The Heywoods terrorised us, *terrorised*, and . . .' She stopped, overtaken by another wave of misery.

'I know it must have felt—'

'And you,' she choked, 'the police – did *nothing!*'

Robin searched for the right thing to say and came up empty.

'They've killed him now,' Emma Renshaw crooned. 'They've killed him. They've killed my baby.'

Chapter Three

West Midlands Police had plenty of interesting stations –
the white Italian baroque number in Digbeth, though yards
from the grungy Rag Market, had an honest-to-God turret,
and Steelhouse Lane had been a stunner, too, Georgian and
elegant, before it was turned into a museum a couple of years
back. Now it traded on its history as the lock-up where the real
Peaky Blinders had cooled their heels.

By contrast, Rose Road, Force Homicide's base in Harborne,
was neither old, beautiful nor possessed of an interesting
history. A nondescript modern red-brick building on an otherwise residential street, there was nothing about it, bar the
blue lamp and signage, to say it wasn't a call centre or any
other bog-standard white-collar business. In recent months,
however, Robin had come to think of it as like Birmingham
itself: not flashy or attention-seeking but straightforward and
hard-working. It got the job done.

For now. Thanks to the hatchet the government had taken
to their budget, plans were afoot to close and sell off twenty-
odd more stations across their patch, Rose Road among them.
Give it two or three years and it likely *would* be a call centre.

Until then, her team was on the uppermost of the three
floors, and as she climbed the stairs, the rather-you-than-me

tone of a 'Ma'am' from one of Webster's DCs told her the news had begun to filter through the building. It could only be minutes until someone dropped a journalist 'friend' a text with Ben's name, if it hadn't already happened.

Malia had called ahead to get everyone together for a briefing, and the hum in the incident room was audible from the top of the stairs. As soon as Robin pushed through the door, Tark, aka DC Les Hargeaves, Half Man Half Chair, reached for his notebook, then, without standing, propelled himself backwards from his desk, through a neat ninety-degree turn and forwards into the area in front of the board, bagging his usual spot dead centre. That keystone *in situ*, other people started filling the space around him, rolling their chairs over or sitting on the desks behind.

DC Varan Patel was at the board, pinning a map of Moseley Bog next to the scene photos. He'd also printed off a head-and-shoulders photograph and Robin went to look at it.

The photographer had caught Ben looking directly into the lens, with the effect that he seemed to be looking out of the picture, seeking eye contact. His own eyes had been large and green-brown and, at least in this picture, faintly imploring. *Here I am*, he seemed to say, *me and my imperfect teenage skin, no hiding, no artifice. Talk to me – confide in me.*

Dry, his hair was lighter than it had looked in the wood, the sort of brown that would turn blond at the temples by the end of a summer, although it hadn't been summer when the picture was taken. His skin had probably been better after a bit of sun, too, but, regardless, he'd been good-looking in a way that she guessed had made him popular with girls his age: full lower lip, arched eyebrows that suggested mischief but no real threat. The word 'cute' came to mind, Corey Haim in *The Lost Boys* grown a couple of years older.

Well, it was all gone now. The boy in the photograph *was* lost, his spirit and personality and everything he might have achieved reduced to a set of remains to be picked off the mud and taken away in a bag.

'You found this online?'

Varan nodded. 'On the *Post*'s website, guv. They did a big feature when StrengthInNumbers.com went live.'

Behind them, the team was quietening down, and when Robin turned, their twenty or so faces were sombre. Even DC Phil Howell, ever the graveside smirker, was wearing an appropriate expression. Possibly he'd just blown a few bob on a scratch card, though.

'Right,' she said, as the last drift of conversation died away, 'let's get started.' She always thought better with a pen in her hand, so she reached for a marker from the shelf under the board. 'As you've all heard, the body found at Moseley Bog this morning is Ben Renshaw,' she began. 'Aged eighteen as of three weeks ago.'

A faint murmur ran round the group at that and Tark bent his head, making a concertina of chins again his collar.

'A lot of you will have recognised the name, but for those who didn't, Renshaw was one of the key witnesses in the Alistair Heywood trial last year.' She looked at PC Dave Hanratty, who'd transferred from West Yorks in September. 'Heywood was at school with Ben. He raped another classmate of theirs, Molly Zajac, and Ben and his best friend, Theo Gillespie, gave the evidence that got him sent down.'

'For eight years' said Malia.

'Afterwards, the three of them – Ben, Theo and Molly – set up StrengthInNumbers.com, which you *will* have heard of, the site where people in sexual-assault cases share their stories.'

Looking round, she saw almost everyone nodding.

'The rape wasn't the only crime, though. Before Heywood's trial, Ben and Theo Gillespie and their families were harassed and intimidated for months, more and more violently.'

'Theo gave evidence in a wheelchair,' Tark, sitting next to Dave, told him. 'Hit-and-run – car mounted the pavement. He nearly lost a leg.' He sniffed as if he were trying to suck his brain back up his nose, and ran a finger under his eyes. The longer she worked with him, the more Robin thought of him as the heart of Homicide. For a man who looked like a Staffordshire Bull Terrier, albeit one committed to a sedentary lifestyle, he was soft as white bread; he'd earned 'Tark' by sobbing over *Tarka the Otter*. 'It definitely wasn't an accident – the car had false plates.'

'And no one was ever *arrested* for any of it, let alone charged.' Phil Howell got in on the outrage. 'Literally *months* of attacks.'

'True,' Robin said. 'Which a lot of people locally were very angry about.'

'*Are* very angry about,' said Tark. 'And can you blame them?'

She held up a hand. 'So this is already a very fraught situation. People are going to think they know who his killer is – or at least their surname – and a lot of them are going to demand know why West Mids didn't prosecute that person – or people – last year. Unfortunately, that includes Ben's parents.'

Roger Renshaw hadn't returned from the kitchen for several minutes. White-faced, he'd barely been able to speak until they'd stood up to leave. Then, voice low and shaking, he'd reached out and gripped Robin's arm. 'There's blood on *your* hands, too – the police. If you'd done your job – even *tried* . . .' His voice had run out.

'However,' Robin looked around, connecting with Phil and a couple of others she wanted to be sure were paying attention, 'we have to keep an open mind. Ben's killing could be *completely unrelated* to the earlier cases. Maybe this was a mugging gone wrong – someone attacked him for his wallet, then ditched it when they realised how hurt Ben was. Maybe Ben was fighting with someone or meeting someone in the woods, and either that person or someone entirely different attacked him. Maybe he was into something criminal. Until we know otherwise, everything's on the table.'

Behind the group, the door opened: Samir. He caught her eye and nodded before taking a spot on a desk at the back.

Robin glanced at Emily Shepherd, the new admin, and lo and behold, there she went, surreptitiously checking him out from under her blunt-cut fringe. Every bloody time. *He's married, love*, she wanted to say. *Has no one told you? Bad luck.*

'At the same time,' she continued, 'it being *Ben Renshaw* who was found dead this morning does feel like more than a coincidence.'

'Yeah,' said four or five voices, and again, almost every head nodded.

'And, given the history, our first priority has to be making sure Molly Zajac and Theo Gillespie are protected. If this *is* the reopening of hostilities, we can't let there be any more victims. This is our watch now.'

'Who are this family anyway, the Heywoods?' asked Dave Hanratty. 'Why *would* they get away with attacking these kids like that – or why would people think they could?'

'Because they're the local great and good.' Tark looked ready to spit on the carpet. 'Big-shot property developers, back and back for generations, loaded, super-connected.'

'So great and good,' said a female voice near the back, 'that even when they spawn a rapist, they just slither away scot-free.'

'Yeah, and it's not every Tom, Dick and Harry who can go round breaking legs to keep their rapist offspring out of jail.' Tark again.

'Stop.' Robin's voice was louder than she'd intended, but no harm done: let them get the message. She held up both her hands now. 'That's *enough*. I don't want to hear any of that again, understood? Yes, of course there should have been charges for what happened, and convictions. But the team who handled that case – they're West Mids, too, our colleagues. Think about it: if we say they didn't carry out a proper investigation' – she looked at Tark, eyebrows up – 'what are we implying? That they're incompetent?' She paused. 'Or bent?' He opened his mouth, but she shook her head. 'No. I won't hear that said by anyone on this team. Understood?'

Some muttering at the back, but more *Yeahs*, including from him.

'All right. The witness-intimidation is *not* our case, Ben's killing *is*, and if *we're* going to get a conviction, we have to be rock-solid. However much pressure we come under, we are going to conduct ourselves unimpeachably, and a major part of that is coming at this the right way: without preconceived ideas. Not least because we know that if this *was* the Heywoods, and their defence gets the faintest whiff we were "out to get them", their expensive QC will tear us apart. So, laser focus. New crime, brand-new set of leads to follow.'

She uncapped the pen and turned to the board.

'What do we know so far – hard facts? Ben was eighteen, in his final A-level year at the Summerfield School in Rotton Park. He lived at home with both his parents and his younger sister, Amy, who's fifteen.' The pen squeaked as she wrote.

'The Renshaws aren't ready for detailed questioning yet, but we're lucky: from what they could tell us, we're already looking at a pretty narrow window for time of death because they last saw Ben at about 8.45 p.m. yesterday when he went out, they thought, to visit a friend or friends. That time is give or take fifteen minutes, though, because Emma, his mother, was on the phone and didn't look at a clock.'

She'd sobbed as she'd told them. 'I wasn't paying attention – the last time I ever saw him.'

'He was dead, or at least lying in the position where his body was found, before the rain started last night, which we think – though to be confirmed – was just before 10 p.m.'

'His parents didn't worry that he wasn't home when they went to bed?' asked Varan, looking up from his notebook.

'No, because it wasn't unusual. He went round to his friends' a lot in the evenings, his mother said. The rest of the family are in bed by ten, but he was a night owl and they trusted him to be back by eleven, which was his curfew on a school night. He had his own key. They didn't realise anything was going on until this morning. When he didn't get up, his mum went to wake him, but his bed hadn't been slept in. She knew something was wrong immediately, she said, because he'd never stayed out overnight before without letting them know. She rang him, kept ringing – straight to voicemail. They got Amy off to school without panicking her, then started calling round. None of his friends said they'd seen him last night and none of them knew where he was.'

Robin tapped the board near the scene photographs. 'Obviously, one of the major questions is what he was doing at Moseley Bog last night. Why was he there? How did he get there? Was he meeting someone, and if so, whom? Did he go willingly, even, or did someone take him there?

'Unfortunately, the rain destroyed any footprints at the scene. I'd thought it would help us – mud – but the area's covered in leaves anyway, and even where it isn't, the rain was so hard, it wiped everything out. Maybe we'll get lucky with the wider search, where there's more tree cover.' She tapped the picture of

Ben's wallet. 'The lab's doing a rush job for us, but I don't think we should get our hopes up. Even if the killer was panicked enough not to wipe it, it's canvas, so not great for prints.'

'No sign of his phone yet, guv?' asked Varan.

She shook her head. 'The CSIs have got their work cut out, though – the undergrowth's very dense and the park's twenty-nine acres. And that's if it's there at all.

'First order of business, then: house-to-house round Moseley Bog and every bit of CCTV we can lay hands on, while it still exists.' A lot of shops and small businesses only had a single tape or two, and with every hour that passed, the odds increased that vital evidence would be recorded over. 'We need witness appeals on social, but we're not going to mention his name outside this room until we have the formal ID. This is a tight ship: no leaks, no mistakes.

'With luck, when we *do* name him, his profile will help – a lot of people will want justice for him, whoever his killer is. And that's what we owe him – West Midlands as a whole and us now particularly, this team. So let's get it for him.'

Chapter Four

Robin watched Samir negotiate the tide of people heading back to their desks, most of them only for long enough to grab phones and jackets. Years ago, in their late teens, they'd been together and, back then, her brother, Luke, had called Samir 'The Shirt', because he was so skinny, Luke claimed, his clothes billowed from the shoulders as if they were hanging on the line to dry. It wasn't true; for all his lightness of movement, Samir had always had muscle, but there was no denying that now, in his late thirties, he was much more substantial, strong-armed, deep-chested. God knows, her brother could never dream of looking as good in a suit. *His* life rarely required one, though, especially these days.

When Samir reached her at the board, they looked at the scene photographs together. 'You're going to need more people,' he said quietly, 'but the only way I can do it is by taking them from Webster.'

Subtext: prepare to be unpopular.

This was the part of his job Robin envied him least, which was saying something. As Head of Force Homicide, he'd largely transcended detective work and morphed into a politician and marshal of their wildly inadequate resources. West Midlands' manpower had been cut to the point where thousands of crimes that would normally merit proper prison time, such as burglaries, had just been written off for lack of anyone to investigate them, and even Homicide wasn't spared. Samir's work now reminded Robin of a recurring anxiety dream she'd had when Lennie was a baby, in which, mythological-punishment style, she was desperate for water but the pool from which she was trying to cup handfuls kept disappearing into the ground.

'We need security for Molly and Theo, too.'

He grimaced. 'I'll try.'

Robin's phone buzzed, Sara Kettleborough's name on the screen yet again. She showed him.

'Has she got his name?'

'I'm not sure, I'm dodging her until his parents have done the ID. But at least if she has, she won't run it without confirming with us.' Unless his family confirmed it, but Sara wouldn't doorstep them. She was an excellent reporter, almost always first with the big local stories, but she was respectful, too, you had to be in local news. National news was a different matter.

Samir nodded. 'Have you spoken to the SIO on the witness-intimidation yet?'

'No. I rang him from the car but got voicemail. I've left a message.'

The bustle behind them stilled abruptly and they turned at the same time to see Assistant Chief Constable Aidan Kilmartin standing in front of the double doors. Pulled up to his full five-feet seven, shoulders back, he was simultaneously scanning the room and displaying himself to maximum advantage, a pocket emperor on opening day at the Coliseum.

'Were you expecting him?' Robin asked under her breath.

'Negative.' Samir's lips didn't move.

Kilmartin located them at the board. 'A word,' he called. 'Both of you. Your office, DCS Jafferi.'

'Yes-*sir*,' Robin muttered.

Almost inaudibly, Samir shushed her.

They followed him out of the incident room and down the corridor. Robin kept her eyes fixed on the floor, averted from his flat little bottom in his too-tight trousers. Once, cruelly, her brain had imagined it naked (no great feat – the trousers were pretty explicit), wrinkled and white as the moon; she'd been off food for a fortnight.

In the small anteroom, Rona, Samir's PA, mouthed Robin a silent hello as they passed.

Once the door was closed, Kilmartin strode to his usual position in front of the window, which he liked for its framing effect. 'Right, well,' he said, stopping bang in the middle and extending his arms to grip the windowsill. 'What an utter shit-show this is.'

'The poor lad,' said Samir.

No acknowledgement from Kilmartin. 'You're leading, DCI Lyons?'

'Yes, sir.' She prepared to fight her corner. 'I know it's a fraught—'

'Good. I want you front and centre on this.'

Startled, she immediately began questioning his angle. In the eighteen months she'd been at West Mids, he'd made no secret of his misgivings about her. They were understandable, she had to admit: she'd first crossed his radar as a person of interest in a murder case, and she'd only returned to Birmingham at all because she'd got into hot water at the Met.

'In this situation,' he said, leaving Robin to supply the *only*, 'you're an asset. You have the summer case behind you, although, as you know,' he frowned, 'I wish you'd been more amenable about maximising that. Yes,' he stopped her, 'I heard why you didn't want to do the TV, but big wins are extremely valuable for positive public perception, especially now.'

It was hardly a 'big win', she wanted to say, *three people died*. But while she hadn't been willing to go full media show-pony, she saw his point about the eventual end of that case and some good publicity for a change.

'This is an opportunity, too,' Kilmartin said. 'We can salvage a PR disaster here.'

She couldn't resist a glance at Samir, who, with an infinitesimal widening of his eyes, warned her to keep her trap shut.

'I want you round at the Renshaws' ASAP, Lyons, as soon as we're done, no delay. We need to look visible.'

'I've already seen them, sir.'

'Have you?' His turn to be surprised. 'Well, all right, good. Optics, optics, optics, here more than ever.'

Optics. Robin barely refrained from rolling her eyes. Had the man ever heard a bit of PR jargon he hadn't immediately clutched to his bosom?

Kilmartin moved away from the window and paced with studied thoughtfulness, hands clasped behind his back.

'I also want you to be the contact with the Heywood family.'

'What?' It was out of her mouth before she could stop it. 'I mean, sir?'

'As you'll both know if you've had a chance to refresh yourselves on the history,' he looked at Samir, 'the Heywoods are very angry at their treatment by this Force.'

Samir's eyebrows drew together in a deep vee. 'Angry?'

'They say they were focused on to an unfair degree.'

'Their son *raped* someone,' said Robin.

'I'm talking about the witness-intimidation inquiry, DCI Lyons,' he said as if she were an imbecile. 'They felt targeted – in fact, Anne Heywood, Alistair's mother, used the word "hounded".'

'But—'

'*Hounded.* I don't want to hear that again, is that clear?' He paced for another moment, head bowed.

Robin and Samir looked at each other.

As if trying to catch them out, he spun around. 'When's your brother's sentencing, Lyons?'

Robin was thrown completely off guard. But of course he knew – how could he not? If it hadn't been common knowledge in Homicide anyway, Samir would have had to tell him.

'Two weeks today,' she said. 'The twenty-sixth.' The date loomed larger and larger every day, the first thing she thought of every morning now.

'So get this wrapped up before then. The last thing we want is that being used against you – I don't even want to *think* about the headlines. God, if we screw this up, the media will want our heads.' He pivoted to Samir, eyes narrowed. 'And I don't expect to be embarrassed by hearing anything for the first time elsewhere, Chief Superintendent. Any developments come straight to me, is that understood?'

Robin waited for the sound of the outer door, then eyeballed Samir. 'Two weeks? For a homicide – when the witness-intimidation has gone unsolved for a *year*?'

He shook his head. 'I wish I could say he was joking.'

'Why does he want me on this at all, Samir?'

'Because you're good.'

'No, come on. So are plenty of other people.'

'He told you himself, you've got the tailwind of the Gisborne Girl case and the other—'

'I've also got a brother on remand for violent disorder with white supremacists.' She'd had months to get used to it, but said aloud, it still shocked her to the core.

'Your *brother*, Robin. *He's* about to be sentenced,' Samir said, 'not you. And you've been totally frank about it.'

'Frank about *that*,' she said, voice barely a whisper. 'You said yourself on the phone: if this *is* the Heywoods, they're going to fight like hell, just like they did before, and if they come after me and find out about Lennie somehow, God forbid' – she felt sick – 'they won't hesitate. I'll lose her. I'll lose everything.'

Chapter Five

Summerfield was a medium-sized private school, but, architecturally, it looked more like a red-brick Oxbridge college. Set back from the road behind glossy black railings and a lawn fringed with rhododendrons, the main building had a central portico whose white pillars reached as high as the second-storey windows. Atop the central gable, the school flag – Robin assumed that's what it was – snapped in the wind as if the building were a ship leading the fleet. *Rule Britannia.*

She gave their names to the intercom and was asked to repeat them. At least two minutes passed before the gates slowly swung open. The driveway took them to the right of the building, where an actual fingerpost directed them to visitors' parking in a small courtyard edged with holly bushes.

They walked back past beds planted with shrubs Robin couldn't begin to name overlooked by tall sash windows. Hard not to compare it with Lennie's school. There was no lawn there or rhododendrons, just an asphalt moat separating a huge, more than slightly shabby sixties construction from an otherwise residential street. No flag, either; shoes thrown over telephone wires was more the vibe. And yet Ofsted graded it 'Good', she reminded herself. It was also free, whereas the fees here were twenty-four thousand a year, they'd just looked it up.

As Varan was reaching for the bell, Robin's phone buzzed: Malia.

'Someone's leaked his name, guv,' she said without preamble. 'It's on social media.'

Bugger. 'Are you with Molly yet?' Robin asked.

'Five minutes away.'

'Well, fingers crossed you get there first. We're probably lucky we've had this long. We'll do the formal release as soon as Ben's parents do the ID.'

As Robin ended the call, a woman in a pencil skirt and pale twinset came barrelling down the hallway visible through the spotless glass. She undid a heavy deadlock, then opened one of the double doors.

After a careful look at their warrant card, she stood aside to let them in, then locked the door again behind them. 'I'm Jane Booth, the school secretary. Please, follow me.'

Wooden boards lined the hallway, painted with names in gold: former headmasters and head boys, scholars. The largest boards, though, were just inside the double doors at the other end, the names arranged alphabetically, not by date like the others: Hastings, Haverton – three of those – Hepworth; two Shepherds, two Stirlings, a Stratford. She was reading the list of the school's Second World War dead. On the board opposite, 1914–1918, the lists were even longer.

Historically, Summerfield had been boys-only, but around the time Robin herself had been the right age, it had started taking girls for the final two years. She hadn't known any boys here, but a girl from her class had got a scholarship and left Camp Hill to come here. Now, as the mother of a teenage girl, it struck Robin as madness, for the final two years – the key, A-level years – to throw girls into a school full of hormone-drenched boys who'd been *Lord of the Flies*-ing it up there since kindergarten. Like tossing a piece of raw meat over the wall into a tiger enclosure. No, even if she won the lottery – and even without a recent rape case – she wouldn't send Lennie here.

The woman led them across a panelled vestibule and up a broad wooden staircase overlooked by beady-eyed oil paintings, all men. Doors off a wide balcony led to classrooms, judging by the single adult voices they heard as they passed. The air held the odd sense of pent-up energy that Robin remembered from being alone in the corridors when she was at school.

Jane Booth stopped outside a door with a plaque that read *Richard Atkinson MA (Cantab), Head of School*, and knocked discreetly. At a muffled 'Come', she opened the door and flattened herself against it. 'Detective Chief Inspector Robin Lyons and Detective Constable Varan Patel, Headmaster.'

'Thank you, Jane.'

Atkinson stood and came around his desk to shake their hands. He was in his early fifties with silver hair cut close to his head and pale blue eyes, the skin around which looked tight, as if he spent his weekends up crags in Snowdonia and was always slightly wind-burned. He was lean, in a worked-on sort of way, the kind of man, Robin thought, who would tell you his splits on the rowing machine and the grams of carbohydrate in any given protein bar at the faintest provocation. The hand he gave them was smooth, his crisp suit more businessman than academic.

Bar the computer and Atkinson himself, the room might have looked the same in 1945 – Robin could imagine the behemoth of a desk being used to plan the Normandy landings. The wall behind it was fitted with shelves, the top three full of leather-bound books that had likely been up there for decades even then. Table lamps cast circles of light onto a Turkish rug in faded blues and greens, and the air smelled faintly of coffee.

'Please.' He indicated the armchairs in front of his desk and withdrew behind it. 'How can we help, Chief Inspector?' He was playing it cool, demeanour unruffled, but his eyes were following them keenly.

'I'm afraid we've got some bad news, sir,' she said. 'As you may have heard, a body was discovered at Moseley Bog this morning.'

He pulled back, alarmed. 'A body? No, I hadn't.'

'We've just had the formal confirmation and I'm sorry to say, it's one of your students. Ben Renshaw.'

'Oh!' He put a hand to his mouth, then closed his eyes tightly and bent his head. 'Oh, no.' He took a deep breath in and let it out. After several seconds, he looked up, face grave. 'I'm so sorry to hear that – incredibly sorry. Can I ask . . . how?'

Robin told him and he shook his head in either disbelief or denial.

'Did you know him, sir? Personally, I mean.'

Atkinson nodded. 'Yes, much better than I can know the vast majority of our pupils on an individual level. He was one of our stars. He and Theo Gillespie both – we were, and are, very, very proud of them. Molly, too, of course, though she's not at Summerfield any more. This – it's a huge loss for the school.'

'Was that why you knew him better than most of your students, what happened before?' Robin asked.

'Yes. I talked to them numerous times, him and Theo.'

'It must have been a very difficult situation for the school.'

With a clink, he lifted the stopper from a cut-glass inkpot and turned it between his fingers, staring into it as if it were a crystal ball. 'The kind you hope you'll never have to deal with. That never happens, I mean, of course.'

She glanced at the wall clock. 'We'd like to speak to Theo Gillespie please. As soon as possible. The news is online, we've just heard, and we'd rather him not find out like that. With phones . . .'

He nodded, picked up the handset in front of him and hit a single button. 'Jane, could you ask Mr Dugmore to bring Theo Gillespie to my office, please? Straight away. My God,' he said, hanging up, 'are you worried that he's in danger, too?'

'Honestly, it's very early and we don't know. Had either of them spoken to you recently about anything worrying them?'

He shook his head. 'That wasn't the sort of relationship we had.'

'I meant if they'd had concerns about their safety, perhaps they came to you about security. We noticed you keep the front door locked.'

'That's standard procedure.'

'And the front gates.'

'Again, standard. We have young children on the premises, four- and five-year-olds.'

'Had Ben been involved in any trouble recently? Had he had any issues here – any disputes?'

'Not that I'd heard, and frankly, I'd have been extremely surprised. He was very popular, especially after what happened. He was kind, full of energy, generous with his time, and he and Theo put a tremendous amount of work into StrengthInNumbers – articles, interviews, school visits. They gave one of their presentations about it in a special assembly, it was impressive.'

'What impact did the rape have here?'

Despite himself, he flinched at the word, Robin noticed. 'In what way?' he said.

'Any that seems significant. An incident like that, the rape of one student by another—'

As if to stop her saying it, he cut in, 'I think it was what you'd expect: disbelief at first, dismay across the board. Summerfield is a close community, however, we pull together, so it was obvious to everyone that it was an isolated incident. Besides, it had nothing to do with the school. It happened at a boy's private home, at a weekend, at the very end of the school year when the Upper Sixth, Heywood's year, had finished their exams and weren't required ever to set foot on school property again.'

'But wasn't everyone at the party a student here?' said Varan.

Atkinson eyed him. 'Not *everyone*.'

'And *was* it an isolated incident?' Robin asked.

He turned his focus to her. 'There was only one assault, Chief Inspector.'

Assault. 'Of course,' she mollified, 'but in terms of the culture generally, especially with girls joining just for their final two years – if we asked them, would *they* say it was easy to be a student here?'

'Yes. I can assure you that our culture is one of equality and respect. Look, Alistair Heywood was found guilty and he's serving his sentence. End of story – the incident rests there. Alone.' His voice had risen and as if aware he'd sounded defensive, he modified it to add, 'We'll do everything we can to help, but there's no reason to think this has anything to do with the school.'

Footsteps on the balcony outside and a low male voice, then a female one – Jane Booth. A knock and then the door was opened by a man in his early forties in a blue-and-black checked shirt and black jeans. His hair was combed neatly from a side parting, his beard short and well-kempt, but his expression was stricken. His eyes flicked over them, then locked on Atkinson.

'Headmaster,' he said quietly, 'could I have a word?'

'Come in, Grant. These are detectives Chief Inspector Lyons and Constable Patel.'

'Grant Dugmore,' the man said, turning to them. Louder, his voice was deep. 'Head of Sixth Form. You're here about Ben.' It wasn't a question.

'You know?'

'I've just heard. At Moseley Bog . . .'

'*How* did you hear?'

'From Theo, just a moment ago. He checked his phone as we came down. Someone had tagged him on Twitter!'

'Oh, for the love of God.' Atkinson sat back in his chair, palms pressed together. 'Where is he now?'

'Next door with Jane.'

'How is he?'

Dugmore made an exasperated gesture, *How do you think?* Then, as if remembering whom he was talking to, 'As you'd expect, headmaster.'

'Bring him in, please.'

Dugmore looked as if he were about to protest, then thought better of it and left the room. It was a couple of minutes, however, before he ushered Theo in.

Robin's first impression was *small bear*. He was medium-sized, five ten or eleven, but solidly built, with a broad face topped with a shaggy load of very straight blond hair. He hadn't been wearing glasses in the picture she'd seen on Varan's screen back at the station, the *Post*'s feature about StrengthInNumbers. com, but today he had on heavy black frames that would have looked cool if the face behind them hadn't been utterly aghast, the skin pale as a church candle. He looked stunned, as if he was the one who'd just taken the blow to the head.

Varan stood and gestured to him to take his chair. Theo looked to Dugmore first for confirmation, then moved towards them as if underwater. Even at this speed, his limp was pronounced. His right leg took more or less normal steps but his left followed gingerly, touching the ground with far less than its fair share of his weight.

'Theo, I'm so sorry you heard like this,' Robin said. 'We'd hoped to reach you first.'

He stared blankly, she wasn't sure he'd even heard her. She remembered how it felt, profound shock, the sense of having been cut off from reality in an instant. She wished she could tell him that she understood, that she'd been where he was now, the post-nuclear landscape after your best friend's murder but bringing that part of her history to light would hardly inspire confidence.

'I only checked my phone to see if my girlfriend had texted,' he said, hands trembling.

'Mr Dugmore said someone tagged you on Twitter. Was it someone you know?'

He shook his head. 'I had thirty notifications – that's why I looked. It was a news blog, people retweeting.'

'This is a terrible shock,' Robin said, 'but time's very important here. We know some of your and Ben's history, but the sooner we have relevant information, the better our chance of catching whoever did this. Do you feel up to answering just a few questions?'

Theo's expression stayed blank, but he gave a small nod.

'Thank you,' Robin said. 'Theo, do you know why Ben might have been at Moseley Bog last night?'

'No.'

'You weren't with him?'

A headshake. 'No.'

'And he hadn't told you he was going?'

'No, he hadn't said anything about it at all.'

'Did he go there otherwise?'

'Sometimes. We both did.'

'Why?'

'Just to hang out. Smoke, sometimes.' He darted a look at Atkinson. 'Just cigarettes.'

'When was the last time?'

'I don't know.' He was crying now, swiping at the tears as if he was ashamed.

'Take your time,' she said gently.

He swallowed. 'September? Just after school started.'

'Would he go in there alone, do you think? In the dark?'

'I don't know. Maybe.'

'OK. Theo, had anything been worrying Ben?'

He didn't bother drying the tears this time. 'No. I mean . . . I don't think so.'

'Would he have told you if there was?'

'Yes. Yes.'

'Had either of you heard from the Heywood family recently?'

'Not since the trial, but that doesn't mean . . .' Now he broke down completely.

'Take a moment, Theo.' Dugmore, standing behind him, put a gentle hand on his shoulder.

A minute or more passed before he was able to speak again. 'Dominic Heywood . . . After the sentencing, he came to find us outside court. He said we'd pay for what we did to their family. "One way or another, sooner or later, you'll pay."'

Chapter Six

As she opened the warm, grease-spotted paper bag, the smell of pastry made Robin's stomach leap as if it were trying to reach up her throat and grab it.

Varan raised another bag into her eyeline. 'I got you two.'

'Thanks,' she said, through a mouthful. She hadn't had any lunch, or even breakfast, in fact the Greek yoghurt she'd brought in this morning was still unopened on her desk. As they'd turned onto King's Heath high street a few minutes ago, her stomach had rumbled loudly enough to be heard over Malia on speakerphone. Varan had pointed at a parking spot just ahead.

'Could you pull over?' he'd said.

'What?'

'Pull over.'

She'd done it, thinking he'd seen something, but before she could ask, he was out of the car. In the rear-view mirror, she'd watched him zip through the drizzle into Greggs. She'd decided to ignore the insubordinate issuing of orders by a junior officer and instead felt a burst of appreciation for the enigma that was Varan, whose character seemed to bend time – at least around her – so that sometimes, like now, he seemed older, nearly parental, other times, so young that although she was less than a decade older than him, she felt like *his* mum. He was almost thirty now, but he could still pass for teenaged. She made a point of driving when they were out together; in the passenger seat, with him at the wheel, she felt like Miss Marple.

The other plus of him riding shotgun was he could research as they went. Even without Kilmartin's ridiculous deadline, time was everything: if this afternoon was in fact the first the Heywood family heard of Ben's death, she wanted to be the one to break the news and witness their reactions.

While it was odd, Kilmartin's ordering her to be their contact did have its upsides. This afternoon, she could put down a marker, let them see who was in charge now and how things would work while she called the shots. She also wanted full knowledge of any exchanges with the family, in case they complained up the ladder. 'Hounded' indeed. *When* had Anne Heywood used the word? That was what she wanted to know.

'So, of the three in the youngest generation,' Varan said as she showered herself with pastry flakes, 'two have got criminal records.'

'Have they? Alistair, obviously, but who's the other?'

'Dominic, the eldest. Criminal harassment of an ex-girlfriend three years ago. She broke up with him and he clearly wasn't happy about it. Phone calls and abusive messages, kept turning up at her office and flat threatening her. Apparently he pissed through her new boyfriend's letterbox.'

'Risky – not one with spring hinges, I take it. What did he get?'

'Restraining order and a two-thousand-pound fine.'

'Hm. How old's he now?'

'Twenty-seven.'

'And the other brother?'

'Marcus, twenty-five. Nothing – he's either better-behaved or craftier than the others because he's the only man in the family who's managed to keep his nose clean. Heywood senior – William, known as Bill – was done for drunk-driving in 2012.'

'And what did *he* get?'

'Fined and lost his licence for a year.'

The bare minimum, then – what a surprise.

'If this *was* them, the obvious question is why now? What was the trigger? Alistair's trial was a year ago – the rape nearly eighteen months.'

'I wondered if it was the anniversary' – he flicked back in his notebook – 'but the trial started the twenty-sixth of November, ended the nineteenth of December. He was sentenced on the eighth of January.'

'So, *almost* a year, but not quite. It seems unlikely anyway, though, don't you think? If they'd got away with it so far, why draw attention by doing it on an anniversary?'

'Unless they wanted to make a point,' he suggested. 'Rub someone's nose in it, send a warning?'

'They're not the Mob.'

'If they're intimidating witnesses and whacking people, you could be forgiven for making the mistake.'

By the time she'd finished the second sausage roll and they'd reached the Heywoods', Varan had morphed into his teenage avatar. 'Whoa! That's all one gaff?'

'Yep.' Robin pulled in across the road. 'Though, again, you could be forgiven for making the mistake.'

In the haters' view (and not only theirs), Birmingham was a dystopian collection of post-war Brutalist arcades, sick-building tower blocks and shabby factories, sixty or seventy per cent of them derelict, all occupied – or abandoned – by people with the UK's worst accent. What the national media never mentioned was how green a city it was, especially here in the south and south-west. Moseley Bog was just one of tens of parks, commons and heaths of varying degrees of wildness and, as ever, the history lay close to the surface: the little local high streets and greens gave a strong sense of the old villages that had stood independently here before being engulfed by a city that had boomed and grown for more than a century before the bust came.

Birmingham's other open secret was its stock of large and beautiful houses, many of them Victorian or Edwardian Arts and Crafts. This particular patch had been developed by wealthy industrialists in Victorian times when the village of Moseley, naturally elevated, was still far enough from the city centre to escape the soot and grime belched out by the factories they owned. The streets were wide and tree-lined, the houses each different, often huge, with three or four storeys. It was more like genteel North Oxford than stereotypical 'Birmingham'.

The Heywoods' house had evidently belonged to one of the wealthiest industrialists. A mellow terracotta brick, it was three storeys high and stretched almost the full width of its substantial plot; going by the windows, the ground floor alone had five rooms overlooking the front garden, all of them huge. Six tall brick chimneys spiked up from various gables. If someone told you it was a boutique hotel, you wouldn't question it. A single black car was parked on the gravel drive, but there was room for seven or eight.

Robin locked hers and they crossed the road. It had finally stopped raining, but the air was chill, and a thick layer of racing cloud was closing the afternoon down too early; just as they'd parked, the street lights had flickered on. The mood suited the house. With its steep dark-tiled roof and long leaded windows, it had a definite gothic feel. Three gnarled yews on the lawn gathered the gloom around them.

No lights in any of the windows, but when they came under the porch, a dim glow behind stained-glass panels either side of the door suggested a lamp on in the hallway.

Varan pressed the button on a small brass plaque and they heard an actual bell ring inside.

'It's like *Downton Abbey*,' he said.

Robin's brain served up a memory of the first time they'd met, when Varan had come with Malia to interview *her*. Her parents' doorbell played an electronic Big Ben chime – she hoped he'd forgotten.

He was about to ring a second time when the light shifted behind the glass. For a few seconds, nothing happened and Robin peered into the little fish-eye on the door so whoever was looking would see her looking back. Then, glancing up, she saw the larger eye of a CCTV camera. A couple of seconds later, a metal bolt rattled.

The door opened on a petite woman in what were undoubtedly premium black leggings and a cloud-like cream mohair sweater that hung to mid-thigh. The feet on the parquet floor were bare and tanned, the nails done in the same burgundy as her manicure. As she tossed her head slightly to move her long brunette bob back from her face, it swung as a single sheet.

'Anne Heywood?' said Varan.

'Yes?'

Robin was slightly wrong-footed. Based on the old-fashioned name and her directorship at Heywood Properties, let alone her three grown sons, she'd expected a woman in the mould of Margaret Thatcher or one of those stern types with spiky no-nonsense hairdos whose very existence seem to imply that everyone else is vain and insubstantial. In the muted light, this woman looked if not soft, then at least young. Robin would have said she was thirty if that wasn't impossible: given that

Dominic, the letterbox pisser, was twenty-seven, she had to be nearly fifty at least. Either the devil had cut her a very good deal at the crossroads or she spent a fortune and many hours on physical upkeep.

'Detective Chief Inspector Robin Lyons,' she said, showing her warrant cards, 'and this is DC Patel. Could we come in?'

'DCI who?' Anne Heywood leaned out to look at it, and blinked as if taking a mental snapshot.

'Lyons,' Robin repeated firmly. She could smell alcohol in the air now.

The woman's eyes met hers unblinkingly. Then she took three short steps backwards, stopping within arm's length of the door. When they followed her in, she made no move to close it or to go any further inside.

They were standing in an entrance hall that was at least thirty feet long, and wood-panelled and beamed to the point of feeling oppressive. At either end were large fireplaces but the only furniture otherwise was a dark wood table that stood against the back wall, bookended by potted trees. There didn't seem enough natural light for plants, but perhaps on a brighter day, the sun pushed through the deep-set windows and flooded the place. It seemed unlikely. Pledge furniture polish – a scent deeply familiar from Robin's mother's house, a stranger to her own – perfumed the air. All it needed to be a boutique hotel were a discreet reception desk and some newspapers on sticks.

On the table were a bottle of white wine and a glass, near-empty.

Varan glanced at the open door as if worried that Greta Thunberg was about to appear and have a go at him about global warming.

'How can I help?' Anne Heywood said, her tone implying she'd rather die.

'We'd like to talk to you for a few minutes, please. Could we sit down?'

'I'm about to go out.'

Robin looked pointedly at her bare feet. 'Right. Well, we're here because a young man's body was found at Moseley Bog this morning.'

The woman frowned, not out of sympathy or regret, Robin realised when she opened her mouth, but confusion. 'Well, it's not one of mine because I spoke to two of them at lunchtime and the other one, as I'm sure you're aware, is in a young offenders institute.'

'I'm sorry, I didn't mean to imply that. The dead boy is Ben Renshaw.'

Another frown and then her expression changed to one of disbelief and outrage. 'You've got to be kidding me. I don't believe . . . You think we killed him!'

'Mrs—' Varan started.

Her eyes flicked his way before snapping back to Robin. 'You people . . . How dare you? How *dare* you come here and accuse me – *us* – of murder?'

'We're not accusing anybody,' Robin said calmly, maintaining eye contact, 'but your family's recent history with Ben means we do need to talk to you.'

The woman looked back at her, completely unintimidated. Her breathing had changed, Robin saw, and she was taking quick shallow breaths she was working hard to control. She was beyond angry – raging – but when she spoke, her words were carefully chosen.

'I'm sorry to hear about his death – anyone's – but I can assure you, DCI Lyons, that my family know nothing whatsoever about it. None of us have laid eyes on Ben Renshaw since his false testimony got my son convicted for a crime he didn't commit.'

'False or otherwise,' Robin said, 'you see why we need to speak to you.'

'I see why *you* think you do. Ever since that . . . cow accused my son, the police have treated this family like we're Myra Hindley and Fred West rolled into one. They accuse us of harassing them, trying to intimidate them – what a joke! *We're* the ones who've been falsely accused and harassed – *we're* the victims here. You've made our lives a *nightmare.*'

'Mrs—' Robin put out her hand, intending a calming gesture, but the woman ignored her.

'Alistair's life is *ruined.* What's he going to do now – or years in the future when he's finally released? University as a mature student, having to explain why he's older than everyone else? Who'd take him anyway, a convicted rapist?' Her face contorted with bitterness. 'And all because that stupid bi—' she stopped herself. 'Because he was stupid enough to have sex with some girl at a party who got embarrassed and cried rape.'

'Alistair's case isn't what we're talking about today, Mrs Heywood, or not directly.' Robin glanced out of the door towards the car, a Lexus. 'Is your husband at home? Or—'

'My family – those who aren't wrongfully imprisoned – are at work, Detective Chief Inspector.' She made the title sound like a slur.

Varan consulted his notebook. 'Would that be at the Heywood Properties offices in Colmore Row?'

She gave him a disgusted look. 'Yes. My two older sons are there. My husband's in Malmö.'

'Malmö?' asked Robin.

'It's in Sweden.'

'Indeed. I meant, *why* is he there?'

'For a meeting. He left yesterday morning if you need him to provide an *alibi.*' Biting scorn.

'We will. You, too, and we'll be speaking to Dominic and Marcus as well.'

Anne shook her head as if the situation beggared belief.

'Where were you yesterday evening, Mrs Heywood?' Varan asked.

'Here. I was here all day. I exercised and read the papers in the morning, then the boys and their girlfriends came over and I cooked Sunday lunch – roast beef and Yorkshire puddings, if you need that for your records, carrots and peas – and we had a quiet afternoon round the fire.'

'So you didn't leave the house at all?'

'Not yesterday, no – unless you count going into the garden to get logs. This morning, I had a meeting with an investor – a *former* investor – who won't do business with us anymore because of the bad publicity. That was pretty shitty, so I decided to take the afternoon off. And now here *you* are, West Midlands Police. *Again.*'

Varan wrote in his notebook. 'Is there anyone who can verify that? Someone outside the family?'

'My sons' girlfriends.'

He frowned. 'What time did they leave yesterday evening, your sons? If they did.'

'Of course they bloody did. They're in their mid-twenties, a bit old to be living at home with your mum, don't you think?' She looked at him pointedly.

'I don't know,' Varan said, unfazed. 'Property prices these days, if you're trying to save up a deposit . . .'

She snorted. 'They're not.'

'So what time did they leave?'

'Eight fifteen, eight thirty? You can check our security cameras if you feel so moved.'

'Thank you, yes.'

'You know, Chief Inspector,' she turned her attention to Robin, 'the Heywoods are an old Birmingham family, we're known here, we go back for generations, and if this persecution carries on, we'll be forced to take action.'

'I'm not sure what you mean, Mrs Heywood.'

'I mean that unless it ends, we'll be forced to make a complaint at the highest levels.' She locked eyes with her again. 'How would *you* like it if someone came after your family and poked into every minute detail of *your* lives?'

Robin felt a wash of alarm sweep her body. Could she know? No – she got a grip on herself – of course not: how could she, even about Luke? She'd never met her before; she'd only just pitched up on her doorstep.

She held her stare steadily. 'We'll send someone round shortly to collect the camera footage for both yesterday and today. If you *are* going out,' she nodded at the wine on the table, 'take a taxi.'

As they crunched back over the gravel, Robin had the distinct feeling of eyes on the back of her neck. When she turned to look, however, the unlit windows gleamed blankly, reflecting the cloud, giving nothing away.

'Well,' Varan said when the car doors were safely closed, 'she was nice.'

Chapter Seven

Recently, in the final few minutes before she saw Lennie, Robin had started to feel the same way she'd used to years ago when she'd been at work all day, Lennie at nursery or at home with Frances, their sweet landlady and babysitter. Back then, she'd had to stop herself galloping down the hazardous stone steps to their semi-subterranean 'garden flat' two at a time, so urgent was her need to see her daughter. As she'd been doing for months now, however, when Robin turned off the engine, she undid her seat belt and stayed where she was until she'd unclenched her teeth and assumed a neutral expression.

Two more weeks and she'll be home and dry.

She just had to keep everything together until then.

With a deep breath, she got out of the car.

As Robin waited on the Appiahs' doorstep, she heard two different lots of music: the *Stranger Things* theme from the sitting-room TV, Wu-Tang from the open window over her head. Wu-Tang would be Austin, but was it the Appiahs senior watching *Stranger Things* or Asha? She and Austin were sister and brother, Lennie's best friend and boyfriend, but Asha seemed to be spending more and more time with their friend Niamh these days or doing her own thing.

Their mother, Anne-Marie, opened the door, smiling. 'Hi.'

She came out and gave Robin a quick hug, pressing her briefly against her bosom, which tonight strained at the buttons of a lavender-coloured shirt. Bar the hairdresser and the dentist, Anne-Marie was one of the few people who touched her these days, Robin had realised recently. She was a social worker in child services, a job that even as a homicide detective she knew she couldn't handle; somehow Anne-Marie had managed it for eleven years without losing all faith in humanity. Her father had been a Brummie, but her mother was Trinidadian and she'd spent her childhood summers there; Austin said her annual trip back 'mended her soul'.

'Sorry, I'm later than I hoped.'

'Earlier than I thought you would be, to be honest. We've just seen you on the news.'

Robin nodded. After leaving Anne Heywood, she'd been back to the car park at Moseley Bog to record a witness appeal for the early-evening slot on *Midlands Today*. The public response hadn't yielded much so far, but maybe they'd be luckier with the ten o'clock.

Anne-Marie's earrings caught the light as she shook her head. 'His poor family, Robin.'

'It doesn't bear thinking about.'

Anne-Marie *was* thinking about it, though, Robin could see, just as she did herself every time they had a young victim: *There but for the grace of God.*

In June, as he'd walked home from their house one night, Austin had been viciously beaten up by a group of thugs. Enflamed by his Black Lives Matter T-shirt, apparently, they'd set about him, breaking his nose, cracking one of his ribs and causing deep abdominal bruising. God knows what would have happened if a passing car hadn't scared them off. No one had ever been arrested for the attack and now, as the months ticked by, it was less and less likely they would be. Another violent crime falling off the radar for sheer lack of police resources. It wasn't her fault, but Robin felt responsible nonetheless. Not just responsible: ashamed.

'If you're going to be working all hours, you know Len's welcome here,' Anne-Marie said. 'We can feed her, make up the futon in Asha's room.' Her eyebrows flicked.

When Lennie and Austin had first got together, Robin had girded herself for a cringe-making conversation, but in the event, she hadn't got further than, 'I wanted to have a word about the age difference . . .' when Anne-Marie had shaken her head. 'No funny business under my roof, don't worry. He knows that. He also knows the law, and she's underage.'

'Thank you,' Robin said now. 'That's kind.'

'Hold on, I'll give her a shout.' Anne-Marie turned and called up the stairs, 'Lennie, sweetheart, your mum's here.'

Nothing overhead for a moment, but then Austin called back, 'OK.'

'I'll wait in the car,' Robin said, 'give them some space.'

'Good to see you. And like I said, let me know if we can help.' Anne-Marie moved to go back inside, then paused. 'I'll let Len tell you the news of the day here.'

Oh no, was her immediate thought, *what now*? But if it was bad, she realised, Anne-Marie wouldn't leave her hanging. 'Good news?'

Austin's mother smiled. 'Yeah.'

Back in the car, Robin put the heater on and settled in for the long separation process, which these days activated the other strand of her disquiet as far as Lennie and Austin's relationship was concerned. She had no worries about Austin himself, he was great, about as bright and socially aware as any boy of seventeen she'd met, and on the sex front, anyway, her anxiety was more about wanting Len to avoid the mistakes she'd made. She'd got pregnant by accident when she was still at university, which was why now, at thirty-seven, she had a child who'd be sixteen next month while a lot of her contemporaries had toddlers. Not that Lennie was a mistake in any other way; Robin had been scared out of her wits, but she'd loved her fiercely from the day she was born.

No, what worried her was how close they'd become. She knew Austin adored Lennie, he looked at her with the same soft eyes Len did him, but these days her mood was so low and, with the exception of Dennis, Robin's dad, Austin seemed to be the only person who could lift it. Lennie had been born self-possessed, even as a small child she hadn't been clingy, but fear was eating away at her, Robin could see it, and she didn't want her to become reliant on anyone, let alone a seventeen-year-old boy; it would be terrible for them both, a disaster.

Robin could see them silhouetted in the glass front door now. Lennie was almost her own height, five seven, but Austin was so tall that when they hugged, he could rest his chin on her head. Lennie put her arms round his waist and angled her face up to kiss him.

Robin averted her eyes and watched in the rear-view mirror as a fox slinked across the road. Her phone rang, a London number she didn't recognise.

'Hello, this is Jeremy Handley from the *Record* in London. I understand you're leading the Renshaw investigation. I wondered if I could ask you about—'

'I'm sorry, no. The press office is handling all media enquiries for now. Thanks.' She cut him off. How the hell had he got her mobile number?

A few seconds later, he rang again, but she ignored him. The phone had been going all evening at the station; they'd released Ben's name officially just before *Midlands Today* at six and the first national paper had called within minutes.

She gave Lennie another few seconds, then sent her a text, *Oi! Home time.*

Fifteen feet away, her shadow daughter reached into her back pocket.

The two shapes melted together again briefly before the door opened and Len stepped out, heaving her backpack onto her shoulder, head down, feet dragging.

Robin's heart sank, hope dying that the news, whatever it was, might have lifted her spirits.

The door cranked open and Lennie landed in the passenger seat, backpack hitting the footwell with a thud.

'Hi, lovely.'

'Hi.' No eye contact.

'All right day?'

Lennie shrugged.

Robin started the car and pulled out, knowing better than to try to talk immediately. Conversations went more smoothly these days when Lennie found her own way into them.

But Len just leaned against the window and trained her eyes on the road. Usually, Robin enjoyed driving at this time of night, when the traffic had died down, her phone had more or less stopped ringing and the city slid past the windows on mute, pubs and houses, people waiting at bus stops and chicken-shop counters like tableaux Edward Hopper might have enjoyed painting if he'd indulged in a spot of time travel and a jaunt to the West Midlands. But it was impossible to enjoy anything when the person you loved most in the world sat next to you in evident distress.

For the thousandth time, Robin blamed herself: if she hadn't been so preoccupied with work, they wouldn't be in this situation. Samir said she couldn't have foreseen what had happened, but it wasn't true. She knew how outraged Lennie had been when Austin was beaten up; she knew her child. But she'd been preoccupied with someone else's.

Emma Renshaw's voice echoed, '*I wasn't paying attention.*'

They stopped for traffic lights, and the silence was broken by shrieks from a group of teenagers on the pavement eating parcels of chips and flinging them at one another. It occurred to Robin that she'd give a lot for Lennie to be out throwing chips; she'd take pretty much any kind of animation over the grey fog that had swallowed her sunny, resilient daughter.

Lennie didn't utter another syllable until they were on Pershore Road. The silence was changing from oppressive to extremely oppressive when she said, 'Austin got an offer.'

Unsolicited as it was, the sentence caught Robin off balance. An offer? 'Oh, for university?'

Her own eyes were on the road, so if Lennie rolled hers, she missed it.

'That's . . .' *Great*, she'd been about to say, but she stopped just in time. 'Where?'

'Manchester.'

Robin immediately brought up a mental map and started calculating. You could get a direct train to Manchester Piccadilly from New Street; how long did it take? How much did it cost? Could she let her go up there on her own? No – she'd still only be sixteen next autumn; it was too young to be hanging round with university students, some of whom would have taken gap years and be nineteen or twenty. *Shit.*

'He doesn't want to go there.'

'Oh.' Robin breathed an internal sigh – thank the Lord, a stay of execution. 'Then why . . .'

'Did he apply? Because it's a great university and a great course. It's a really solid option, but he wants to be in London, you know that, I've told you. He wants to go to LSE. The point *is*,' Lennie said, no longer trying to mask her frustration, 'it means he's going *somewhere*.'

Chapter Eight

When they'd first moved back to Birmingham, they'd lived with Robin's parents in Hall Green, sharing not just a room but the bunk beds Robin and her brother had shared when they were growing up. The day they'd finally got their own place again, this little terraced house on Mary Street, the sense of liberty had been dizzying. It had felt like the start of a brand-new era, a much better one.

Tonight, that seemed a long time ago.

After the outburst, Lennie had gone silent again. Robin had racked her brain for something helpful to say, but if she said they'd always known Austin would go somewhere, she'd come off as insensitive; if she told her she was sure their relationship would be fine wherever he went, she'd look as if she wasn't taking her worry seriously. And she couldn't say that anyway, because she was living proof it wasn't true. However much you loved someone, it was no guarantee.

Lennie yanked her bag off the floor, got out of the car and slammed the door shut. As Robin followed her across the road, she noticed how spindly her legs were. Despite a sweet tooth, Len had always been slim, but since the summer, her appetite had dwindled to the point where, if left to her own devices, she'd barely eat at all. 'I can't, Mum,' she'd said last week when Robin had asked her if she'd like a slice of toast. 'I'm trying, but I just can't.'

As she hung up her coat, Robin tried to think of something appealing for her now, easy to get down but with some protein and vitamins.

'Would you like some hot chocolate, lovely?'

Already halfway up the stairs, Lennie spun around. 'Stop it! Just stop . . . *fussing*!'

Too late, Robin realised her mistake.

'You're making it worse! You keep saying there's nothing to worry about, but everything you do says the opposite. How can I forget for a *minute* when you're tiptoeing round me like I'm some . . . *glass figurine* all the time?'

'I'm sorry. I just thought maybe with Austin's news, you might not have been hungry at the Appiahs', and—'

'I'm not talking about Austin!' Lennie's eyes burned. 'When were you going to tell me?'

'What?'

'That you're doing the Ben Renshaw case? I saw you on TV – because that's how I find out what's going on with my mother. Two weeks! Two weeks 'til the sentencing and now – *surprise!* – you're going to be working round the clock. So don't pretend you care about me, because when it *really* comes down to it, you don't give a shit!'

The words landed on Robin like a punch.

'It never occurs to you that *I* might need you, does it?' Lennie spat down. 'Time after time. Yeah, sure, of course I can take care of myself – I've been doing it for fifteen years because you were too busy!'

She turned her back and marched up the rest of the stairs. Her bedroom door slammed so hard, the floor shook.

Robin stood still for a moment, the air vibrating with her

daughter's anger. Then she went to the kitchen, poured a large glass of wine and sat at the table. Lennie's room was directly overhead and the ceiling trembled as she stamped from one side to the other, underlining her point.

Robin put her head in her hands. *Had* she deliberately held off telling her about the case? No – in the car she'd just been trying to give her space to talk.

Either way, Len wasn't wrong about the timing: it was appalling. If there were two weeks when she needed her not to be at work every hour God sent, it was these.

You were too busy.

In June, days after Austin's beating, a group of highly organised Neo-Nazis had pitched up outside the station gates in Rose Road to protest the blind eye they claimed Robin and her team were turning to suspects of colour as white women were murdered. Though there'd been relatively few of them to begin with, thank Christ, they'd put the word out online and a motley bunch of sympathisers had turned up, too, swelling the numbers. Then a group of counter-protestors had arrived, most of them student activists from the local universities.

Things had quickly turned violent.

From the incident-room window, Robin, Samir and half of Force Homicide had witnessed a man on the white-supremacist side drive a plywood protest sign straight into the face of a black student, nearly costing him an eye. When the man had turned in amazed horror at what he'd done, she and Samir had recognised him at once: Luke, her brother.

Robin had run downstairs and into the fray to try to drag him out, but within minutes, one of the riot police had been stabbed. When the crowd scattered, leaving the injured officer fighting for his life, only one of the counter-protestors had stayed with him: Lennie.

Until that moment, Robin had had no idea she was there and she'd been so proud of her for confronting Neo-Nazis and staying with the injured man that she'd almost forgiven her for bunking off school and getting involved. Afterwards, though, in Samir's office, literally sick with fear, Len had confessed to hurting the *other* person who'd been severely injured, a skinhead left lying in the street unconscious: she'd thrown a large stone and hit him on the head. The man had been unconscious for hours, and it was weeks before they'd been sure he wouldn't have long-term brain-damage.

As far as they knew, in the chaos, only two people had actually seen Lennie throw the stone. One of them was Samir. The other was Luke.

When she'd heard, Robin's blood had run cold. Her brother had boiled with jealousy of her since the day she was born, and he'd made her life as unpleasant as possible, with petty acts of cruelty and physical violence when they were children, scorn and psychological abuse as teenagers and then, when she was nineteen, a lie whose impact she was still living with now, nearly twenty years later.

She'd girded herself for him to use Lennie as a bargaining chip to reduce his prison sentence, but to her astonishment, the exact opposite had happened. Their mother, Christine, who had coddled and apologised for Luke every day of his life, blind to his faults, apt to take his word over Robin's in every altercation, had finally reached her limit. She'd been disgusted by what he'd done, his appearance alongside shaven-headed fascists in the paper, and she'd demanded he make amends by confessing to the stone as well. He was going to prison anyway, she'd told him, as he deserved to, and she wouldn't stand by and let her granddaughter's life be ruined as well. In a state of shock, he'd done as he was told.

At the time, Lennie had gone along with her grandmother's plan. She'd been so scared and overwhelmed, she'd needed someone to take charge. But she'd always had a developed sense of right and wrong, and the more time passed, the more her fear was replaced by guilt. Over the past month, as Luke's sentencing grew closer, she'd grown more and more preoccupied and anxious, until one night last week, when, in a moment of relative calm – they'd been watching a documentary – she'd said suddenly, 'I don't think it's right.'

Until she spoke again, Robin had thought she was talking about the programme.

'To let Uncle Luke take the blame, Mum.'

Her stomach had dropped. No, of course it wasn't right – morally, legally, at all – but the stone had been the work of seconds, driven by righteous anger at people, who, like the ones who had hurt her boyfriend days earlier, hated other people for the colour of their skin. And she was fifteen! Was it right to upend a whole life – a good, kind, thinking life – for a few seconds and an act that, thank God, had had no lasting consequences?

Last week, she'd managed to re-convince Lennie with the arguments she'd been repeating to herself for months: Luke was going to prison anyway, by doing this he was helping himself, too, restoring some balance to his own conscience. Nevertheless, she'd gone to bed feeling sick, and she felt sick every time she remembered. They were far from out of the woods. So many things could still go wrong – Luke could change his mind, an eyewitness could come forward or even hand in phone footage.

And now there was the new worry that it might be Lennie's own conscience that blew the whole thing sky-high.

If Robin was working round the clock – she *would* be working round the clock – she wouldn't be here to help her daughter hold the line.

*

Robin stuffed down a couple of slices of toast and quickly called the station, but when she came upstairs, the line of light under Len's door had gone out. She hovered on the landing for a minute, debating whether to knock and try to talk, but she was afraid Lennie would interpret that as yet more 'fussing', more evidence of her anxiety. And if by any slim chance she *had* fallen asleep, Robin didn't want to wake her. Sleep was no longer easily come by in this house.

Instead, she changed and got into bed with her notebook. In the key days of a case, she spent a few minutes every night writing down what they had so far, the day's new developments. Sometimes a random juxtaposition uncovered a connection or shook something loose in her brain. Not tonight – her mind kept skipping elsewhere.

She reached for the glass of wine on her bedside table – red with a white duvet cover; life on the edge – and took a sip. As she put it down again, she saw the time: 11.05. Already, Ben had been dead for more than twenty-four hours. This time yesterday, while his mother slept, he'd been lying out in the wood, alone in the wind and the rain.

On the bed next to her, her phone lit up. Samir.

'Hey. Sorry it's late, we had dinner with one of Liz's clients.' Liz, his wife, was a partner at a local law firm. 'I wanted to check in quickly before calling it a day.'

'Well, nothing much to report, I'm afraid. Just a handful of calls after the ten o'clock, the usual nutters and a few pensioners with vague accounts of "youths". Same with the house-to-house so far. It was Sunday night, dark, cold, about to chuck it down, so it sounds like everyone just stayed in and drew the curtains.'

'You spoke to the Heywoods?' He'd had meetings at Lloyd House, West Midlands' city-centre HQ, in the afternoon; they'd only messaged since.

'Well, Anne, yes – she was home alone. Her husband's in Sweden, apparently, and he was already there when Ben died, so if that checks out, *he's* off the hook – at least as the physical perpetrator.'

'What was *she* like?'

'Unsympathetic. In both senses.' Robin took another sip. 'She told me that if we bothered them, she'd shop me to the brass. Was Kilmartin at your meeting?'

'Yeah, and I had a quiet word afterwards. He told me they'd "met socially" at fundraisers and charity events.'

Of course, where else? He loved that stuff: profile-building, networking.

'Ugh, the high-powered rich-people gala routine,' she said. 'It sticks in my craw. I know it raises the "real" money, but sometimes it seems like another opportunity for people to connect strings to pull later. It's not far off pay-for-play.'

'It amazes me that you think this,' said Samir, and Robin heard a smile in his voice. 'I'd never have guessed. You know, it's a shame you weren't around for the revolution, I've always thought; the Bolsheviks could have used you.'

'They did all right on their own, didn't they? And I don't see *you* on the other side.'

'Oh, I'm not.'

She hesitated. 'Samir, do you think someone else *should* take this one?'

Silence, then, 'Has something happened?'

'No.' *How would you like it if someone came after your family?* 'No, it's not that. It's just – these two weeks. If it was any other time . . . Len's in a state, she needs me.'

His pause told her he knew what she was trying to say. 'But Kilmartin's adamant he wants you on this. He said it again this afternoon.'

Robin felt a flare of disquiet. 'But *why?*'

Samir gave a sort of half-snort. 'We've had this conversation.'

'But I don't buy it.'

'Whether you do or not—'

'Come on! He knows these people, it's a political hot potato and yet he's *adamant* he wants me rather than his beloved Webster? Tell me you don't smell a rat.'

'Webster's only a DI. Kilmartin needs to tell everyone he's got his top people on it – he needs a Chief Inspector, and he's specifically asked for you. I'm sorry, Rob, without provoking all kinds of questions you don't want, there's nothing I can do.'

She glanced towards the door, making sure it was closed. 'I'm scared for her,' she murmured.

'I know. I know you are – and *you* know I'll do whatever I can to help.'

Somehow, the words only served to highlight how little that was.

When they hung up, Robin did her teeth, then got back into bed. She'd closed the door earlier in case Samir rang, but she left it open this time for Lennie. Whatever happened, whatever she said or did, Robin wanted to signal, she would always be available.

What could she do, though, in any real terms? Lennie had hurled her lightning bolt of anger and frustration tonight because, at this crisis point in her life, she was discovering that her mother was powerless. *God, Len*, Robin thought, *what wouldn't I give to fix it for you, to rewind those seconds, catch the stone mid-air and put it safely back down on the ground?*

She glanced at the clock: late. More and more these days, she was postponing the moment she began the work of trying to sleep, but she couldn't afford to be exhausted, especially now, so she turned the light off and burrowed down. After ten or fifteen minutes of flipping from side to side, however, she gave up and turned on to her back, eyes open.

A car passed on the street outside, heading downhill towards the city centre. As the sound of its engine faded, she felt suddenly and intensely alone. What was she doing here on her own in this bed, this room, this house? Who was really hers in the world apart from Lennie, who these days could barely bring herself to look at her?

Until the summer, Robin had been having – what, a fling? Casual relationship? *Thing*? – with Kevin Young, a mutual friend of hers and Samir's from back in the day. Then, though, she'd recognised what she'd still felt for Samir and she'd had to call it off and wrestle with that instead. It wasn't fair to Kev, who definitely deserved better. And yet she missed him, his easy company and kindness. And warmth, not least here in bed. It wasn't about sex, even though that had been good; she'd just like to reach out and find someone next to her for a change, not feel like she was hurtling through space on her own.

Two more weeks, she told herself. Then, either way, the uncertainty would be over.

She turned onto her side again, curled up and closed her eyes. A few minutes later, when her hands started to ache so tightly she was clenching them, she sat up, turned on the light and reached for her laptop at the side of the bed.

Opening a new browser, she typed in StrengthInNumbers.com.

Under the title, the top half of the homepage was taken up by a video, the freeze-frame of which showed Ben, Theo Gillespie and Molly Zajac sitting on a trio of stools, Molly in the middle, the boys either side, all three in white T-shirts printed with the site's logo, a pair of hands clasped together.

Robin had seen photos of Molly in the *Post* feature earlier, and she'd seen her on TV when she'd spoken briefly outside court on the day of the verdict. She'd been amazed at the time by her confidence, remarkable for a seventeen-year-old full stop, let alone one who'd experienced what she had. She'd spoken clearly and calmly about her determination to prosecute Heywood and thanked her team but most of all Ben and Theo for supporting her despite the price they and their families had paid.

She had light brown hair that fell two or three inches below the shoulder, naturally wavy, and large dark eyes in a freckled open face. On the court steps, she'd been wearing a dark jacket and shirt, but here she was in jeans, stacks of bangles on both wrists, the heels of her boots hooked over the rung of her stool.

Robin hit 'play' and the three of them came to life.

'Hi, hello. I'm Molly, I'm Ben, I'm Theo.'

She'd expected the production quality to be Upper School Presentation, as it would have been in her day – terrible sound quality, worse lighting – but though they'd evidently made it themselves, enlisting other friends to help, it was surprisingly professional. For the umpteenth time, Robin was aware of her own obsolescence.

Ben took the lead, and whoever was operating the camera moved it on to him. 'Welcome to StrengthInNumbers.com. We're really glad you found us.' He was wearing jeans as well, and the same trainers – or at least the identical model – as the ones she'd seen this morning in the wood. Skinny and earnest, he looked even younger than in the picture Varan had put on the board.

The camera swung to Molly in the middle. She shook her hair back over her shoulders and looked into the lens with the same directness she'd had on the court steps. 'Last summer, at a house party where we should have been celebrating finishing exams and breaking up for the holidays,' she said, 'I was raped by someone we were at school with, a boy – no, not a boy, a man: he was eighteen – from the class above. A group of us had been outside, but suddenly, I'm not sure how much later, everyone else had vanished and I ended up alone with him in a summer house at the end of the garden. I found out later that my drinks had been spiked. When I realised what was going on, I tried to get away, but he was stronger than me and I couldn't stop him. It only ended when Ben and Theo here heard me scream from the other end of the garden and came running to help.'

The camera moved to Theo, but he spoke just to Molly. 'Thank God we did hear you.'

'I was lucky,' she said to him, 'really lucky,' to the camera. 'Not only did Ben and Theo see what happened, when I told them I wanted to prosecute and hold my rapist accountable, they were behind me one hundred per cent.'

'What none of us realised then,' Ben said, 'was how hard we'd have to fight.'

'I'd expected the trial to be tough,' Molly continued, 'my team had tried to prepare me, but nothing could have, really. With my rapist looking at me all the time, I was forced to relive the attack step by tiny step. His barrister implied I was mentally unstable and had a dodgy relationship with my dad. It's supposed to be illegal to go through a victim's sexual history, but he did it anyway – what there was of it – and accused me of leading my rapist on and "liking it rough", then changing my story "when the Southern Comfort wore off".'

'As witnesses,' said Theo, 'we expected to be questioned – even interrogated. We didn't expect to be terrorised.'

'In the months leading up to the trial,' Ben took over, 'Theo and I were bombarded with anonymous hate mail: threatening letters, abusive letters, parcels of rotting food and maggots. On my birthday, I opened a parcel that I thought was from my gran. It was a lunch box full of dog shit.' He looked slightly defensive, as if, despite the broader subject matter, he half-expected a grown-up to come and reprimand him for the language.

'And it wasn't just us,' Theo said. 'Our families were targeted, too: they were followed and spat at, our car was vandalised. My mum was mugged by a man in a balaclava.'

'And then,' Ben again, 'things escalated. Six weeks before the trial, a burning rag was dropped through my family's letterbox one night. Without smoke alarms, we would all have been killed. But you got even worse, Theo.'

'Well, I don't know about that, but, yeah, a month before the trial, when I was walking to the bus stop after school, a car came off the road onto the pavement and hit me. It pinned me against a wall and shattered both my legs – one of them nearly had to be amputated. That only didn't happen because I had a brilliant, brilliant surgeon.'

'It was a campaign of terror designed to silence us,' said Ben, 'but it failed.'

'In the UK,' Molly said, 'the vast majority of rape and sexual assaults are never even reported, let alone make it to court, and one of the main reasons – *the* main reason – is fear. People who are raped or sexually assaulted – I don't say victim, I am not a victim and I refuse to let *him* label me – are afraid. Afraid of their attackers, either physically or psychologically or because they hold power over their lives in some way – your husband, your boss, a member of your family. People are afraid of having to relive their attacks in court, afraid of shame and judgement. They're afraid of not being believed.

'We're founding StrengthInNumbers.com as a stand against fear. We hope this site will be a place for people affected by rape and sexual assault, whether as survivors, their loved ones or those who support them in court, like Ben and Theo did for me, to share their stories and find a sense of community and strength. You aren't alone – *you're not*. Together we're stronger, together we can stand up to fear and intimidation and make sure that rapists and the sexually violent end up where they belong: behind bars.

'This is my story, and it's Ben's and it's Theo's. We hope that by telling it, we can help you tell yours.'

Chapter Nine

The knuckle rap on her office door yanked Robin out of an intense bout with her emails. Expecting Samir or Malia, she looked up to see a tall man in a charcoal suit holding two take-away coffee cups. He was in his early forties, she guessed, with slightly dishevelled dark hair and thick brows over eyes that, even from a distance, were visibly green. Faint lines bracketing his mouth gave his smile a wolfish quality.

'DCI Lyons? DCI Hailey.'

The SIO on the witness-intimidation case – she hadn't been expecting him until eight.

He saw her glance at the clock above the door. 'Sorry, I'm early. I can come back, but I had a feeling you'd be here and I passed Nero so . . .' He raised a cup in her direction.

'Thanks. And it's fine – you've rescued me from my inbox.' She gestured to the chairs in front of her desk, feeling the usual embarrassment at the state of them. The blue fabric had worn through to crumbling sponge on both now but of course, new ones were a pipe dream.

Hailey gave her a cup, waited for her to put it down, then shook her hand. 'Sorry I couldn't get back to you straight away yesterday. I was at the prison all day.'

'Home turf?'

'Sorry?'

'You were at HMP Wakefield, you said in your message. You sound like a Yorkshireman.'

'Oh.' He smiled again, the corners of his eyes crinkling. 'Yeah, guilty as charged. East, though, Scarborough. I've been down here since university, but you can take the man out of Yorkshire . . .'

Robin nodded. 'I was in London for seventeen years, not that you can tell from my accent, either. I'm sorry I left the news in a voicemail – you must have known Ben pretty well.'

'I did, and I liked him a lot, he was a good lad.' He prised the lid off his cup and put it on the edge of her desk. 'Honestly, I'm gutted. And if this *was* the Heywoods and I didn't nail them, I'm going to live with the guilt for the rest of my life.'

He sounded genuine and, to her surprise, Robin felt sorry for him. In his position, she'd have started blaming herself immediately, too. But there was so much wrong with that line of thinking, not least, of course, that Ben's death might be completely unconnected.

Hailey was watching her. Feeling self-conscious, she looked away and made a show of taking the lid off her own coffee.

'Do you think it *is* connected?' he said, as if he'd heard her thinking.

'The million-dollar question. We're trying to come at it fresh, but it feels like a huge coincidence, doesn't it – a witness in a highly controversial case, a schoolboy with a stable family background, no gang ties as far as we know and no other record, killed for a totally unrelated reason?'

He nodded.

'But then, coincidences *do* happen. When did you last speak to him?'

Now he definitely looked sheepish. 'A month ago. A brief check-in on the phone.'

'So you weren't actively working on it any more?'

'I won't need to tell you why,' he said. 'We'd had nothing new in months, everyone was burned out, and with multiple other serious cases on the books . . .'

'It's the same here – sheer amount of work. Did he mention any new harassment that last time?'

'No. We would have been on it straight away.'

'When we spoke to Theo yesterday, he said Dominic Heywood threatened them after the sentencing, that "one way or another, sooner or later", they'd pay.'

'Yeah, and we were all over that. Heywood admitted it. He said he hadn't meant it, he'd just got carried away, seeing his kid brother sent down.'

'Did you believe him?'

'I was sceptical, let's say, but there's been no trouble since. At least, until now – maybe.' He made a face.

'DCI Hailey . . .'

'Peter, please.'

'Peter – thank you – I have to ask, was there ever any suggestion that Ben and Theo's evidence wasn't completely truthful?'

'Plenty of suggestion, from the Heywoods and their team.'

'But grounds to believe it? Why *would* they lie, Ben and Theo, especially when it cost them so much?'

'Well, they hated Alistair, even before it all happened.'

'Did they?' She hadn't known that. 'Why?'

'A better question would be why they wouldn't. You clearly haven't met him. He's a hideous, arrogant little creep, and obviously predatory. There were other girls who'd had bad experiences with him before Molly, but they were too scared to testify.'

'Scared of what? Or whom?'

'The family.'

'So you *do* think it was them, the witness intimidation?'

'Yeah. They had a clear motive, ample means, and they were about as angry as I've ever seen people, but we could just never catch them out. They always had alibis.'

'Isn't *that* odd, though? I mean, multiple incidents against Ben, Theo and their families over a period of several months – who can tell anyone where they were every hour of every day?'

'The Heywoods. After the first couple of times we questioned them, they started keeping records of all their movements, hourly if necessary. Anne's idea – she said she wasn't having us pinning it on them.'

Robin could imagine. 'Say they *were* behind it, then who was physically doing it? I mean, I can't picture Anne packing lunch boxes with dog shit.' Though dropping burning rags through someone's door she *could* – it was the low-rent grubbiness that didn't seem her style.

'If they were doing it themselves and getting people to provide false alibis, our money was on the boys. The few times we had CCTV, we were definitely looking at males.'

'The twenty-something *boys*.'

His eyebrows flicked, amused. 'But, more likely, they contracted it out – the risk of being seen, all those different occasions, especially the car? Though we couldn't find any evidence of that, either – no covert meetings, no odd financial transactions.'

'Given their work, could they have people who handle this kind of thing for them anyway? Big-time building industry, massive sums of money involved – I wouldn't be surprised if there was a bit of "security" involved occasionally.'

'Thugs on the payroll, you mean, rather than specially hired? Yeah, we looked.'

'How deep did you go?'

'Deep,' he said, sounding a bit defensive. 'But they employ a lot of people.'

'Maybe not so many these days – it sounds like Alistair's case has hit their business pretty hard. Whoever actually did it, though, how did they pull it off? I mean, with CCTV, even just the car . . .'

'Tinted windows, sunglasses, false plates. We spent *weeks* tracking where it came from, where it went afterwards – zilch, dead end after dead end. It was stolen, of course, and afterwards it was driven deep into the country, off-grid, and it vanished. The whole thing was a masterclass, really, all of it – that, the fire, the mugging. Quite often, we had CCTV of the attacker nearby, but then, *pouf*, he was gone and the trail went cold.'

'So how did the Heywoods explain it?' she asked. 'That the very people they might want to nobble were conveniently getting nobbled by someone else.'

'A big boy did it and ran away.' He snorted. 'Someone else wanted to hurt Ben and Theo and the Heywoods were the fall guys.' He saw her face. 'I know, ridiculous.'

'Unless someone else implicated in it all wanted to hurt Ben and Theo because they were testifying? Friends of Alistair's – accomplices?'

He shook his head. 'Nope. And no one else with a beef with either of them. And we looked, bloody hell we did – we spoke to everyone they'd ever come into contact with, from the Gillespies' cleaning lady to the blokes who'd run their respective scout troops back in the day. No one had a bad word to say about either of them.'

'Hm.' Bugger – she'd hoped there might be *something*, some way in.

He sighed. 'I don't envy you. Our case was a nightmare – pain from all angles. We were working round the clock but getting nowhere, beating our heads against the wall, and the more the Renshaws and Gillespies got harassed, the more *we* got harassed by the *Post*. And from inside, too.'

She looked at him. 'Kilmartin?'

'All his usual guff about the reputation of the Force, and then Anne Heywood on top of that. She was on the phone to him every day, then he was on the phone to me. I mean, how could I investigate if I wasn't allowed to talk to the bloody suspects?'

Robin hesitated. She needed to tread carefully. 'Peter, how did you get the case?'

She saw his defences go up – he actually pulled back. 'What do you mean?'

'Sorry, that came out wrong. I just meant, did it come via your gaffer, as per?'

He softened slightly. 'Yeah, but I think Kilmartin tipped me for it. I reckon that's the only reason I was never kicked off it when we didn't get anywhere – it would have been too much of a personal climb-down after he'd banged on about having his "best people" on it. Why?'

'Just curious.' No, that wasn't fair, he'd been straight with her, or she thought he had. 'Honestly, I wondered because Kilmartin's keen on me handling this one, and I've never had the impression he's much of a fan of mine.'

'Really?' Hailey looked puzzled but he sounded almost teasing when he said, 'After the summer, I'd have thought you were the golden girl round here.' His paper cup was empty when he put it down. 'Look, just take it steady, that's my best advice. About the only thing we came out of it knowing for sure is that the Heywoods are not good people. They're all scumbags in their different ways. I found Anne the hardest, personally, because she dresses it up in righteousness. "The family"' – he pronounced it East End-style, stretching the a – 'that's what she's *all* about. I mean, I get it, family's family, but where does it end? In her mind, there's no line between looking out for your own and using it to justify doing whatever the hell you like to other people.'

'We got a taster yesterday – Lady Macbeth minus the soft edges.'

He huffed, amused. 'Exactly. Have you seen the transcripts of the trial yet? The Heywoods' QC just tore Molly to bits, and Ben and Theo. I mean, yes, they smoked a bit of weed, but from the way he carried on, it was like they ran a crack house. He even dragged up that Theo's dad was done for fraud a few years ago – the judge had to remind him it wasn't Theo on trial, let alone his parents. But all totally defensible when you're protecting your son, eh?'

'What about the brothers, Dominic and Marcus? What do you make of them?'

'Useless, entitled, self-satisfied wankers.'

'No, be honest.'

He grinned, showing pointed white canines. 'As the day is long.'

At quarter to seven, when she'd arrived, the incident room had been near-empty, but by the time Robin walked Hailey to the lifts, everyone was at their desks. Coming back, she went to the window and watched as he crossed the car park with long strides, got into a 5 Series BMW, then drove away. When she turned, she caught Malia's eye and saw questions: what had she made of him? Was he competent? Straight up? Observer of protocol that she was, Malia wouldn't ask – especially after Robin's warning yesterday – but if she actually *knew* what she'd made of him, Robin thought, she'd tell her. She trusted Malia, one hundred per cent.

She fetched her cup with its last couple of inches of luke-warm coffee, then came to perch on the spare desk next to Varan's – her spot when she talked to her core crew.

'Morning. How are we getting on? Anything from the appeals overnight?'

'Well, we've got a man who says he was on Yardley Wood Road on Sunday night and saw a lad he thought might have been Ben,' Malia replied. 'He was driving, though, and his description's pretty vague – tall, dark clothing – so it could have been anyone. There's a couple of other things, but that's the most promising.'

'Hm. How about the neighbourhood team? Did you hear back from them?'

She nodded. 'Two things, potentially. One, they've had a spate of car jackings round Moseley Bog over the past two or three months. People getting back to their cars after a walk, knock on the window all of a sudden and there's blokes with baseball bats: get out and give us your keys.'

'Baseball bats?'

'I know. And the other thing: last month Organised Crime got a tip-off about a Luger buried there, and bullets. They think it was gang-related, but no arrests yet.'

'Imagine,' Varan said. 'First he saw the rape, then he happened to be in the wood and witnessed something totally different going down? How unlucky would you have to be?'

'Unlucky enough to get murdered,' said Tark, uncharacter-istically dry.

'We've got to find out what he was doing there,' Robin said. 'Let's follow up with this potential witness, see if we can get more detail. Ben left home voluntarily, we know that, but we still don't know whether he was in the park under his own steam or whether he was intercepted en route somewhere else. If he *was* there of his own accord, why? Was he meeting someone in secret for whatever reason? Someone else's girlfriend? Or a boyfriend?'

'We know he didn't have a girlfriend,' said Malia, 'or not that his family or Theo knew about, but could there be someone more casual or new?'

'Maybe it was like a Tinder thing – just sex,' suggested Varan.

'Oh, you know about stuff like that, do you, young 'un?' Tark said.

He knew he was being teased, but Varan still looked a bit embarrassed. 'I've *heard* about it, old man. Surprised *you* have.'

'All right,' said Robin. 'Either way, yes, romantic or sexual connections. We'll need to talk to Theo and Molly in more detail, now they've had a bit of time. Malia, could you speak to the Renshaws again, Amy, too, the younger sister? We need a list of who else he was close to. Tark, you and Jo go to Summerfield, talk to his classmates. Let's ask everyone about drugs. Ben and Theo were smoking weed the night of the rape, and though Theo said cigarettes yesterday, if they were going into the woods to do it, it probably wasn't. Just weed, then, or something else? Where did they get it? Was Ben buying on Sunday – was that why he was there? All questions we need answered.'

'We really need the search team to find his phone,' said Tark.

'Yeah, but at this stage, I'm not feeling optimistic. The post-mortem's at twelve – Varan, if you could speak to Theo this morning, I'd like to talk to Molly and then we can do that together. Afterwards, we'll pay the Heywood "boys" a visit.'

Chapter Ten

'Please can you put someone outside our houses? *Please*. Mine and Theo's – we're scared out of our minds.' Molly Zajac held out her hands as if she were literally begging. 'What if they come here? What if we're next?'

She'd been up all night and she said, it showed – she looked like a shadow of the girl from the video. Her nose was raw from repeated blowing, and though her eyes were pink and painfully swollen-looking, the hollows below them were pencil-lead grey. She hadn't been still since Robin had arrived. They were at the table in her parents' little kitchen, sitting in theory, but Molly had been up and down near-constantly, standing and going to the window, then sitting again, bouncing her knee, picking up her mug of tea, then putting it down without taking a sip. Her agitation was exhausting even to watch.

'I'm working on it,' Robin told her. 'But until we know Ben's death is linked and there's reason to believe the two of you—'

'Oh, come on!' Molly shut her down, thank God. Even as the words left her mouth, Robin hated herself. First they cut your resources to the bone, then you were the one who had to justify it. 'Dominic told them they'd pay and now Ben's paid! What more reason do you need? Who *else* would have wanted him dead? He was at freaking *school*.'

'Molly, look, the Heywoods are absolutely top of our list, but we can't jump to conclusions.'

She gave a snort of derision. 'I wouldn't call a year "jumping". Hailey had months to make sure this didn't happen and—'

'So why now?'

Molly stopped, flow interrupted.

'Why now?' Robin repeated. 'If they've had a year, the Heywoods, why have they done this *now*? What triggered it?'

'Time. They've waited until it all died down – they basically said they were going to "sooner or later". They waited 'til people had moved on so that it didn't look like them.'

'Do you really believe that?'

'What?'

'Do you think that in a year – not even – people round here have forgotten what happened to you all? Because I can tell you they haven't, and they're angry – take a look at the comments on our witness appeals on social media.' *Take a look in my incident room.*

'They *should* be angry. My legal team was brilliant – it's nearly impossible to get a rape conviction, I know *that* now – but Ben and Theo . . . All they ever did was help me.' Her eyes welled. 'I know it isn't, I do know, but this feels like my fault. If I'd just let it go, not insisted on prosecuting . . .'

'No. No way. You did the right thing.'

'Did I? Theo'll never walk normally again and Ben's *dead.*'

'So help me help him, Molly. Think – why now?'

Molly looked at her, then pulled a tissue from the box and blew her nose. 'Seriously, I don't know.'

Despite the hard time she was giving her – because of it, maybe – Robin could feel herself warming to Molly more and more. She respected her – if that wasn't an odd thing to say about someone half your age. She was fierce – grieving and afraid for her safety, and yet she'd still come out all guns blazing. She was right about not being a victim – she hadn't let Alistair Heywood put her light out. Good for you, Robin wanted to tell her, get your revenge by going out into the world and swinging it by the tail. Be the biggest, brightest success you can.

Maybe it was why Alistair had picked her in the first place – he was enraged by her strength. How *dare* this girl from an ordinary background – Molly's dad worked for Network Rail, her mother for an estate agent three days a week – come into *his* world and make him feel small? Molly had got eleven A stars at GCSE and a scholarship to Summerfield; it sounded like she'd knocked him into a cocked hat intellectually *and* she was good-looking. Even with a face swollen by hours of crying, she was vivid.

'Tell me about Ben,' Robin said. 'What was he like?'

Molly dropped the tissue in the basket at her feet and pulled another from the box. 'Amazing. Really, really kind. After it happened, some people acted like I was unclean or something – even people who believed me went weird, like I was a freak all of a sudden. Ben wasn't like that, or Theo. They didn't treat me like a victim. And he just refused to be intimidated, *refused*, even at the end, even after they tried to burn his parents' house down. He wouldn't let them stop him doing what was right.'

'Brave.'

She nodded. 'Very.'

'The headmaster said he was popular at school.'

'Even more now, apparently. Theo called him Babe Magnet.' The faintest hint of a smile.

'He didn't have a girlfriend at the moment, though. Did he ever?'

'He went out with this girl called Abby Purcell for a few weeks last year, but it kind of fizzled out.'

'Do you know why?'

'He just wasn't that into it. He was only seventeen then, he wasn't looking for a serious girlfriend. And honestly,' another half-smile, 'he was a total flirt.'

'Did he flirt with you?'

Molly looked at her. 'No.'

'Really?'

'Really we were friends.'

'Was it only girls he liked?'

'Yeah. He was straight.'

'OK. What else was going on in his life? Anything new? Anything worrying him?'

'No, he'd been fine, same as always. He was doing his university applications.'

'Sports Science, right? Where did he want to go?'

'Loughborough was his first choice. He wanted to be the next Joe Wicks – sports and fitness, his own brand.'

'Good for him.'

'It combined what he was good at – sport – and the media experience he had from StrengthInNumbers. We've run the site and done so many interviews and articles, plus the events – school visits, talks.'

'You obviously put a huge amount of work into it, the three of you.'

'We wanted something good to come of it all. The Heywoods tried to silence us, so we wanted to stick it to them by giving voices to other people, or at least a place where they could feel heard.'

Amazing, Robin thought, after everything she'd been through. 'Molly, you said Ben refused to be intimidated. Do you think if he'd run into trouble at Moseley Bog on Sunday he'd have refused to back down?'

'What sort of trouble?'

'If he'd come across someone doing something criminal or if someone tried to rob him, for example. We found his wallet some distance away, which makes us wonder if he'd been mugged. Would he have stood up to someone in a situation like that?'

'Probably. He believed in standing your ground.'

'How about risky behaviour? Would he have gone into the wood alone, after dark?'

'Maybe, but for a reason – he wouldn't just go off to be alone. He was an extrovert, he liked to be around people.'

'But you don't know that he'd been meeting someone like that recently? Someone he shouldn't have, maybe?'

'If I knew, I'd have said. We didn't speak every day now anyway.'

'Really?'

'I'm not at Summerfield any more, I'm at Sutton Coldfield Grammar, and the website more or less runs itself now it's set up. If there's gossip, Theo fills me in.'

'So you speak to him more often?'

'Well, yeah, we're going out so . . .'

Robin frowned. 'Are you? I didn't know that.'

'Why would you?'

'Well, when we spoke to him yesterday, he didn't mention it.'

'Is it relevant?'

'I don't know.'

'It's not.' Molly dropped another tissue into the bin and fixed Robin with a stare. 'Look, I'm telling you, we know who did this. We *know*. All you have to do is prove it.'

Chapter Eleven

The morgue was in the very centre of town, tucked away behind the Victoria Law Courts. Varan had met her there just before twelve, but it felt as if a whole day had passed by the time they emerged again from a world in which a young man's heart had been lifted from his chest and weighed in the scales like an Ancient Egyptian ritual to one where two men at the kerb were fighting over who'd been first to hail a cab.

'Let's walk,' Robin said as the wind swirled litter round their ankles. 'It's only five minutes, and I need some fresh air. We'll get the car afterwards.'

The Heywood offices were on Colmore Row, of course – the best business address in town. By some miracle, this small area in the heart of the city had dodged the bombs during the Second World War and survived to represent Victorian Birmingham's elegant business district. The westerly end of the street came out on Victoria Square with the Town Hall and the famous 'Floozie in the Jacuzzi' fountain, the east near Snow Hill station. Midway along was St Patrick's Cathedral, whose bells struck the half-hour as they passed.

The Heywood Properties building looked like a town house – sash windows on all four floors and a heavy front door whose black paint gleamed almost as brightly as its brass fittings. A few seconds after they rang, it was opened by a woman in her late fifties with a silver-blonde bob. As soon as Robin said 'Detective', she hustled them in off the street before giving her own name: Claire Philips, Bill Heywood's personal assistant. Her silk scarf, Robin noticed, combined the navy and paler blue of her trousers and blouse with a terracotta that perfectly matched her lipstick. The level of attention was probably the same across the board; she had the air of someone who'd been doing her job for a very long time to a very high standard. Let alone the Heywoods' clients' favourite restaurants and brands of Scotch, she probably knew the names, birthdays and favourite colours of all their children.

As they stepped inside, the scent of furniture polish enveloped them, as it had done yesterday in Moseley, redolent of order and expensive continuity. The reception desk was a burnished mahogany, the heavy glass vase on the corner filled with huge cream flowers – camellias, maybe, or peonies, one or the other – and glossy evergreen foliage.

They hadn't rung ahead, but evidently they'd been expected to turn up at some point. Claire Philips had shown no surprise when she'd opened the door, and now, as they followed her in, she maintained an untroubled patter about the city-centre traffic. They refused the offer of tea, and she retreated with a smile. 'I'll let them know you're here.'

They waited beneath an antique chandelier in a parlour-like reception room. On the wall above the white marble fireplace was a large oil painting of an undeniably British landscape, rolling pasture and trees and scudding cloud, the kind of green-field site that Heywood Properties probably loved getting their earth-movers on.

For a couple of minutes, faint street noise was all they could hear. No one passed the doorway, and the telephone on the reception desk down the hall stayed silent. Varan looked at the painting, moving in close enough to study the brush marks. His interest in art was another thing that had taken Robin by surprise before she'd really got to know him.

Somewhere overhead now, feet descended carpeted stairs at speed, two pairs, *duh duh, duh duh, duh duh.* A brief hiatus – a landing – and then another cascade. *The boys* – Robin imagined them at six or seven, thundering down to tea from a lavishly equipped playroom at the Moseley house.

A moment later, two dark-haired men appeared in the reception area's arched entrance. In terms of stature, they had to take after their father. Both were over six feet and athletically built, rugby players to their mother's figure skater. It was hard to believe people this size had sprung from that tiny, probably intensely Pilates'd body. This was what generations of a top-quality diet did for you: turned *you* into prime rib.

'Dominic Heywood,' said the one in a navy jacket, proffering a large hand. 'And my brother, Marcus.' His expression wasn't actively hostile, but it certainly wasn't friendly.

Facially, the brothers were similar, and similar to Alistair, too, in the photographs Robin had seen of him. A consensus would say Marcus was the best-looking of the three, though, his cheekbones higher, eyes a little less deep-set. Dominic had a neatly trimmed dark beard and his nose had been broken at some point. Robin wondered if that was the handiwork of his ex-girlfriend's new partner, then saw a mental image of him at the letterbox and felt an urgent need for some hand sanitiser.

Marcus was looking at her in a way that was frankly assessing, and not of her professionalism. She was twelve or thirteen years older than him, a senior detective here to talk about a murder, for God's sake. She gave him a hard look back: *Yes?*

Dominic indicated the pale sofa just behind them, then took the one opposite with his brother. Knees apart, forearms resting on his thighs, he stayed at the edge of the seat as if ready to spring up again at any second.

'So, you visited our mother yesterday,' he said before Robin had a chance to get a word out. 'First of all you lock up her son on a bogus rape charge and now you're after the rest of us for murder. We had nothing to do with what happened to the Renshaws or the Gillespies back then, and . . .' He stopped himself. 'We see why you want to talk to us now, Alistair's in jail because of Renshaw's testimony, but—'

'Strictly speaking,' Varan said, 'he's in jail because he was convicted of rape.'

Dominic gave him a look that could light a fire. 'I'm *saying*, we understand why you're here, but we had nothing to do with his death.'

'I assure you, Mr Heywood,' Robin said, 'if that's the case—'

'It is,' put in Marcus, speaking for the first time. In contrast to his brother, he looked relaxed – so relaxed, in fact, he was starting to recline. His legs were crossed, the upper foot casually swinging in its black lace-up and matching wool sock. He wasn't wearing a jacket and the sleeves of his white shirt were rolled, displaying muscular forearms, tanned in November. 'As we've said since the so-called witness intimidation started, someone tried to set us up.'

'Someone else who wanted to hurt Ben and Theo. It was perfect – they'd hurt them and it'd look as if *we'd* done it because we had a motive. And it worked: they got away with it.'

A big boy did it and ran away.

The brazenness. 'And who would this be?' Robin couldn't quite contain her scorn. 'They were seventeen – how many mortal enemies could they have had?'

'How the hell would we know?' cut in Dominic. 'We didn't know them from Adam until they decided to wreck Alistair's life. You're detectives, maybe you can work it out.' His tone implied he doubted it.

'We will,' she said, looking him straight in the eye. 'Whatever's going on here.'

'Glad to hear it. Your reputation goes before you, anyway. You did that case in the summer – the girls. We know who you are.' He looked back, holding the eye contact.

Robin's skin prickled. 'Where were you on Sunday night, Mr Heywood? Sunday as a whole, actually.'

'Well, I woke up at my apartment around ten or ten thirty – we'd been out the night before.'

Apartment? Spare me. 'We?'

'My girlfriend and some friends. We'd had a few drinks. Caitlin stayed over and we went to Mum's for a late lunch. Dad's away, and she likes having people around.'

Varan scribbled a note in his book. Robin bet it was along the lines of 'Girlfriend? Despite harassment conviction?' Well, money talked, she thought. Loudly, to some people.

'What time did you leave there?' she asked.

'Eight? Eight fifteen? Something like that. Cait put the TV on when we got back for the end of *Dynasties,* that Attenborough thing. She loves animals.'

'Evidently,' smirked Marcus.

Robin pretended she hadn't heard him. 'And after that?'

'Nothing,' said Dominic. 'It was a school night.'

God, Robin hated that expression. The constant infantilising that went on these days, as if everyone wanted to wash their hands of being adults and retreat to perpetual childhood. You're twenty-seven sodding years of age, she wanted to tell him; you don't go to bloody school any more, in case you hadn't noticed.

86

'How can we confirm that?' Varan asked, pen hovering.

'Caitlin can tell you.'

'Apart from her.'

'There's CCTV at my place. I got home and I stayed there 'til the morning when I came to work.'

'How about you, sir?' Varan angled his knees towards Marcus.

'Same as Dom,' he said, foot still swinging. 'We were out on Saturday, my girlfriend stayed over, then we went to Mum's for lunch. Chloe had to leave at five, she had some work to finish, but I stayed until Dom did, then went back to mine.'

'What did you do once you got home?'

'Played on the Xbox until about midnight, then went to bed.'

'Right. Could you give us numbers for Caitlin and Chloe, please?'

They pulled out phones and read them off. Not memorised, then, Robin thought. But how many numbers did anyone know these days?

'When was the last time you both saw Ben Renshaw?' Varan looked between them.

'At the sentencing,' said Dominic.

'After which you threatened Ben and Theo Gillespie, I understand,' Robin said.

He shook his head as if it had been blown out of all proportion and she was being ridiculous. 'As I've explained, I didn't mean it. It was a stupid remark made in the heat of the moment.'

'And you've neither seen nor spoken to either Ben or Theo since?'

'How many times do we have to tell you? No'

'These are beautiful offices.' Varan made a show of looking around.

Well, of course, Dominic's face said. *Do you think we'd settle for anything less?* 'Yeah. We've been here since 1923. Our great-grandfather bought the building.'

'Long time. What do you do here?'

'We develop property.' Slowly, for the hard of understanding.

'You specifically?' Varan said. *Don't even think about patronising me, sunshine.*

'Nominally we're in sales,' Marcus said, 'but we're jacks of all trades. It's Mum and Dad's show.'

'At the moment,' said Dominic quickly. 'We're learning from them. Financing, relationships, project management. When they retire, we'll take over.'

'Will Alistair join the company when he's released?' asked Robin.

'Probably,' he snorted. 'I mean, who else'd have him now, with a criminal record?'

'How's business these days?'

'Fine.' He blinked.

'Your mother told us you'd lost an investor. We got the feeling it wasn't the first.'

'Well, mud sticks, doesn't it? We've been running this company since the 1880s without any issues beyond the usual – planning, conservation. We're doing fine, but thanks to my brother's wrongful conviction and this knee-jerk cancel culture, yeah, you could say we're learning who our real friends are.'

He met her eye and held it again.

Our friends, your enemies, was that his point? Robin stared back until he broke the contact, then she glanced at Varan and stood up. 'Well, I'm afraid there's more turbulence ahead, one way or another,' she told them. 'You'll be seeing us again, so don't go too far away.'

'Oh, we're not going anywhere.'

Chapter Twelve

They were on the stairs at the station when Robin's phone rang, a mobile number she didn't recognise.

'DCI Lyons? Jeremy Handley from *The Record*, we spoke very briefly last night. I wondered if you had a moment now to comment on—'

'I'm sorry,' she told him, 'I really don't. As I said yesterday, all media enquiries are being handled by the press office. Thank you.'

She pressed the button, cutting him off mid-sentence. Bloody hell.

On the top floor, Varan went to the incident room and she carried on to Samir's office. Rona wasn't at her desk, so she knocked and went in. Samir stopped typing straight away.

Robin closed the door behind her. 'What's going on?'

'Kilmartin rang a few minutes ago.'

'Surprise – we left the Heywood brothers half an hour ago. What did he say?'

'Did you see your TV bit last night?'

'Second-to-top billing, right after the multi-car pile-up on the M42.'

He beckoned her behind the desk and clicked out of his email onto the *Midlands Today* homepage, where Gemma Blockley, the youngest of the reporting team (and the hottest, according to Phil Howell, no doubt one of her thousands of Facebook followers) was freeze-framed in the car park at Moseley Bog with her mouth half-open.

Samir hit 'play' and she widened her big blue eyes. '. . . shockwaves across the region and beyond because of his impact on so many people's lives, as a key witness in the high-profile rape trial of Alistair Heywood and then as co-founder of StrengthInNumbers.com. I'm joined by Detective Chief Inspector Robin Lyons, leading the enquiry.'

Samir was in shirtsleeves, no jacket, and Robin could feel his body heat against the top of her arm. As she appeared on-screen, she batted him, 'Ugh. I know what I said – stop it.'

'No, I won't,' he said, putting his elbow out to block her from reaching the keyboard, and so she was obliged to watch and see how wan she looked compared to Gemma, who was ten years younger and wearing nuclear-grade TV make-up. Her coat looked terrible, too, she realised, almost as knackered as she was. 'You're great at the media stuff,' he said afterwards. 'Much better than me.'

She looked at him. 'Have you done some sort of management course? *Boost your team's confidence and improve results by 17.3 per cent!*'

A huff. 'Wish it was that easy.'

'So what did Anne Heywood take exception to?'

'That the report mentioned them and we're bringing it all up again, "dragging them into this when it's nothing to do with them."'

Robin moved away to the other side of the desk and sat down in one of his chairs. 'Well, you can see her point about the rape, but their having something to do with it is absolutely on the table.'

'She told Kilmartin their solicitors are "on speed-dial".' Samir made a face; he couldn't stand corporate-speak.

'Business as usual, probably. So what does he expect us to do?'

'"Tell Lyons to tread carefully."'

'I am, but I'm not going to be pushed around, Samir, I won't. When I spoke to Peter Hailey this morning, he said he was barely allowed to talk to them. I'm going to investigate this case like I would any other, whoever the hell they are.'

He nodded. 'Which is why you're the right person for it. How was the post-mortem?'

A memory of Ben's pale body on Faulkner's table. So young – she shut the door on it quickly. 'Well, there were particles of soil in the wound, so we know for sure now that it wasn't an accident.'

'They couldn't have got in when he fell?'

'No. The wound was on the upper side of his face as he landed, and the particles were deep in, they had to have been pushed in by the blow, Faulkner said. There were tiny bark splinters as well, and under the microscope, he saw signs of decay. He reckons Ben was hit with a branch that had been on the ground for a while and started to break down. Whoever it was, they're clever: we're never going to find it. What's easier to hide than a branch in a wood? At least a needle's distinguishable from a haystack.'

'Any help on gender?'

She shook her head. 'Because the bone at the temple's comparatively weak, any able-bodied adult could have done it, he said, "if they'd put a bit of welly into it". He's prioritised the bloods, but in the meantime, no alcohol or pills in the stomach, no defence wounds, no evidence of any sexual activity, consensual or otherwise. Overview: not much help at all.'

Chapter Thirteen

'It's time to get your head in the game.'

Robin dropped her bag at the foot of the stairs as the front door closed behind her. Was it? Now? It was nearly ten o'clock and she'd been at work for fifteen hours; any chance of a five-minute breather now she was home?

On the plus side, at least she was being spoken to again.

She put her head around the sitting-room door and saw Lennie sitting on the sofa with her laptop, legs crossed under her yogi-style, Austin's *Trump for Jail 2020* T-shirt on. Her dark hair was tied in a wispy topknot that exposed her slim white neck.

Lennie didn't look up. 'I watched your *Midlands Today* bit again. You need a new coat, Mum.' Now she eyed her over the lid of the laptop. 'Yeah, *definitely*.'

'I didn't know it was *that* bad.' Well, after seeing it on-screen earlier, she did, but recently she'd been trying to get her financial act together and build some savings for when Len went to college. A new coat was a big-ticket item.

'The good news is, it's a quick fix,' Lennie said. 'Once you've got a sharp structured coat on, you'll look totally pulled together, whatever you're wearing underneath.'

Structured? Pulled together? Where was she even getting this language?

Len picked up her phone and handed it to her. She had Instagram open, the picture on-screen a woman in a chic mid-length coat standing in chiaroscuro, chin jutting, like a cover image for *The Fountainhead*.

Hm. Robin clicked 'Shop now to see the price'. 'It's nearly eight hundred quid! My first car didn't cost much more.'

'I'm not suggesting you get that precise one, *obviously*, just something like it.'

'Len, I—'

'I'm on eBay.'

She turned back to her laptop, *You are dismissed*, and Robin took the opportunity to leg it to the kitchen where she poured a glass of wine, leaned against the counter and exhaled. The coat talk was an olive branch, albeit well camouflaged. She'd take it.

On Sunday evening – at about the same time Ben's family must have made the last meal they'd ever eat all together, she realised now – she'd cooked a sausage and pasta bake. The scent of it was on the air, Lennie had had the leftovers for dinner. Robin had eaten part of a jacket potato from the canteen – microwaved, of course: damp on the outside, still hard in random patches inside – but even that had been three hours ago. The casserole dish from the pasta wasn't soaking in the sink, so she looked in the fridge. Joy, there was a small corner left.

She gave it a quick blast in the microwave and ate it straight from the dish, standing up. Then she girded herself and went back to the sitting room. Engrossed, Lennie didn't acknowledge her reappearance, so she drank her wine and feigned interest in a quiz rerun on the TV.

After another five or six minutes' intense clicking and scrolling, Lennie handed over her laptop, open to a page showing a coat very similar to the one on Instagram. 'Here,' she said. 'French navy, twill, barely worn – it's Stella McCartney. If you put the collars up, you'll look like the model.'

'I doubt that. No disrespect to the coat.'

'A hundred and thirty pounds to buy now. Give me your card, I'll do it for you.' She held out her hand. 'Come on, Mum. You want to look sharp for work, don't you? Impress your commanding officer?'

Was she implying something? Unclear. Robin decided to ignore it either way, heaved her weary carcass off the sofa again and went to fetch her purse. A hundred and thirty pounds for a subtextual apology and the pleasure of seeing Lennie distracted from her angst for twenty minutes? Cheap at the price.

Chapter Fourteen

The noise pulled Robin from total oblivion to a place in which numbers glowed through the dark: *3.27.* It took her a couple of seconds to separate them from the sound – not the alarm ringing: her phone. Fumbling for it, she blinked at the screen. The station.

She pulled herself upright. 'DCI Lyons.'

'It's Phil, guv.' He sounded flustered. 'There's a fire.'

For a moment, still half-asleep, she wondered what it had to do with them – fires were for the Fire Service and Response, even Phil knew that. But then she remembered the burning rag pushed through the Renshaws' letterbox.

Shit – Theo, Molly . . .

'Where?' She braced herself.

'Moseley,' he said. 'It's the Heywoods' place.'

Though their houses were a world apart by every other metric, geographically barely a mile separated them. At this hour, the roads were empty, and it took Robin just minutes to thread her way south from Balsall Heath. On the last stretch of Alcester Road, an ambulance tore past, lights on, siren wailing. It turned a few seconds ahead of her.

Emergency vehicles filled the Heywoods' street, their lights staining the leafless trees red then blue against the dull orange of the night sky. She parked three houses down, well out of the way, and grabbed her coat.

Frost glittered on the verge. The curve of the road meant she couldn't see the house yet, but the smell of burning hit her the moment she opened the car door. House fires didn't smell like log fires, wholesome and natural, they were acrid and chemical, your nose and throat knew they were poisonous, told you not to inhale, to get away. She could see the smoke in the sky, a thick column in roiling shades of dull orange and grey.

Up ahead, people huddled in the street and on the pavement, heavy coats over pyjamas, arms wrapped around themselves, their stunned joyless faces turned towards the house as if they'd been summoned from bed for a mandatory fireworks display on a dictator's birthday.

Robin ran, but when she passed the line of monumental conifers between the Heywoods' property and their neighbour's, she stopped short. The entire central gable was engulfed, all three storeys, fire visible in every window. On the ground floor, heat had shattered the glass and great tongues of flame flared from the openings. Wicked – the word arrived in her head. In a house, where it shouldn't be, fire wasn't an inanimate thing, morally neutral, it was wicked. And intelligent.

Suddenly, three years vanished and she was standing outside Corinna's house again, the burned-out, skull-like house that had belonged to the best friend she'd ever had.

Snap out of it, Robin! Now!

Four fire engines skewed at angles across the drive and the top of the lawn. Firefighters were everywhere, she could see ten or twelve even from here, dragging hoses, raising a second hydraulic platform, another ladder. Weighted by their suits, others carried hooks and poles from the engines like a small, grim mob about to ransack a village.

Above it all roared the fire, full-throated.

Robin ran towards the Response officer stationed at the bottom of the drive and flashed her warrant cards. 'Where's your guv'nor?' she yelled.

He pointed over the lawn to a man talking into his radio, uniform tinged orange by the fire despite the spotlights from the engines.

As she jogged across the grass, she could feel its heat pressing against her face and arm, but what she felt inside was relief: Anne Heywood's black Lexus wasn't there.

Thank God.

'Sergeant Collins?' She had to shout to make herself heard. He was a fit-looking man of about thirty-five, and as he turned, Robin saw the fire reflected in his eyes. 'DCI Robin Lyons, Force Homicide. I'm SIO on the Ben Renshaw case – the family here are people of interest in the—'

She was interrupted by the sound of shattering glass: one of the windows on the top floor had exploded, sending out a hail of shards. Seconds later, the one next to it went, too. Shouts from the firefighters.

'They haven't found anyone?' Robin yelled.

'Not so far,' Collins yelled back, 'but they're still checking.'

The garage doors were open, and the car wasn't in there, either.

More breaking glass but deliberate now: firefighters axing the frames out of two first-floor windows. Once a fire reached this size, toxic gases and extreme heat made areas too dangerous to enter even with full protective kit and breathing gear.

The heat and smoke were drying her eyes and Robin blinked to try to moisten them. 'How did it get so bad?' If the house was out in the country, miles from anywhere, she'd under-stand, but here, a couple of miles from the city centre, surely someone would have raised the alarm before it could take hold like this?

'Very quiet street,' Collins shouted. 'No through traffic at night. Next door are away and the man opposite sleeps at the back. His dog woke him up, but it was in the kitchen with the door shut so it took a while. Plus, the house is wood-framed.'

'No alarm?' Given the CCTV system, she'd assumed the house would be wired up like the National Gallery.

'If there was, no one seems to have heard it.'

A bellow from the foot of the drive. Turning, they saw a man grappling with the uniformed officer Robin had spoken to and then with a second man who rushed to help. 'Get off me – get your fucking hands off me! That's my house! That's my fucking house!'

Dominic Heywood.

Robin ran, Collins right behind her.

'Dominic!'

He turned, face aghast. 'What the . . .? Where is she? Where's my mother?'

'Sir,' Collins said, 'if you could—'

He shoved his face right up in Robin's, teeth gritted. 'Where's my mother?'

'I don't know, but, Dominic, her car's not here.'

'No, it's at my place! She had wine at dinner – we made her get a taxi home.'

Robin's stomach plummeted.

He looked back at her and then at the house. He pointed to the trio of windows directly above the front door, all three filled with billowing rolls of flame. 'That's her bedroom.' His voice was full of fear.

Collins' radio crackled and he strode away from them just as an almighty wrenching noise overhead sent a spray of sparks into the sky. Flames leaped after them, liberated. When the first flare died back, the roofline was jagged – one of the gables had collapsed. *Please*, Robin thought, *please don't let anyone have been up there.*

Next to her, Dominic was shaking. 'What's going on?' he demanded. The fire showed the glint of tears in his eyes. 'What's happening?'

'I don't know.' She tried to sound gentle while shouting to be heard. 'I'm not the one with information here, I'm CID, not Response – this isn't my—'

'Then why are you here? No' – he pulled back a few inches, suspicion flaring in his eyes – 'I know why! You know someone did this – one of *them*! Payback!'

'No!' *Shit – shit.* 'Dominic, no. We don't know what happened. It could have been an accident – a candle, an electrical fire! Until Fire Investigation can get—'

Attention caught by something else, he broke eye contact and looked past her, over her shoulder. Robin turned to see Collins returning. From the way he was walking, eyes fixed on the ground, she could tell he had news and it wasn't good.

'What's happening?' demanded Dominic again, but his voice was so fearful now that the question sounded existential.

Collins indicated a length of low wall around a flower bed. 'Why don't you sit, sir?'

His eyes were huge in the gloom. 'No. Just tell me.'

'The firefighters have found a woman in a room at the back of the house – a sitting room? A den?'

'The family room, Dominic said.'

'She was on a sofa, under a blanket, so they didn't see her straight away.'

'Is the fire there? At the back of the house?'

'Not all the way back, no,' said Collins. 'Not in that room.'

'Is she burned?' Dominic's voice was full of fears

'No.'

'Oh, thank God.' He sagged.

Collins shot Robin a pained look and her stomach sank. 'I'm sorry, sir, I wasn't clear. I'm afraid she's dead.'

For a moment, the word didn't seem to register – Dominic's face was blank. Then, fleeting, horror – a realisation of impending pain. Then, again, seconds later, as if he'd remembered he was dealing with idiots, he was back, raging. 'How?' His nostrils flared. 'If she isn't burned, then *how* is she dead?' He jabbed a finger at Collins: *What aren't you telling me?*

'Without a post-mortem—' Collins began.

'*How?*'

'Sir, most likely she died in her sleep from inhaling smoke.'

Dominic pulled back, then shook his head vehemently. 'No. Not possible. She would *never* have slept through it – she's a light sleeper, really light. When we were kids, it was always her who woke up for us. She would have woken up.'

Collins' chest rose. 'Again, we'll need a post-mortem, sir, but it looks as if alcohol might have been involved.'

'Alcohol?'

'They found wine bottles next to her. Two.'

For a moment, Robin thought Dominic was going to hit him – he was up in his face, *How* dare *you?* – but then he heard movement on the lawn behind him.

Paramedics were wheeling a gurney across the grass.

As suddenly and completely as if a power cable had been cut, Dominic's rage died. Before her eyes, as his own followed the gurney, he transformed from a towering physical menace into a boy.

'They're going to get her,' he said. 'Aren't they? That's for her.'

Collins nodded gently. 'Yes, sir.'

Dominic's chin was trembling. He closed his eyes, as if by shutting out its image, he could make the gurney itself cease to exist. He spun away from them – from it – hands in fists, not for hitting now but for holding on. To himself. To reality.

'Dominic.' Robin put out a hand and gently touched his arm. 'Why don't you sit down for—'

'Don't you fucking *touch* me!' He shook her off. For what seemed a long time, half a minute or more, he didn't move, but then, as if remembering something of great importance, he fumbled in his jacket pockets, one then the other, and took out a pack of Marlboro Lights. He snapped the first cigarette he tried to get out and his hand was shaking so much, he couldn't work the wheel on the lighter to light the second. Without touching him, Robin held out her hand, and after three more attempts, he gave up and dropped it into her palm. In the flare of light as she lit his cigarette, she saw terror in his eyes.

Dominic inhaled like his life depended on it, the coal barely dimming from one drag to the next. He used the stub of the first cigarette to light a second.

Then, from behind the far end of the house – a gate there, or a way round to the back – the gurney returned, more slowly this time, lifted across the thick gravel by the paramedics and two response officers, and set carefully back down on the lawn. Even at a distance, the body bag was clearly visible.

Dominic watched as if he were watching his own death approaching. When it was close enough for him to see that the bag was zipped closed, he gave a guttural roar and fell to his knees on the grass, arms wrapped around his head as though he were trying to keep himself physically whole. 'Mum,' he shouted into the earth. '*Mum!*'

*

Robin stayed with Dominic while Collins detailed two members of his team to attend to him. When she was sure he was properly taken care of, she walked quickly back up the road to her car, from where, door closed, she called the station. Phil wouldn't have been her first choice, far from it, but he was on nights this week so he was what she had.

'I need you to get over to King's Heath straight away,' she said, 'and make sure the Renshaws are at home.'

Chapter Fifteen

If the mood on Monday had been sombre, this morning the incident room crackled with energy. When Robin had called the team together, they'd assembled in a matter of seconds.

At least two phones had been ringing somewhere in the room from the moment she'd walked in: no hiding a 'deadly inferno on one of the city's most exclusive streets' as the *Post* had put it on their homepage. The piece was short, nearly all the facts taken from the Fire Service's website, but alongside a bystander's shaky phone video of the fire at its peak, flames leaping against the night sky, they'd published Anne Heywood's name and, in a sentence carefully worded and positioned to avoid the possibility of any legal comeback, the information that the body of a key witness in her son's trial last year was discovered at Moseley Bog just two days ago.

So much for salvaging a PR disaster; Kilmartin's 'shit-show' had just added a whole new act.

'OK,' she said, looking round at the expectant faces, 'so things are a lot more complicated this morning, but a note of caution before we start: however sceptical we are of coincidences, it wasn't arson until we hear it from Fire Investigation and we can't waste time speculating. For now, we need to stay focused on Ben. This is day three.' Even Phil would get the subtext:

the key first forty-eight hours after a killing, when the odds of a solve were by far the best, were over. 'That said, as you might have heard, I asked Phil to check the Renshaws were all at home in bed, just in case.'

She'd thought he was paying attention, but Phil blinked hard, as if the sound of his name had called him back from somewhere more exciting. He was tired – he'd stayed on past the end of his shift to be here for this.

'Yeah,' he said. 'It took me three goes on the bell to wake them up – they'd taken sleeping tablets.'

'The doctor prescribed them yesterday,' said Sandy Kelman, their Family Liaison Officer.

'They came to the door looking like zombies; I felt really bad for waking them up. I mean, if anyone needs a break from reality . . . No one had been out – you could tell from the frost on the ground, too.'

'Right. Which is not to say we won't need to take a much closer look at them if it *is* arson, but for now, check what time the frost settled, will you?'

He nodded.

'Thanks. OK, Ben. What we *do* know for sure is, this makes our lives much harder: whatever the cause turns out to be, Dominic Heywood was there this morning and, under-standably, he's beside himself and the rest of the family will be, too.'

Dominic, she'd heard, had refused to leave the premises until the fire had been completely extinguished. He'd been there for hours and the paramedics had ended up checking him for hypothermia.

'We'll need to be incredibly sensitive. Even if one or more of them *was* involved in Ben's death, they're grieving now, too, so anything related to them has to be done in as careful a way as possible. If we need to be in contact with them directly, I'll handle it.' She saw a momentary twitch cross Tark's face – *Yeah, more special treatment* – but ignored it. 'How are we getting on with their alibis for Sunday evening?'

'Well, Bill was definitely in Sweden,' Malia said. 'We checked with the airline and his hotel, and we spoke to him on a Swedish landline number.'

'Anne's car stayed put all night,' said Tark, the team's de facto head of CCTV on account of his ability to stay alert during brain-killing hours of it, 'and we've got Dominic at the Moseley house and the garage at The Mailbox, as well as ANPR along the route he gave us.'

'Marcus?'

Tark tipped his head from side to side. 'Not there yet. We've got him at Moseley leaving when he said he did, same time as his brother, but his fob for the snazzy parking at The Cube has him arriving thirty-seven minutes *after* Dominic, and their two places are basically the same block, aren't they? Two minutes apart, absolute max.'

'What about ANPR?'

'He's on the same first one as Dominic, still in Moseley, but none of the others, even though they set off from the same place, headed to the same place, more or less.'

'Try tracing backwards from The Cube and see where that gets us.'

He nodded. 'On it.'

'Good. What about CCTV round Moseley Bog?'

'Nothing interesting yet. We've made a start, but we haven't had that much in. Given the size of the perimeter, I thought we'd be swamped, but so far, we've only got about twenty tapes, and most of them are from the opposite side to where Ben likely went in, if he was coming from home.'

Robin turned to Malia again. 'How about the guy who thinks he could have seen him on Yardley Wood Road?'

'We spoke to him again, but he really couldn't give us any more detail. When pushed, he eventually admitted to being on the phone while he was driving.'

'Does he know what time it was?'

'About nine o'clock, he said, "give or take ten minutes."'

Meaning at least fifteen, then, probably. Great. 'We need to do another round of house-to-house,' she said, 'catch anyone who wasn't in the first time, and go after every last bit of tape: CCTV, bus cameras, dashcams, the lot. Let's get on to the taxi firms, too, see who was in the area. It was a storm, not an air-raid warning: someone else must have seen him. What about Ben's phone?'

Malia's face said it before she did. 'We got his records in last night, Varan's going through them, but the phone was still in the wood when it pinged for the last time. It triangulates to pretty much exactly where the body was.'

In other words, the SIM card had been taken out either in the clearing or very near it. Robin sighed inwardly. 'Who was the last person he spoke to?'

'Pierre Kaplan,' said Varan, 'school friend, who called him. Seven thirty-four on Sunday night, a few minutes before the Renshaws sat down for dinner.'

'Reason to call, rather than text?' In their day, she and Corinna had spent hours on the phone, but if Lennie was representative, communication with anyone but Austin happened by WhatsApp now. The *ping* of messages sound-tracked their evenings.

'Psychology coursework, Kaplan said, they were stuck. I spoke to him last night.'

'Right. And how about Ben's laptop?'

'Tech say no red flags so far,' Malia answered, 'and there's nothing untoward in his recent email or social media. If he was using WhatsApp on his phone, he didn't have it synced.'

Bugger. The phone records would tell them whom he'd been texting but not what was said; without the phone itself, the last hope of seeing any messages was that he'd used WhatsApp or Messenger on his computer as well.

'OK. Jo, how did you and Tark get on at the school?'

Jo – DC Joanna Kowalska – tried not to look too pleased to be called on. She was really coming into her own these days and quickly becoming one of Robin's favourites. Twenty-eight, she had an open face and straight blonde hair that she redid in a messy bun fifteen times an hour with the hairbands she kept round her wrist. She was slightly overweight and self-conscious about it, starting each week with brutally spartan lunches before flaming out, usually mid-morning Wednesday, in a blaze of Cadbury's Dairy Milk. She didn't miss a thing.

'Well, the Renshaws sent over a list of Ben's regular crew, and the school gave us one, too,' she told them, 'and it was the same names on both, which was helpful: Theo, obviously, then four other boys . . .' She glanced at her notebook, 'Mo Abadi, John Waller, Pierre Kaplan, Chris Chan, and two girls, Lily Halliday and Ava Morris.'

'You talked to them all?'

'Apart from Theo, yes, because he was at home.'

'Anything strike you?'

'Not really. They all seemed like good kids. Given the state of the place, I was expecting crown princes and the like, to be honest – they've got a ton of overseas students boarding there – but the ones we spoke to were just normal. They're all gutted, all said they didn't think anything weird was going on. The only thing either of us noted' – she looked at

Tark – 'was that Lily admitted she and Ben "had a night" a few weeks back.'

'"Had a night?"'

'Her words. I thought she meant just got off with each other or something, but when I asked her to clarify, she told us they'd slept together. Just once. I pressed her a bit and she said she'd liked him – quite a lot, I got the impression – but he'd wanted to leave it at that. Apparently he was nice about it and went on about their friendship and how he didn't want it to change.'

'Should have thought of that before giving her one,' snorted Phil.

Robin fixed him with a hard look. 'What was she doing on Sunday evening?'

'She was at home all night, she said.'

'Hm. Did any of the others mention her and Ben?'

Jo shook her head. 'We definitely thought it could be worth looking into his love life, though, guv. Three of the lads said he got about a bit.'

'Agreed, yes. Molly did, too.'

'Chris Chan described him as "Summerfield's answer to Harry Styles".'

'Good local boy, Harry Styles,' said Tark. 'Born in Redditch.'

'Was he?' Varan looked amazed.

Robin raised her eyebrows. 'A little focus here, perhaps?'

'Sorry, guv,' Tark said. 'My niece told me – she likes him.'

'Right. Let's find out if Ben's popularity was a problem for anyone, either someone who liked him but wasn't getting anywhere, like Lily, or maybe a jealous boyfriend. Maybe it was an angry father: found out his daughter had been meeting Ben secretly in the woods, sorted him out? Or just went there to catch them and lost his cool. Underage daughter? Religious objections? Let's see who else he'd been involved with recently. Sandy, could you ask the family?'

'Yes, guv.'

'I'm going to talk to Theo this morning, so I'll ask him. We're also overdue a visit to Alistair Heywood at Brinsford. Let's see if he's got anyone on the outside who might have taken care of business for him. Malia, would you do that, you and Jo?'

She nodded.

'OK, so that's the order of business for now: CCTV, Marcus' whereabouts during the missing minutes, Ben's love life, Alistair. And I know I don't need to say it again, but I'm going to anyway: this was a delicate situation before and now it's hair-trigger. So whatever you're doing, please do it gently.'

When her desk phone rang, Robin reached to pick up and caught the smell of fire again. She got it every time she moved her head, but it wasn't coming from her clothes or body, it couldn't be. As soon as she'd got home from Moseley, she'd stripped in front of the washing machine, stuffed everything in, then taken an extra-long shower – she'd shampooed her hair twice. The smell was either trapped in her nostrils or it was a trick of the mind. The same thing had happened after Corinna died, she remembered.

'Robin?' A Yorkshire accent. 'It's Peter Hailey.'

'You've heard?' Stupid thing to say, she thought; how could he not?

'Anne – Jesus. I mean, we had our moments, but . . .' He tailed off. 'Any word yet on what happened? It's got to be arson, hasn't it? Two days later?'

'If it isn't, it's another hell of a coincidence.'

'Will you let me know when you find out?'

Robin made a noise she hoped he'd interpret as yes.

'And how are you getting on with Ben? Any news?'

'We're chipping away,' she said. 'Making progress.'

Ha – standing on the Heywoods' lawn this morning, more than anything she'd had the sense that they were teetering on the edge of a fast-deepening sinkhole.

Robin sat in one of Samir's chairs, elbows on her knees, fingertips pressed against her lips.

'We need people outside their houses,' she told him. 'All of them. I know, the budget, but the situation's so volatile. I'm scared of what Dominic's capable of – he was unhinged this morning. If he was done for criminal harassment when a girlfriend dumped him, God knows what he'd do to avenge the death of his mother.'

Samir rubbed a hand across his mouth. 'The Gillespies, too, though? Wouldn't the Heywoods assume the Renshaws were behind this?'

'Without knowing what kicked it all off again, I'm not sure. What I *do* know is they're all scared out of their minds.'

Samir picked up a pen and spun it round his thumb. He didn't take his eyes off her, but the distance in them told Robin he was imagining chains of possible developments, conditional clauses, *if x, then y*. He'd been silent for ten seconds or more when a cursory knock at the door heralded the advent of Rona and her little wicker-edged tray.

'Thought you could do with coffee and a biscuit, love,' she told Robin. 'Bit of sugar.'

Disproportionately moved by the kindness, Robin took the smoked-glass cup and saucer, finding a custard cream tucked in under the handle. The seventies had never ended in Rona's world. 'Thank you.'

'You're welcome, bab.'

Rona put a cup in front of Samir and left again, shutting the door quietly after her.

'We'll do it,' Samir said. 'All four families.'

'The Heywoods, too?'

'I'll find another corner to cut. Somewhere. I want eyes on them.'

'For their protection or other people's?'

'Both.' He looked at her. 'And ours. If they were angry before . . . We can't let them feel we've left them swinging in the wind.'

'I'm surprised they didn't have their own protection. The money, Samir. Guess where Dominic lives, age twenty-seven.'

'The Mailbox.'

'Ah, too easy.' If you were a flash young bachelor with a big budget, The Mailbox would be top of your list. On the site of the old Royal Mail sorting office, right on the redeveloped canals in the city centre, it was a huge complex of upscale shops and restaurants, a Malmaison hotel, the BBC studios, offices and flats. Harvey Nicks could be your corner shop. 'Marcus, age twenty-*five*?'

'The Cube.'

'Right again.' The Cube – appropriately – was the Mailbox's younger sibling, equally flash. 'Bill's going to stay with Dominic for the time being. He got a cab to the airport as soon as he heard about Anne and his flight took off from Malmö a couple of hours ago, so he'll be landing at Birmingham about an hour and a half from now. Have you heard from Kilmartin?'

He sighed. 'Three times in the past hour.' The phone on his desk buzzed – Rona, from the other room. 'Probably him again now.' He picked it up and listened. 'Of course, thanks.' He put the receiver down again. 'Not him. Liz is on her way up – she's coming with me to a lunch.'

Robin felt a weird pang at being excluded followed by the pressing need to be elsewhere. 'I'll leave you to it.'

'No, don't – just say a quick hello. She'd like to see you.'

Really? She nearly said it out loud.

Even though she'd come to terms with the way things were now, she still found Liz difficult. It wasn't remotely Liz's fault, she'd never been anything but kind and friendly. In fact, if it wasn't for her, Robin would be back in London leading a different life because before he'd asked Robin to apply for her job, Samir had asked Liz if she was all right with it. If she hadn't been, he'd said, he wouldn't have done it.

Liz had also been gracious when Robin's past with Samir had been dragged up by the media, including one particularly egregious photograph of them together at eighteen in which they'd been wrapped around each other, Samir's lips on her neck, her boobs bulging under the pressure of his arms. 'I'm so sorry,' Robin had said when they'd next seen each other. 'I'm mortified.'

Liz had waved her away. 'Don't worry! It was years ago, you two, before Samir and I even met. I felt bad for you – there's no picture of *me* at eighteen I'd want bandied about, believe me.'

Robin didn't, really. She'd met Liz for the first time when they were all twenty-three, and she'd been as lovely-looking then as she was now.

That first time had been Corinna's wedding, and happy as Robin had been for Rin, it had been one of the worst days of her own life. That she'd smiled all the way through was still one of her proudest accomplishments because it had also been the first time she'd seen Samir since he'd summarily dumped her five years earlier. She'd spent weeks nerving herself up, especially after hearing he was bringing a girlfriend.

Even so, across the sun-bleached lawn at Josh's parents' house in Edgbaston, she'd seen him reach for Liz's hand and felt as if she'd been kicked in the chest. They'd had their backs to her, but Robin knew Liz would be gorgeous. She was tall and athletic, with glossy brunette hair that over the course of the day had slowly slipped loose from its updo, somehow making it look even more chic. Robin had had a hideous mental image of the pair of them, Samir pulling out the last grips so it fell between her bare shoulder blades before he pushed her back on his bed. The way he'd used to do to her.

Knowing – *seeing* – that he'd moved on was bad enough, but worse was a sense of her own utter isolation. That day, she'd seen that she lived in a different reality from him now – from all of them. She was the same age as Samir and Liz, Corinna and Josh, but they'd still been young, at the start of their adventure, together. Robin was alone, a single mother, a *matron;* she'd already made her choices.

For a good chunk of that day, she'd been literally isolated: Lennie had been eighteen months and she was so amped up after her turn as a mini flower-girl, it had taken ages to calm her down for a nap in a quiet bedroom upstairs. Later, she'd hared around the lawn and into Josh's mother's flower beds, gleefully trampling and picking, and Robin had run after her in the heat feeling middle-aged and overweight, sweating in her too-tight dress, a wild extravagance at the time – she'd been in her first year as a PC at the Met – that nevertheless looked as cheap as she'd felt, sticking to her C-section paunch like cling-film on custard.

Samir had said four words to her that day – 'Hello, how are you?' – then, before she could reply, he'd moved away to give Liz her drink. Four months later, Corinna told her they were getting married and Robin's exile became complete and permanent. For a while then, Lennie had felt like the only reason to get up in the morning.

Now, Robin saw Liz beam at Samir as she came in and walked round his desk to kiss him hello. For all her maturity these days,

she couldn't quite make herself look at him and see the corresponding expression on his face. Liz looked as stylish as ever. She
was in business gear, an olive silk shirt with navy trousers and a
navy three-quarter-length *structured* coat that would certainly pass
muster with Lennie. From what Robin knew of Liz, she doubted
it had cost anywhere near eight hundred pounds but she made it
look as if it had. Her hair was tied back today, emphasising her
elegant face with its high cheekbones and large eyes.

'Robin!' she said. 'Lovely to see you.' She approached in a
subtle cloud of orange blossom and they did the cheek-kiss
thing. Robin wished she'd had more than three and a half
hours' sleep. Well, at least she'd washed.

'I was just listening to the radio,' Liz said. 'The fire sounded
horrendous.'

'It was. The whole case is.'

'Well, if anyone can sort it, it's you, I'm sure, The Star.'

'Star?' On the heels of the wedding memories, it seemed
especially ridiculous.

'Lean in, sister! No false modesty. I've seen you doing your
press conferences.'

'Well, we've been having a good run lately, let's hope this
isn't where it all comes unstuck. Speaking of which' – she
glanced at Samir – 'I'd better get back to it and let you two
get to your lunch.'

He nodded. 'OK. Let me know how you get on with Bill.'

'You should come over for dinner one night,' Liz said. 'You
and Lennie.'

'That'd be great,' Robin said as her gut yelled *No*. She gave
Liz a big smile, then scarpered in case the social blandishment
became a reality.

*

As Robin was making her way back along the corridor, her mobile rang. An 0207 number, London, and corporate-looking, going by the round 400 of the central three digits.

'Jeremy Handley, Chief Inspector, from the *Record*,' said the smooth voice.

Oh, for crying out loud. 'Mr Handley, with respect, I've asked you twice now to—'

'I'm aware, but before you cut me off again, DCI Lyons, I wondered if you'd like to comment on your brother's upcoming sentencing.'

Robin was momentarily speechless.

'It's quite a contrast, isn't it,' he said, 'you the high-flying detective on this big case – and *so* much bigger this morning – with him on remand, waiting to hear how long he's going to do for violent disorder with a gang of white supremacists. Who were protesting one of *your* cases. It's a decent story, even without throwing in your old skeletons – and that's just the ones I found with a quick google.'

Over the sudden pounding of her heart, Robin tried to think. *Calm wisdom, calm wisdom – what would Samir say?* 'I wouldn't like to comment, I'm afraid,' she said, 'no. And, Mr Handley, I'm not sure how you came by this number, but I'll ask you not to call it again. Goodbye.'

Chapter Sixteen

Varan was coming with her later to see Bill Heywood, but Robin was glad to be alone as she drove to the Gillespies'. She'd felt her face redden during the phone call with Jeremy Handley and she'd seen Malia clock it when she'd gone back briefly for her coat. As she'd been coming from Samir's office, as far as Malia knew, she'd probably thought he'd just torn a strip off her.

Your old skeletons.

That she'd been iced at the Met, that her best friend had died a violent death for which she herself had briefly been in the frame, yes, that was public domain if you went looking, but, as far as she knew, the connection between her and Luke had never been explicitly made in the media or online. People knew at West Mids, though – had this Jeremy Handley spoken to someone about her? Maybe he had regular contacts here – if crime was his beat, it would make sense: apart from Police Scotland, West Midlands was the biggest force outside the Met.

And it *was* a good story, she knew it. Rape and murder, a high-profile website, #MeToo, and now the devastation on Millionaires' Row. Feeling sick, Robin remembered the photograph that had been splashed across the papers after the riot: her brother side by side with the white supremacists' leader and a man in a balaclava. Especially with his guilty plea, she'd been praying the sentencing would pass unnoticed, a sordid little footnote, but if this guy dug it all up again, harnessed it to *this* case, and if the story went viral . . .

The thick snake of anxiety, never dormant now, coiled and uncoiled in her gut. Twelve days from today – both Luke's sentencing and Kilmartin's stupid deadline for her to present him with a solve, all neatly wrapped up with a bow on top, or else.

I don't even want to think *about the headlines.*

Oh, for the love of God, just stop, she ordered herself. She could actually feel her blood pressure rising, the squeeze at her temples. If she panicked, she wouldn't be able to think straight and then it'd all be over. She needed to focus.

When she reached Shirley, a leafy area of the city south of Hall Green where her parents lived, she took a minute to compose herself and check her colour in the mirror. Normal, or normal enough to pass for someone under professional strain. Before she could go back down the rabbit hole, she got out of the car.

Samir rang as she was crossing the road. Robin could hear cars in the background of his call and she guessed he'd come outside wherever he and Liz were for their lunch. 'No surprise,' he said, 'but it's looking like arson. I've just spoken to Fire Investigation and to be confirmed, of course, but they think it started at the front door. From the intensity of the damage there, most likely an accelerant was involved.'

Petrol, for example.

'You're opening an investigation?' she asked.

'I am, yes.'

'And I'm running it, aren't I?'

*

Two locks were undone before the Gillespies' front door opened, and the chain stayed on. The face that appeared in the six-inch gap belonged to a woman with the same straw-shade hair as Theo's and blue eyes that took a careful look at Robin's warrant card before withdrawing again.

Carolyn Gillespie was about forty-five and – thought Robin, when the chain dropped and she saw all of her – probably exactly what you'd want your mum to look like if you were a teenage boy: attractive but not sexy, stylish rather than fashionable. She was wearing good jeans – mid-blue, form-fitting but not skinny – and a simple caramel V-neck sweater. Her left hand reached for a gold heart locket just under her clavicle.

'Is Theo here?'

'Yes, he's in his room,' his mother said. 'I'll go and get him.'

She was halfway up the stairs when another woman appeared from the door to what Robin guessed was the kitchen. She was about the same age as Carolyn with a crisp blonde bob and a similar basic-but-elevated style: the sweater over *her* good jeans was navy and oversized. 'Caro, I'll leave you to it,' she said with a trace of Scots. 'I can let myself out.'

'Please don't go on my account,' Robin said. 'It's Theo I need to speak to.'

'No, I have to get on anyway. I was just dropping something off.'

'Thanks, Izz,' Carolyn said from the top of the stairs. 'That was really sweet of you.'

'Oh,' she waved it off. 'Keep me posted, and anything we can do, just let us know. Awful, the whole thing,' she said *sotto voce* to Robin as she passed. 'I hope *you're* planning to actually *do* something and let these poor people get on with their lives.'

The door shut behind her emphatically, the flap of the letterbox giving a final clap a half-second later. A wire cage had been added around it on the back of the door, Robin noticed.

The house was a large double-fronted Victorian terrace, and a glance was enough to tell you that someone here – given her clothes, probably Carolyn – cared about design. The hallway was laid with highly glazed tiles – original, Robin guessed, but carefully restored – and the walls picked up the creamy colour in their pattern. The spiky lampshade overhead, a kind of glass mace on a chain, echoed their shape. From a wide-necked bottle on a polished side table, a spray of eucalyptus perfumed the air.

Theo took the stairs one at a time, holding on to the bannister and leading with his right leg. When he reached the bottom, she saw how exhausted he looked. Doubtful he'd actually done any sleeping in his jeans and T-shirt, but they were wrinkled enough, and his hair looked unwashed since she'd seen him in Richard Atkinson's office at the school. Behind the heavy frames, his eyes were pink.

Carolyn followed him down. 'Would you like coffee?' she asked Robin. 'I'll put the kettle on. Izzy made you some of her chocolate biscuits,' she told Theo, touching his arm.

He shook his head. 'I can't. I feel sick.'

The kitchen was a large room with units whose deep green matched a ceramic bowl on the table and the frame of a still-life line drawing on the opposite wall. No jars or bottles cluttered the counters, even by the stove; everything was either put away or decanted into canisters. Pride in her own paltry domestic achievements at Mary Street, Robin understood, had been wildly premature.

Carolyn indicated a sofa tucked into a nook overlooking the garden. 'It's warmest in here during the day, but if you need somewhere more formal . . .?'

'Theo? Where's most comfortable for you?' Robin asked.

He cleared his throat and nodded. 'Here's fine.' He gave her the sofa and took one of the pair of wicker armchairs either end of the tea-chest coffee table. It was a snug fit for him, especially with the sheepskin draped over the back, but perhaps that was the point: furniture as protective exoskeleton.

'It's just a few questions,' Robin said, 'I know you spoke to DC Patel yesterday, Theo, but first I want to say to both of you that if you have reservations about the police because of last year, I do understand. If you can find a way to trust us now, though, me and my team, it could make a huge difference.'

Theo said nothing. He met her eye briefly, then looked away.

'You and Ben were friends for a long time,' she said. 'Before Summerfield.'

'Since primary school.'

'What was he like then?'

He shrugged a little. 'I don't know. Normal. Fun. We liked the same stuff – Lego, bikes, the aquarium. He was really into football – playing, watching. I remember we went to a match for one of his birthdays.'

'Villa or Blues?'

'Villa.'

'Was he still into it?'

'Watching. He only played at school these days – he gave up his outside club at the beginning of this year, there wasn't enough time with the work on the site.'

'He did love sports,' Carolyn said over the low rumble of the kettle, 'but on the inside, he was always a softie. They had a cocker spaniel called Bess who had to be put down when the boys were nine or ten because she went senile and bit his sister. He was devastated – I think he cried solidly for a week.' She took a tissue from her pocket.

'Did it make the two of you closer, Theo, what happened last year?'

'Yes,' he said. 'Ben and me, *and* us with Molly.'

'How long have you known her?'

'Only since she started at Summerfield.'

'She was the academic year above, is that right? You and Ben had just finished your GCSEs when the rape happened; she'd just finished her first year of A-level work, and Alistair Heywood was the year above her?'

He nodded.

'But you and Molly weren't together at the time of the attack or the trial?'

'No. We started going out in February. This year.'

Nine months ago, then.

'How was that in terms of the three of you?'

'What do you mean?'

'Three's a crowd – Ben wasn't ever jealous? Or he and Molly didn't ever—'

'No,' Theo said, emphatic.

'I'm sorry, I had to ask. From what we've being hearing, he was popular with girls. Molly said you called him Babe Magnet?'

'Sometimes.'

'He recently had a thing with your friend Lily?'

'Yeah, that was a bad idea.'

'Why?'

He looked at her as if she was thick. 'Because she was a friend. You don't mess around with your friends.'

'Molly *wasn't* a friend, then?'

The look turned immediately defensive, as if she'd tried to catch him out. 'Molly's different. *Things* are different with someone who's been through what she has.' He shot a glance at his mother, who tactfully kept her eyes on the coffee she was spooning into a pot. 'The whole thing's different.'

He loved Molly, Robin realised. For him, it was the real thing. 'I understand,' she said.

Theo looked away, out of the window, and she saw a broken blood vessel at the side of his eye. Like Molly's yesterday, the sides of his nostrils were raw from blowing.

'What happened with Ben and Lily?' she asked.

'She really liked him, and she asked him out, afterwards' – another glancing look at his mother – 'thinking it was on. He had to let her down gently.'

'How did she take it? Was she angry? Or . . .'

'Angry? No. Embarrassed and a bit— Wait, are you driving at whether she killed him?' The hint of a smile. 'No. No way.'

'Lily's a sweetheart,' Carolyn said.

'OK. Was it definitely only girls he was into, Theo?'

'Yes.'

'You're sure?'

'He would have told me.'

'Really? If he wasn't out? You don't think he would have felt ashamed or . . .'

He looked at her as if she'd suddenly started speaking Chinese. 'Ashamed? It's the twenty-first century.'

'And yet people are still attacked for their sexuality.'

'Yeah,' he accepted the point, 'I know. But no, with me – especially after all this – we could talk to each other about anything. If he'd thought he was gay or bisexual or questioning, he would have told me.'

'We're trying to establish why he might have been at Moseley Bog on Sunday night. We know men meet there sometimes for sex and we need to rule it out as—'

'You can rule it out,' he said. 'I'm sure.'

'Right. At school, you said the two of you went there to smoke. I'm guessing it wasn't really cigarettes.'

His mother spun around, a coffee cup in her hand.

Theo lowered his head. 'Sorry, Mum. It wasn't a lot.'

'But you promised—'

'I'm not interested in the drugs, Mrs Gillespie, just in whether it might have been why Ben was there.'

'That's not the point. Or not the only point.'

Robin's look asked her to stay out of it for now. No doubt Theo would hear about it later. 'Ever at night?' she asked him.

'A few times, in the summer. It was quiet, no one bothered us, no one could smell it. We took torches, but once we were there, quite often we turned them off and just let our eyes get used to the dark. It was peaceful.'

'But *you* weren't there on Sunday evening?'

'No. It's too cold now.'

'When you *were* there, did you see other people?'

'Some – a few couples messing around: women and men, men and men. A couple of times we saw people doing drugs. *Other* drugs.'

'Did you ever see anything else criminal?'

'I don't think so. No.'

'There have been car jackings recently, some gang activity . . .'

'Never anything like that.'

'Did you ever do drugs other than weed?'

The look he gave her now was pained.

'Again, purely for this investigation,' Robin said. 'My team and I investigate homicides, that's it. And none of this will reach school, I promise.'

Eyes down, he mumbled, 'Sometimes.'

'Theo!'

'Please, Mrs Gillespie . . .'

'We did E three times,' he told Robin quickly, 'and acid once. We just wanted to know what that was like, we won't do it again.' He seemed to remember. '*I* won't.'

'Where did you get it?' He got in before his mother could. He turned to the window again.

'Theo?'

Nothing for several seconds, then a long out-breath. 'If I tell you, he won't face any consequences, will he? It's just for this?'

'I don't know. Honestly, I can't promise that.'

He said nothing.

'We need to eliminate every possibility,' Robin said softly. 'I'm not suggesting he's a suspect, your guy, just that if he was there, he might have vital information.'

'He's at the university.'

'Which one? Birmingham? Birmingham City? Aston?'

'Birmingham.'

She waited.

'Martin,' he said without looking at her. 'Spencer.'

'Do you have his number?'

He hesitated again, then took his phone in his pocket.

Robin wrote it down. 'Was it just the two of you, or other people as well?'

He sighed. 'God, you want me to throw *everyone* under the bus?'

'We won't say it was you who told us.'

He closed his eyes as if it actually pained him. 'Pierre Kaplan and Chris Chan. Only ever weed, though.'

'Thank you.' She made a note. 'Theo, you said Ben had to give up his football club to work on the site – all three of you must have made sacrifices.'

He shook his head. 'Not really. I mean, at the beginning it was a lot of work, but it never felt like a sacrifice. If we could help even a handful of people who'd been through something like Molly . . .'

'Was there ever any trouble? Sexual assault, rape – they're

contentious, I don't need to tell *you*. Had anyone ever had a problem with it? Someone who felt wronged, maybe – falsely accused?'

'No. We're extremely careful. Everything's legally vetted before it goes live.'

'Who does that?'

'Three postgraduates at the university. That's what the site's sponsorship money is used for.'

Carolyn brought over two mugs. Her hand shook as she put them down on the tea chest, splashing coffee over a copy of *World of Interiors* and the toes of Robin's boots. 'I'm so sorry.' She pressed the tips of her thin fingers against her forehead. 'I'm a wreck, we all are. Emma and Roger – I don't know how they're holding it together. We thought it was over . . . Please – make this stop. We can't go through it all again, waking up every day afraid for our son's life. And Anne – if they think one of the families did it . . .'

Robin nodded. 'I've spoken to my commanding officer and he's agreed that we'll post cars outside all your houses – yours, Molly's, the Renshaws'.'

Carolyn pressed her eyes closed. 'Thank you.'

'In terms of the fire, though,' Robin seized her chance, 'I'm sorry, Theo, but I know you'll understand I have to ask: where were you last night?'

Chapter Seventeen

Bill Heywood was moving as if he were a puppet, abruptly and slightly out of sync, eyes wide with the effort of trying to hide that, mentally, he was elsewhere. With his house destroyed, he was literally dislocated, and he looked it – a sixty-two-year-old man in a brushed-cotton checked shirt and a burgundy V-neck stranded on the white leather sectional sofa, reflected pitilessly back at himself by a wall-mounted television the size of a single bed. His suitcase was in the hallway, the airline tag still attached. At least he had a change of clothes, Robin had thought.

Dominic's flat – she refused to say apartment – was where Bill would stay for the foreseeable future, but it'd be cold comfort. If she had to describe it with a single word, she'd choose 'surface'. The huge white-walled living space was paved with a faintly sparkling marble that matched the kitchen countertops, the two items visible on which – a Gaggia coffee machine and a giant Dualit toaster – were stainless steel. The only picture on the walls, a black-and-white photograph the same size as the television, showed a powerboat shaped like a missile. Sofa aside, not one thing was soft, and, apart from the Heywoods themselves, nothing even had any colour except for the glasses of amber Scotch on the coffee table.

Bill Heywood reached for his now and took a shaky sip. Robin was reminded of her own father's bewildered fragility when her mother had been ill last year and felt a new stab of pity. This morning, she'd imagined him hearing the news thousands of miles away in a foreign country, his harrowing flight back knowing what waited for him here. Anne had been his wife for thirty years, the mother of his children; he had loved her.

Dominic and Marcus flanked him on the fifteen-foot length of the sofa as if to defend him against her and Varan from their positions on the sections at either end. Marcus was transformed, the lounging, foot-swinging man of yesterday gone. Dominic radiated hostility; when he'd opened the door to them, his expression had been so hate-filled, she'd thought for a split second he was about to launch himself at her.

'We're going to post officers outside,' she told them now. 'For security. They'll be in place soon.'

'Too fucking late,' he said. He'd finished one Scotch since they'd been here and poured himself another twice the size. He looked wild. 'Where were they last night when my mother was murdered in her sleep?'

Bill Heywood flinched.

Robin nodded, trying to communicate understanding without committing herself to words. 'Marcus, if you're really thinking about moving here for a few days so you're all together, it would work well logistically.' Samir would be thankful: it would mean they only had one location to secure overnight.

'If it's all right with you, Dom?'

'Of course it is. We need to stick together. Before any more of us are picked off.'

Robin turned to his father. 'Mr Heywood, when DI Hailey was investigating, he found no evidence to link you to the attacks against Ben and Theo before the trial—'

Dominic's voice was a growl. 'How many times? *Because. We. Didn't—*'

With a half-second time-lag, his father reached for his wrist and gripped it tightly.

'Please hear me out,' Robin asked. 'Last year, you thought someone else wanted to hurt them and saw a convenient opportunity to put you in the frame for it, yes? To me, it seems much more likely the other way round: that someone had a grievance against *your* family.'

'Because we're successful,' said Dominic. 'Because people can't stand tall poppies.'

Because one of you raped someone. Because people can't stand arrogant little gits who think they're special because they were born rich.

She kept her face neutral. 'Can you think of anyone in particular?'

'What, like we'd know and not tell you?' said Dominic, incredulous, his father's hand still clamped round his wrist. 'Sit back and let this drag on and on, destroy our business and now . . .' He swallowed. 'For fuck's sake!'

'Witness intimidation, GBH, attempted manslaughter, Ben's murder if it's the same person – for someone to try to frame you for all that, it would have to be a serious grievance.'

'No shit, Sherlock,' snorted Marcus.

Robin ignored him, too. 'Which is why I find it hard to believe you don't have any idea who it might be. So much effort, so much risk and they're not even on your radar?'

'Who knows what goes on in people's minds?' said Dominic. 'It could be any pathetic little loser.'

Robin eyed him. *He's just lost his mother, he's just lost his mother.* 'I doubt that. Apart from anything else, to have avoided being caught, he – or she – was absolutely meticulous. Please – help us end this. Tell us who has reason to cause you this much pain.'

'Molly Zajac, her family, the Renshaws, the Gillespies – they *think* they have reason.'

'And no one else? No one who feels you wronged or slighted them? Former employees, investors, ex-lovers? I'd rather be able to eliminate something unlikely than not hear about it at all.'

Bill Heywood met her eye and, for a moment, he seemed fully present. '*I* think Renshaw was killed because of that fucking, *fucking* website.'

She frowned. 'What makes you say that?'

'Because, in this family, we know how it feels when someone you love is accused of something they didn't do.'

Momentarily, despite the DNA evidence, the eyewitnesses, the unanimous guilty verdict, Robin caught herself wondering: what if Alistair *hadn't* raped Molly? If it *had* been consensual?

No – no, no, no. That way madness lay.

'If the root of the problem *is* with the website,' she said, 'we'll find it.'

'Forgive my lack of confidence.'

'Why do you dislike it so much, sir?' Varan asked.

Bill Heywood looked at him with contempt. 'Because every time anyone mentions it, my son's name is dragged up again, isn't it? Other people are found guilty – rightly or wrongly – they get their sentence and they serve it, but *my* son? Oh no. His crime – his *alleged* crime – is rehashed over and over and over again; they just won't let it lie. Articles in the paper, interviews, sodding *podcasts* – whatever the hell they are – every time they talk about that website, everyone's reminded again. And it's not just them – the *Daily Mail* does a piece on #MeToo in schools? StrengthInNumbers. Some little reality-television *tart* decides to boost her public profile by crying rape and, look, here it is again, StrengthInfuckingNumbers.'

'Reality TV?' said Varan.

'Marni Weston,' said Marcus. 'The "singer". She was laughed out of court, but she still managed to namecheck the site on her way out. More publicity, more and more people hearing Alistair's *story*.'

'How many other rapists – *alleged* rapists – can the general public name?' demanded his father. 'Murderers, yes – they're basically celebrities, some of them. Rapists? No. But *my* son's name's continually dragged through the mud because of that site, and there's not a thing we can do. So if someone killed Renshaw because of it, I wouldn't be surprised. Honestly, today, I'd shake their hand.'

Dominic showed them out. As he stood, Robin saw Heywood Senior shoot him a warning look, *Watch yourself*, but when they rounded the corner in the corridor, out of sight of the main living space, he turned to her, pushing his face right up in hers, finger aimed at her chest.

'Last year,' he said, eyes locked on hers, voice shaking, 'I know you weren't involved. But *this* – my mother – *this* is on you.'

'Dominic,' she said, putting up a hand, feeling Varan move closer to protect her. 'Take a step back, please.'

He shook his head infinitesimally, not refusing but talking to himself: *Not now, not yet, wait.*

'Be careful,' he warned. 'That's all I'm saying. My mother's dead and I don't even know what I'm capable of now.'

Chapter Eighteen

The light had been fading when they left The Mailbox, and though it was still barely half past five when they got back to Rose Road, it was dark. Many of the houses in the street were dark, too, but the station was lit up like a cross-Channel ferry, light pouring from every window. Samir's car was in its spot, two along from her own, and Robin felt an odd sense of homecoming.

Tiredness washed over her as they went through the turn-stiles and her legs were heavy on the stairs, but the moment she put her hand on the incident-room door, Tark spun his chair round, face aglow. Robin knew that look, he might as well have had his hand up, *Pick me, pick me.* She'd have liked to have taken her coat off first, but it would have been cruel to make him wait.

'Go on then, what have you got?'

'Ben on Sunday night,' he said, trying and failing not to look too pleased with himself. 'The number 11 route anti-clockwise goes from near the Renshaws' to Moseley Bog, so I called the bus company and found out which drivers were on and Dave went to speak to them.'

Hanratty looked delighted with himself, too. 'When he saw the photo, the second one said he wasn't positive, but he thought Ben had got on his bus on Sunday, just before nine.'

'So we got the tapes from the bus,' said Tark, 'and look.'

He had it up on-screen, ready to go, and the core crew huddled behind him and watched Ben in grainy black and white as he boarded the bus wearing the same thin hoodie Robin had seen in the wood. He showed the driver what she guessed was a 16–18 photo-card, then tapped another card on the reader and loped out of view.

Tark toggled to footage from a different camera, in which Ben sat in the first row of raised seats to the right of the aisle, just past the middle doors. Two other passengers: a man in his thirties on the back seat with his head against the window, eyes closed, and a woman in a hijab, who, by the speed of her thumbs on her phone, was either playing a game or having an extremely animated text conversation.

Ben stayed in the outer seat. 'No point getting settled in,' Tark said, 'because he was only going five stops, Melton Road to Swanshurst Lane. It's about a mile, just over, could have walked it and saved the money, it wasn't raining yet.'

'Maybe he was pushed for time – said he'd meet someone at nine and he's running late?' suggested Malia.

'What do you think?' said Robin. 'Does he look relaxed?'

'I can't tell if he actually is,' Tark said, 'or he's pretending – you know, teenage cool? I've watched it nine or ten times and I'm still on the fence. Look.' He dragged the cursor along a little and they watched Ben pull a hand out of the hoodie pocket and lean forward to press the request button. A few seconds later, he stood up, waited for the doors, then swung himself down the steps to the pavement in a single fluid move. 'Cool? Playing it cool? I can't decide.'

'Let's see him again?'

Tark dragged the video back and they watched Ben drop into his seat a second time. 'He's bouncing his knee,' Tark pointed, 'but, again, you could take that either way: anxious or teenage energy, can't sit still? Whichever, though, we've got him going voluntarily – or at least not physically coerced at this stage – to the south-west corner of Moseley Bog. Progress.'

'*Excellent* progress.'

'Interesting he's not on his phone when he's sitting there,' said Malia. 'I can't do that anymore – as soon as I'm at a loose end anywhere, my hand goes for it automatically.'

'Has he even got his phone with him?' Varan asked. 'He's not holding it, is he, when he gets on?'

Tark went back to the first camera and they watched Ben board the bus again, pay and turn. 'There,' he said, pausing it. 'What's that in his back pocket?'

'Phone,' said Robin and Malia together.

'Might suggest he's got something on his mind, that he's not looking for a distraction?'

'Impossible to know,' Robin said. 'How was Alistair, Malia?'

She shook her head. 'Not good at all. Distraught about his mother – he was crying almost the whole time, hardly got his words out.'

'You told him his father was going to see him later?'

'Yes, but honestly,' she frowned, 'I don't know if it was good news.'

'I thought they were close. Senior was definitely defensive of him.'

'Jo and I both got the impression he was ashamed.'

'But isn't he still saying he's innocent, the sex was consensual?'

'No, not that. Because he'd been beaten up – he had the remnants of a massive shiner and two of his fingers were strapped, they'd been stamped on. When we said his dad was coming, he put his hands over his face, then sort of gestured at himself, "Look at the state of me." We reckoned he didn't want him thinking he can't hold his own.'

133

For a couple of seconds, Robin felt sorry for him, too. To have to think like that the day you lost your mum. But standing your ground and being the alpha were doubtless core tenets of Heywood family code, whatever the situation. *We're not going anywhere.*

'When did it happen, this beating? What day?'

'Last Thursday.'

Six days – almost a week ago. 'Did he tell you why?'

'"Same as it always is. Posh boy needs a kicking." I pressed him because of the timing, but we both thought he was telling the truth. God, I hate those places,' she said, 'they're worse than adult prisons. There's always a couple of psychos, but the rest are just kids who never really had a chance.'

Lennie's had a chance. The thought arrived in Robin's mind without warning. If everything went sideways, and the plan fell apart, was Len posh enough to be the 'posh girl'? In a young offenders institute, yes. And – much worse – her mum was police.

'Not saying it's OK for him to get the living shit kicked out of him,' said Tark, pre-empting a warning, 'but you can see why they'd hate him. He basically had everything handed to him on a plate, then took the one thing that wasn't.'

No one disagreed.

'So the beating happened,' Robin said, 'then Ben was killed three days later.'

Malia nodded. 'We checked his visitors. Anne went every week, but no one else had been for nearly a month. The last person otherwise was Marcus, then Dominic two weeks before that. The visits are definitely tailing off. A friend went at the beginning, but that was a one-off, probably scared the living bejeezus out of him, and his solicitor went four times. Since April, though, it's only been family, and the visits from his dad and brothers were getting further and further apart.'

Robin thought about Dominic's 'luxury' flat and wondered what he felt when he went to see Alistair. Brinsford was just north of Wolverhampton, twenty miles away, max, but he hadn't been for weeks. She'd be willing to bet he'd only gone at all under duress from his mother, then came home and showered, like she had this morning, scrubbing to get the place off his skin, un-sully himself.

But as he'd said at his office, mud stuck. Bill had had to go to Sweden to woo an investor who wasn't au fait with their particular brand of it – though in these days of the internet, surely anyone investing money would do a cursory search. The story of Alistair's crime would live forever online, and every time Ben or Theo or Molly talked about the catalyst for StrengthInNumbers, it was refreshed, just as Bill had said.

Chapter Nineteen

When her mother put the plate in front of her, Robin felt an excitement more appropriate for a hot date than a hot dinner. Cottage pie and peas – no, petit pois: ordinary peas were 'too mealy', in her mother's view. She put her face over it and breathed in: actual home-cooked food.

Her mother sat with her while she ate, nursing the last half-inch of the small glass of red wine she now drank daily 'for medicinal purposes'. Following a stroke in the summer, she was all about the Mediterranean diet (the weekly cottage pie, Robin's father's favourite, was an act of love), water aerobics and countless thousands of daily steps. She claimed the exercise was for the cardiovascular benefits, but Robin and her dad had talked a couple of weeks ago about whether she was using exercise to control her anxiety about Luke.

Circles under her eyes notwithstanding, her mother was attractive, and losing a few pounds had given her a jawline women fifteen years younger would envy. She'd always had good skin, and she'd started lightening her hair several years ago so that, in her mid-sixties, she was going blonde rather than grey. She was a careful dresser, too: not by chance were the leaves in the pattern on her shirt the same blue-green as her eyes.

Lennie and Robin's dad, Dennis, were next door in the sitting room. Since the summer, whenever they were together, the two of them had started watching 'our programme', as they called it, which wasn't one thing in particular but one mutually agreed-upon series after another. They'd done five seasons of *Friends*, *Rising Damp* – her dad's suggestion, of course, but Lennie had loved it – *Ab Fab* and now *Miranda*. Comedies only, nothing dark, no crime. As an initiative, it was pure Dennis, low-key and gently self-indulgent, but consistent, reliable. The series element was important, Robin understood, because episodes were something, however small, to look forward to, a bread-crumb trail through this dark and frightening time.

Lennie had come to say hello when she'd arrived. The cast-iron stability of this house and its routine always raised her spirits. When *she* was a teenager, Robin had found it stultifying, but then, she'd had the benefit of its stability all her life and you only went looking for what you were missing.

She still had the benefit of the stability now, and its chief architect. She hadn't minded when Lennie sloped back off to the television, because it was her mother Robin needed to speak to.

Christine was a creature of the era she'd been brought up in, a firm believer that the best use of any woman's talents was in the home, the support of husband and children, but since she'd turned her focus to protecting Lennie instead of being Robin's (formidable) adversary, Robin was profoundly grateful. She'd always recognised the strength of her mother's will – she'd had no choice – but after the Rose Road riot, Christine Lyons had revealed herself in a whole new light. She was no *hausfrau*, however dominant; she was Don Corleone in a pinny, and with Lennie's future hanging by a thread, she was exactly what Robin needed.

'Delicious, Mum.' She put down her knife and fork. 'Thank you.'

Her mother had made the pie probably a couple of thousand times over the past forty years, but she looked gratified nonetheless. 'Glad you enjoyed it, love. I know I'm always nagging, but you have to make time to eat decently, however busy you are. You'll be no good to Lennie if you die of scurvy, will you?'

'Scurvy!'

'Well, you laugh, but the old diseases are coming back, the way people eat now. Unless you're actually lactose-intolerant, this squeamishness about dairy – there's children with *rickets*.'

Robin nodded. 'I know. And you're right.'

Her mother dropped her voice a little. 'How's the case?'

'Not great,' she admitted. She pointed at the sitting-room wall and mouthed, 'How's she been?' Sound travelled so efficiently in her parents' little house that you could stand in their kitchen at the back and hear someone turning a page upstairs in the master bedroom at the front. With all the doors shut.

Her mother tipped her hand from side to side, then, stealthy as a street dealer, nodded towards the conservatory. They slid off their stools and tiptoed out, pulling the door silently closed behind them. Then her mother headed for the outer one, to the garden. She'd deliberately left the outside light off, but in the glow coming through the conservatory from the kitchen, Robin saw her touch a finger to her lips to caution that next door might be listening, too. Over-caution in this case: unless you were a smoker banned from the house – which, as she remembered from her teenage years when they'd shopped her, the Richards emphatically were not – there'd be no reason to be lurking in your garden at night in these temperatures.

Her mother checked around as if the Flying Squad might be lying in wait behind the shed.

138

'Look, it might not mean anything, but . . . I don't know. I've gone over it, back and forth, and . . .'

'What? Come on, love, spit it out,' Robin told her in a voice that sounded a bit like Peter Hailey's. Putting on accents to diminish serious things was a tic Corinna seemed to have bequeathed her when she died. The strange dints and scratches other people left on you as they hurtled on *their* solo journeys through space.

Her mother's voice dropped. 'Luke doesn't want to see me this week. I heard from them this afternoon – he's cancelled my visit.'

Robin stiffened. 'What?'

'He doesn't want to see me, or talk – he didn't even ring to let me know.'

Her mother couldn't say the word prison, but every week since Luke had been arrested, without fail, she had steeled herself and gone up the road to Winson Green to visit him there. Of course, he wouldn't see Robin, and he'd refused offers from his estranged wife, Natalie, to bring their toddler, Jack, to see him, too. 'I am not having my son coming into a prison. Not happening.'

So, when his life had fallen so dramatically apart, their mother had been his constant and his line to the outside. Single-handedly, she'd kept him going. And resolved. Every week, she'd reassured him he was doing the right thing, that by serving the time for Lennie's crime, he could atone for what he'd done and – probably more important to him, Robin thought – he could make things right with *her*.

'Why?' she asked in a whisper.

'Apparently he needs time to think.'

'He's got nothing *but* time!'

Her mother's face said she'd had the same thought.

'Mum,' Robin made herself ask, 'is he OK?'

'I hope so. I really hope so.'

'I meant,' she lowered her voice another, 'is he still . . . solid?'

'I know what you meant.'

Shit – shit.

Robin paced, careful to stay out of potential sightlines from the sitting room. If Lennie saw them out here, she'd know immediately something was wrong. She stopped moving when she realised how loud her feet sounded – apart from the distant swish of traffic on Stratford Road and canned laughter from inside, the garden was silent.

Then, another thought, horrifying. 'Mum – a journalist hasn't contacted you?'

'Journalist?' A hiss of alarm.

'From London. The *Record*. He's called about the case before, but this morning he talked about Luke.' Her voice wasn't much more than a whisper. 'Me and Luke.'

'Robin! Why?'

'Said it would make a good story, the contrast in situations. And my skeletons.'

Her mother was silent. Then, almost inaudibly, she said, 'Did he mention her?'

'No, but if he goes looking . . .'

In the semi-dark, she saw her mother's thoughts cycle across her face: the new danger, the realisation of what it could mean for the family and then, in a second, her own feelings sublimated so she could do what she needed to do now: make things better, help her own daughter.

'No,' she murmured, reaching out to grip Robin's upper arm, 'no. It'll be all right, love – it'll be fine. You don't need to worry about that. Apart from us, no one else knows, do they? How *could* he find out?'

Chapter Twenty

When they arrived home, Lennie made a cup of tea, then disappeared upstairs. Seconds after her bedroom door closed, her muffled voice reached Robin through the kitchen ceiling: the late-night call with Austin. The lulling effect of her parents' house had meant a peaceful drive home, and in the olden days, pre-boyfriend, pre-riot, Lennie would have drunk the tea down here, with her. For once, though, Robin didn't mind being left in the dust; it was a relief to drop the nothing-to-see-here façade.

She poured herself a glass of wine and took it to the sofa, where she let her head fall back and closed her eyes for a minute. What the hell was going on? What was Luke playing at? 'Time to think' – the words turned her stomach. Think about what?

Well, what might it be? said a sarcastic voice in her ear. *A week and a half before being sentenced for something he didn't do?*

Could that be all it was? Just the closeness of the date now?

Quickly, she stood and went back to the kitchen for her personal laptop. In the sitting room again, she opened a browser and typed in 'Jeremy Handley *Daily Record*'.

The search returned a lot of hits, almost all bylines on articles he'd written. She clicked around to get a sense of them. From what she could tell, he was relatively junior, but he'd been promoted in the past year or so. On a couple of the earlier pieces, he was credited just for 'additional reporting', but then he became 'Jeremy Handley, *Record* News Desk', then 'Jeremy Handley, News Reporter'. In the past three months, he'd written two 'news features', too – one about a junior cabinet minister caught expensing flights to the British Virgin Islands with his mistress, the second about the mishandling of resources by a local education authority that had led, among other things, to students being fed out-of-date food.

She found him on Twitter, worried he might have posted about her, but no, someone at work (probably Kilmartin) would have seen and brought it to her attention. Also, if he was planning a scoop, he'd play his cards close to his chest until he was ready: any blood in the water would attract other journalists. A quick scroll through just a couple of hundred of his four thousand followers turned up several reporters on different papers.

Two of his tweets this week linked to stories he'd written about the case – one yesterday, one today – and there she was: 'DCI Robin Lyons, leading the inquiry, was unavailable for comment'. Well, it was factually accurate, even if it sounded like she'd been off having her nails done.

She double-clicked on the round circle with Handley's headshot, a professional photo, maybe taken in anticipation of picture bylines. He was younger than he'd sounded on the phone, mid to late twenties, though that made sense of where he was career-wise: climbing the ladder, beginning to make a name for himself. Brown hair, brown eyes, pink shirt – more pleased with himself, at least in the instant the picture had been taken, than Robin had ever been in her life.

It was easy to find him on Facebook because he'd used the same profile picture. He'd grown up in Twickenham, gone to university in Newcastle, but that was as far as his details went.

Based on how often he posted, it looked like Twitter was much more his bag; he'd only added a single update this year, a picture from May showing him in jeans and a shirt standing next to a black Mazda MX5, '*New wheels!*' The comments were from friends, not professional contacts: '*Nice, mate!*' '*Designated driver for the next ten years!*'

Robin found she'd emptied her glass. She stood up again and fetched the bottle and her notebook. Then she opened a new window and typed in 'Marni Weston'.

The X Factor, *The Voice*, *Britain's Got Talent* – she didn't watch them, so she struggled even to keep track of which was currently on, but she remembered from Lennie and her school friends back in London that Marni Weston had reached the final rounds of one of them three or four years ago. She was a singer – small, dark-haired and pretty, a sort of poor man's Ariana Grande from somewhere in the south-west – Avonmouth, Portishead? No, *Weston*-Super-Mare – of course. After she'd been eliminated, she'd been on magazines by the tills at the garage for a few months and then, as these things went, she'd dropped out of view. Until Bill Heywood had said the name, Robin had forgotten all about her.

About half the first page of hits were to do with her stint on the show and her fledgling romance with a member of a wannabe boy-band who'd been rival contestants: *Love or War? Marni and Danny!*

The other half were from last month. Marni Weston – real name Rachel Dobbs, twenty-five – had been the victim of an alleged attack by the owner of a venue in Somerset where she'd been performing. After the club closed, Weston said, the man had locked the doors and raped her.

Robin added 'StrengthInNumbers' to her search terms. The first hit was a news article from the *Bristol Post* three weeks ago

– *Not Guilty: Verdict in Marni Weston Rape Case.* Robin hit the 'play' arrow on a video beneath the headline, and an older and thinner-looking – much thinner – Marni appeared in front of microphones on the steps of Bristol Crown Court, flanked by her parents and lawyer, Robin guessed, but touching none of them. Everything about her body language said *Get away from me.*

'Today, the court chose not to believe my testimony – testimony it was beyond traumatic to give – and decided to acquit. Tonight my attacker will be celebrating getting off scot-free while I go on living with what he did. Since that night, I've lived in constant fear – I have PTSD and flashbacks, I can't perform. Most days I find it hard to leave the house at all.

'We didn't get the right result here, but I want to thank everyone who tried and who supported me: my family, my legal team, and everyone who shared their support on social media. I'd also like to thank StrengthInNumbers.com and the people who shared stories like mine there and inspired me at least to try to bring my attacker to justice. Thank you.'

The video ended and the arrow obscured Weston's face again.

Robin remembered Heywood's words: '*I think Renshaw was killed because of that fucking, fucking website.*'

Could that be right? And if it was, had it been something specific, or was it just because, as he'd said, while the site was running, Molly, Ben and Theo giving interviews, visiting schools, writing articles, Alistair's case would never be allowed to slip out of view?

Had Ben been killed to kill the site?

The phone made Robin jump.

'Hey,' Samir said, 'calling the night shift for any late-breaking developments.'

'Nothing major to report, I'm afraid,' she said, pulling her feet up under her, 'but, you know, thinking.'

'Anything interesting?'

'Well, one way or another, I don't think *Bill* Heywood killed Ben. Obviously, he'd have to have farmed it out, but I don't think he knows anything about it.' Yes, marooned on the sofa in that god-awful flat, angry as he was, he'd been telling them the truth, she thought. 'I'm not ruling out one or more of the others, but *he* didn't know.'

In the background at Samir's end, Robin heard footsteps on tile and, a second or two later, the unmistakable sound of a kettle being filled and replaced on its stand.

'Robin,' he said, she guessed in response to a gestured enquiry.

'Hi-i,' Liz called.

'Hi back.' If not Bill then, Robin thought, what about Anne? What if her death wasn't just a general counter-strike but *she specifically* had been the target? Had whoever fired the house done it because they'd known that *she* had killed Ben?

Samir listened then was quiet. 'You're saying Anne might have killed Ben without her husband knowing? Or sons?'

'Not saying, wondering, but yes, as a theory. *Why now?* That's the question I keep asking. Bill said he thought Ben was killed because of the site – if he was dead, he couldn't keep spreading the word, refreshing Alistair's story, could he? Maybe, after a year, Anne had realised it wasn't going to go away while the site was still active and she decided to do something.'

Maybe seeing Alistair last week had been the final straw, finding him broken-fingered and black-eyed as his friends disappeared and even the rest of the family left him to rot. As Heywood Properties failed and they had to go further and further afield to find new investors.

'*Could* she have done it, logistically?' Samir asked.

'Faulkner said it could have been a woman, and she was very fit-looking for fifty-three. She said she was at home on Sunday night, and Tark says her car didn't leave the house, but that doesn't mean anything. She could have left on foot, from the back or in a CCTV blind spot, if there was one, caught a taxi.'

From Samir's end, behind him somewhere, she heard the soft bump of a cupboard door and the chink of a teaspoon in a china mug. 'But isn't your thinking that Ben went to Moseley Bog of his own accord? He wouldn't have gone to meet Anne, would he?'

She sighed. 'I doubt it, not wittingly, but maybe she tricked him somehow. We still don't know *what* he was doing. He wasn't meeting any of the friends we've spoken to. Our best guess at this stage is he went to meet their dealer; we're still trying to track him down.'

'Then how would Anne have known he'd be there?'

'How did whoever attacked the boys and their families over and over last year know where they'd be?'

'So you *do* think the same person, or people, did both?'

Robin took a deep breath and blew it out. 'Honestly? I haven't got a clue.'

'Well, it doesn't matter,' he said. 'That's not our case.'

'True. All we have to worry about is solving two murders in a handful of days. Thank God, eh?'

He was quiet long enough for her to know he'd guessed something else was afoot. 'Anything you want to tell me about?'

Yes, she wanted to say. She wanted to tell him about Handley at the *Record* and Luke, suddenly incommunicado at Winson Green; she wanted reassurance that everything would be fine, that Luke was bound to be jittery, that there was no way Handley could have got to him in prison. With Liz hovering, however, it was impossible.

'Nope,' she said, 'all good. See you tomorrow.'

Chapter Twenty-One

Robin had been so tired when she'd finally switched off the light that sleep had dragged her under without too much effort on her part (at least by prevailing standards), but, as also happened more often than not these days, it spat her back up too soon, so that by five o'clock, she'd been wide awake and girding herself to check the *Record*'s website. Her heart had thumped as she'd refreshed the page, but though Handley's piece had been updated, *Arson Confirmed in StrengthInNumbers Case*, and there was a big new photo of the fire at its height, being unavailable for comment was still the extent of her role.

She'd made good use of the time, though, ploughing through some of her email backlog and making notes for the day. She'd been at the station by seven, called The Mailbox at eight and, at nine thirty, Varan stuck his head round the door to say that Marcus Heywood had arrived downstairs.

He'd brought a solicitor, William Seymour from Seymour Cowper Price, one of the top local firms. Robin had never met him before – his rates put him beyond almost everyone's reach – but she'd heard he was sharp as cheese wire.

She requested the dingiest interview room and kept them waiting forty minutes – time she enjoyed significantly more than they did, by the look of it. When she and Varan went to find them, both were pink in the cheeks, debatable whether from the deliberate overheating of the room or the insult to their dignity. Maybe, as she'd intended, Marcus had been put in mind of his handful of visits to Alistair in Brinsford.

'Chief Inspector,' Seymour said as he sat again after a terse handshake, 'I understand you're busy, but my client is grieving.' He was tall and very thin, dry-handed despite the heat.

'Yes,' Robin said. 'My team and I are investigating Anne's death, too, as I'm sure you're aware. Both cases.'

He frowned slightly. 'You regard them as separate?'

'Let's talk on the record.' She nodded at Varan to start the tape. 'We're treating the deaths as separate, yes,' she said, 'until we learn otherwise. Which is why, Marcus, we need to talk to you.' She let her eyes linger on his face, making sure he felt it. Under the flushed cheeks, his skin was pallid and his forehead shone. Not so confident now. 'As you say, we're extremely busy, so I'll get straight to the point. On the evening Ben Renshaw was killed, you told us that you were with your mother, your brother Dominic and his girlfriend, Caitlin, at your family house in Moseley. *Your* girlfriend, Chloe, had been with you earlier in the day but left at 5 p.m. You, Dominic and Caitlin stayed until a little before eight thirty then left at the same time as one another, you alone, the two of them together. We were able to confirm all that with CCTV from the house.'

'Right. Good.'

'What we need now is to hear why it took you thirty-seven minutes longer to get home.'

The Marcus of Tuesday might have rolled his eyes, but this one looked uncomfortable. 'I went a different way and got stuck in traffic,' he said.

Robin tipped her head to one side. 'Sunday night in November, after eight o'clock? Even if we allow ten minutes extra for the minimal distance between your place and Dominic's, it's a significant discrepancy.'

'Different route, traffic,' he said, emphatic.

'You didn't stop to get petrol or a pint of milk?'

He hesitated a second as if realising first that he'd missed a trick, then that they'd be able to check anyway. 'No.'

'In a criminal investigation, Mr Heywood,' she locked eyes with him, 'the next best thing to evidence of guilt is catching someone in a lie. I'd bear that in mind, if I were you, while you consider whether traffic is the answer you want on the record.'

'Chief Inspector, this is really not—' began Seymour.

Robin cut him off. 'The reason the time bothers us so much, Mr Seymour, is that it's when Ben Renshaw died.'

Both reacted, Seymour with a small jolt, Heywood by closing his eyes. Robin watched his chest rise and fall before he opened them again.

'I want to speak to my solicitor,' he said.

Fifteen minutes passed before he was ready again. When Robin and Varan re-entered the room, Marcus was sitting with his forearms against the table's edge, fingers tightly interwoven. He didn't look up, but Robin could see enough of his face to know he was crying.

Varan restarted the tape.

'DCI Lyons,' Seymour began, 'Marcus has asked me to speak on his behalf. On Sunday evening, he didn't go directly home to the city centre. After leaving his parents' house, he visited an acquaintance in Spark Hill and bought a quantity of diazepam. He returned to Moseley to give the tablets to his mother, Anne, *then* drove home.'

Robin saw a tear fall from Marcus' chin onto the front of his shirt. As it seeped, darkening the pale-blue cotton, she felt a corresponding sinking in her stomach.

'You supplied your mother with tranquillisers, Marcus?'

A nod, barely perceptible. He mumbled something, then cleared his throat. 'She asked me to get them for her. When things were bad after Alistair . . . She didn't want anyone else to know – our doctor's a family friend and Dad thinks pills are for weak people.'

'Was she using them regularly?'

'Not always, she tried not to, but . . . She made me promise not to tell anyone.'

Robin thought of Anne unresponsive in the family room, knocked out hard enough with wine and pills to sleep through the fire. Through the end of her life.

Marcus raised his head and in his eyes, she saw fear. 'Is there any way my father couldn't know?' he said. 'Please?'

Robin considered, then shook her head. 'No, I don't think so. It'll come out – there'll be a post-mortem, an inquest. Tell him, Marcus. It'll be better if he hears it from you.'

Chapter Twenty-Two

The news settled on the team like a weight. 'God almighty,' said Tark, dropping his chin. 'Unless her bloods show she hadn't taken any on Tuesday night, he'll be living with that forever, won't he?'

'Unless his dad kills him first,' muttered a male voice at the back.

'What it means as far as the inquiry is concerned,' said Robin, getting them back on track, 'is that *all* the Heywoods now have solid alibis. Bill was in Sweden, we can track Dominic on ANPR and CCTV, and – subject to our corroborating it, of course, by looking later on the house footage from that night – Marcus' information gives us not only *his* whereabouts but Anne's: she couldn't have got to Moseley Bog, killed Ben and been back at the house in time to get the pills.'

'There's still the possibility they contracted the work out,' said Malia.

'Yes, or that Alistair pulled the strings from Brinsford somehow, but both of those still leave our question: Why now?' She paused for emphasis. '*Why now?*'

'So, next move: we need to drill deeper into Ben's life. We keep hearing everything was normal, and yet he went out to Moseley Bog alone, apparently of his own accord, in the dark and cold on a Sunday night? Back to basics: more interviews, more social media, another go at tracking down any CCTV we might have missed. I also want to take a much, much closer look at StrengthInNumbers.'

She looked at Malia. 'Let's speak to the accused in the Marni Weston case – did *he* think she went to the police because of the site? Or was there someone *else* who's been called out or identified or prosecuted? Did someone use it to settle a score? We need to ask Molly and Theo, and these graduate students – maybe they caught something before it went live.'

'Or missed something,' said Malia.

'If it *is* the site, though,' Varan asked, 'why Ben, and not the others? Last year, *both* boys were attacked.'

'Very good question – needs answering.'

Malia nodded. 'This time, Theo wasn't even aware of anything going on.'

Jo looked up from her notebook. 'The dealer Marcus got the diazepam from – it's not the same guy Ben and Theo bought from, is it? Could that be how the killer knew he was in the wood?'

'Another good question,' Robin said. 'It doesn't sound like it – different names, different numbers – but we need to lay eyes on them both and make sure.'

'There's thousands of stories on the website,' said Tark. 'Maybe tens of thousands.'

'And all the stuff *around* the site, too,' Malia said. 'Talks, articles, interviews, social media. There's a ton on his computer, apparently.'

Looking round, Robin saw consternation at the sheer scale of the work in front of them. Hard as the Heywoods would have been to nail, at least they'd been a concentrated focus. Now the case was blown wide open.

*

As she made her way back to her office, Robin had a mental image suddenly of an old-fashioned inkpot, like the one Atkinson, the Head at Summerfield, had had on his desk. In her mind's eye, it had been filled with jet-black ink but had tipped over – no, it had been *knocked* over – and the ink, set free, had spread in a glinting pool across the surface. It was spreading still, she thought, reaching for the next thing it could touch, then the next, completely uncontained.

At her desk, she checked the *Record*'s site again, then rang Peter Hailey.

He picked up almost immediately, his voice conjuring a vivid picture of his wolfish teeth, as if he'd smiled when he'd heard her. 'How are you getting on?'

'Well, the body count's still two this morning, as far as we know, so that's a victory, but it's about the only one.' She told him about Marcus and the tranquillisers. 'What it means is that none of the Heywoods themselves can have done it. I thought you'd like to know.'

If this was *the Heywoods and I didn't nail them* . . . She'd thought about that since they'd met, how she would have felt exactly the same.

'Thank you,' he said, 'I appreciate it. Though I could still be on the hook.'

'If the death's related to StrengthInNumbers, which is a main line of enquiry now, you can't be, because the site didn't exist then.'

'Hm. What about the fire? Anything?'

'No, we're drawing blanks. Given how much there is to protect on that road, you'd be amazed how little CCTV we've got. Theirs was destroyed with the house, and a lot of the neighbours' cameras are so focused on their own properties, they don't even catch a street view.'

'What's important finishes at the end of their drive?'

'You'd think so, given the responses from the house-to-house, too. No one heard anything, no one saw anything, no one had much to do with the Heywoods despite having lived across the way for fifteen years.'

'How about the other families?'

'The Renshaws were home in bed, I sent one of my DCs to make sure. The Gillespies and Zajacs say they were, too, though we'll need to check that.'

But if the fire wasn't retaliation for Ben, then a whole other vat of worms yawned open.

'I had a question for you, Peter,' she said. 'With the witness-intimidation, Ben and Theo were put through hell, but Molly *wasn't* targeted, was she? At all?'

'No.'

'What was your thinking on that?'

'You mean, why not? Our best guess was, because of the DNA evidence – sex definitely took place – the question was only whether or not it was consensual, and beyond he said/she said, Ben and Theo were the ones who were able to speak to that.'

Robin frowned. 'Hm.'

'Not convinced?'

'Not really.'

He huffed, a half-laugh. 'No, we weren't, either. Look, would it help to talk it over more in person? We could grab a drink one evening?'

Caught off guard, Robin didn't immediately reply. 'A drink?'

'I know you're under the cosh, and I've got a ton on, too, so we could do a later one.'

'I . . .' She had the sense – she was sure she was right – that he was talking about more than a chance to discuss things at greater length. After all, they could meet at either of their stations. He was talking about a date.

'Just an idea,' he said.

'No, that sounds . . . good – just, as you say, busy, so . . .'

'Well,' Hailey said, drily, 'you know where to find me. Here, around the clock.'

Robin made some notes, answered a couple of pressing emails, then called Sandy Kelman, the Renshaws' Family Liaison, to say she was coming.

Just as she was leaving her office, however, the phone rang, an outside call. She reached across and answered it from the wrong side of the desk. 'DCI Lyons, Force Homicide.' As the words left her mouth, she thought of Jeremy Handley – had he given up on her mobile and gulled someone into giving him her direct line?

'Robin? It's Liz Jafferi.'

Whether because she'd been thinking of Handley or because she'd never called her before, it took Robin a second to compute. Liz Jafferi – Samir's Liz.

'Hi.'

A laugh at the other end said her confusion had registered. 'Sorry, I caught you unawares.'

'No, not at all. I was just . . . away in my head. Crazy here today.'

'I can imagine. And that's partly why I'm ringing. What I said about dinner – why don't you come over on Saturday night? You and Lennie.'

Robin was momentarily lost for words. 'I . . . Honestly, Liz, it's really kind of you, but at this rate, I'll probably be *here* on Saturday.'

'Oh, I know the score' – another laugh – 'I was a DCI's wife once. So come over later, eight-ish. You have to eat and I'll be doing dinner, so you won't even have to think about it. No big deal, just casual, have a couple of glasses of wine, take the pressure off a bit. And if you *do* get called away in the middle of the main course, you know we'll understand.'

Robin scrambled for an excuse. 'Lennie might already have plans, I don't know – with everything that's happened this week, I've barely seen her.' She regretted the words as soon as she said them; she was sure Liz would never neglect her children.

'Well, that's OK. Just let me know when you do. Harry and Leila would love to meet her, though, and so would I. Eight, then?'

'I . . .'

'Looking forward to it already – it'll be great to get to know you better. We should have done it ages ago.' And then she was gone.

Shit, thought Robin as she put the phone down. *Shit, shit, shit*.

Chapter Twenty-Three

When Robin stepped inside the Renshaws' house this time, the air was hospital-warm. No cosy food scents lingered now, though, and aside from her own movements and Sandy's, who'd answered the door, the house was silent.

The Renshaws were waiting in the sitting room, the three of them huddled onto a two-person sofa and holding hands tightly, as if prepared for a game of British Bulldog in which she'd charge and try to rupture their line.

Ben's sister, Amy, was pressed between her mother in the middle and the arm of the sofa, where a dark patch on the fabric suggested that, until very recently, she'd had her face there. She was still crying; Robin saw her wipe her cheek surreptitiously as if she were somehow letting the side down. She was blonder than Ben, and slight like her mother. Robin knew that she went to Camp Hill, her own old school, and she tried to imagine herself in the same position at fifteen. Bad as things had always been between her and Luke, the seismic rupture of him dying at that age – let alone being killed – was hard to fathom. It would have changed everything, ruined them as a family.

Sleeping tablets or no, Ben's parents looked exhausted. The slow erosion process she'd imagined on Monday when she'd first met Emma was under way, her eye sockets visibly deeper despite her swollen eyelids. No skirt-and-shirt work clothes today but a pair of loose-fitting jeans and a sweatshirt that was far too big, with a fluorescent graffiti-tag design. It must have been Ben's, Robin realised.

She and Sandy took the sofa opposite.

'Mr and Mrs Renshaw, Amy,' Robin began, sitting forward, 'thank you for seeing me. We've had a development in the case this morning and I wanted to talk to you in person.'

Roger Renshaw looked at her with large eyes. His jaw was clenched, the muscle wadded.

'We've had new information that makes it impossible for any of the Heywoods to have been directly responsible for Ben's death.'

She'd expected the news to go down badly – it was partly why she'd come herself – but she wasn't prepared for the explosion from Roger. 'What? What the actual . . .' He remembered his daughter was there. 'You're joking – tell me you're joking.' Only the tightening of Emma's hand stopped him surging to his feet.

Robin shook her head. 'No, sir.'

'You . . . How much are they paying you, you and your . . . overlords? They've crossed your palms with their stinking silver again, haven't they? Justice for sale at fucking West Midlands Police!'

'Roger . . .' Emma tightened her grip again.

'No.' He shook his head as if trying to shake off a buzzing insect. '*No*. I can't take any more, sitting here listening to how people who harassed and terrified then *murdered* my son are going to walk away scot-free *again*.'

'Not scot-free,' his wife croaked. 'Not this time. Anne . . .'

'Mr Renshaw,' Robin said, 'I understand your frustration, but please believe that I'm running this enquiry free from any undue influence. What we learned this morning is true.'

'Then what is it?'

'I'm not at liberty to say, I'm afraid.'

'Not at liberty to say,' he mimicked. 'But you're at liberty to come here, to my house, and tell me that those *people*,' he spat the word, 'are going to get away with murder.'

Amy made a painful gulping sound.

'Roger, please,' Emma begged. 'Please, just listen. Chief Inspector . . .'

Robin gave her a look she hoped combined thanks and apology. 'All I can tell you at this stage is that none of the Heywoods can have been in the woods at Moseley Bog when Ben died. It isn't possible.'

'Then who?' Roger challenged. 'Who *else* would want to kill our boy? Our kind, lovely boy, who spent the last eighteen months of his life doing everything he could to help other people at the cost of his free time, his schoolwork, his physical safety? Who else?'

'We don't know yet, but we will.' Robin wanted to promise him, she badly wanted to, but with the way things were going, she couldn't let herself.

Roger snorted with scorn.

'Who else could it be?' asked Amy in a small voice. 'If it really wasn't them.'

'We're investigating the possibility it was connected to the website in some way. The man Marni Weston brought her case against, for example . . .'

'Him?' said Roger. 'He was guilty as hell and he knew it. No one'll hear from him again – he knows how lucky he is. Another bastard set free by the great British justice system. Well done, everyone – nice work.'

'Were there other cases where StrengthInNumbers was explicitly mentioned?' Robin asked Emma.

'One,' she nodded. 'A girl on Humberside. Ashley . . .' She closed her eyes. 'I'm sorry, I can't remember her surname. My brain . . .'

'Marsh,' said Amy. 'Ashley Marsh.'

'Thank you.' Robin made a note. 'It's been to court already?'

Emma nodded again. 'He got off, too. Not guilty.'

'OK, we'll talk to him. Speaking more broadly, had any sort of trouble stemmed from the site? They did a lot of events – did anyone ever approach them with a grievance? Obviously these are contentious issues . . .'

'Ones they should never have even had to *think* about at their age,' said Roger, 'and here's my fifteen-year-old daughter, too, now, telling you about rape cases. The damage Alistair Heywood's done to this family . . .' His left cheek turned concave, as if he'd bitten the inside to keep himself under control.

'I don't think it's StrengthInNumbers,' said Emma. 'It can't be – they'd done so much less of it lately.'

'Really?' Robin turned to her. 'I don't think we'd heard that.'

'Is it important?'

'Perhaps – it might be. Why had they done less?'

'Ben's AS results. He did worse than expected – a lot worse. He needed decent grades for Loughborough and the school said he had to cut back and focus.'

'How did he feel about that?'

'Angry. He was committed to the site – he thought it was important.'

Robin nodded. 'Did Theo cut back, too?'

'They both did. Theo's academics are fine – better than – but he was applying for Oxford and that's a lot of work in itself, there's exams. They agreed to do fewer events and media things until the end of the academic year.'

'How about Molly?'

'She'd already pulled back a bit. She took a year out after the attack so she's doing A levels, too. I don't know if she chose to or her new school said something. Because she's not at Summerfield any more, she's beyond their jurisdiction now.'

Ben's room had been searched thoroughly on Monday, but Robin asked his mother if she'd show her.

Familiar as she was with the layout of this kind of semi-detached house, and given his status as the older sibling, she'd guessed Ben would have the larger of the two non-master bedrooms, but Emma brought her to the smaller, which shared its longest wall with the landing. Robin took a couple of steps in, then stopped and looked. She and Luke had shared a room not much bigger, but it was still close quarters for a teenage boy, and tidy, too. A single bed was tucked into the corner, the headboard against the wall with the window, which looked down the side return then out across the Renshaws' small garden at the one directly behind and its mirror-image house.

On the wall opposite the bed was an Ikea desk that Robin recognised from when they'd bought Lennie's, a Danish Modern design in pale wood. On its surface, the light angling through the window showed outlines in a fine layer of dust.

'The search team took things from here? Was it his box files?'

At her side, Emma nodded. 'All the printouts and press cuttings about the site, and the correspondence he wanted to keep.'

A pin-board directly above the desk was covered with a neat single layer of papers and photographs, including the *Post*'s article with the picture Varan had printed. Stepping closer, Robin saw a class timetable, a reading list for essay topics on Carl Jung and a flyer for a nightclub in the Jewellery Quarter.

He'd been eighteen for just three weeks; she wondered if he'd ever got there.

A family photo showed the four Renshaws on the beach two or three years back, judging by the relative ages of Ben and Amy, sand under their feet, the horizon a hazy afternoon blue behind them – Mediterranean somewhere, Greece or Turkey perhaps. Both the senior Renshaws were holding books – Roger, who was wearing a long-sleeved shirt with his swimming trunks, had two plus a newspaper. Robin imagined the pair of them coated with Factor 50 reading under umbrellas while the kids swam and messed about. She'd bet they'd insisted on touring the ruins of the local amphitheatre for a bit of improving culture first.

Another photo showed Ben and Theo in a little boat, a white sail behind them, Ben at the helm, Theo on the ropes, both squinting into the sun and grinning, teeth slightly too big for their faces.

'Sailing camp,' Emma said. 'They were thirteen, it was the first time either of them had really been away from home. Two weeks in Cornwall sleeping in little chalets, sailing all day, campfires – Carolyn and I were worried it'd be too long, but they had the time of their lives. Ben was so sunburnt when we picked them up, I thought he'd done permanent damage.' She blinked, then blotted a tear with her cuff.

'You and Carolyn are friends?'

'Yes. Do you have children?'

Robin nodded. 'A daughter, sixteen next month.'

Emma looked surprised. 'You don't look old enough.'

'I wasn't.'

A slight twist at the corner of her mouth, an attempt at a smile. 'But you know what it's like, then: if your children are friends when they're young, you end up spending a lot of time together. It's a bond.'

'Are your husbands friends, too?'

Emma appeared to hesitate. 'Not as much.'

Robin waited, leaving the air empty.

A faint sigh. 'Rog is very fond of Theo, but as the boys got older and there wasn't as much ferrying in the car, standing round together at practice, all that, he let things . . . tail off.'

'What was the issue – if there was one?'

Now Ben's mother looked uncomfortable. 'I don't want to speak ill of Eddie, but you probably know he went to prison for fraud.'

Yes, Edward Gillespie's conviction – Hailey had mentioned that coming up at Alistair's trial, Robin remembered. The QC had used it to question Theo's credibility as a witness.

'He'd been filing false business records. After he was released, Rog said he felt differently about him. It was his cousin's business, they were struggling, he understood the family-loyalty angle, but still . . . He's moral, Rog.'

'Has it affected your relationship with Carolyn?'

'Not now, we're fine, but to start with, it was tricky. They kept inviting us to dinner and I had to keep fending them off because Rog wouldn't go and it just got . . . awkward. After a few times, she asked me outright and I had to tell her. Being Caro, she didn't blame me and she and I are still friends.' Emma blinked and two big tears ran down the sides of her nose. This time she brushed them away with her fingers. 'Please make sure nothing happens to Theo – I couldn't bear it if *both* of them . . .' She turned back to the photograph with the boat. 'Look at them – that was only five years ago. They were children.'

Chapter Twenty-Four

Back at the station, Robin beckoned Malia to her office. Thinking about Summerfield as she drove, she'd been struck by a memory from the Head's office, an image of the Sixth Form teacher's hand on Theo's shoulder. 'His name's Grant Dugmore.' 'Let's get him in,' she said.

Malia nodded and made a note. 'How were the Renshaws?'

'Distraught, angry and sceptical about the website line of enquiry. But I'm not so sure. When we went back to Summerfield on Tuesday, did anyone there mention Ben and Theo had done less work on it recently?'

'Not that I heard.'

'Will you check with Tark and Jo? Apparently it was the school who asked them to cut back – crunch time, exams, it all sounds reasonable – but Summerfield would benefit from things quietening down, too, wouldn't they? Their application numbers must have dropped way off, for a start, but maybe there's more to it.' She tapped the end of her biro against her pad. 'How've you been getting on here?'

'Two bits of news,' said Malia. 'First, we've tracked down the defendant in the Ashley Marsh case. He's in Grimsby – shall I send someone to talk to him?'

Robin considered. It was a good way north – well over a

hundred miles, maybe a hundred and fifty. Round trip, it'd be a whole day's manpower and that seemed too big an investment. 'Let's get in touch with the SIO at Humberside who handled the case, get the lie of the land first.'

'Right. The other thing is, Varan's downstairs with Ben's dealer.'

'At last! Great.'

Malia pulled a face. 'Only from an elimination point of view, I think. I've been watching on-screen and he's got an alibi for Sunday night – he was playing snooker at a hall in Small Heath from six until close. It was busy, he said, loads of potential witnesses, and they'll have CCTV. Unless Ben was buying from someone else as well, I don't think it was drugs that took him to Moseley Bog.'

At five, Lennie texted: *Going to G&G's again, hope OK. Gran doing chkn kebabs.* Robin felt the usual push-pull, glad she'd have company and a proper meal, regretful that yet again it would be her parents who'd spend time with her, her mother who'd feed her. Over the past couple of months, she'd worried that one day, not even in the heat of a moment, Lennie would turn round and say she wanted to move back in with them. They'd have her in a heartbeat and if it was what she needed, Robin would agree, even if the idea alone was a stab in the chest.

For tonight, though, they'd keep her busy, stop her stewing.

Downstairs, Jo was starting an interview with Kaia Powell, one of the graduate students who vetted posts for StrengthInNumbers.com, and Robin turned on the stream, both to listen and to remind herself why she did this job while she faced down the five messages from the bloody woman in Human Resources whose sole pleasure in life seemed to derive from chasing her for annual Performance Development Reviews. *Christ on a bike, love,* she was tempted to write back, *have you seen the news at all? Little tied up here at the mo.*

On-screen, sitting on a sofa in one of the 'soft' interview rooms, Kaia looked like a slightly older version of Lennie. She was a similar build, and, given the size of the bun she'd pinned with a pencil, her brunette hair was probably a similar length. Her clothing budget looked about the same, too: black leggings, black DMs. Judging by the matted fake fur, her parka was a veteran of several winters.

Papers squared on her knee, Jo explained they wanted to know more about Ben's work on the website.

'How did you get involved? How did they find you – or you them?'

'Through our department at the university. All three of us – Dave and Suriaya, too – our PhD supervisor suggested us. He's a friend of Roger's, Ben's dad, and he'd given them legal advice early on. He told them they'd need to legal the posts before they went up and he put them in touch with us. He asked me because it ties in with my doctorate and he was sick of me moaning about being broke, I think. It doesn't pay much, it's a non-profit, but it helps. Or it did – I hope Molly and Theo won't stop now.'

'Just to confirm, when you say "legal" new posts, you mean check they don't contain anything libellous?'

'Yes. Names, obviously – people, companies, places – but anyone could take those out, you wouldn't need a law degree. The stuff we're really looking for is the more subtle bits of information that could *imply* an accusation against someone.'

'Do you have an example?'

'Well, say someone wrote they'd been staying at a bed-and-breakfast, gave enough detail to make it identifiable, and said that they'd woken up to find a strange man in their room who then assaulted them but the police found no evidence that the door or windows had been forced. That would imply the attacker had access to a key and then, if the number of people who had keys was very small, perhaps even just one man if the B & B was run by a husband-and-wife team . . .'

'Then, legally, that could read as identifying the husband as the attacker.'

'Exactly.'

Robin thought of the thousands of posts on the site. Dear God, let it not be something like that.

'Did you get posts that identified people?'

'We got *emails* like that, yeah, but we couldn't post them.'

'What did you do with them?'

'We had a form response letting people know why we couldn't post and giving them information on how to report the crime or find support.'

'Could something have slipped through the net?'

Kaia thought for several seconds, then shook her head. 'No, I really doubt it. We're so careful, the three of us, we never forget the potential repercussions, not just legally but the impact on people's lives.'

'You mentioned the work ties in with your PhD?'

'Yes. A lot of the stories on the site have to do with victims' experiences of the justice system, not just the assaults them-selves. I'm writing on Section 41 of the Youth Justice Crime and Evidence Act, what it's *supposed* to do and how, in reality, defendants' counsels deliberately misuse a clause and completely subvert it.'

'What's in Section 41?'

'At trial for a sexual offence, "except with the leave of the court", it's illegal to cite evidence or ask questions in cross-examination about the victim's sexual past, i.e., use it against them. But then there's a clause, 3c, that says if it's a question of consent and the behaviour of the complainant is "so similar" to their previous sexual behaviour "that the similarity cannot reasonably be explained as a coincidence", then it's allowable.'

'Leaving it wide open to abuse.' Jo nodded.

'*Wide*. There was a survey recently and collectively, ISVAs – that's Independent Sexual—'

'Violence Advisers, yes, who support victims through the legal process.'

Kaia looked surprised, as if she'd forgotten she was talking to a detective. 'Right. They said that the victim's sexual history was brought up in nearly three quarters of cases they'd seen. Three quarters! And apart from in exceptional circumstances, it's not allowable. They're just doing it anyway.'

'They did it to Molly,' said Jo.

'Yes. I was there, in court, for research. I'd been following the witness-intimidation in the papers, so I knew it would be bad. The Heywoods' QC – fucking hell. Sorry. He tried to say her behaviour was the same as when she slept with her boyfriend the first time – her *only* boyfriend then, the first time she'd ever slept with *anyone* – because she'd been nervous. And, of course, they just sprung this stuff on her. The law says if you *are* going to bring up the victim's previous sexual conduct, you have to notify them beforehand, but hey, why ruin the surprise?'

Kaia's voice was rising as she warmed to her theme. 'There's no other crime where the victim, usually a woman, has to prove *they're* innocent. Not just innocent, either: *virtuous*. The equivalent in Homicide would be the victim proving they didn't deserve to be murdered – in fact, that they deserved it less than the average person.'

'When did you last see Ben?' Jo asked, bringing her back down.

'Not for a few weeks, any of them. The site runs smoothly, we don't have to talk much. If there's something to say, we normally email. People send their stories in, Dave, Suraiya and I legal them, then Ben, Theo or Molly post them. Theo's dad's an accountant, so we email him our invoices for hours worked, and the money comes directly to our accounts.'

'Had you spoken to any of them? Was there anything going on, out of the ordinary?'

'No, none of us can think of anything. And if we could, we would have come straight to you.'

'What was he like, Ben?'

'Great – so full of energy. When the others got disheartened, he was the one who got them fired up again.'

'Did they get disheartened often?'

'No, but there was this one week over the summer when two cases they'd been following – people who'd got in touch to say they'd reported after posting on the site – got dropped. It wasn't that the police didn't believe them, just that the bar's so high. A case basically has to be cast-iron even to proceed, doesn't it, let alone get a conviction. Perish the thought that a "promising young man" might have his rep tarnished.'

'Molly and Theo were more affected by the failing cases?'

'No, they were all affected – I think they were all coming to see what a massive feat it was, actually getting a conviction in Molly's case. But Ben bounced back fastest. They were a good team, the three of them. Ben was the energy, Theo was the methodical, wise one, and Molly was the heart, the seed for the whole thing. And they're all still so young.' She stopped, and Robin heard a silent *were*.

'What's *she* like?' Jo asked. 'Molly.'

'Amazing – I love her. She's a case study in my dissertation. I don't know if she'll do more activism, but I hope so. We need voices like hers. We need *change*.'

Chapter Twenty-Five

Dunnington Road was long quiet by ten o'clock, everyone safely gathered in for the night, doors locked, soft lamplight or flickering television finding the edges of curtains and blinds. 'They're just finishing their episode,' her mother said, opening the front door to Robin, 'three minutes left. She's all ready to go otherwise – it's late.' In the past, Christine had expressed perhaps thirty or forty times her view that fifteen-year-olds should be tucked up in bed, lights off, by ten, and any mother who wasn't able to achieve that – *Robin* – was failing.

'I know,' she said, following her into the kitchen. 'This case – the timing's terrible.'

'It's not your fault, love, and she knows that.'

Robin was startled. Had her mother gone hog-wild tonight and had a glass and a half?

Christine tapped a Tupperware box on the kitchen island. 'Chicken and vegetables for you.' Silently, she nodded towards the back door as she'd done last night.

'Thanks, Mum,' Robin said loudly, tiptoeing after her.

She'd taken her coat off inside, and within seconds the air started to strip away her body heat. She crossed her arms and shivered.

Her mother closed the conservatory door and beckoned her further away from the sitting-room window. 'Have you heard from that journalist again?' she muttered, barely audible.

'No.'

In the dim light, her mother's face showed confusion. 'But that's good, isn't it?'

'I don't know. Maybe it means he's working on something big – a full-scale exposé: *Robin Lyons, Crookedest Cop.* Have you heard from Luke?'

'No. And I rang Nat – she hasn't heard from him, either.'

Shit.

Robin jumped as the door behind her cranked open.

'What are you doing out here?' Lennie's voice, accusatory.

'Hi, lovely!' Robin turned.

'Mum, Gran, what are you doing? It's Baltic. And dark.'

'Just talking about Christmas, love,' said Christine. 'Presents. You know what it's like in the house – no keeping a secret in there!'

Pure scepticism, Lennie gave them a long look, one then the other. 'Well, we've finished our episode.'

'OK, then, home time!'

As Robin passed her on her way in, Lennie's expression warned her not even to bother. A few seconds later, behind Len's back, Christine pulled a face: *Damn.*

When her parents' front door shut behind them again, it sucked all the warmth back inside. Robin knew it was ridiculous, but she felt guilty for making Lennie leave, taking her away in the dark and cold. On the silent street, their footsteps had a ring of exile.

She started the engine quickly and pulled off, hoping that driving would work its magic, moving the world past them, obscuring the fact that it was just the two of them side by side in a steel box, eyes front, unspeaking.

Lennie wasn't done, though, she was just gathering herself, and as they passed Hall Green station, she reached boiling point. 'What's going on?

'What?' Robin said brightly. She knew she was being performative, but she couldn't stop.

'What were you talking about in the garden? Bollocks it was Christmas presents.'

'Len . . .'

'Oh, come on.'

Robin took a silent breath. *No lies to Lennie* had always been her mantra. 'We were just letting off a bit of steam about next week. We didn't want to worry you.' Was that a lie? Yes, but well-motivated and truth-adjacent, at least.

'Is *Gran* worried?' came the immediate response, subtext loud and clear: if *she* is, then we're doomed.

'No,' Robin said, looking over, pleased by how confident she sounded. 'No, she was just reassuring me.'

'Why are *you* worried?'

Oh, bloody hell. 'I'm not, love. I mean, not for any reason. Just, you know, until it's all done and dusted . . .'

'Done and dusted,' Lennie intoned. She turned her face towards the window.

A fox darted across the road ahead, a low-slung orange flash. Robin touched the brake. Desperate to stop Lennie slipping away, she said quickly, 'Liz and Samir have invited us over for dinner on Saturday.'

'Have they?' She actually turned back. 'Why?'

'Liz says she wants to get to know us.' From the corner of her eye, she saw Lennie frown.

'That's . . . weird.'

'We don't have to go. We can say we're busy.'

'We're not, though, are we?'

'Well, there's work.'

'Of course.' Bone dry.

'Aren't you seeing Austin?'

'No, tomorrow. Anne-Marie says we can blow up the mattress again if I want to stay over. And Sunday, but just the afternoon.' She paused. 'You don't want to go.'

It wasn't a question, and for the umpteenth time, Robin marvelled at her daughter's powers of perception and emotional wisdom. At thirty-seven years of age, Lennie would not be playing pin the tail on the donkey with her feelings, as *she* so often had to. 'In a way, I actually do. It's just . . .'

'Weird?'

'A bit. So . . . And, you know, I can totally go on my own as well. You can say no.' If she did, thought Robin, perhaps they could postpone it, maybe indefinitely . . .

'I don't want to say no. I *want* to go. He was, like, this whole massive part of your life and now he is again. I want to see what he's like.'

'You know what he's like. You've met him.' *He's covering for you, saving your future.*

'But I've never spoken to him for more than a minute,' Len said. 'I want to see why you like him so much.'

'As a *friend*.'

'Yes, as a *friend*.'

'What?'

'Nothing.' Lennie put her hands up, all nothing-to-see-here. 'I was agreeing with you.'

Their house was dark, of course, and though the radiator in the hallway was still warm, the air had a chilly edge. Robin bustled ahead of Lennie, snapping on lights in the sitting room and kitchen as if she could create the illusion of a warm family evening in progress.

'I'm just going to make a cup of tea and go straight up,' Lennie said.

'Sure.' Robin swallowed her disappointment.

She couldn't face real food, it was too late, so she put the Tupperware of chicken and vegetables in the fridge and got a crumpet out of the freezer. When it was toasted, she buttered it, added some Marmite for the B vitamins – who said she didn't look after her body? – and sat at the table with her laptop. She did the *Guardian* Sudoku, then opened Google and typed in 'Edward Gillespie Birmingham UK fraud'. Thousands of hits, so she added '2015'.

She'd just fetched her notebook and pen when her phone lit up, a text. Expecting it to be Samir or one of the team, she was surprised: *Kevin Young.*

Kev.

Hi Robin, hope you're well. Wondering if you're around?

They'd known each other for years, since primary school in fact, so she'd been sure they'd find a normal, platonic footing again at some point, but even though he knew she was a night owl, eleven was late to get in touch after months of silence.

She put the phone down and jotted a couple of notes, but she'd lost her focus. Well, fine – enough for today. She picked up the phone.

Hi Kev, good to hear from you. All well – you?

What was going on? Was he out somewhere, a few drinks down and hoping for a hook-up? They hadn't done that at all since the summer, it had been a clean break. Plus, it was Thursday, and Kev didn't usually go carousing during the work week. *Would* she hook up with him, if that *was* what it was about? Not tonight, of course, Lennie was here. That had been an issue at the time; she hadn't wanted to get Lennie's hopes up that Kev was a serious boyfriend. But could he actually *be* one now? She'd ended things then because she hadn't sorted out her feelings for Samir (not that Kev knew that) but she'd faced those now and she was ready to move on.

Another message arrived: *Yes, all good. I wondered if you fancied a drink tomorrow?*

She sat back again. Three invitations now? This was getting ridiculous. *A drink.* Yes, sure, why not? If he was just being friendly, trying to get things back to normal, she didn't want to rebuff him. And if he was up for trying again, well, they could see. Either way, she'd go for a drink: she liked him and it would be nice to have his company, with Lennie over at the Appiahs'.

Yes, sounds great, she replied.

The dots appeared almost instantly.

Excellent! I'll come your way, shall I? Expect you're v busy so 9.30? 10.00?

OK 9.30 perfect, she typed. *See you then.*

Chapter Twenty-Six

There'd been a sea change in Bill Heywood since Robin had last seen him. Gone were the bewilderment and the checked shirt and jumper that had made him look almost grandfatherly; this man was at least fifteen years younger and he'd either taken a suit to Malmö or bought one since because he was wearing it now like custom-made charcoal-wool armour. His entire bearing was different; he hadn't struck Robin as especially tall last time, but today he looked every inch the same height as his "boys" and almost as beefy.

Kilmartin was having to use all the weapons in his arsenal not to look pathetically runty by comparison. He was quick to put physical distance between the two of them and take up his magnifying position by the window. Robin caught his eye as he was pulling his shoulders back and lifting his chin and an uncomfortable moment passed between them. She'd pay for that later; for now, it was the least of her worries.

'Detective Chief Superintendent Jafferi.' Samir shook Heywood's hand. 'And you've met DCI Lyons.'

Robin moved to shake, too, but Heywood didn't budge. 'Yes.'

'Good. You're in very capable hands.'

Heywood shook his head. 'No, Superintendent. No. I see zero evidence of that. My house has been burned to the ground and my wife is dead.' He quavered slightly at 'dead', but otherwise he was rock-solid. He'd dissociated himself emotionally, Robin thought, at least for as long as it took to do what he'd come to do. Or maybe it was the other way round: he'd come here in *order* to dissociate. He was a man used to being in control, and this gave him purpose, the illusion of *doing something*. Bill Heywood would not enjoy being a victim. 'And *now*,' he said, 'having jailed one of my sons for a crime he didn't commit, you're insinuating another is some kind of . . . *pusher*.'

Samir looked at Kilmartin, giving the senior officer a chance to speak first, but Kilmartin demurred, *Oh no, all yours*.

Before Samir could get a word out, however, Heywood spoke again. 'Which is why Assistant Chief Constable Kilmartin and I are here. To find out what the *fuck* is going on.'

Robin glanced at Samir, *May I?*

'Mr Heywood,' she said, 'I can't begin to imagine the pain you're feeling—'

'Oh! Have you *tried*?'

'But as far as the tranquillisers are concerned, there's no insinuation. Marcus himself volunteered that information.'

'*Volunteered*? You dragged him in here when he was grieving, kept him waiting for nearly an hour, then subjected him to extreme pressure!'

Nearly an hour! The indignity. 'No,' she said, 'I just asked him to account for his whereabouts for thirty-seven key minutes on the night Ben Renshaw died and told him why we needed to know. We're conducting a homicide investigation – a young man has lost his life and we have to find his killer.'

'Are you according my wife's case the same priority? Anne's?' This time, the shake in his voice was unmistakable. 'Well, are you? Have you had *them* in here, the Renshaws? Kept *them* waiting, put the thumbscrews on *them*?'

'The Renshaws weren't responsible for the fire, Mr Heywood.'
'Bullshit!'
'No. They were at home all night. No one left the house.'
He snorted. 'And where was our security *that* night? Oh, we've got it *now*, a couple of useless fuckers hanging round the corridor at Dominic's, but where was it when we actually needed it?'
'We had no reason to suspect your family was in danger, sir. Until Wednesday morning, every act of aggression from the beginning – wherever we count that as being – had been directed against Molly, Ben and Theo or their families.'
'Is this your way of making us pay? The total destruction of *our* family, one by one?'
'Sir, I—'
'Even though the so-called *witness intimidation* had nothing to do with us. You couldn't get us legally, so when you saw an excuse, you—'
'Mr Heywood,' Samir cut in, voice a balance of calm and warning, 'I understand you're under enormous strain, but I can't let that accusation pass.'
'Ben Renshaw's death has *nothing* to do with us,' Heywood spoke over him, slicing the air with his hand, 'and our solicitors have been instructed that anyone who suggests it will be pursued to the very end of the law. *Anyone.*' He let the word linger.
Kilmartin's gaze, Robin noted, had barely left the carpet since Heywood started talking. Creep.
'If it wasn't the Renshaws, *Chief Inspector*, then who *did* kill my wife?'
'We don't know yet,' she admitted, 'but we're making progress.'
'What progress?'
'I can't give details, I'm afraid. We have to conduct our inquiries in a way th—'

'Oh, spare me.' He turned to the window and glared at Kilmartin. 'Aidan, who's your top man?'

Oh, yeah, thought Robin, *get a* man *on it, Aidan.*

Caught on the hop, Kilmartin looked up and gathered himself quickly. 'Detective Chief Superintendent Jafferi here is Head of Force Homicide, hence—'

'Then *he* should be handling this. For god's sake, give *him* the case, can't you?'

To his credit, even Kilmartin looked embarrassed. He opened his mouth but then hesitated, clearly flailing. 'I . . .'

'With respect, Mr Heywood,' said Samir calmly, 'that isn't possible. I'm afraid to say that despite its importance, Anne's is only one of several active and time-sensitive cases Force Homicide's currently dealing with. Robin's one of our most senior detectives, and our best, and I have complete confidence in her. Her results speak for themselves.'

'And she and DCS Jafferi work very closely together,' put in Kilmartin.

'Oh yes,' Heywood said, 'we've read *all* about that.' He fixed her with a stare. *We know exactly who you are.*

Stomach flipping, Robin made herself hold the eye contact.

Samir looked at Kilmartin first, then Bill Heywood, making sure both were listening. 'What we can't afford here, any of us, is an accusation of bias. To speak frankly, Mr Heywood, at the time of Alistair's trial, as I'm sure I don't have to tell you, a lot of people – very *vocal* people – believed your family *was* responsible for what happened to Ben and Theo.'

Incensed, Heywood burst out, 'What the—'

'If I could finish, sir?' Samir's tone was cool water. 'They also believed you weren't prosecuted because of your financial and social standing in the city.'

'Bullshit – utter crap.'

'*If* your family has no involvement in what happened to Ben, we want to make sure you're fully exonerated and those rumours are dispelled once and for all. But for that to happen' – he looked between them again – 'Force Homicide has to conduct this inquiry as we conduct all our inquiries: properly, and without a *hint* of undue influence. I'm sure you understand what I'm trying to say.'

Heywood opened his mouth to speak but thought better of it. He gave Samir a blistering look, then spun to face Robin.

'So we're in your hands, God help us. Go ahead and conduct your enquiry – and yourself – with your famous *propriety*. But let me tell you this, DCI Lyons: my sons loved their mother – *loved* her – and they're angry. *Very* angry.'

Far enough back from the window that they could see without being seen, Samir and Robin watched the exchange in the car park below. They couldn't hear it – Robin doubted it was being conducted very loudly – but the body language told them all they needed to know. 'Big dog, little dog,' she said. 'God, his face when Heywood ordered him to make you SIO.'

'Like he'd just been handed the bill for some very expensive dinners?' said Samir. 'You know, we're the rock, but what's the betting there's an even harder place? You think Heywood's satisfied with having the Assistant Chief Constable "on speed dial" when there's a Chief Constable and PPC?'

They stayed where they were, side by side, neither of them moving.

'Think he'll come back up?' she asked.

'Probably, vent some spleen. I'd leg it if I were you.'

'Definitely, let you deal with it.' She grinned. 'Seriously, though, thank you, Samir, for backing me.' For not caving, either – she'd had bosses before who wouldn't have done that. *Hadn't* done it.

He looked at her as if she were daft. 'Of course I'm going to bloody back you.' He paused. 'How *are* you getting on with Anne, though?'

'Frankly? We've got nothing – CCTV, witnesses, literally nothing. Despite all the appeals we've put out, all the media attention.'

'If Heywood accused you of prioritising Ben, Rob, would he be right?'

'Yes. But we can't do it all, Samir – we can't. It's just not possible to cover everything on two huge cases with the staff we have. I *have* to prioritise, especially since, apparently, I've got to get a solve on Ben in just over a week now. We're working round the clock, you know that.' She knew he was genuinely asking, not criticizing, but she still couldn't quite keep the defensiveness out of her voice.

'Yes,' he nodded, 'I do know.'

'We're human beings, unfortunately, with inconvenient needs, like eating and sleeping, occasional interaction with our families.'

'I'll talk to Kilmartin.'

'Thank you.' Without knowing she was going to, Robin said, 'Liz invited us for dinner with you on Saturday night. Lennie and me.'

He moved away and picked up his phone. 'Yes, I know. Obviously.'

'You don't mind?'

He frowned. 'Why would I?'

'Mixing personal and professional?'

He rolled his eyes. 'I think we're a bit past that, aren't we?'

Are we? she wanted to ask. *You and me, perhaps, but Liz?*

'Why didn't she just ask you to ask me?'

'Because it was her idea? She mentioned it when she was here the other day – she was following up.'

But why does she want *us to come for dinner?* How could she ask without sounding weird?

'She wants to get to know you,' he said, as if he'd read her mind. 'We're friends, you're my only significant ex, you're in all the old stories from back then, and now we work together. You're a major part of my life.'

'Oh.'

'Plus, she was organising some things last week and found my photographs from our gap year.' He smiled.

'You kept them?' Robin was startled.

'You didn't keep yours?'

'No, I burned them.'

His turn to look taken aback. 'All of them?'

'Every single one.'

Their eyes met again and, for a moment, she had the impression she'd hurt him. Then he nodded and moved away again, turning his back. 'Makes sense.'

Chapter Twenty-Seven

Grant Dugmore stood when Varan and Jo entered the room. Watching on-screen upstairs, Robin saw him offer them his hand, Jo first. Confident. His outfit was similar to the one she remembered from Monday afternoon at the school: black jeans and a dark plaid shirt. The beard and 1940s side-parting had more than a hint of hipster, but though he wasn't particularly tall – probably five ten at most – he looked 'a bit useful', as her mother would say – physically strong, someone you'd want on your side in a fight, not the other.

Varan indicated that he should sit again, and he and Jo took the sofa at the ninety-degree angle across the coffee table. 'Thanks for coming in.'

'I'm sorry it wasn't until now.' He glanced at the clock over the door. 'As I said on the phone, the history teacher for the fourth and fifth forms is off with bronchitis and I'm covering. It's been a godawful week.' His voice was deep and resonant, as if it bounced around his slightly barrel chest building up texture before launch. 'It's shocking when a student dies.'

'You've had it happen before?'

'At my previous school, a group of boarders got tanked up and climbed onto their dorm roof. One of them slipped.' He shook his head. 'Horrendous.'

'When was that?'

'In 2012 – so six years ago. I moved the year after.'

'To where you are now?'

'Yes. Promotion – bigger school and Head of Sixth Form. We wanted to be further south, too, nearer my wife's family. Her father's got Alzheimer's.'

'That's hard, I'm sorry. Where were you before?'

'Lake District. The Chapel Hill School.'

Jo made a note. 'How's the atmosphere at Summerfield now?'

'Still much as you saw on Tuesday – there's been a lot of tears. We told the Sixth Form that anyone who wanted to could take a day or two off, but everyone's been in. I think they all want to be around each other. They're shell-shocked, honestly. As am I.'

'They're tight-knit, as a group?'

He nodded. 'Partly because of what happened last year, I think – a lot of them were frightened by it. They talk the talk, but they're still seventeen and eighteen. I'm not saying they're saints, this lot, there's all the usual vaping and underage drinking and bunking off at lunchtime, but they're nicer to each other. The dominant personalities always set the tone, and this year's are kinder. *Were*.'

'Mr Dugmore,' said Varan, 'in that vein, we wanted to ask you about Ben and Theo's StrengthInNumbers work. We heard the school asked them to cut back.'

'Yes, that's right. Largely so Ben could focus on his academic work.'

'So that *was* the reason?'

He frowned. 'Did you suspect otherwise?'

'Not necessarily. But we heard he wasn't pleased about it.'

'No, nor Theo, but Ben less so. Theo had the Oxford exams last week, so he had a pressing reason to knuckle down, but

Ben definitely saw A levels as way off in the dim and distant.'

'Who did it come from, the suggestion – if that's the right word?'

Robin saw Dugmore smile slightly. 'As opposed to edict or diktat? We heard both of those. It was a team decision. Atkinson's very keen on Theo getting into Oxford, for obvious reasons . . .'

'School glory?'

'Yep. And Ben was struggling. We just didn't think he would pull off the grades if he was out doing events every week, trying to cram in his academic work round the edges. We had a meeting – me, Atkinson and his subject teachers – and we all agreed.'

'When was this?'

'Start of the academic year – second week of September?'

'Was he still angry?'

'I think so, but he knew we weren't going to budge and his parents were on board, so he just had to deal with it.'

'When we came to the school,' Varan said, shifting tack, 'the Chief and I, we thought we detected a bit of tension between you and the Head.'

Robin watched Dugmore nod slowly, as if he were making a connection. 'Hence your asking me to come here.'

'In case you felt able to speak more freely.'

Dugmore covered his mouth with his hand and looked at them. Perhaps ten seconds passed before he said, 'Atkinson and I don't always see eye to eye, it's true.'

'In what way?'

He exhaled a long breath. 'He's ambitious. He *did* teach, but he's far more interested in the business side of the school and, to be fair to him, he's done a lot to make it better. When he took the headship, Summerfield was a bit run-down, the facilities needed updating and we were slipping down the academic league tables. If people are paying as much as they do, you need to provide a top-class experience. He's turned things around.'

'But?'

'But sometimes there's a cost, and he's more flexible about that than I would be.'

Varan waited.

Another sigh. 'It's very difficult to be even-handed if you're dealing with the children of people who've given the school tens of thousands of pounds. Or more than that. Things were allowed to go by the board that shouldn't.'

'Go on.'

'The photographs – you know about those? It was a couple of months before the rape – two or three of the girls in Alistair's year were daft enough to send naked pictures, or let them be taken, and Alistair and his mates shared them around.'

'That "went by the board"?'

'Detentions.'

'*Detentions?*' Jo couldn't hide her outrage.

'I strongly advocated for more, let's put it that way. Strongly.'

'But the Heywoods,' guessed Varan, 'were major donors to the school.'

Dugmore nodded. 'Going back decades. They always gave money, always sent their boys there. All three of this generation, their dad, their grandfather. Their great-uncle was head boy in the fifties – he's on the board in the lobby.' He huffed slightly. 'I should think that's the end of it, though.'

'How so?'

'All hell broke loose after the trial. Heywood Senior had paid for the new athletics centre, but after Alistair was convicted, the school took the Heywood name off it. You can imagine how that went down – Senior demanded his money back.'

When Varan and Jo came upstairs, Robin went out to talk to them. Malia and Tark paused what they were doing, too, and spun their chairs round.

'Thoughts?' Robin said.

'You think something was going on at the school, guv?' asked Varan.

'That's what I'm wondering, yes. You?'

He nodded. 'We don't reckon Dugmore knows about it, though.'

'We were talking about it on the way up,' Jo said. 'Maybe something new's going on, another assault or abuse, perhaps, and the Head's trying to keep it on the down-low to protect the school reputation, especially after last year. Maybe Ben got wind of it.'

'And was threatening to expose it?' Malia suggested. 'Doubly motivated, maybe, by being angry about being shut down?'

'Molly and Theo don't know about it, though, do they?' asked Tark.

'Meaning he hadn't told them, or hadn't told them *yet*,' Varan said.

'Or he *had* told them but they're too scared to say anything, given what happened to him,' said Jo.

'It could explain why Ben was in the woods, couldn't it?' said Varan. 'If he was talking to someone who didn't want people to *know* they were talking. Privacy.'

'Yes,' said Robin. 'So, back to the school we go, Atkinson top priority. This time, let's find out who's been donating money, too – especially significant amounts. Speaking of which, Bill Heywood was in first thing with the Assistant Chief.'

Malia did a double-take. 'What?'

'Yes, and I told him we were making progress on Anne's case, so if anyone could make me feel less like a liar, I'd be grateful.'

Radio silence.

'CCTV, Tark?'

He grimaced. 'Hide nor hair, sorry. Plus, having said we didn't have much to go on, now look.' He pointed to seven cardboard boxes on the table against the wall. Three of them were full, another two getting there. Black marker on the front said where each batch had been collected: Chesterwood Rd/Wheelers/Coldbath; Yardley Wood Rd/Swanshurst; Alcester Rd/St Mary's Row (the roads around Ben's house and Moseley Bog. Turning his chair, he pointed to the empty desk that had belonged to Niall before he'd left Homicide for a sergeant's job in Organised Crime) without being replaced, needless to say. Another two boxes were there. 'Those are the ones from round the Heywoods' place. I don't mean to complain, guv, I really don't, but there's work for three *teams* here, not three people. We're drowning.'

Chapter Twenty-Eight

'Shall I cook?' Robin had asked when she'd rung Lennie at six thirty.

'No,' Len had sounded confused. 'You won't be getting back 'til late, will you, why would— Wait, you've forgotten I'm round at Asha and Austin's, haven't you?'

'No, no, of course not,' Robin had floundered. 'I just thought you were going over there later.' She'd kicked herself for the mistake, then been disappointed. Failing a last-minute crisis, her idea had been to leave the station at seven, stop off at M&S for some fresh ingredients and make something decent, part apology (for the week in general and because she was out for a drink later), part demonstration that she, too, could make nutritious meals, and part just something nice for the two of them.

Well, she thought as she put her key in the door at eight thirty, the white plastic bag from the Lebanese down the road dangling from her wrist, it was more business for Ahmad – she was on first-name terms with him now, both she and Lennie were; after Christine, he was the person who fed them most often. *Oh bollocks* – too late, Robin remembered the box of leftover chicken and vegetables her mother had given her.

Along with the free newspaper and the usual drift of flyers on the doormat was one of the red-bordered cards from the

Post Office, *Something for you . . .* What, she wondered. She wasn't expecting anything, but maybe Len had ordered something online. Their postman, bless him, was not of the sadistic ilk who gleefully ticked the box to inform you that your parcel was going back to the depot and your Saturday morning would thus be spent queuing with equally pissed-off strangers, he'd left it with the Spencers next door. Their lights had been on just now, but it was dinner time, Robin didn't want to interrupt them. Tomorrow would be soon enough.

She transferred her own food from its foil dish and gave it a twenty-two-second zap in the microwave – the exact sweet spot, she knew from too much experience, between replacing the warmth lost in transit up the hill and turning the chicken stringy. When it was ready, she carried it to the table and ate while poking around on Twitter for mentions of Summerfield. She checked Jeremy Handley's feed and the *Record*'s website for perhaps the twentieth time of the day, then got out her large notebook where she found a couple of questions about Eddie Gillespie that she'd written down last night.

Given he had a fraud conviction and yet was working in finance again, she'd wondered whom he was working for. A company called Myrmidon Logistics, Malia had told her, and looking it up now, Robin learned that it was based just past Longbridge on the west side of the city, probably for easy access to the M5 and the docks at Bristol. It had been founded in 2003 by a man named Alun Morgan and, if the website was anything to go by, it was now a substantial business offering shipping and transport services to customers including major international brands.

Did Myrmidon know Gillespie's history? Yes, surely – as with the Heywoods and their investors, no one would employ a finance guy without due diligence, would they? So who there had hired him?

Gillespie's LinkedIn profile gave his job title as 'Finance Manager' which was about as opaque as it got. The only thing she could tell by cross-referencing with Myrmidon's site and other personnel with LinkedIn profiles was that at least three other people in the department were senior to him: a CFO, a Finance Director and Deputy Director.

As he'd worked for his cousin's business previously, she'd wondered if someone at Myrmidon was a personal connection, too, but apart from looking for other Gillespies, there was no easy way to check that just now.

A glance at the clock at the corner of the screen told her she was running out of time, so she put her plate in the dishwasher and went upstairs to shower.

As she shaved her legs, foot on the edge of the bath, she had a moment's déjà vu, a mini flashback to an evening in the spring when she'd done exactly the same thing before meeting Kev for dinner. What was she doing *now*, shaving her legs? They were going for a friendly drink after not seeing each other for months – was she going to need smooth legs? Well, if she did, would that be a bad thing, now that she'd come to terms with her emotional baggage? She liked Kev – a lot – and he was a good man, kind, very bright, family-minded.

Hair dry, she dressed in her best black jeans and a soft grey fitted jumper, then put on silver hoops and a small amount of perfume. Back in the bathroom to brush her teeth, she caught her eye in the mirror. *Who are you kidding?* asked her reflection. *Friendly drink!*

At 9.29, she heard a car and looked out of the sitting-room window to see Kev's Mercedes estate in his old favourite spot across the road. By the otherworldly glow in the front, she guessed he was texting. She waited a minute to avoid looking too keen, then put on her coat and went out. Just like old times, he reached across to open the passenger-side door as she approached.

The cracked leather seat shaped itself around her rear end in its familiar way. The car smelled like Kev, or, rather, like his aftershave, which was definitely heady but also good. It was the grown-up, successful man's version of the clouds of Gillette body spray that followed groups of lads out on a Friday night, all ironed shirts and fresh shaves.

'Hi'

'Hello.' There was a smile in his voice and on his face as he leaned over to kiss her cheek. His brown eyes twinkled in the ambient street light. 'How are you?' he asked.

'OK, yes, fine. You missed the view, then?' She gestured at the windscreen, beyond which the lights of the city centre lay sparkling. She'd chosen the house for its position here, close to the centre and on an elevation, but it was Kev who'd made her really appreciate this vista of central Birmingham, its mad mix of ancient and modern, on evenings when they'd sat here together either because they were on their way into the house, snogging like teenagers first, or because she'd had to sneak out so she could send him on his way without tipping off Lennie.

'Well, it's a good one,' he said. 'Do you fancy the Old Mo?'

The Mo? Robin was surprised. Kev was the MD of his family's sizeable scrapyard and when they were seeing each other, he'd always gone for far fancier places. She'd only been to the Mo – The Old Moseley Arms – a couple of times, but it was familiar to her on a molecular level, essence-of-the-Midlands. It wasn't a cool place, there was no attitude there; it wasn't trying to say anything other than *We're a friendly pub, come and have a drink.* A lot of the men would be wearing polo shirts with company logos. But it was two or three minutes away, on Tindal Street, and maybe that was the attraction: if they needed to, they could get back here *prontissimo*.

'Sure,' she said. 'Shall we walk?' If they were drinking, better not take the car.

'Nah, let's drive, it's cold.'

She laughed as she reached for her seat belt. 'Wimp. Maybe they'll have lit the fire for you.'

'Bloody hope so.'

'I've been following this new case of yours,' he said, as he pulled away from the kerb. 'Well, hard to avoid it. What a nightmare.'

'Nightmare's one word. Snowballing's another. But enough of that, it's Friday night. How've *you* been?'

'Oh, all right, at work, same old. We're expanding again, I've just bought that bit of land next door I had my eye on, you remember, and I'm more or less keeping Dad out of the office and out of trouble. Not *criminal* trouble,' he added quickly.

Robin smiled again. Kev was totally legitimate, but his father, Morris, had done a short stretch for fencing stolen metal years ago. Kev had been in secondary school at the time, but it still weighed on him. 'Don't worry,' she said, 'I know what you meant.'

Morris was an expansive character, apt to make large scrap deals on a handshake after a couple of whiskies, and Kev's management of him was one of the things that Robin found most endearing. He achieved a fine balance, somehow reining Morris in without ever making him feel like a liability. The two of them were incredibly close.

'It's good to see you,' she said.

He smiled across at her again. 'You, too.'

Less than a minute later, they were in Tindal Street.

Kev was big – not overweight but solid, tall and large-handed, long of stride. As they crossed the road, his black wool coat billowed and she remembered him enclosing her in it when they'd kissed on a cold night in the spring. The thought sent a shiver through her, not unpleasant.

Friday night, the pub was busy and all the tables were taken. Kev insisted on buying the drinks, then carried them over to the mantelpiece. The fire was indeed lit and putting out so much heat Robin had to stand away from it. She'd never been anywhere like The Old Mo in London, it was proper old-school. The carpet was an intensely patterned red and blue and bore no relationship to either the spotted wallpaper or the pale striped curtains. The seats were old red leather, the tables wrought-iron-framed like garden furniture. A one-armed bandit spun its wheels in the corner, lights cascading in invitation across the touchpads.

'I've always liked this place,' Kev said, hoovering off the top half-inch of his pint of Butty Bach. 'It's comforting. Does what it says on the tin.'

She nodded. 'Kev,' she dropped her voice, 'you've heard about my brother?'

'Yeah, of course. I'm so sorry, Rob, what a . . . He was on the edge, though, wasn't he, you don't have to tell me. It wouldn't have happened if he'd been in a better place mentally.'

'Maybe not the violence – I hope not – but the fact he was there at all . . . Well, you know he's got form on that front. That *National* kind of front.' If their roles were reversed, Luke wouldn't be trying to see the best in Kev, she knew, but making sly comments about what he believed – wrongly – to be Kev's Romany blood and how it was bound to come out. Kev was the better man, no doubt about it. Despite Luke's long-time hostility towards him, he had helped him on a very tough day in the summer. His kindness then had given Robin an insight into what it would be like to have him as a real partner.

'Maybe it'll be good for him in the end,' Kev said. 'Make him sort himself out.'

'Maybe.' She sounded about as convinced as she felt. 'Can I ask you something, Kev?' she said over the plangent opening bars of 'Total Eclipse of the Heart'. She wasn't sure if it was her imagination that he suddenly looked a bit shifty. 'A work thing.'

'Go on, then.'

Relief? Again, she wasn't sure.

'I just wondered if you'd ever come across a man called Edward Gillespie – Eddie?'

He thought. 'No, I don't think so. Who is he?'

'His son was the other witness in the Heywood rape case. Ben, and Theo Gillespie.'

'No, sorry.'

'That's OK. How about Myrmidon Logistics?'

This time, the thick eyebrows lifted a little. 'I've used them for a couple of jobs before, but their rates are a bit punchy. They're upmarket from scrap, really – smarter vehicles, you know, not the rough old things I normally deal in.'

'Do you know the owner, Alun Morgan?'

'No, but I've met him a couple of times, round and about.'

'What's he like?'

He twitched his shoulders. 'I don't know – I mean, literally, I've met him.'

'Any impressions?'

'Not really. I was introduced, we said a couple of words, then he moved off. I wondered if it was me, but my mate Terry said no, he's just like that, a bit . . . stand-offish.'

'Rude?'

'No, just keeps himself to himself. You know what this city's like, Rob. It's big, yeah, but it's not really, is it? People go back here, lot of the businesses, particularly – old families. There's a lot of relationships.'

'He started Myrmidon, though, didn't he?'

'As far as I know, but I think his dad was in haulage, too. Smaller way of business, from what I understand. But that's about all I know, sorry.'

'It's plenty. Thanks.'

He smiled. 'Any time.'

'How are the girls?'

'All right, yeah, good. So grown-up. Shocking, isn't it, how quickly it all goes? Sasha phoned me yesterday to say she'd bought Anna a bra, but I wasn't allowed to mention it. As if I was bloody going to!'

'I envy Liz and Samir having Leila, still little. Have you seen *them* recently?'

Now Kev looked undeniably shifty. 'I haven't seen *him* for two or three weeks We were supposed to have a pint the other day, but he had to bail last minute because of work. Your fault, I expect.' He raised his eyebrows. 'I saw Liz yesterday evening, though.'

'Oh yeah?'

'In Waitrose.'

He stopped and reached for his pint, avoiding her eye.

'Come on, Kev. Out with it.'

'Rob,' he said, and she recognised that he was buying time, choosing his words, 'she mentioned you're going over there for dinner tomorrow night.'

'Well, a bite to eat, anyway, I don't know if it's as fancy as dinner. She said it'd be fairly casual. Why – will you be there?'

Was that why he'd suggested a drink? So they wouldn't have to meet again for the first time in front of other people?

'No, it isn't.' The shiftiness increased. 'I just didn't want you to get caught out if she mentioned it. I mean, there's no reason why it would bother you, I don't reckon myself *that* much, and *you* dumped *me*,' he laughed awkwardly, 'but yeah, just in case, I didn't want you to be surprised if you heard it from them first . . . I was with Vic in Waitrose. Victoria. My new girlfriend.'

Robin felt herself redden, and not because of the heat from the fire. She remembered shaving her legs less than an hour ago and fought an urge to close her eyes with shame. God, she was excruciating – *excruciating*.

'She's fantastic,' she heard Kev say, 'I think you'll really like her – all the gang will.'

'Brilliant news!' She reached out to rub his arm. 'Great. I'm really happy for you. I can't wait to meet her!'

Kev looked chuffed. 'Thanks, that means a lot. You know, I'm glad we can get things back to normal now. It's been great, having you back here, and I didn't want what happened to make things awkward between us. You're a good mate.'

Chapter Twenty-Nine

Robin woke just before eight, skin clammy, heart bumping. She'd only had one drink with Kev because he'd been driving – or had he been driving so that he could only have one drink? Either way, feeling oddly wounded despite his kindness, she'd come home and finished the rest of the bottle of wine from the fridge. That wasn't making her heart race, though, it was the dream she'd just had. She'd been opening a cardboard box – cutting the tape, opening the flaps – and then, without warning, a ball of flame had burst out of it, exploding upwards in a column before furling back on itself, a huge mushroom cloud.

'*Something for you . . .*'

The phrase struck her suddenly as deeply sinister. What if the parcel delivered next door wasn't an Etsy order but something like the Renshaws had received last year? Was she about to open a lunch box full of dog shit? Or – *Jesus* – what if they'd upped the ante? What if they'd sent some kind of incendiary device and, in holding her parcel for her, the kindly Spencers had endangered themselves?

Robin got out of bed so quickly she gave herself a head rush. Throwing on last night's jeans and jumper, she ran downstairs and grabbed her keys. The Spencers were early risers, she heard them moving about on the other side of the wall from six every morning, so it didn't feel unreasonably early to knock.

Val opened the door in her housecoat and slippers. 'Morning, love.' Her face was round and puffy as a ball of pizza dough, but behind their big pink-plastic frames, the blue eyes were keen.

'Sorry it's a bit early,' Robin said, 'but I've got to go into work so . . .'

'On a Saturday?'

'No peace for the wicked.'

'Or those that have to catch them, eh? Well, you take care of yourself. I saw you on the news the other day. Proper nasty, isn't it? Are you going to get them?'

'Them?'

'The Heywoods.' Val looked up and down the street. 'It *is* them, isn't it?' she said, lowering her voice. 'They've always been horrible. One of my cousins used to work for the current one's dad in the seventies. Sharky, they used to call him. Mean as hell, apparently.'

Robin had to suppress a smile. On several occasions before, she'd thought what a shame it was she couldn't share any details of her cases with Val, she'd get such a kick out of it. Apparently unshockable, she'd seen every police show there was, no matter how brutal. When they'd first met, she'd confessed she was excited to live next door to a 'real homicide cop'.

'Well, you know how it is, Val' – Robin drew an imaginary zip across her lips – '*omertà*. But we'll get a solve one way or another, keep the faith.'

'Ooh, I will,' she said, thrilled. She looked at the red slip in Robin's hand. 'You've come for your parcel. Hold on a sec.'

She retreated into the house, reappearing thirty seconds later with a cardboard box the size of the ones the CCTV tapes were in – the same size as the one in Robin's dream. It was quite heavy, whatever was inside, and soft, rather than rigid like a lunch box. There was no return address on the box and the postmark was a pink smudge.

Back home, Robin walked it straight through the house and out of the kitchen door to the small backyard. Quickly, she covered the rickety metal table there with yesterday's free newspaper and brought out sunglasses, a Stanley knife and a pair of nitrile gloves. On further consideration, she went back into the house for a scarf to tie over her nose and mouth. If Val and Trev looked out of their upstairs window, they'd think she'd lost it, but so be it. Val would enjoy seeing police work in action, and if it *was* an incendiary device and she turned into a Roman candle, they could call the fire brigade.

Gloves on, she gingerly cut the brown packing tape, being careful not to go too deep. She took a breath, then opened it. When she saw what was inside, she actually laughed.

It was her new coat, the one Lennie had found for her on eBay.

Back inside, she texted Malia to see if she was up, then, as soon as she replied, she rang her. 'Saturday morning – sorry.'

'No problem. I'm actually heading in. Tark's already there, and Varan's on his way. Jo's popping in to see her mum at ten, but she'll be in straight after that.'

For far from the first time, Robin felt deep gratitude for them all. 'Thank you.'

'Of course,' Malia said, as if it were a given that a bunch of people who'd worked twelve-hour days and more all week would be in at the weekend without overtime pay, without even being asked.

Chapter Thirty

'Where did *you* go?' asked Robin as the gates in front of them began to swing open.

'Me?' Jo said, looked across the wide lawn to Summerfield's main building. 'St Peter's RC for primary, then South Bromsgrove High. Nowhere like this – normal schools.'

'Good ones, though? I don't know the primary, but South Bromsgrove's decent, isn't it?'

'Outstanding, according to Ofsted – my little brother's still there.'

'You've got a brother who's at school?'

'Yeah. We call him "the Afterthought".' She grinned. 'Which he loves. Seven-year age gap between him and the next youngest.' She reached for her bag and pulled out a bar of Dairy Milk. 'Bit of energy before we go in, guv?'

'Go on then, just a square. Thanks.'

She parked in the small court yard again and they got out. Jo retied her ponytail, then brushed down her slightly bobbly pea coat. 'Not sure I'm dressed for the occasion.'

Since it was Saturday, they'd called in advance, but Atkinson told them he'd see them in his office again, and when they rang the bell this time, it was he who came to the door. He was wearing what Robin guessed was his 'weekend but on school premises' outfit: olive chinos and a navy sweater, the collar of a flannel shirt just visible at the neck. He'd recently showered – comb-marks were still visible in his hair and as they followed him up the stairs, he trailed the scent of herbal soap.

'I hope you haven't made a special trip in?' Robin asked.

'Only across the lawn. The headship comes with a house on the grounds.' He ushered them inside his office and closed the door after them. On his desk was a tray with a Thermos jug and cups. 'Coffee?'

'Yes, thank you,' said Robin, and Jo followed her lead.

'Please,' Atkinson said, 'take a seat.'

Jo sat down but Robin took a couple of steps to the window and looked out. Back in her day, the school had a fearsome reputation for sports on the boys' side. Summerfield had regularly thrashed the boys' grammar at rugby; Samir had played and she recalled him coming back from a match one afternoon with an eyebrow split badly enough to need stitches. He still had the scar if you knew where to look. Had it been against Summerfield, that match? She couldn't remember. Their team was playing now, from the looks of it, little Subbuteo figures moving round a muddy pitch visible beyond the tennis courts closest to the lawn.

'So how can I help?' Atkinson asked, turning a cup upright in its saucer and filling it.

'A couple of things have cropped up as we've spoken to people over the past few days,' Robin said. 'We wanted to ask you about them.'

'You spoke to Grant Dugmore yesterday, I believe.'

She was surprised. Dugmore had come to the station, of course, and they'd made a point of calling him on his own number rather than the school's. Had he told Atkinson he'd come? Or had someone else? And what was Atkinson's angle in mentioning it?

'It's a comprehensive inquiry,' she said. 'We're talking to anyone who was in contact with Ben. Our first question is about his StrengthInNumbers work – we heard from the Renshaws that the school had asked him and Theo to cut back on press and events.'

'That's right.'

'I'm curious to know why you didn't mention it before. Not on Monday, that's understandable, but the following day, when DC Kowalska here and one of my other officers came to talk to you.'

'They didn't ask.'

Jo shifted forward in her seat. 'We asked if there'd been any significant changes in Ben's life recently.'

'Is that significant?'

'In the circumstances, I'd say so, sir.'

'So was there a reason?' Robin asked.

'Of course not.' He gave her a hard look, then picked up a spoon and stirred his coffee vigorously.

'It wasn't that you were trying to distract us from further sexual misconduct at the school?'

The spoon clattered in the saucer as he put it down. 'No. The website has nothing to do with the school and nothing posted on there has anything to do with us, either.'

'Though, given the stories are anonymous,' said Jo, 'there'd be no way of knowing if they have or not, would there?'

Her logic earned her a cold look from Atkinson before he turned back to Robin. 'As I told you on Monday, Chief Inspector, the party where Alistair assaulted Molly—'

'*Raped* Molly.'

'The party,' Atkinson's voice was adamantine, 'was off school premises, at a weekend, after Heywood had ceased to be a student here, technically speaking. He'd finished his exams, he was done.'

'But that *wasn't* the case when the naked photographs were circulated some months before the rape.'

Atkinson took a deep breath. 'The boys involved in that – who, yes, included Alistair Heywood – were disciplined.'

'With three after-school detentions.'

'The girls involved had sent the photographs, or agreed to them being taken.'

'Had they agreed to them being shared around?' Robin asked.

No response.

'We heard,' she said, 'that there were questions at the time about whether the penalty should have been more stringent. I imagine if it was my daughter, I'd certainly have asked that.'

'The matter was discussed at length.'

'And at that time, the Heywood family were major donors to the school, is that right? They'd just built the new athletics centre. Is that the building I could see from the window? It's big.'

'Parents who send their children here have expectations. Working in the public sector, Chief Inspector,' Atkinson said as if handling the words with gloves, 'I imagine financial realities are outside your purview.'

'Do you?' she said, dry.

'While Summerfield is a place for education – one we're incredibly proud of – the reality is, it has to be self-financing. It's a business, not a charity. Sometimes that means difficult decisions.'

'Blind eyes?'

'No!' He slapped his hand on the desk then, as if realising that he'd given himself away, he softened his tone. 'I have to make decisions based on what is most beneficial for the school as a whole.'

'Meaning sometimes individuals pay the price.'

'If you're implying that Alistair Heywood raped Molly Zajac because he wasn't sufficiently punished for sharing some risqué pictures, then I'm afraid I find that very naïve.' His tone now was almost pitying: poor old her, so unfamiliar with the ways of the world.

'Perhaps, in that case,' she said, disingenuous, 'I'm also being naïve in questioning whether that sort of behaviour – inadequately punished – was really indicative of a culture of, what were your words on Monday, "equality and respect"?'

Chapter Thirty-One

Liz and Samir lived in Bournville, just off Selly Oak Road. Samir had texted the address, and the satnav brought them to a three-storey red-brick semi-detached house surrounded by a cluster of the type of giant straight-trunked pines that always reminded Robin of the campsite in the South of France where they'd stayed on their gap year.

It'd be a good house at Christmas was her first thought: solid, spacious, warm-looking. Yellow light shone from the fan above the front door and over white wooden shutters in the large bay window, as well as in a wide dormer near a brick chimney of dimensions Father Christmas himself would approve of on his annual mince-pie and sherry bonanza. The boy had done good, Robin thought.

'OK?' said Lennie. On the drive over, she'd been quite upbeat by recent standards, actually volunteering information about a local band she, Austin and Asha had been watching on YouTube. Robin had wondered if she'd picked up on *her* nervousness, and her question now seemed to confirm it.

'Yep, fine. Let's do it.' She cranked the door handle and got out before she could listen to the voice telling her she shouldn't be here, to turn the car round and hightail it back to Balsall Heath without delay. She was glad she'd taken a leaf out of Kev's book and driven to make sure she'd have to stay sober.

Under the carriage lamp, Lennie gave her a quick once-over. 'You look good, Mum.'

'Thank you. It's the coat.'

'It's not. Though if you get compliments, you're banned from saying it's second-hand or making some daft self-deprecating remark, all right? I know you. *"What, this old thing? A tramp found it, but he didn't want it so he slept on it for a couple of months, then gave it to me."* None of that.'

'Yes, boss.' Robin smiled: the old Lennie was still in there, still kicking.

'Good. Glad we understand each other.'

'You look beautiful, Len.' She really did. When she'd got home from Austin's, she'd showered, then changed into her best jeans and her favourite faded blue-and-white-striped shirt. She had on some mascara and grey eyeliner, enough make-up to say she was her own woman now, not a child, but not enough to throw shade on Robin's parenting. Robin fought an urge to get out her phone and take a picture, try to freeze the moment. She still couldn't shake off the sense that time was running out.

Oblivious, Lennie waved the compliment away and rang the doorbell.

Within a few seconds, they heard footsteps and the door swung open to reveal a smiling Samir in jeans and a tight-fitting navy T-shirt. Used to his suits these days, Robin was thrown. He looked – different. Usually, at work, he looked sophisticated; like this, he looked . . . able. Broad shoulders, flat stomach, strong arms. *Fit*, said a voice in her head before she could stop it.

'Hello, Lennie, Rob. Come in – Liz is just stirring some-thing time-sensitive.' He stood back to let Lennie through, then leaned to look out of the door. 'You drove then,' he said to Robin. 'Why did you park out there? I left my car on the road so you could have the other parking spot.' He indicated the empty space next to a silver Honda CRV, presumably Liz's.

'Oh.' It hadn't occurred to her that he would do that – it was the sort of thing her dad did – but also she'd never have thought to drive onto their property. It would have felt presumptuous. Invasive.

'I hoped you'd get a cab, though.'

'Well, I just thought if something happens with the case . . .' But what she would do about Lennie in that situation, she didn't know.

'You need an evening off,' he said. 'You're a workaholic.'

She snorted. 'Pot, kettle.'

'Wait, there's *two* of you?' said Lennie.

Samir grinned at her. 'Afraid so. Come on then, come in.' He moved past Robin to close the door and she caught the scent of Old Spice. He'd worn it even when they were teenagers and she'd teased him about it – 'Old Dude!' – while secretly loving it. Back then, if she hadn't seen him for a couple of days and she was in Boots, she'd open up a stick of deodorant just to remind herself. Those memories were overlaid by another, more recent one now. Five months ago, she'd stood with his arms wrapped tightly around her, her cheek on his shoulder, and just breathed him in.

'Hi!' One oven glove on, the other tucked under her arm, Liz appeared at the far end of the hallway, followed a second later by Leila, who ignored Robin entirely but looked at Lennie with undisguised curiosity. 'I'm so glad you're here – thanks for coming.'

'Thank you so much for inviting us.'

'I'm sorry I didn't do it ages ago. Do you mind being in the kitchen? We've got drinks and snacks in here and then I can talk to you while I finish cooking. That's a gorgeous coat, by the way.'

Robin could feel the weight of Lennie's stare. 'Thank you.'

'Give it to Samir, though, and come through.'

There, that wasn't so hard, was it? said Lennie's look as Robin took it off.

Like the Gillespies', their hallway was tiled, though whereas the Gillespies' shoes were tucked away in a cupboard somewhere, here boots and trainers and shoes in four different sizes were stowed on a long rack underneath a row of jackets and coats. Leila, Robin noticed, had a pair of pink leopard-print Converse high-tops very similar to ones Len had had when *she* was eight.

She waited for Samir to lead the way. When she caught herself admiring the shape of his shoulders in the T-shirt, she started self-flagellating, then decided to cut herself some slack. What was life if you couldn't appreciate the male form?

The house had been extended at the back, making a huge square kitchen, the rear half of which was glass. A spotlit island dominated the space, with more spotlights along a beam above a wooden table near the far wall. Six places were laid at the end nearest the garden, the visible part of which, as far as Robin could see with the play of inside-outside light, was a sitting area surrounded by lush green plants.

'Your house is lovely,' said Lennie, taking it all in.

Liz beamed. 'Thank you. We've done quite a lot of work on it over the years. We bought it from an old lady who'd been here since the dawn of time and hadn't managed the stairs for ten years. It was a state.'

'There was only one loo in the whole house!'

'Headline facts first, Leila?' Liz laughed.

'It's one of the Cadbury houses?' asked Robin. The Cadburys, of chocolate fame, had moved their factory out from the city centre in the late 1800s and gradually built a whole village of good-quality housing for their workforce. Given the size, this one must have been a foreman's house, or a manager's. But Liz and Samir had two salaries to conjure with 'a lawyer's and a Chief Super's' so, of course, their house was a good size.

'Yes. We've got paperwork about it, past residents, et cetera. I'm a bit of a local history fiend; I went to the records office and copied everything.'

'You should meet my grandpa,' said Lennie. 'Local history's his thing, too, big time. Mum's getting more and more into it as well, though, the longer we live here. Give her a couple of years and she'll be really, really boring.'

'Instead of just really boring,' Robin said.

Leila giggled. Robin had met her two or three times before when an issue with her after-school babysitter or a last-minute change of plan had meant her coming into the station to 'help Rona'. She was a delightful creature, full of spirit, who looked at you unabashed with her big brown eyes before zipping off again so quickly that you almost hadn't realised she'd gone before she popped up elsewhere. Tonight she was barefoot in leggings with panda-face patches on the knees, a ribbed vest top clinging to her little round tummy.

'Mummy made cheese puffs,' she told Lennie. 'Goo-jere.' She made little hand movements at the side of her face as if she were twiddling the points of a waxed moustache.

'Yes, dive in.' Liz directed them to the island, where, behind a large vase of greenery, Robin saw the bowl of puffs and a huge wooden board of cheese, charcuterie, nuts and dried fruit.

'Drinks,' said Samir.

'Can we open the Orangina now, Daddy?'

'Yes, but first ask your guest if she'd like some or if she'd prefer something else.'

'You'd like Orangina, wouldn't you?'

Lennie tried not to laugh. 'Yes please.'

Samir took a tall bottle out of the fridge. 'Ice for you, ladies, or no? Rob, what would you like? We've got red, white, Prosecco, gin and tonic, vodka? You can leave the car if you change your mind, come and pick it up tomorrow, but either way, you can have one, can't you?'

'Have a cocktail with me?' asked Liz. 'I've got a passion for gimlets, it's reaching danger level. Hence all the limes.' She pointed at a fruit bowl that held ten or twelve.

Samir looked at Robin, eyebrows up.

'Sure – yes. Sounds great. Thank you.'

'Grab a pew.' Liz gestured at the stools along the side of the island before looking at the bowl of puffs. 'Leila, how many of those have you had now? Is that your *tenth*? She had six before you got here,' she told Lennie. 'And those were just the ones I saw.'

Leila glugged down the top three inches of the drink Samir put in front of her as if she'd just staggered in from the Outback. 'Do you want to play Sylvanian Families with me?' she asked Lennie, wiping her top lip. 'They're just through there in the playroom, so we can come back for snacks whenever we like. I got the tree house for my birthday.'

'Can I take my drink?' Len asked as Leila took her hand and started pulling her away.

'Of course,' said Liz.

Leila spotted an opening. 'Can I, too?'

'No. *You* can come back when you need some.' She went to the stove, looked under the lid of a large casserole, then came to sit on the stool next to Robin's, where they watched Samir squeeze limes for the gimlets, muscles moving in his forearms. He added the gin to the shaker by eye, no measure.

'You're well practised,' Robin said.

'Vital life skill round here.'

Liz nodded. 'Key Performance Indicator. Goo-jere?' She twiddled one side of her own imaginary moustache. 'While the locust's back is turned. Lennie's a good sport,' she said more quietly. 'We'll give them a few minutes, then rescue her.'

Robin shook her head. 'She'll be loving it.' Lennie had always wanted a younger sister. Plus, while she was out of the room, she couldn't go on watching every interaction between her and Samir as if they were on Centre Court.

'Did you call Harry?' Liz asked Samir.

'I did.'

'He'll be reading,' she explained. 'He's just moved to the top floor and now we hardly see him – he just wants to lie on his new carpet and read round the clock.'

'I would, too, if I could get away with it.' And Harry was much shyer than she'd ever been. He was eleven but the one time she'd met him before, with Leila, it was his little sister who'd done the talking.

'God, yeah,' said Samir. 'Reading. The dream.'

'Only ten years until the children go to college and we can read all we want,' said Liz. 'Though I'm actually already dreading it – wah!'

'Same. And I've only got *three* years left. Not even – Len's doing her GCSEs in the summer.'

'Is she? I mean, yeah, of course she must be, but, God, where did the time go? I still think of her eating those rose petals as she went up the aisle at Josh and Rin's wedding.'

Robin had to stop herself staring. Liz had seen that – Liz? She'd known who Lennie was that day – she'd noticed her and *remembered*? She felt a revolution in her inner landscape, an actual physical sensation, like the time a couple of weeks before Lennie was born, when, at thirty-seven weeks cooked, she'd done a 180-degree turn from breech position and Robin had seen the bulk of her own stomach quite literally shift from left to right.

'Top-quality mothering on my part,' she managed to say. 'One of her five-a-day.' She could feel Samir's eyes on her; she kept hers down.

'Honestly, I don't know how you did it,' Liz said. 'And the job at the same time?'

'Hilary's poor flower beds were representative, if you remember Lennie rampaging through them? It was firefighting all the time in the early years. All. The. Time.' *And now, these past few months, it's been disaster management.*

She managed to lift her head and saw Liz shaking hers. 'I had so much respect for you. Running round after a toddler all day in that heat – do you remember how hot it was? – *and* you were matron of honour. Your speech was brilliant – actually funny, which is so hard to do.'

So she'd known who *she* was, too – Robin had never known that. Liz had seen *her* that terrible day, and she'd never realised. Matron of honour or not, she'd felt invisible, like she could just float away and no one bar Lennie would notice she'd gone.

Now Robin made the mistake of looking up and caught Samir's eye.

'*Hello, how are you?*'

Four words. The memory hung in the air between them, so clear it was amazing Liz couldn't see it, too.

Samir broke eye contact first, picked up a lime-half he'd already squeezed, then put it back down again.

'Even more respect with hindsight,' Liz was saying, 'now I've had small children myself. We were so young, just out of university. I couldn't have done it *at all* and you were there running around, doing everything and acing it. You were like bloody *Superwoman*.'

To her horror, Robin felt tears in her eyes. *Pull yourself together*, she ordered herself, *for Christ's sake, right now!*

'Thanks,' she croaked. 'It was hard at the time – the single-mum thing, I mean – but I've never regretted it.'

'I'm not surprised – she's fantastic.'

'Thank you.' She nodded. 'Biased, but *I* think so.'

Samir broke the silence that followed with a deafening rattle of the shaker. He filled the trio of martini glasses he'd set out, then carried two over to them.

'Thank you, lovely.' Liz put her arm around his waist and pulled him in next to her. Feeling awkward, Robin looked away.

'Any time.' He went back for his glass and brought it to the stool across the corner from them.

'Cheers.' Liz held up her glass to clink.

Robin took a large sip and felt the gin hit the centre of her forehead within seconds. Bliss. If she hadn't had to conform to societal norms, she'd have downed it.

'Delicious,' she told Samir. 'You're wasted in the police.'

'What, I've missed my true calling as a bartender?'

'That's what I've been saying,' said Liz. 'Will you eat some of these things?' She slid the giant wooden board across the counter in front of her. '*He* says I went over the top and I don't want to give him the satisfaction of being right.'

Samir grinned. 'Right *again*.'

Harry came downstairs thirty seconds before Liz put the tagine on the table, still carrying his book. She gave him a look that said *OK, but put it down now.* Reluctant but familiar with the drill, he put it on the corner of the work surface next to a pile of paperwork. A second later, he turned back and pushed the papers over the top, and Robin guessed he didn't want to answer lame adult questions about what he was reading. Fair enough: books had always felt very personal to her, too, still did if they were good.

Harry looked like his mother, though his colouring was his father's, his hair the same near-black that Samir's had been when Robin first knew him, before the silver. He was going to be tall like Samir, too, perhaps even taller, given the relative heights of Liz and Samir's mother, Padma, who was several inches shorter.

'We ate all the cheese puffs,' Leila told him, remorseless, 'and it's your own fault for being a *hermit*.'

He looked outraged until Liz said she'd put some aside for him.

Resolve blurred by the gimlet and still feeling as if Liz had torn her shell off, Robin let herself be talked into getting an Uber so she could 'help her finish what was left in the shaker' and have a glass of wine with dinner. '*One* glass, or I'll be wrecked tomorrow, and I just can't handle hangovers any more if I've got things to do.'

'God, I hear you. One too many and I'm a hundred and nine the next day.'

The tagine was predictably delicious, as was the raspberry pavlova that followed, Lennie a little too appreciative for Robin's liking. *Don't be* too *complimentary*, she wanted to hiss, *she'll think I don't feed you at all, let alone like this.*

Leila's boldness had been increasing in inverse proportion to Liz's relaxation level now the food was all served, and halfway through her meringue, she announced, 'You used to be Daddy's girlfriend.'

Liz snapped to full attention. 'Lei! Sorry,' she said to Robin. 'That was out of left field.'

'That's OK,' she said, smiling, as blood rushed to her face. 'It was a long time ago,' she told Leila. 'Before your daddy met your mummy. Before Lennie was born, even.'

She was undeterred. 'You went on a really long holiday to lots of different places.'

'It's called a gap year,' Harry told her.

Leila gave him a withering look, as if to say, *I know that, fool.* 'I saw some of the pictures.'

'Did you? Yes, we went travelling together. It was a lot of fun.'

Leila nodded, considering. 'I think I'd like to go on a really long holiday one day.'

'Well, I recommend it.' Again, she could feel Samir's eyes on her, and Lennie's moving between them. *Christ on a bike.* Her cheeks burned.

'It's all right,' Leila said, 'I don't mind – about you and Daddy. I think you're quite nice.'

'Thank you. I think you're quite nice, too.'

'So have you got a boyfriend now?'

No, but I'd quite like someone to kill *me now.*

'Not at the moment,' Robin said. She thought of Kev and the Vic woman, and one of her stupid throw-it-all-up-in-the-air urges came upon her. Before she could stop herself, she said, 'But someone asked me out the other day and I think I'll say yes.'

'Who?' said Lennie, instantly alert. She was sitting next to Samir, so Robin had to be very careful to avoid his eye.

'The DCI on the case Ben Renshaw was involved in last year. He's called Peter.'

'I don't think that's a good idea,' said Samir, shaking his head, avoiding *her* eye now. 'At all.' He reached for his wine and drained it.

Liz looked at Robin and pulled a conspiratorial face: *Uh-oh, the guv'nor's not happy.*

*

Five minutes later, Leila yawned like the MGM lion and Robin seized her opportunity. The love-life interrogation had put paid to the easy atmosphere, and Samir still hadn't met her eye. 'We should make a move,' she said, 'and let you tuck this one into bed.'

'I'm not tired!' Comical indignation.

'Can we help tidy up before we go?'

'Absolutely not – after the week you've had? Go and tuck *yourself* in.'

The Uber took seven minutes to arrive, time during which Robin was grateful for Leila's impromptu comedy routine, the area of the landing visible from the bottom of the stairs becoming the stage for a cops-and-robbers type routine in which Leila, in rabbit-print pyjamas, was on the lam from Liz and 'bedtime prison'.

When they heard the car outside, Samir opened the door. 'I'll walk you out.'

'Oh, it's ten yards, don't worry.'

'I'll walk you out.' He put the door on the latch and pulled it closed after them.

They were almost at the car before he turned to Lennie. 'How are you doing?' he asked quietly. 'Are you OK?'

They both understood him immediately. Robin tensed but Lennie gave him a small nod. 'Well, kind of. I'm so nervous – I feel sick a lot of the time. It just feels really wrong.'

'I know,' he said. 'I know it does. But I promise you, Len, it isn't. It's the right thing. You've got your whole life ahead of you, you can do good things in the world. Just hang in there.'

To Robin's amazement, Lennie stepped forward and hugged him. Then, slightly embarrassed, she stepped away again, thanked him and got into the car.

'Yes, thank you,' Robin said. 'Really. And thank you to Liz. She's brilliant, Samir.'

He nodded. 'Yeah, she is.' He nodded up the road towards her car. 'See you tomorrow.'

As the taxi moved off, Lennie leaned her head against the window. When they were safely two streets away, she said, 'She looks like you.'

'What?' Robin's voice sounded startled enough momentarily to interrupt the driver's rapid-fire phone conversation. 'No, she doesn't.'

'Oh, Mum, she *so* does.'

Chapter Thirty-Two

Robin stood at the door, looking past her reflection into the dark back garden as the new version of history impressed itself on her again. Liz had seen her at Corinna's wedding. On that appalling day, she had known who she was.

She'd been so focused on just getting through it, she barely remembered it herself. Apart from her happiness for Rin and Josh, it existed in her mind as a small collection of very painful images and her own grinding internal monologue. *Keep going, keep smiling – don't ruin Corinna's day, don't let Len wreck the flowers, don't let anyone see your insides are on fire.*

'Mum? Are you all right?'

'What?' She turned to find Lennie looking at her strangely. 'Yes, of course. I'm fine.'

'Are you? You've hardly said a word since we left their house. Here – your tea.' She put the mug on the table and went to get her own. Robin assumed she'd say goodnight and spirit away upstairs to phone Austin, but instead, mug in hand, Lennie returned to the table and sat down. 'What's going on? Did it upset you, going there?'

Upset? In the sense of knocking her over, maybe, yes.

'Earth to Mum – are you receiving?'

'Sorry.' She moved towards the table and pulled out a chair.

Looking at her daughter's face, she felt a rush of pure love and, for perhaps the hundred thousandth time, thanked God for the sudden mad conviction she'd had that, at twenty-one, unqualified, unemployed, she should have her baby, she could make it work, however hard it was. 'No, I'm OK,' she said. 'Just thinking. While you were in the other room with Leila, Liz was talking about Rin's wedding.'

Lennie took an exploratory sip of her tea – too hot – and waited for her to go on.

'It's hard to explain. I was so tired then – I'd started working at the Met, you were still tiny, obviously, and I just felt really . . . past it. Old and tired and frumpy.'

'That was the first time you saw Samir again, wasn't it? After you broke up.'

'And he basically ignored me. I didn't even meet Liz, just saw them across the garden all afternoon while I kept an eye on you. Corinna and Josh were too busy to talk much, obviously, Kev had brought someone, too – I didn't know that Liz even knew I existed that day. In my mind, she was like this . . . turned back and I was just . . . irrelevant.'

'Oh Mum.'

'But it wasn't like that. Tonight, she was talking about you eating the rose petals – she saw that and she knew who you were. She saw me charging round after you like a sweaty pink hippopotamus in my awful dress and—'

Lennie's eyebrows lifted. 'Her words, obviously, "sweaty pink hippopotamus"?'

'Obviously. But what I'm saying is *I* felt like a disaster area and *she* thought I had it all under control. She even thought I was funny – she said she laughed at the jokes in my speech. I'd more or less forgotten I'd even *done* a speech; Rin asked me at the last minute, when she realised that otherwise, it was only going to be men talking. Of everyone to notice, *Liz*.'

Lennie was nodding slowly.

'When she asked us over tonight, Len, I assumed she was just supporting Samir, you know, inviting one of his senior team to dinner, but I think she actually wanted us to come.'

Now Lennie laughed out loud. 'Oh my god, Mum, you are *such* a basket case. Like, why would anyone ever want *you* to come to dinner?'

'Well, I always thought she kind of . . . pitied me. Not even at the wedding, but in the past few years. I mean, compared to her, I was chaotic, single, in trouble at the Met to start with . . . I knew she was decent – Samir wouldn't have married anyone who wasn't – but I had this picture in my mind of her saying, "Yes, let her apply for the job at Force Homicide, Samir; give the poor woman a chance."'

'You're ridiculous.'

'It's what I thought. And it's hard to like someone if you think that.'

'But you did like her, didn't you, tonight?'

'Yes.' Robin didn't hesitate. 'She's one of the best people I've met – well, met properly – in a very long time.'

Robin lay in bed, sleepless yet again. Grateful as she was for the evening – a new version of the past, Lennie distracted for hours from her dread – she'd walked into her room and felt a wave of anger sweep over her. At the top of the stairs, before turning to go into her own room, Lennie had given her a hug and Robin had remembered the one she'd given Samir before diving into the taxi.

Suddenly she was furious with him – beyond furious. She wanted to scream at him, thump her hands on his chest. You *idiot!* You stupid *idiot!* To have all that, that brilliant woman and Leila and Harry, that whole *life*, and to jeopardise it. His job, his reputation, the income that raised his children – he'd put it all on the line to protect Lennie.

And Liz didn't know.

'I'll walk you out.' The door pulled closed behind him.

Oh, Samir.

Because she got it now – she understood why Liz had been OK with her applying for the job. It wasn't because she'd pitied her or wanted to support the sisterhood, or even make the point that she was cool and above such petty rivalries. It was because she trusted Samir completely. He could work alongside the only other woman he'd ever had a long-term relationship with, she could invite Robin to dinner at their house and make friends with her without hesitation because she was one hundred per cent sure of him.

Despite how much she'd liked Liz, despite having finally confronted her feelings for Samir, the realisation hit Robin like a punch.

Chapter Thirty-Three

In the Uber back to Bournville in the morning, Robin felt like a child being strong-armed back to a shop to return something she'd stolen. The voice last night had been right: she shouldn't have come here.

She shouldn't have come, full stop, not just to Samir's house, but to West Mids; she should never have taken a job working with him.

When she'd woken up this morning, she'd lain in the semi-darkness and the old feeling had come creeping round, the conviction that something was profoundly wrong with her. She wreaked destruction wherever she went: because of her dismal parenting, Lennie had got into a situation she should never have been in, and now, as a direct result, everything was in jeopardy, not just Len's future and Robin's career and reputation, potentially her freedom, but – if their plan came to light – Samir's, too.

Liz didn't deserve this. She didn't deserve to have her life as she knew it put in jeopardy because her husband's stupid idiot ex was a bad mother and her stupid idiot husband was protecting the ex's daughter.

She should leave – West Mids, Birmingham as a whole – before she destroyed anything else. She'd thought about it last night, lying awake past two o'clock. But, no, she'd realised then, she couldn't: Lennie had GCSEs in the summer, Asha and Austin were here, and her grandparents – Len's relationship with them was vital now. It would have to wait, at the very least until the summer, when her exams were done and Austin was on his way to university. Maybe if he did get a place at LSE, Lennie would actually welcome the idea of moving back to London.

But maybe it would be too late by then. If they were discovered, Lennie might not be moving on to A levels at all, at least not in school, and Samir might have no job to save.

As the taxi made the turn into his street, Robin touched the key in her pocket and entertained a brief fantasy of just hopping in the car and going. But that would look terrible and she wasn't a coward.

This time, the car parked on the drive was Samir's. She said a prayer that they were all out together in the Honda and, having knocked, she could send a text saying she was sorry to have missed them. Of course, though, she wasn't that lucky.

'Hello,' Samir said, opening the door. He was in jeans again, though with a white T-shirt this morning and bare feet. She hadn't seen his feet in nearly twenty years, but she'd still be able to pick them out of a line-up, those long straight toes with the tufts of dark hair. 'It was fun last night, wasn't it? Thanks for coming.' He indicated the empty spot. 'Liz has taken Harry and Leila ice-skating, friend's birthday party. She'll be sorry to miss you.'

'And me her. I enjoyed getting to know her.' Robin heard how stiff she sounded – they both did. They were talking like people who barely knew each other.

Samir frowned. 'Come in a moment.'

'No, I should get on. I'm on my way to the station and—'

'Robin. Two minutes – one. Can we not have this conversation in view of the neighbours?'

She hesitated, but then stepped inside.

Samir closed the door. The pink leopard-print high-tops had gone to the party, she saw.

'What conversation?'

'You're angry with me.'

'I'm not angry.' She glanced down the hallway to the kitchen, from where she could hear voices. 'No one's here?'

'I'm on my laptop, the rugby's on in the background.'

'I'm not angry, Samir. I'm livid.'

He frowned. 'Why?'

'Because you're lying to Liz!' she hissed.

'I'm not.'

'Oh, come *on*, you absolutely are. You're risking all this' – she gestured around them – 'your job, your salary. If it comes out you knew, forget your job, you could face jail time! And she doesn't even know you're doing it.'

'She does know.'

Robin stopped, sure she'd misunderstood. 'What?'

'I told her.'

She stared at him.

'I couldn't not, Rob, she's my wife.'

Robin struggled to compute: Liz knew?

'You can trust her,' he said. 'One hundred per cent.'

Now she was even more wrong-footed. 'Why? Why can I? How is she OK with this? She's a lawyer, for God's sake; we're perverting the course of justice!'

'Are we?'

'You know we are!'

He shook his head. 'No, I don't. I really don't. Is it justice to ruin a fifteen-year-old's life for something she did in the heat of a moment, faced with Neo-Nazis – when he made a full recovery and your brother's going down anyway?'

Questions she'd asked herself over and over and over again.

'Robin, I didn't *choose* to see Lennie throw that stone; the only choice I had was whether or not I was going to throw *her* to the wolves. *Your* daughter.' He let his hands drop and looked at her, eyes dark in the hallway's muted light. The space between them seemed suddenly to come alive. 'It wasn't a choice,' he said. 'I didn't even have to think about it.'

For several seconds, they looked at each other, and Robin felt their past breathing with them, the love and hurt and regret, and the relief, too, of finally knowing what had happened and finding each other again.

'It's too big a risk, Samir,' she said. 'It's a risk *I* have to take, but you . . . Look at all this – everything you've worked for. Both of you.'

'That's why I had to tell her.'

'What, that you'd jeopardised it all for someone else's child? Not just anyone's, either – mine.'

'If I *hadn't* told her, I'd have jeopardised it all. A marriage with a secret like that . . .' He shook his head. 'I told her that while there was a way out for Lennie, I believed the right thing to do – morally, if not legally – was to let it happen. No one's looking at what she did, no one's asking me about it. I'm not actively lying, but if I said anything, I'd be actively choosing to hurt her. I know she's suffered for it, I saw it last night, and you've told me. She's had months of mental anguish, she's done her penance.'

'What did Liz say?'

'She panicked, she'd be the first to tell you, but then she thought about the reality, what it would mean for Lennie. She knows the risk to me is minimal. The only people who know I know are you and Len, and neither of you'll say anything.'

'Of course not. Ever.'

For a few seconds, the only sound in the house was the faint babble of rugby commentary.

Robin felt a mounting pressure in her chest. Before she could stop herself, she said, 'Why didn't you talk to me at the wedding?'

'What?'

'Four words, *Hello, how are you?* then you moved away like I was someone you'd met once before at a cocktail party.'

He shook his head slowly. 'I didn't talk to you because I couldn't, Robin, OK? I couldn't. Seeing you again, after four years, and Lennie, and being there with Liz – I felt like I was being torn in half. It was one of the worst days of my life.'

Chapter Thirty-Four

Robin pulled into the station car park with deep relief: Sunday, at the oasis. She'd long ago made peace with people thinking she was a workaholic – she *was* a workaholic. It was an addiction, a real one, not something she mouthed off about to show how important she was. She self-medicated with work in the way that other people did with drink and drugs, and it damaged her and the person she loved most in the world.

I felt like I was being torn in half.

Today, as so often before, she wanted to check out of her personal life and sink into work as if it were a warm bath. Or the Dead Sea, more accurate – nothing grew here but it kept you afloat.

Varan and Jo were both in again as was Tark, but Malia had rung while Robin was in the taxi to Samir's. 'It's my birthday,' she'd said. 'Normally it wouldn't matter, but other people have made plans for me, and I feel like I can't let them down.'

With a small spike of curiosity about these 'other people', Robin had told her she couldn't believe they were even talking about it and wished her happy birthday. 'Now be gone.'

At her desk, she opened her notebook to a new page, smoothed it down with unnecessary force and tried to get her head back in the game by making the notes she hadn't done last night.

Summerfield – something else going on there?
General culture? Single attack/incident? Longer-term abuse?
Ben's AS results – convenient excuse?

She scribbled for a few minutes, adding details and questions, then went out to talk to the others. Jo was working with such focus, they had to say her name twice to get her attention.

'"Friends of Summerfield",' she told Robin, tapping the printout on her desk, 'aka the donors' list. Atkinson emailed it over late afternoon yesterday.'

'Anything strike you?'

'Not yet, but I'm only a little way in. I can't believe how many people have spare money for this kind of thing. Most of it's only smallish amounts – five hundred here, two-fifty there – but just on this page, there are three people who donated five figures.'

'While the rest of us wonder if we can afford the dentist,' said Tark, running his tongue alongside the inside of his cheek. 'Different world.'

'Nothing on CCTV?' Robin asked.

He shook his head.

'OK. Varan, could you give Theo a ring? If he's at home, let's pop over there.'

Theo was at home and, as he'd told Varan on the phone, Molly was with him. Carolyn made them a pot of tea, then retreated elsewhere in the house, leaving the four of them in the kitchen.

Molly looked better today, less raw around the nose, eyes less swollen, but although his clothes and hair were clean, Theo looked much the same as he had on Wednesday. He told them he couldn't sleep, which Robin had detected for herself without drawing too deeply on her training.

'We're looking specifically now at whether Ben had heard about something else at Summerfield,' she told them. 'A new case – or cases – of assault or abuse. Please – if you know but you're afraid to tell us for fear of repercussions, we can make sure you have security. More security – the cars outside are still in place, as you know. We *can* keep you safe.'

Neither quite hid their scepticism, but Theo shook his head. 'It's not that – we just don't know anything. Honestly. If he'd told us, we'd have told you.'

'Which leads to my next question. We've heard a couple of times that he was the one who really resisted cutting back on StrengthInNumbers work. Did that cause tension between you all?'

'In what way?'

'Was he annoyed you didn't fight it as hard as him?'

'A bit,' said Molly. 'To start with. He was so passionate about it. He didn't like writing articles very much, Theo and I did most of them, but when we were talking to schools and colleges, as soon as he was up on stage, it was like a light came on. He loved it, and he really believed it was important.'

'And you?'

'Of course I think it's important.' Impatience.

Varan nodded. 'We heard you'd already started doing less, though, before the school asked the boys to scale back. Did your school suggest it, too?'

'No, it was my choice.'

He waited, and after a few seconds, Molly sighed.

'I needed a break for my own sake – my mental health. The rape and then afterwards, with what happened to Theo and Ben, it was like I was living on this constant adrenaline rush. Then the trial and launching the site and everything that came with that. The idea of being a "victim" was so offensive to me, I'd decided I just wouldn't be one.'

'Did that change?' Robin asked gently.

'No. I did. I've been seeing a counsellor and a few months ago, over the summer, it was like the adrenaline suddenly wore off. I realised I was hurting myself by pretending it hadn't affected me. I was just shoving it under the carpet, never giving myself an opportunity to process it, and at some point, if I didn't deal with it properly, it was going to hit me really badly. I needed time.'

Theo reached for her hand.

'Time to absorb it, you know? And for other stuff, too, just . . . *life*. Suddenly it felt like everything revolved round that one fact about me, that I'd been raped – it drove everything. We were getting home at ten or eleven at night after events, doing interviews at weekends – it was too much.'

'I can see that, definitely. Did Ben?'

'After a couple of weeks. He couldn't really argue with me much because it was me it had happened to – you can't bully someone who's been raped into talking about it. That feels like another sort of attack.'

Robin nodded. 'How about you, Theo? What were your feelings about it?'

'I was with Moll,' he said. 'It was her thing.'

'No,' Molly protested, 'that's not true, it *wasn't* just mine. And it wasn't just me who was physically attacked.' For a moment, Theo looked confused. 'The car?' she said. 'Your leg?'

He shook his head. 'But that's different. It's different.'

'Was Ben harder on you about it, Theo?' Varan asked. 'If he didn't have the same worry about pushing you?'

'A bit,' Theo conceded. 'He tried some emotional blackmail – I'd be doing it for Molly, et cetera. But school laid the law down and I was tired, too. And we always planned to go back to it afterwards – it was just a break, not an end. And the site itself is still live, obviously..'

They were interrupted by the doorbell. Theo and Molly both jumped. Hand on the arm of the sofa, Theo listened to hear if anyone was coming, then relaxed a little when his mother started moving across the room overhead.

'Your leg still really bothers you?' Robin asked.

He nodded. 'It hurts to stand up from a low seat. I'll need at least one more surgery, they think, before it's as good as they can get it. Probably two.'

Carolyn reached the bottom of the stairs and paused for a moment. Then they heard the locks and the rattle of the chain.

'Al! Nice surprise – good to see you.'

'You, too. How are you, Caro?' A male voice, forties or fifties, unaccented and warm, as if it really was good to see her. Another pause, Robin guessed a hug. The voice was lower when he said, 'I was so sorry to hear the news – I asked Ed to let you know I've been thinking of you all.'

'Thank you. Yes, it's been a very tough week.'

'Is Theo all right?'

'Very sad,' she said. 'Very, very sad. We all are. They'd been friends for so long. Look, don't stand on the doorstep, come in. Ed's just here – I can—'

'No, you're all right, I've got to get on. I just came to drop these off for him. Figures for the meeting tomorrow.'

'OK, I'll pass them on.'

'Thanks. Can we see you, the two of you, when the dust settles a bit? Dinner?'

'We'd love that, yes.'

'I'll be in touch in a few days, get it in the diary.'

It wasn't until they'd said their goodbyes and the door clicked shut that Robin realised the four of them in the kitchen hadn't spoken since it opened; they'd all been listening.

Carolyn's footsteps approached briskly down the hall but diverted before reaching them and were swallowed by the sitting-room carpet. Her voice reached them, however, her tone faintly questioning. 'That was Alun, Eddie.'

'Yeah,' said a male voice, dry. 'I heard.'

On their way out, Robin put her head round the sitting-room door. Eddie Gillespie was sitting in a wing chair set a little way into the bay window, a laptop open on his knees. 'Mr Gillespie? I hadn't realised you were here, sir,' she said, going in. 'Detective Chief Inspector Lyons – Robin. I'm leading Ben's case.'

Eddie put the computer on a covered stool next to the chair and stood to shake her hand. 'Sorry,' he said. 'I would have introduced myself earlier, but it was Theo and Molly you were after so . . .'

His handshake could have done with a bit more muscle, for Robin's taste, and she had the impression that he pulled back a fraction of a second earlier than most people would. He was in his mid-fifties, she guessed, but his hair, mostly grey, had receded in deep Vs from the temples and his face was lined. When he removed his glasses, he looked slightly pissed off, as if annoyed at the interruption.

'Working?' She nodded at his laptop.

'Always. Same as you – Sunday afternoon?'

'Time is of the essence.'

'Glad to hear it. Perhaps you'll actually get somewhere – we're still waiting to hear that the Heywoods are going to pay for nearly crippling my son. It's only been a year, though, so no rush.'

Robin left the station in time to do what she'd planned on Friday evening, stopping at M&S on her way home to buy ingredients for a big batch of chilli and enough roasted vegetables to last them the week.

She had everything ready when Lennie arrived back from Austin's, and when Len saw the laid table and candles, Robin panicked that she'd made a mistake. She waited for the outburst about fussing, but instead, to her surprise, after a moment's hesitation, Lennie came across the room and hugged her. 'Thank you, Mum.'

After dinner, they cleaned up together, then watched *Dynasties*, letting Attenborough's voice wash gently over them. Robin remembered Dominic, how Marcus had snickered that his girlfriend loved animals.

Later, in bed, the faint sound of the conversation with Austin reaching her from down the landing, she opened her laptop. Since the visit to the Gillespies' house, she'd kept thinking about Eddie. It seemed most likely now that Alun Morgan himself was his connection at Myrmidon, and that was how he'd got his job despite the fraud conviction. She put their two names together in a search, but, apart from a few lists of company personnel, found nothing.

Searching for 'Morgan Myrmidon Logistics Birmingham', she got pages of hits and a strip of thumbnail images of a man in a suit posing either with enormous lorries or other men in suits.

She clicked on a photo of him in black tie and it opened as a bigger image on a page of others from the same event, apparently a gala dinner at Birmingham Botanical Gardens. If you were going in for that sort of thing, it looked a nice place for it, she had to admit. This particular event had happened in the summer, drinks with a backdrop of Victorian greenhouses and scarlet geraniums, clusters of men in black and women in jewel-coloured occasionwear and blistering heels.

The photo was dated last year and Morgan looked to be in his late forties. His hair was brown, short and brushed to one side at the front, with a hint of red that showed most in his eyebrows and the shorter patches round his ears. He was squinting slightly in the late-afternoon sun, a hand up to shade pale eyes, smiling in a way that accentuated a generous lower lip.

In three of the other pictures, he stood close to a woman with a sharp blonde bob. Frowning, Robin clicked one with a better view of her face. When it enlarged, she was sure: yes, she *had* seen her before, and recently. *Alun and Isabel Morgan*, read the caption. Isabel – Izz. It was the woman she'd met briefly when she'd first gone to talk to Theo at home, the one who hoped *she* planned to actually *do* something.

They met socially.

Opening a new window, she typed in 'Alun Morgan Bill Anne Dominic Marcus Heywood' but got nothing.

She kept going for another twenty minutes or so, nonetheless, her eyes flicking to her phone on the duvet every couple of minutes. It stayed silent, though. At eleven thirty, too late for Samir to call, she closed her computer and turned off the light.

Chapter Thirty-Five

As the days had passed, one by one, the grace period between waking up and remembering the situation had been shrinking. This morning, Robin had had barely a couple of seconds before she realised it was now only a week until Luke's sentencing. A week today.

To try to control the anxiety, she'd got out of bed immediately and started making a mental list of actions for the day, among them her own first port of call.

She was in the car on her way there when her phone rang: *M&D*.

Her mother's voice filled the car, high and fast. 'That journalist called me, love. Jeremy Handley at the *Record* – that's him, isn't it? I know it is.'

'What? Hold on.' Seeing a space at the side of the road, Robin pulled in without indicating, earning an angry blast on the horn from the car behind. 'When? What did he say?'

'Just now. He wanted to ask me questions about you and Luke.'
Oh, Jesus Christ.

Over the weekend, she realised now, without any further calls and nothing on the *Record's* website, Robin had allowed herself a scintilla of hope that he'd moved on to something else. She should have known better.

'What did you say to him, Mum?' Her heart was bumping. 'I said, "No comment."'

Amid the panic, Robin detected a note of pride. She exhaled. 'Thank you. Thank you, that was exactly right. Nothing else?'

'No. I said I had no comment now and that wouldn't change, so there'd be no point calling again.' She swallowed. 'Rob, he couldn't get to Luke, could he? In there? He couldn't reach him?'

'No, Mum, no one can – not even *you*.'

'Yes, that's right, of course. Sorry, I'm not thinking straight.' A momentary pause. 'But, Rob, he could have contacts there, couldn't he – people on the inside who could phone out? People with secret phones – or wardens, even.'

She couldn't reassure her without revealing she'd had the same thought, but there was no way round it. 'I don't think it's likely. He's young, this guy, only a handful of years into his career, and he's not from around here. I looked him up – he grew up in West London.'

'OK, that's good, isn't it? That's good.'

'Mum, you said exactly the right thing and no one else will talk to him: Luke's incommunicado, and the rest of us – you, me, Lennie, Dad – we're all solid. We're going to be fine.'

'Yes, you're right, I know you're right.' She blew out air, a single long breath. 'I'll tell you what, though, love: my nerves. If it wasn't nine in the morning, I'd have my wine.'

'Don't put ideas in my head.'

Her mother half-laughed, the most she could muster, and after agreeing to be in touch, they said goodbye. As she was indicating to pull out, however, Robin felt the dread start to creep in again. She was transported back to Samir's hallway in Bournville, his bare feet and T-shirt, the rack of his children's shoes against the wall behind her.

If it comes out you knew, forget your job, you could face jail time.

*

Carolyn had seen Robin through the peephole, so she'd had a second or two, but she still seemed surprised when she opened the door. 'DCI Lyons, hello again.' She pushed a pair of emerald-green reading glasses to the top of her head. A Breton top accompanied the jeans today and a pair of Ugg slippers. 'Theo's not here, I'm sorry, he's gone back to school today.'

'That's all right, it's actually you I was hoping to talk to.'

'Really? Oh. Right. Well, come in. It's freezing out there.'

'Sorry for the interruption,' Robin said as she followed her down the hall.

'No, you're fine. I'm working, but I'm freelance so it's no problem.' She indicated two neat stacks of paper on the kitchen table. 'I'm in here trying to keep warm.'

'What do you do?'

'Editing. Mostly academic papers, but I also do some projects for a small history press, which I like. That's a book on the canal network. Sounds boring as hell, I know, but it's quite lively, particularly the snippets from contemporaneous accounts – some of the voices. Would you like coffee? I've just made a pot.'

'Thanks, yes, a quick one.'

When it was poured, they sat in the window where she and Varan had sat with Molly and Theo yesterday. 'How did he feel about going back this morning?' Robin asked.

'It was his idea. Staying home was just making it worse, he said – at least at school there'll be structure to the day. I think he's right, but I'd be amazed if he manages to concentrate at all.'

'Does he enjoy school, normally?'

'Yes, he always has.'

'He's been at Summerfield long?'

'Since he was eight.'

'Mrs Gillespie—'

'Carolyn, please.'

'Carolyn – thank you, and I'm Robin – I don't know whether Theo and Molly mentioned it after we left yesterday, but we're currently looking at whether Ben had discovered evidence of more sexual wrongdoing at the school.'

'They did mention it, yes. They don't know of anything, obviously.'

'No. I wondered what your impressions of the school were, though, as a parent. After last year, you weren't tempted to move Theo for Sixth Form?'

'We talked about it, but academically he was very happy there and he loves some of his teachers – Dugmore, as they call him, and Mrs Foster, his English teacher. And the school's gone to great lengths to reassure us all that they're on top of things now.'

'Right.'

'The education's just so good – since Atkinson took over as Head, they've been soaring. Plus, in our case, there's the scholarship issue. After having that all the way through, we didn't feel it was right to turn around and leave.' She hesitated. 'They also hadn't made a big stink during *our* troubles.'

'Meaning your husband's conviction?'

Carolyn nodded and looked away into the garden, where, beyond the patio, the lawn was crisp with frost.

'I'm sorry to drag it up again. I know the bare bones, but could you tell me about that – how it affected you as a family?'

'You know he was working for his cousin's company and he filed a fraudulent tax return?'

'Yes.'

'They were both convicted, him and Chris. They were only trying to keep the company afloat – Chris and Fran had just had a third baby, we had the mortgage here and Theo at Summerfield . . .' She shook her head. 'It was a stupid thing to do, *stupid* – I could have throttled him. And the business ended up folding anyway, of course.'

'Fourteen months, he served?'

'Yes.'

'And he got out . . .?'

'A year and a half ago – more now. The seventeenth of March last year. Then, four months after that, all hell broke loose a second time, with Alistair and Molly and everything that ensued. Theo's accident.'

'You've had a rough time.'

'I'd hoped we were out the other side – finished with police on the doorstep.' She attempted a smile.

'You managed to keep everything together, though – the house, and Theo stayed at Summerfield.'

'Barely. One of my aunts died and what she left me was just enough to cover the fees for that year. It came into my account, thousands of pounds, and I just forked it over, chunk by chunk, until it was gone.'

'You didn't ask the school if there was any more leeway?'

'I didn't dare. Given Eddie's situation, I was scared they'd throw us out. For the rest, the mortgage, money to live on, I took on more work – a lot more – and we ate jacket potatoes and beans and we just got through it.'

'Your husband is working again now, though, despite the conviction.'

Carolyn Gillespie frowned. 'Is this relevant?'

'Frankly? I don't know.'

She sighed. 'I was terrified he wouldn't find another job. During his last months in prison, he'd talked about retraining for something else, but what? Then, thank God, Alun got in touch.'

'They were friends?'

'Yes. They'd lost contact over the years, but, lucky for us, he'd heard on the vine about the mess we were in, he needed someone, and he sent Eddie an email.'

'How did they know each other?'

'School. Apparently they used to vie for the maths prize – one year one of them would get it, the next the other . . .'

Yes, it *was* lucky, Robin thought, very – jobs for the boys, a safety net in every situation. No doubt that was why Theo's school fees had been the priority even if it meant beans for a year – at Summerfield, the old school tie would be silk, not polyester. 'It must have been a huge relief.'

'It meant we could breathe again – financially and otherwise. Work is a big thing for Eddie, not just keeping us all going, but for his own self-esteem. The job offer was pure relief for me, though, on that level, I think it's more of a mixed blessing for him.'

'Really?'

'Masculine pride,' she said with the hint of a smile. 'I think it's like having to concede the maths prize on a permanent basis. Alun's told him countless times he's not a charity case, but it rubs Ed the wrong way, feeling "beholden", as he says.'

'When we were here yesterday, Mr Morgan dropped round some papers for him.'

'That's right.'

'You answered the door – you came from upstairs to answer it.'

'Yes.'

Was she being deliberately obtuse? Robin wondered. 'Despite Eddie being in the next room – when it was his boss who was here?'

'Oh, Alun's a family friend now.'

Robin waited, and after a few seconds, Carolyn sighed. 'He gets a bit jealous sometimes – Eddie, I mean. He thinks Alun fancies me. Flirts with me.'

'Does he? Flirt?'

'No.' Carolyn waved the idea away, nose wrinkled. 'Well, maybe a bit, but it doesn't mean anything. I'm sure he's the same with everyone. It's not like I'm going to have an *affair* with him, is it?'

Robin drained her coffee cup, hoping she'd feel obliged to fill the silence again, but she didn't. 'You said Alun's a family friend "now" – when did *you* meet him?'

'Last year.'

'Only then? You didn't know him at all before they lost touch?'

She shook her head. 'No.'

'OK. Did they go to Summerfield, your husband and Alun?'

Carolyn looked slightly surprised. 'Summerfield? No. They went to Clarendon – do you know it?'

Chapter Thirty-Six

The good news of the morning was that Samir's petition to Kilmartin had resulted in him finding them an extra PC and two civilian staff, one of whom, in his late fifties, was a retired DS who'd got bored of sitting round at home on his pension. Robin directed the three of them straight to Tark on CCTV. 'There has to be someone or something in all of that,' she said, pointing to the brimming boxes. 'Two killings in central Birmingham in the Year of Our Lord 2018 without anything caught on camera? No way. We just have to find it. Malia, on a different note, let's get in touch with Jane Booth, the secretary at Summerfield, and ask for the names of anyone who's left unexpectedly in the past five years. We'll also need someone to track down some people who went to the Clarendon School.'

'Clarendon.' Malia wrote the name down, frowning. 'Where is that?'

'Between Henley and Solihull, out in the country. Eddie Gillespie went there, and Alun Morgan, his boss.'

'You think something's going on *there* now?'

'Not now, no. I'm interested in their time, when *they* were at school.'

Varan turned in his chair.

They'd talked yesterday afternoon on the drive back to the station and he'd also picked up on the strangeness of Eddie not coming to the door when, from the sitting room, he must have heard Alun or even, as Robin had thought as she'd noted the position of his chair in the window, seen him coming up the path. And, Varan had pointed out, who needed to bring papers round at all, anyway, in these days of email?

'I've just dropped back in there for a word with Carolyn,' she told him. 'She said Eddie thinks Alun flirts with her, so it could be not coming to the door was a protest.'

'Though if it *was* jealousy, wouldn't he have wanted to cut her off at the pass and get in first, if he'd seen him coming?'

'True. Either way, though, there's something else. She told me that when Alun first contacted Eddie with the job offer, they'd been out of touch. Before last year, she'd never met him.'

'Never?' said Malia.

'I know.'

'How long have she and Eddie been married?'

'Twenty-one years.'

Malia, Varan and Tark looked at one another.

Tark said it: 'Why would he get in touch after that long to offer someone with a conviction a job?'

'You have to wonder, don't you? I think to start with, we should come at this from two angles. Let's see if we can find out what their relationship was at school beyond a maths rivalry. Maybe this is nothing at all: they used to be close, just fell out of touch, no ill will, and when Alun heard about Eddie's straits, he remembered him fondly and wanted to help out of the goodness of his heart.'

'Or,' said Malia, 'a crooked accountant was just what he needed.'

'Yes. So, on the quiet, two prongs: their relationship and a look at Myrmidon Logistics. Something here doesn't add up.'

Robin closed her office door and sat down at the desk. She needed to talk to Samir, but she wasn't ready, so when she picked up the phone, she called Peter Hailey instead. Like last time, he answered almost immediately.

'Robin, how are you?' Again, he sounded as if he were smiling. 'How can I help?'

'I've a question for you: in your investigation, did you ever come across Alun Morgan?'

'Remind me who he is?'

'Eddie Gillespie's employer, Myrmidon Logistics.'

'Oh, yeah. No, beyond that I don't think so. There's nothing on HOLMES?'

'No.'

'I'll ask my DS in case she remembers anything. Theo's dad's boss, though? What's your thinking? What's the connection to Ben?'

Stated baldly, it did seem straw-clutchingly tangential. 'I don't know,' she said. 'Maybe none at all, we'll see.' She paused. 'Peter, the other thing I was calling about – I wondered, if you were still up for it, should we have that drink one night?'

Robin had just put the phone down when it rang again, this time an internal call.

'It's lunchtime,' said Samir, 'and I haven't seen you yet today. Are you talking to me?'

'Of course.'

'Well, come and do it in here then. Rona's just zipping out for some sandwiches – do you want one?'

Rona was gone by the time she got there, so Robin let herself in and closed the door.

Samir watched her as she crossed the room and sat down. 'OK?' he said quietly.

She nodded. Back in a jacket and tie, he was easier to look at. 'You?'

'Fine. How are things next door?'

She told him the latest lines of enquiry and watched him frown. 'You're thinking, what does this have to do with Ben?'

'I am,' he admitted, 'but if your antennae are up, then go for it. I trust you.'

'Just make it bear fruit before Kilmartin asks?'

'If you wouldn't mind.'

I trust you.

'Look, Samir,' she lowered her voice, 'I've got to tell you something.'

'I don't like the sound of that.' He put an elbow on the desk and rested his head against his fingertips. 'Go on then.'

'There's a journalist, Jeremy Handley from the *Daily Record*. He's done their news coverage on Ben and Anne, but I think he's working on something else, too.'

'What? What do you mean?'

'He rang a few days ago and told me he was doing a piece about me and Luke, his sentencing for the riot while I'm leading this case. He said it's a good story even without my "skeletons".'

Samir's hand moved to cover his mouth. 'For God's sake, Rob, why didn't you tell me?'

'I couldn't – when you rang me after that, Liz was with you. At that point, I didn't know you'd told her. And then I didn't hear from him again, so I hoped maybe something else had come up and bumped it down the list.'

'But it hasn't?'

'Mum rang me this morning. He'd just called her.'

Samir was silent for several seconds, hand back over his mouth, eyes on her. Then he said, 'What's his angle? It's not much of a story, *Detective With Some Personal History Also Has Nasty Brother.*'

'Oh, I don't know – I've seen stories about less. Much less, in the *Record*.'

'If he's a news reporter, he needs a hook.'

'"DCI Robin Lyons, leading the inquiry, was unavailable for comment."'

'Meaning what?'

'We're not doing anything. We failed before and we're failing again – it's a week today since Ben died – more than – and we've got nothing. Nothing on the witness intimidation last year and now nothing on this – *What The Hell's Going On At West Mids? Incompetence! Crime-ageddon!* I'm an SIO with what looks like a shady past . . .'

'But isn't.'

'And a brother who definitely *is* about to be sentenced for violent crimes. And this shady SIO also happens to be the Head of Force Homicide's ex.'

'Corruption – that's his angle?'

'I think that's what he's looking for, yes. And honestly,' she lowered her voice again, 'with Bill Heywood in Kilmartin's ear all the time, who's to say he's wrong, even without *my* contribution.'

'Your "contribution" isn't going to come to light. I promise you.'

'You can't, Samir, because you're forgetting someone. Someone who's completely shafted both of us in the past and is fully capable of doing it again.'

*

As Robin made her way back along the corridor, head down, uneaten pack of sandwiches in hand, she almost collided with Tark coming the other way.

'Guv,' he said, hands up to stop her, 'I was just coming to find you.' His expression was grim. 'There's something you need to see.'

In the minutes she'd been in Samir's office, the mood of the incident room had changed entirely. When she'd left, the double doors had closed on the hum of twenty-five people at concentrated work, typing, talking, a printer chuntering. As she came back in, the room was quiet and the faces that turned to her were solemn. Phil looked particularly stricken.

Dave Hanratty was waiting at his desk, an empty chair pulled up next to his, grainy black-and-white paused on-screen. When Robin sat, Tark, Malia and Varan gathered behind her.

'Where is this?'

'Alcester Road,' Hanratty said. 'Just round the corner from the house – cross over, take a left and you're in Salisbury Road. The tape's from a café.'

'Let's see it, then.'

He hit 'play' and the fuzzy picture became a length of street, a strip of road taking up the top third, the rest pavement. For five or six seconds, nothing moved apart from the digital seconds following the time in the bottom corner: 02.12. A car came and went, left to right, ghostly in the grey silence, and then, also from the left, a figure appeared.

Slight, somewhere between five two and five four, Robin would say, wearing jeans and a dark puffer jacket, a sweatshirt underneath with the hood up. Even without the strand of long hair that escaped at the front, it was obvious they were looking at a woman. No, not a woman, a girl.

Skinny legs, white Nike trainers, a pale backpack that looked heavy, the straps over both shoulders. She was walking quickly, eyes down, face hidden by the hoodie until, suddenly, another car passed and she startled. Had it beeped at her? There was no way of knowing, but either way, she raised her head and followed it with her eyes. A second or two later, as she turned back, her attention was caught by something else, maybe her own reflection in the café window, and she looked in their direction.

Hanratty hit 'pause.'

Robin looked, then closed her eyes. Dear god.

'And this is definitely Wednesday morning?' she said.

'Yes, guv.'

Robin was in the corridor again, this time on her way back to Samir to break the news, when she heard the doors open behind her. She guessed whom it would be before he said a word.

'Guv?'

She turned, but Phil Howell stayed back as if he were actually physically afraid of her.

'I'm sorry,' he said. 'Really sorry. I made a mistake – I thought it was Theo who had the little sister.'

Chapter Thirty-Seven

No black umbrella today, the air was dry and so cold that their breath was visible in the thickening twilight, but as Robin and Varan walked the slight incline to the Renshaws' front door, she remembered the image of the judge's black execution cap. For the second time in just a week, she was bringing disaster to their doorstep.

They hadn't called ahead, so Emma Renshaw was surprised to see them. Robin watched her read their faces and saw the hope that there was news on Ben's killer turn quickly to trepidation instead.

'Are you all here?' Robin asked.

'Yes. Roger and Amy are upstairs.'

'Could you ask them to come down, please?'

'What's it about?'

'I want to speak to you all together, Mrs Renshaw.' She saw the trepidation become frank fear.

Once she was gone, Robin pointed to the kitchen and in a voice barely above a whisper, she broke the news to Sandy. As Family Liaison, she was only supposed to be a conduit for information, but warm-hearted as Sandy was, it was hard for her not to feel for bereaved families. From her horrified expression, Robin could tell she'd become fond of the Renshaws.

The sound of feet on the stairs and Emma appeared in the

kitchen doorway, the look on her face reminding Robin of Lennie's when she'd cranked open the conservatory door and demanded to know what she and her mother were talking about.

In the sitting room, the Renshaws took the same spots on their sofa, Emma in the middle, Roger and Amy wedged in between her and its high arms. Emma reached for both their hands and gripped them tightly. Amy was crying silently, tears slipping down her cheeks undisturbed.

At the thought of what she had to do, Robin's whole body felt heavy. '*The total destruction of our family, one by one,*' Bill Heywood's words echoed in her ears.

But there was no way round it. 'Emma, Roger, Amy – we're here because this afternoon a member of the team discovered CCTV footage that presents some very difficult questions.'

A sound escaped Amy, a sort of painful gulp swallowed the wrong way. Emma glanced at her, *OK?* She didn't know, Robin realised – she had no idea. Oh God.

'The CCTV's from a camera on Alcester Road,' she went on, 'a minute's walk before the turn into Salisbury Road, where the Heywood family home is.'

Amy was shaking visibly now and, feeling it, Emma looked at her, concern mixed with the first intimation that something was wrong. Very wrong.

'The footage is from just after 2 a.m. on Wednesday morning,' Robin ploughed on, 'which, by the Fire Service's estimate, was about half an hour before the fire really took hold.'

'For the love of *God,*' Roger Renshaw spoke for the first time, gripping Emma's hand so hard she gave a yelp of pain. 'Just say what you're trying to say!'

'I'm so sorry.' For the content more than her delivery. 'Mr Renshaw, the film shows Amy. It's Amy, walking towards the Heywoods' house just before the fire started.'

He snorted, derisive. 'Don't be ridiculous, she was here! At two in the morning? What the hell would she be doing out in the streets at *two in the morning*? She's fifteen! For fuck's sake, is no one over there capable of doing anyth— Your man *came* here – at the crack of dawn. He got us out of bed to make sure we were here!'

'He got *us* out of bed, Roger,' Emma said quietly. 'Just us.'

Robin had a sudden flash of memory: Phil's blink as she'd told the team she'd asked him to check the Renshaws were *all* at home in bed. '*I made a mistake.*'

Emma turned to her daughter now, white with fear. 'Is it true? Amy, tell us it's not true.'

In response, Amy curled over, hiding her face, hands laced over her head as if she expected blows to come raining down. Her back heaved as she struggled to get a breath.

Fifteen. She was a child. The exact same age as Lennie.

'It's all right,' Sandy said. 'Amy, it's all right—'

'For fuck's *sake*.' Roger was on his feet. 'For fuck's *sake*, woman, shut up! Just shut up! It's not all right – it'll never be all right. Nothing will *ever* be all right.'

Amy sounded as if she were choking. Sandy went to her, down on her knees on the rug. She murmured something that Robin couldn't hear over the ragged sounds now coming from Emma. Roger alone stood, a man on the deck of a ship before the last of it slipped beneath the water.

Between giant gulps at the air, Amy tried to speak.

'Take your time, love,' said Sandy. 'Just take your time.'

It was a minute or more before she could get the words out, but when she did, they sent a shiver down Robin's arms. 'It was only supposed to be a little fire – like they did to us. A little fire. There were no cars – I thought the house was empty.'

Chapter Thirty-Eight

From his position at the window, Kilmartin looked between Robin and Samir, letting his gaze rest on one of them, then the other. The silence stretched, interrupted only by the distant ringing of Rona's phone outside.

'Well,' he said at last. 'You got a result, DCI Lyons.'

Braced for a first-class bollocking about an elementary cock-up, Robin was thrown. Then thrown again: a 'result'? Was it? She hadn't once thought of it like that – it felt the very opposite. The scene at the Renshaws' yesterday afternoon had been one of the most distressing of her career, its shadow over her and the team so dark that even now, with a night's distance, they were chilled by it. The mood in the incident room this morning was muted in the extreme.

'It's not a result I wanted, sir,' she said.

Samir shook his head. 'It's a disaster for Amy and her family.'

'Well, yes, from that point of view, but at least we've been able to go back to *Anne's* family with some closure.'

Robin and Samir looked at one another.

'That *is* your job here,' Kilmartin said, impatient. 'To find out who committed the crime and ideally – which you've done – secure a confession.'

'Yes, sir.'

'I just wanted them to know what it felt like,' Amy had sobbed last night. 'To be scared, just once, to know that everything could be taken away. I thought they'd killed him. I loved my brother, I *loved* him. I thought they'd killed him.'

With that, Robin had felt the poisonous seeping ink of this case touch her, too. If she'd been able to rule out the Heywood family more quickly, Amy would never have done it – Robin had had a chance to stop the poison spreading and she'd failed.

But never mind because the Heywoods had got what they wanted.

Yes, what a result.

'And the press,' Kilmartin was saying, 'at least online – it's too early for hard copies yet, that'll be tomorrow. I presume you've seen?'

Fatal Birmingham Blaze Arrest: Sister, 15. The piece on the *Record*'s site had been short, still 'developing', but a spokesman for West Midlands Police had confirmed that Amy Renshaw, sister of Ben Renshaw, found dead last week, was in custody. Over the next few hours, the story would grow and grow, spread until it was everywhere.

'Yes, sir.'

'You know, Lyons,' said Kilmartin. 'There have been times when I've dreamed of hearing you just saying "Yes" for once, but now it's actually happening, it's falling flat.'

'Sorry about that.'

Samir flashed her a warning.

'What I'm *trying* to say,' Kilmartin finished, exasperated, 'is well done. Good work.'

In their own usual post-game spot at the window, they watched the entrance below to make sure Kilmartin was out of the building. As he minced across the tarmac to his car, Samir said, 'You know, it *is* a result, however much we hate it. Whether or not she meant the whole house to go up, whether or not she thought it was empty, she went there in the dead of night with a towel and petrol and matches and set fire to it. It was premeditated arson.'

'I know. I do know.'

'I can see what you're thinking, but you *haven't* done what *they* wanted, Rob, and hung the Renshaws out to dry. You just solved that part first.'

She looked at him. 'Thank you.'

'And the best way to make it feel better—'

'Yeah. I know.'

As she turned to go, Samir put out a hand to stop her. 'One thing I don't understand – Phil said there were no prints in the frost at the Renshaws' on Wednesday, didn't he? How's that possible, given that Amy left after the dew fell?'

'Because she went out through the back gate,' Robin said wearily. 'Across the lawn. He didn't think to check the bloody back garden.'

With the obvious exception of Phil – who spent the day with his eyes glued either to his screen or, when compelled to leave the safety of his desk, to the carpet – it was a day, like Saturday, when Robin felt deep gratitude for her team. Without prompting, they seemed to have taken a decision to kick things up yet another level. The focus in the room was visible – even the CCTV crew appeared animated. Looking out into the main room just before six, Robin pictured the case as a gigantic land-fill with her team a crew of hungry scavengers picking it over for anything of value, selecting items, scrutinising them, then tossing them over their shoulder: no, no, no.

After a terse exchange with the headmaster, Malia had addressed a special assembly at Summerfield in the early afternoon, asking anyone, student or faculty, with any knowledge or concern about impropriety at the school to contact them on either the dedicated number or email they'd set up. Varan was contacting pupils who'd left at unorthodox points, scouring social media and StrengthInNumbers.com. Malia had tasked Jo with researching Eddie Gillespie, Morgan and Myrmidon.

What were they missing? Robin asked herself. Where else should they look? She was concentrating so hard, she jumped when her phone rang, a mobile number she didn't recognise. Jeremy Handley's latest gambit? Well, she couldn't take the risk that it wasn't. She steeled herself and answered.

'Robin?' said a panicked voice. 'It's Carolyn Gillespie.'

'Carolyn, hello.'

'I'm so sorry to call,' she said. 'It might be nothing – I really hope it's nothing – but Theo hasn't come home.'

Chapter Thirty-Nine

'I've always been an anxious person, but after the car incident, it reached a level I couldn't manage on my own any more. I take medication and I see a counsellor, and normally that helps but . . .' Carolyn pressed a hand against her chest. 'My heart's just all over the place, I—'

Her husband interrupted. 'I don't think it's a *psychiatric condition* if you're worried when your son's been incommunicado for hours when he was nearly killed before and his best friend actually *was* killed last week.'

'Eddie, *please*. Don't. I'm just trying to say maybe I'm over-reacting. Maybe after the news about Amy he needs some time alone or—'

'Then why not just tell you? He knows you'll be frantic. All he has to do is send a text. It's so thoughtless – completely bloody selfish.'

'Don't! In case . . .'

In case, when it came, the news was bad and he'd have to live the rest of his life knowing that while his child was in mortal danger or dead, he'd been criticising him.

Denial, thought Robin, in two different guises. Theo's mother's was simple, his father's cloaked with anger that masked a howling sense of powerlessness.

Eddie was still wearing work clothes, suit trousers and a shirt. On her way in, Robin had seen the jacket and a striped tie on the newel post at the bottom of the stairs. He was fifty-one, she knew now, younger than she'd thought on Sunday, but tonight he looked every bit of sixty. He'd run his hands through his remaining hair so many times, it literally stood on end.

'It's impossible not to panic,' she said, 'I know, but if there's anything you can try . . . As you say, he's dealing with a monumental amount.'

But they knew as well as she did that none of this was good, and even information that might have been reassuring – that they'd launched a search, that all neighbourhood policing teams had been briefed – struck them only as evidence that he was in terrible jeopardy.

Earlier, judging that haring over at the drop of a hat might alarm them, she'd sent Varan and Malia instead. At eight thirty, however, Kilmartin, who'd just heard, had called with orders that she was to get over here herself, quick-sharp.

'Optics, optics, optics.' Samir's eyebrows had flicked.

Under normal circumstances, Carolyn said, Theo being late home wasn't extraordinary; as they'd heard from Ben's parents before, their group of friends often hung out after school or, as most of them lived close by, later on. 'But ever since the accident, he texts me. Always. I try not to drive him mad with my nervousness, he's got enough to deal with, but at five, I couldn't wait any more, so I texted him: no response. At half five, I rang him and that's when I started getting *really* worried. Normally if he can't answer the phone or he's already talking to someone, I get his voicemail, *Hello, this is Theo Gillespie, leave me a message*, but it just went straight to a recording saying number unavailable.'

She'd rung Molly, then Eddie, then a friend nearby whose son was two years below at Summerfield and took the same bus home. Theo hadn't been on it.

So she'd started ringing the friends whose numbers she had from when they used to come and visit him in hospital. One by one, they'd told her the same thing: they'd last seen him outside school. 'All of them,' she said, 'Pierre, Mo, John, Lily. He said goodbye and that was it.'

When Robin heard about the 'number unavailable' message, her heart had dropped. It was what you got if the SIM card had been taken out. It was what *Ben's* mother had heard when she'd called his phone last Monday.

And time was racing: every time she looked, another quarter-hour was gone. It was already nine forty-five.

'I know Varan and Malia asked you all of this earlier,' Robin said now, 'but tell me again how Theo was when he left for school this morning.'

'Devastated – beyond – because he'd just heard the news about Amy.' Carolyn's bottom lip disappeared between her teeth.

'Do you think he had any clue before today that Amy was responsible?'

'What?' they said together. 'No!'

'Of course not.' Carolyn's voice shook. 'He was horrified – horrified. He sat for a few seconds just staring, then he pushed his chair back with this terrible screech and stumbled to the loo. We heard him throw up and he was white when he came back out, shaking. He could barely speak.'

'But he still went to school?'

She gulped. 'I tried to make him stay off, I told him he wasn't in a fit state, but he insisted. "I'm just clinging on to what's left of normality, Mum." That's what he said. "Clinging on."'

'This is a nightmare,' Eddie Gillespie said. 'Alistair Heywood trapped us all in a nightmare and it's never going to end. Never.'

Malia and Varan had done a preliminary search of Theo's room, but Robin asked to see it, too. She followed Carolyn's neat figure up the stairs, then along a wide carpeted landing to a door at the end. It was ajar, but Carolyn stopped outside for a second, as if she'd been about to knock before sticking her head round.

The room was square and generously sized. A big window overlooking the back garden was set between sloping gables so that sitting at the long wooden table with its piles of books and papers you'd feel tucked in and focused. As a teenager, Robin would have killed for a work spot like it; she'd done her homework on a tiny desk that she'd shared with Luke. Crammed between the door and the wardrobe, there hadn't been space to keep two textbooks open at the same time.

Against one wall was a single bed covered with a pale grey seersucker duvet cover, cushions at either end making it an ersatz sofa by day. Above hung a large black-and-white poster of sixties Bob Dylan, all beetling brows and dangling cigarette.

Two large speakers squatted in the corners, and on top of a wooden chest in front of the fireplace was a record player with a box of LPs.

'He's into music?' Robin asked.

'Loves it.'

She moved to look at the bookshelves. The sixties were here as well – a cluster on the second shelf included Kerouac, Salinger, *Catch 22* and *A Clockwork Orange*, although there was all sorts of stuff, old and new, a history of growing up in books. Faded *Hardy Boys* and Willard Prices shared the shelf nearest the floor with all seven Harry Potters and *The Ghost of Thomas Kempe*. Tolkien, a collection of Arthurian legends, *Maus*, Dickens,

Brighton Rock. Robin took down a copy of *Cyrano de Bergerac* in French and a bookplate with the Summerfield crest told her he'd won it as a prize last year. She slid it back into place.

His mother moved towards the bed, where, from among the cushions, she lifted a battered stuffed creature – a dragon, maybe, or a dinosaur; green or once-green, anyway. She held it tightly against her chest.

'Carolyn, Theo was here the night Ben was killed, wasn't he?' Robin asked.

'Yes. Up here, in fact – he came up after supper to finish some work.'

'Alone? Molly didn't come round? Or any of their other friends?'

She shook her head.

'You and your husband were in?'

'Yes, downstairs. We were watching a film.'

'Anything good?'

'*Sabrina.* It's one of my favourites, and, of course, Eddie loves Audrey Hepburn.'

A folding wooden frame on the bedside table held two photographs. Robin picked it up. The picture on the left was a recent shot of the family at a formal occasion in summer light: Theo and his dad in suits, Carolyn in an umber silk dress with a matching hat. Theo was in the middle, his arms round his parents' shoulders.

'His cousin's wedding,' Carolyn said. 'The first day he walked without a stick again.'

The second picture showed Theo and Molly. They leaned together, grinning. Both were in T-shirts, Theo's plain grey, hers printed with a slogan. Robin peered, trying to make it out.

'*What would Margaret Atwood do?*' Carolyn supplied. 'She wears it a lot.'

'Do you like her – Molly?' She put the frame carefully back down.

'*Love* her – both Eddie and I do. Robin, tell me honestly – do you think he's in danger?'

The abrupt change of direction took her by surprise. 'Honestly? Perhaps. But we can't afford to speculate, Carolyn. Without any—'

'He could have gone into hiding, couldn't he? Maybe he's terrified the Heywoods are going to come after him again now – after Amy? He went to school so he'd be surrounded by people, safe, and now he's hiding?'

Please, said her eyes, *just tell me my son is all right*.

Robin wished she could.

'It's possible,' she said, 'When you looked earlier, did you notice any of his things were missing – clothes, medication, anything significant to him?'

Carolyn gave the smallest possible shake of the head, as if anything bigger would somehow make it more true.

Malia had taken his toothbrush for the DNA sample and though she'd reassured her multiple times it was standard misper procedure, Carolyn had been very upset.

'And his passport's still here?' Robin asked.

'Hm.'

'He's got a laptop?' She pointed to a trailing white cable. 'Apple?'

'MacBook Air. He'll have it with him – he takes it to school.'

'Is his phone an Apple, too?'

'No, Samsung Galaxy. It's new, we've just got upgrades.'

'What's his case like?'

'Pale green with line drawings of flying saucers – alien space-ships. His wallet's not here but he always takes it to school for anything he needs at lunch or afterwards.'

'Do you know how much money he had on him, or what he has access to?'

'Some, not a lot. I don't know what he's got in cash, but there's only about two hundred pounds in his account – I saw his statement the other day. He spends too much – books, music, trainers – we're always having a go at him.' Her expression now said she'd sell the house to buy him the music he wanted if only he'd come back. Eyes filling with tears, Carolyn sat on the edge of the bed and put her face in her hands.

Surprising both of them, Robin sat down next to her and put her hand on her back. Through the soft wool of her sweater, the sobbing woman's vertebrae moved like stones under her fingers.

Robin's phone rang as they were coming back downstairs. Eyes huge, Carolyn spun around before she'd even had a chance to get it out of her pocket.

On the screen was another mobile number she didn't know. 'Robin Lyons.'

'DCI Lyons,' said the smooth voice, 'Jeremy Handley at the *Record*. Sorry to call so late, but I wanted to confirm something. Theo Gillespie's missing now, too – is that right?'

'Hold on a moment, please,' she said. She muted him, then told Carolyn she needed to step outside.

Terror flooded the woman's face. 'Is it Theo?'

'No,' she said. 'No. Don't worry.'

For the first time, the battery of locks and chains weren't on and Robin let herself out of the house and pulled the door closed behind her. Across the road, in a space equidistant between street lights for maximum gloom, she saw a man sitting at the wheel of his car. The surveillance detail – God.

Unmuting, she put the phone back to her ear. 'Mr Handley, I have a question for *you*: where are you getting your information?'

A small huff, amused. 'In this case, Twitter. His friends are very worried, as I imagine you are. Would you like to comment for the piece?'

'The press office will tell you everything we're releasing at this time.'

'Yes, got all that. But, Chief Inspector, while I've actually got *you*, to confirm, your daughter Elena, known as Lennie, age fifteen, same as Amy Renshaw, was at the Rose Road Riot, is that right?'

Robin felt heat rush to her face. 'Yes,' she said, amazed at how calm her voice sounded. 'It is. As was reported at the time. Goodnight, Mr Handley.'

After she'd cut him off, she made an exaggerated display of dialling another number and held the phone to her ear while she tried to calm down enough to go back inside. Lennie's presence at the riot was no secret, it *had* been reported that she was the one who'd stayed with the fallen officer. But that wasn't the point. Handley wasn't fact-checking: he was letting her know which way *his* investigation was going.

It was ten twenty by the time Robin left the Gillespies, and as she crossed the road to her car, she went to her recent calls and scrolled down. *M&D.*

'How are you doing, love?'

Her mother's voice caused Robin a pang of longing for her world of order. She got into the car and pulled the door closed after her. 'All right,' she said. 'Long day, but I should be there in fifteen minutes.'

'About that,' her mother's tone turned apologetic. 'I was just about to ring you.'

Translation: *Because Lennie doesn't want to.* Robin swallowed a sigh.

'We were wondering if she should stay over here tonight? With Theo missing now – in case you get called away.' Her mother lowered her voice to the point of near-inaudibility. 'She's feeling vulnerable, Robin.'

Oh really? she bit back an impulse to say. *Why would you think that? And why do you think* I *wouldn't know – my own child?*

But her mother wasn't trying to make a point, she recognised, just stating a fact.

'Yes,' she said, 'I know. And thank you, Mum.'

'Look, why doesn't she stay tomorrow, too? Unless he turns up – and let's pray he does – you're not going to be home 'til the dead of night then, either, are you? She can come straight over after school – we'll invite Austin and Asha for dinner as well if they fancy it.'

'That sounds lovely,' Robin said and she meant it. 'Mum, before you go – have you heard anything from Luke?'

Her mother's voice dropped to a whisper. 'No, love. I haven't.'

Chapter Forty

Robin woke with her alarm at six and by that fact knew at once that Theo hadn't come home: she'd asked the duty team to call her, whatever time it was. She'd gone to bed still clutching a thin strand of hope that the surveillance car would see him staggering up the pavement in the small hours drunk out of his mind.

Since nine last night they'd been hammering their social media accounts with witness appeals, but for all the tweeting and sharing and an appeal on the *Post*'s website, so far it was slim pickings. By the time she called the team together, only two members of the public had rung in with plausible sightings and both had been within the quarter-hour after Theo left school yesterday afternoon. A woman taking her toddler for a walk two streets away from Summerfield said he'd passed them 'walking quickly and looking preoccupied'. The second was a driver who'd been waiting for the lights on Hagley Road when he'd crossed in front of him.

'He's distinctive-looking,' he'd told Jo. 'Bit like Ed Sheeran with all that hair and the glasses.' He'd said more or less the same: Theo had been alone and looked 'serious'.

With Theo's disappearance, the story – which was literally how some people seemed to regard it – had reached a tipping point. Online threads of fifteen and twenty posts speculated about what had happened and what was going to happen next, comments on the threads numbering hundreds.

The traditional media was all in now, too. Malia had arrived at seven with a copy of the *Mail* and opened it to a double-page spread. They'd tracked down a picture of Amy looking young and vulnerable and printed it with photographs of Ben and the Heywoods' house at the peak of the blaze: *StrengthInNumbers: Devastation.* Reporters were camped outside both the Renshaw and Gillespie houses, and as people gathered at the board, Robin heard Admin Emily complaining of RSI from transferring too many calls to the press office.

Any hope that her own newsworthiness might fade was truly dead now.

'OK,' she said when everyone was settled. 'New territory this morning and I know none of you needs telling how critical it is we get things right. Until we know otherwise, Theo is alive and our job is to find him. Attention to detail, everything followed up, not a single corner cut. If you've got more work than you can handle, tell Malia because Sod's law guarantees that the one thing we don't do will be the key.'

She'd let Samir know she was about to brief the team and he came quietly in now and leaned against a desk at the back.

'So, our working hypothesis: *Ben* discovered something, either at Summerfield or elsewhere, and was killed for it. And now, given Theo's disappearance, it looks likely that he knew, too, or found out, and was too afraid to tell us. Why? Either because he himself had something to hide *or* he didn't trust us to keep him safe.'

'Because we couldn't protect them last year?' asked Hanratty.

'Either that or – and I do think we have to consider the possibility now – because he suspected that whoever killed Ben had connections inside the force.'

She watched an uneasy ripple move through them. Easy at the beginning, she thought, to cast aspersions on Hailey and his team for their lack of success, but a different matter when suspicion fell on your own.

'Clearly, we very much hope that isn't the case, but if any of you know or hear anything along those lines, please come straight to me or Superintendent Jafferi. Anything we hear will be treated in complete confidence.'

She looked around, seeing solemn faces.

'Right, so, what have we got to go on? Varan, are Theo's phone records in yet?'

'Just now, guv.'

'Good.' That had been her first job this morning, done before she was even out of bed. Accessing a missing person's phone records needed a superintendent's authority, but in a high-risk case, phone companies could send them over very quickly once it was given. She'd texted Samir at 6.03 a.m. and he'd responded immediately.

'I'll start going through them as soon as we're finished here,' Varan said, 'but straight off: the phone was on Norfolk Road when it pinged for the last time.'

'Where is that?'

'Directly off Hagley Road, about three minutes' walk from the crossing where the driver saw him. The ping was about five minutes after he said goodbye to his friends.'

'What's the street like?'

'I've just had a look on Google Maps. Wide, residential, plenty of trees. Detached houses, pretty big. But not a thoroughfare – it's quiet.'

Damn. On a residential street during working hours, it would be much easier for something to happen unwitnessed. Something like opening the door of a Transit van and pulling someone in off the pavement, for example.

'Right. So, top priority, CCTV collection and house-to-house there.' She glanced at Malia, who nodded, *On it.* 'Let's find out if that was a normal direction for him. His bus stop isn't that way, we know, but did he regularly cut through there en route somewhere else? Or, if he's hiding, as we all hope, was it a quiet spot to put a hat on, change his jacket – get in a cab, even?'

'In that case,' said Tark, 'do we think he took out the SIM himself?'

'We'd have to assume, to avoid anyone tracking him. And then, of course, the question is, who? Whether he's been abducted or chosen to disappear, who's behind all this?'

Silence again.

Day ten, thought Robin, *ten*, and they were still no closer to answering that question. 'How much tape's left to go through from Moseley Bog last Sunday, Tark?'

'Not a lot. Six or seven?'

'Right. Malia, could we do a final round of house-to-house and collection round there, just in case? I know, ten days later, but if there's anyone who was marked as away or didn't answer the door last week, let's go back to them.'

'Guv,' said Varan, 'just now, while I was waiting for Theo's records, I went back to Ben's.' He reached behind him and retrieved a carefully marked-up printout from his desk. 'It's not massive, you wouldn't see it unless you were specifically looking because they were in contact so much anyway, but there's a slight uptick in calls between the two of them after their last event, in Worcester.'

'OK,' Robin encouraged.

'The fact that it's *calls*, not texts, so no record anywhere of what was actually said? And some of them are longer. Normally if they are calling, it's two or three minutes, but there's a seven-minute one, then an eleven. Teenage boys – however empathetic – chatting on the phone?'

Robin nodded. 'Let's get over to the Worcester school *tout de suite* then, see if anyone knows anything there. Good, Varan. And on a school note, what about Summerfield – anything on the dedicated line?'

'No. Not yet.'

'Malia, we need to talk to Molly again ASAP. Maybe something will shake loose now. Will you do that? Ask her to come here, in case that helps as well. One thing that still bothers me, especially if something's happened to Theo: why, when she's such a key player in all this, isn't *she* being targeted, too? It was the same thing last time.'

Malia nodded. 'Yes.'

'Jo, how are you getting on with Eddie and Alun Morgan, and the Clarendon School?'

'Well, interesting. I've contacted some of their classmates – those I can track down – and I've just had a bloke call me back who said he didn't remember them being friends at all.'

'Didn't remember they were friends or remembered that they *weren't*?'

'That they weren't. Apparently they moved in totally different circles. Eddie was Mr Popular, and Morgan really wasn't. This guy described him as being "infra dig", if anyone here born after 1975 even knows what that means. When I asked him, he said he was ashamed of the meanness now, but though Morgan was very clever, he was "one of the Untouchables".'

'*Untouchables?*'

'Total losers.'

Funny, Robin thought. Based on the picture and what she'd seen and read about Morgan, she wouldn't have guessed that. 'Did he say why?'

'He didn't really know. He finally came up with him being "one of those people with slightly greasy hair who don't look comfortable in their own skin"' – she glanced at her notebook – '"and when you're a teenager and you've got your own issues in that direction, you don't want any part of it".'

'Hm.'

'The other thing is, guv, in their final year, a boy in their class died. He was an overseas student from Milan, boarding. Stefano Fiore.'

'What happened?'

'The verdict was misadventure. He'd been drinking and drowned in the Avon.'

'Any suggestion of foul play?'

'Not in the records. Do you want me to keep going?'

Robin heard the real question: with the new urgency of Theo missing, weren't there bigger, less tangential fish to fry now?

'I think so,' she said. 'Yes. Keep going. See if you can find anyone else who was there.'

Chapter Forty-One

Five or six journalists scuffed about on the pavement outside the Gillespies' house, their breath making clouds. Robin scanned them quickly, but to her enormous relief, none of them looked like Jeremy Handley, or at least the version of him she'd seen posing with his Mazda on Facebook. One had a cigarette and the smell caused her a fleeting nostalgia. 'Excuse me,' she said, barging past to reach the gate.

A man in a black puffer jacket had clearly done his homework and recognised her. 'Detective Chief Inspector – any news? Is he dead?'

Another stuck an iPhone in her face and took a picture.

'For God's sake, have a heart.' She rang the bell, then ignored them, making sure her body blocked their cameras when the door opened on Carolyn Gillespie, her expression fifty per cent hope, fifty per cent abject terror.

Robin ushered her backwards and quickly closed the door.

'There's no news,' she told her straight away and watched her sag with relief and disappointment. She was wearing the same outfit she'd had on last night, so if she'd slept at all, it had probably been in a chair. 'How are you?' she asked, following her into the kitchen.

'I feel sick,' Carolyn said. 'Just sick.'

'Are you here on your own?'

'Eddie's out in the car, driving around looking. He couldn't stand it, just sitting doing nothing. I'm here in case Theo comes home or phones the landline.'

Robin thought of Bill Heywood, his grief buttoned away inside a suit while he marshalled his considerable resources, human and otherwise, to try to assert some control. 'I think it's harder to be the one at home,' she said.

'Yes. The silence.'

A cluster of dirty mugs and side plates had accumulated next to the sink, nothing compared to the chaos that ruled in *her* house at the moment, but striking by the standards of this one, where Carolyn seemed to operate at a similar perfection-level to her mother.

'My daughter was kidnapped,' Robin said before knowing she was going to. 'It was nearly three years ago now. By someone I was investigating.'

Carolyn turned sharply, eyes wider. 'Did you get her back?'

'Yes.' As she said it, she was aware of how unassailable that privilege must appear. 'But the hours she was gone were the worst of my life.' If she didn't get Lennie back, she'd wondered in that time whether it would even be worth going on living.

'I thought I'd *done* the worst hours of my life when Theo was hit by that car. Waiting while he was in surgery, not knowing if he'd ever walk again. If they'd have to amputate.'

'I'm so sorry this has happened. All of it.'

'Thank you.' Carolyn broke eye contact and turned away again. 'I keep calling his phone,' she said as if to the garden, 'but it's the same message: number unavailable, number unavailable.'

'Come and have a seat.'

When she was tucked into the wicker chair that Theo had chosen last week, the sheepskin rug giving it the appearance of a sort of fur-lined eggshell, Robin took the one next to her.

'Carolyn,' she said, 'we're looking at the possibility that Ben and Theo knew something that someone strongly wants to keep quiet, and we're wondering about their last event, at the school in Worcester. Ben's records show they started talking more on the phone directly afterwards. Did Theo tell you about anything that happened there? A case that came up, maybe.'

She thought, hands gripping her thighs just above the knees. 'He couldn't. Everything to do with StrengthInNumbers has to be confidential.'

'I understand. Did you suspect something had happened, then – get a sense of anything?'

'No.'

'Did they engage with people who approached them at events, typically? In person?'

'They tried not to. They were seventeen, eighteen – they weren't equipped, even if they did know far more than anyone should have to at that age. They said they couldn't get involved personally, but they were very kind about it, obviously – they'd seen what rape and sexual assault could do. If anyone came up to them, they put them in touch with people who were qualified to help.'

'Do you know whom?'

'There's a couple of national organisations they link to on the site and a couple of local ones as well. I can give you their details, but I'm not sure they'd be able to share information.'

'Thank you, we'll talk to them.' Robin made a note in her book and scanned the top of the page where she'd written questions before getting in the car. 'Carolyn,' she said, 'when did you and Eddie meet – what age were you?'

The woman looked at her, curious at the change of tack and the personal question. 'When I was twenty-five and he was twenty-eight. It was at a friend's party. Why?'

'We're just doing a bit of lateral thinking,' she said, avoiding eye contact. 'So, about ten years after Eddie left school?'

'Yes, it must have been.'

'I know he and Alun had dropped out of touch until recently, but I wondered, has Eddie ever mentioned the name Stefano Fiore?'

Carolyn frowned but at least appeared to be trying to think. 'No, I've never heard of him. Why? Who is he?'

'He was in Eddie and Alun's class at Clarendon; he died the year they finished.'

'Oh.' The frown deepened. 'How?'

'He drowned. He'd been drinking and he either fell into the Avon or went swimming and got caught up in reeds underwater.'

'Hideous – the poor boy.' She shuddered. 'But why are you asking?'

A cover story wouldn't make much sense, but nor would the truth, so Robin flannelled. 'At this stage of the inquiry – for Ben, it's day ten now – we're looking at anything and everything, no stone left unturned.'

Carolyn looked unconvinced, but it was the best Robin could do.

She pressed on. 'Does Eddie enjoy his job with Alun?'

'Honestly – don't let on to anyone I said this because I'm incredibly grateful to him – but I don't think always, no. Ed had a lot of autonomy in his cousin's business, he was CFO, but he's junior in the department at Myrmidon and he does a lot of the grunt work. I keep telling him it'll get better once he's proved himself again, he'll move up once there's an opening and what happened before begins to fade.'

'Is he decently paid?'

'*Decently*, but that's about it. Alun *is* a businessman, and he knows Eddie's stock is down at the moment. We have to be very careful, and I still take on a lot more work than I used to.'

'You mentioned on Monday that Eddie thinks Alun flirts with you. I'm sorry to have to ask, but you *aren't* having an affair? He's an attractive man and you've had such a hard time – I can see how some flattering attention—'

'Stop,' Carolyn's voice had surprising force. Her fingers gripped her thighs tighter. 'Just stop. Alun and my friendship has nothing to do with this – nothing at all. Please, I'm begging you – stop asking these irrelevant questions and just find my son.'

Robin had hoped that the social media would have garnered multiple new witnesses, but when she called from the car, Malia told her that, so far, they'd had just one more, another driver who'd seen Theo coming round the corner onto Hagley Road. 'So, between the other two – after the woman with the baby, before the first man, who saw him on the crossing. Molly's on her way in, though – she should be here any minute.'

By the time Robin arrived back at the station, she was there and ensconced with Malia in the 'soft' interview room with the sofas and terrible watercolours. At her desk, Robin turned on the monitor to listen while she answered some of the two screens' worth of emails that had arrived since she'd left an hour and a half earlier.

Even remotely, it was apparent Molly hadn't slept much, either. She'd come from home, she wasn't in any fit state for school today, she'd said, and that was certainly borne out by her demeanour. Sitting forward on the sofa's edge, feet on the floor, the shredded knees of her black jeans almost touching the coffee table, she held her eyes on Malia with such focus that the phrase 'as if her life depended on it' came to mind.

'Molly, were you aware of any tension between Ben and Theo?'

Robin watched her frown, vertical lines appearing between her eyebrows. She was thinking as hard as she could, special-subject round on *Mastermind*, clock ticking. No Margaret Atwood T-shirt today, just plain white, and none of the bangles Robin remembered from the StrengthInNumbers mission video, either. Subsistence dressing.

'In the past month or six weeks, for example.'

More thinking. 'About six weeks ago,' she said suddenly, 'yes, there was some tension then. That was when Ben was still annoyed about having to cut back.'

'But they'd sorted things out by the time of the Worcester event?'

An earnest nod. 'Yes.'

'Molly, from their phone records, we know they talked more directly after that event. Do you have any idea why?'

This time the answer was a head-shake. 'No.'

'Did you have a sense something might have happened in Worcester?'

Molly thought again. Robin was impressed by her self-possession, her refusal to rush. Finally, she let out a controlled breath. 'No. The only thing I can think of at all,' she said, 'was the weekend before Ben was killed.' She swallowed. 'We were over at Theo's house. I wasn't in the room, I was just coming back from the bathroom, but I heard them talking really quietly.'

'About what?'

'I don't know. I could hardly hear the words, it was so quiet.'

'Did you catch anything at all?'

'Only something about "talking the talk" and then they heard me.'

'Did you ask them about it?'

'No.'

'Really? Your boyfriend and his best friend, whispering while you were out of the room? When I was your age, I would have wrestled it out of them – I wouldn't have been able to stand

277

the mystery. Or the paranoia that they'd been talking about me.' Malia made a face, self-deprecation trying to build fellow feeling, trust.

But Molly looked at her almost wistfully. 'There are things I don't *want* to hear now. Can't hear. I don't read any posts on the site – it's too triggering. If there was something like that, distressing, they didn't tell me, to protect me.'

'Do you think that's what it could have been?'

'I don't know. If it was, I didn't *want* to know.'

'Do you think Ben could have been irritated with you both still "talking the talk" but not walking the walk so much any more?'

'Maybe. I don't know.'

'What was the atmosphere like when you came back into the room?'

'It felt a bit . . . tight. Like, *Oh hey, Moll*, which made me think it *was* something distressing, actually.'

'Were you and Theo open with one another?'

'Yes.' No thinking time.

'So if it was important and he didn't think you'd find it painful, he'd have told you?'

'Yes.'

'How had things been between the two of you recently?'

'Good,' she said automatically. 'Good. We haven't seen as much of each other as we usually do, but that's because of the Oxford exams. He'd been working really hard for them – he really wants to go.'

'You're sure that's why?'

'Yes.' Again, emphatic.

'Molly,' said Malia gently, 'this is very hard, I know, but we have to consider the idea that Theo wasn't being completely frank when we've talked to him since Ben died. I'm not suggesting he's done anything wrong, but we think it's possible he knew something he didn't feel able to tell us. We know how close the two of you are – would you have known if he was hiding something?'

She bent her head and looked at her hands in her lap. 'I would have said yes.' There was a shake in her voice. 'Until last night.'

Chapter Forty-Two

The incident room was operating on what felt like a collective adrenaline rush. People seemed to talk faster, type faster, move around more quickly than usual. Robin was too jittery to sit down for long. She knew that if anyone heard anything significant-seeming, they'd bring it to her immediately, and yet she couldn't stop herself pacing the room asking. Even though working at her computer and on the phone *was* work, it felt ineffectual, far too little. She wanted to be moving, keeping pace with her mind and its questions. Where was he? What was he doing now, if anything? Could they still find Theo alive or were they already too late?

The phone line they'd set up for Summerfield had stayed quiet and no further eyewitnesses had come forward or been located. Robin had sent a FLO to the Gillespies and she was in touch with Carolyn every hour, though with the same awareness that if there was any news at all, *she'd* contact *her* straight away. Though Amy was in custody now, Sandy had stayed on with Roger and Emma Renshaw but there was nothing new to report there, either. Nothing, nothing, nothing. With every hour that passed, Theo seemed further and more away, the likelihood of finding him alive more and more remote. And as the afternoon ebbed away, the energy ebbed with it.

She'd asked Varan to call when he left Hillier, the Worcester school, and at quarter past five, her phone rang.

'I don't know, guv,' he told her, tone a mix of frustration and apology, as if it were somehow his fault. 'Honestly, I liked the place more than Summerfield, definitely the atmosphere there. It feels a lot warmer, and open. The Head's a woman, Margaret Leonard, and I thought she was totally straight. She seemed genuinely upset by what's happened. She went to their presentation and thought they were great, she said, "really accomplished and fluent speakers". She got all the year groups they'd spoken to together in the gymnasium and while I was talking to them, they printed flyers with our hotline numbers and my mobile to give to them on the way out.'

'So nothing at all?'.

'Not yet, unless you've heard anything on the numbers. Ironically,' he said, 'the only person who had anything even remotely negative to say was the bloke who'd arranged the visit – Paul Whittaker, the social studies teacher. He's in charge of this kind of thing, talks and special events on social responsibility and equity. "Good citizenship, basically, or being a decent human being," in his words.'

'What did *he* say?'

'Not much. Just that they were very sincere – he managed to make it sound slightly negative – and he thought Ben liked the attention.'

'Justice campaigner as rock star?' said Robin, remembering him as Summerfield's Harry Styles.

'Pretty much. It sounded like a few of the girls were quite smitten.'

'What about Theo?'

'"Lower-key."'

'Which ties in with what we've heard from other people.'

She thought back to Jo's interview with Kaia.

'*What was he like, Ben?*'

'*Great – so full of energy. When the others got disheartened, he was the one who got them fired up again. Before Ben was the energy, Theo was the methodical, wise one.*'

Had Ben got them caught up in something Theo didn't like, or tried to handle something in a way Theo didn't think was right? But what the hell could it be, if even after Ben's murder, Theo felt he couldn't say?

'Has Hillier had any trouble with sexual harassment or assaults?'

'I had a look online before I went, to see if there was anything to that effect, but I didn't find anything and no one I spoke to there said so.'

'You think they would have?'

'Today, with Theo missing? Yes, I do.'

Robin pulled up a chair next to Jo. 'How are *you* getting on?'

'Well, I've spoken to four more of Eddie and Alun's class-mates, but they all said the same thing: they didn't remember them ever interacting. Alun would have been completely beneath Eddie's notice at the time, one of them said. All of them said Eddie was super-popular, and two of them didn't remember Alun at all until I emailed them a picture from 2003 when he started Myrmidon, which was the youngest one of him I could find online. Then they said more or less the same as the guy who called him an Untouchable.'

'What about Stefano Fiore? Any more on him?'

'Well, it's tricky because it was 1985, so it's not like now, obviously, with everything online, but I called an archivist at Warwickshire Libraries and she managed to find a bit about it from the *Stratford Herald*.' She rustled about in a small pile of papers and handed Robin a printout of a short newspaper article.

Misadventure Verdict in Clarendon Student Drowning.

Robin skimmed it and read an expanded version of what Jo had told them this morning in the briefing – that Fiore had been an Italian boarder at Clarendon, sent to the school to make sure he spoke fluent English when it came time to apply to British universities and then, afterwards, when he took over his father's private-investment business back in Milan.

The inquest into his death, she read, had heard that on the fourth of May, a Saturday, Fiore, eighteen, had left the school for the day, as Sixth-Form boarders were permitted to do. He'd been seen alone during the day in Stratford and he'd bought a bottle of vodka at an off-licence in the town. The staff member who'd served him had remembered him because of his accent and because she'd asked to see his ID. She'd been the last known person to see him alive.

He'd been reported missing by the school early the following morning, the piece said, after he'd failed to return overnight, but his body hadn't been discovered until three days later by a fisherman at Bidford-on-Avon. At post-mortem, his blood-alcohol level was found to be 104 mg/dL. He must have been wasted.

Robin felt her phone buzz in her pocket and pulled it out. *Lennie.*

'Hold on,' she told Jo. 'I'll be back.'

In her office, she closed the door, then answered. 'Hi, lovely.'

'Mum?'

The word sent a jolt of fear through her. 'What's happened?'

Lennie could hardly speak, she was snatching at air as if she'd been sprinting. 'A journalist just rang me. On my mobile. He said he wanted to talk,' she made an ugly swallowing sound, 'about the protest. About what I'd done there.'

Robin felt herself go cold. *Oh no, please God, no.* 'Len, what did you say?'

'He knew I was there.'

'That's OK, that's OK, people knew that because you stayed with Shaun, remember?' Her own voice was barely more than a murmur, but Lennie's words sounded siren-loud. With a minimal movement of her head, Robin glanced through the internal window to see if any of the team were watching, but they seemed oblivious, either on their phones or focused on their screens. 'What did you say?'

'I admitted it, I said I was there,' a clutching breath, 'and I told him why. About Austin.'

Shit. So her motive for throwing the stone. 'Len, after that?'

'Just that I stayed with Shaun, nothing else. I hung up. He phoned back, but I didn't answer. Mum, I'm scared, I'm so scared. I feel like I'm going to have a heart attack. Where are you?'

Robin told Malia she had to go out briefly. 'If anything happens,' she called over her shoulder as she tried not to run, 'I'm on my phone.'

To her surprise – Robin had assumed she'd go straight to Dunnington Road and her grandparents – Lennie had gone home to Mary Street. As soon as Robin closed the door behind her, her daughter ran into her arms.

'He's just fishing, lovely,' Robin told her, feeling her skinny torso trembling. 'He's hoping there's a story, that's all, he doesn't know anything – he couldn't, there's no way.'

Lennie's hands shook so much that when she tried to drink the tea Robin made, the mug's china rim chattered against her teeth. Taking her upstairs, Robin packed her own night things and an outfit for tomorrow. Then they drove over to

Hall Green.

After telling her grandparents what had happened and a new round of reassurance, Lennie disappeared with Dennis to watch an episode of *Miranda*, and Robin and her mother slipped out to the back garden, where, despite it now being fully dark, Christine looked over the fence to make sure the Richardsons weren't down on kneelers in the shrubbery.

'You've got to speak to Luke, Robin,' she hissed. 'You've *got* to. We're five days away from the sentencing and Lennie's whole future's in the balance. You're a detective, for God's sake – if you said you needed to interview him for this case—'

'Mum, don't think I haven't thought of it – believe me, I have, every possible version – but I can't, I just *can't*. It's a career-ending offence – game over, immediately, and I can't look after Lennie if I don't have a job.'

'But if he told anyone . . .'

You wouldn't need *to look after Lennie because she'd be in a young offenders institute with a couple of psychos and the kids who were never given a chance.*

'I know.' She slid her hands into her hair and made fists until the roots hurt. The pain felt good, a distraction. 'Yes, I know.'

Chapter Forty-Three

When she was confident Lennie was safely cocooned and as calm as she could be, Robin told her she'd be back later on to spend the night with her in the bunk beds and then she headed back to work. From the car, she called Jo and asked her to meet her at the Gillespies' house.

It was half past seven when they arrived, and seeing Robin, two of the same journalists she'd seen in the morning jumped out of an old BMW where they were keeping warm. 'Chief Inspector – what's the latest? Have you found him?'

She'd asked Jo to call ahead, but nevertheless when they rang the doorbell, it elicited a muffled cry of alarm inside the bay window on their right. 'I'll go, love,' said Eddie's voice. Seconds later, on the other side of the door, they heard him clear his throat before turning the lock.

When he saw them, his face dropped and Robin realised that even though he'd known they were coming, he'd still been praying that when he opened it, he'd see his son.

Carolyn stood in the entrance to the sitting-room with a similar expression.

'I'm sorry, there's still no news,' Robin said when the door was closed. 'As Jo said on the phone, just more questions.'

The sitting room was in evening mode, lamps on and the

television, too, some sort of antiques programme on mute, a small majolica pot under consideration on a baize table. The Gillespies were going through the motions, she thought, clinging on.

'Please.' Carolyn ushered them towards a sofa upholstered in the same white and green bamboo print as the armchair in the bay.

'Our questions are really for your husband, Carolyn,' Robin told her, 'since you and I spoke this morning. Would you mind if we spoke to him alone?'

'I . . . Oh.' Carolyn looked at Eddie and then back at Robin. She was alarmed, she couldn't hide it. 'No. Of course.'

Theo's father waited until she'd retreated to the kitchen. 'What's this about?' he demanded.

'We wanted to ask you about Alun Morgan, Mr Gillespie.'

'Why?' He frowned. 'What's he got to do with this?'

'We don't know yet,' Robin said. 'Perhaps nothing. We'll find out.' There was a coolness in her voice that she hadn't intended, but now, having noticed, found herself resistant to changing it. 'You knew each other at school, correct? Clarendon. You were in the same year.'

'Yes.'

'And you were friends?'

'Yes. Yes, of course.'

'Though you fell out of touch when you left.'

'That's right.'

Robin wondered about his curtness. Was he annoyed, thinking they were wasting valuable time, or was he being defensive?

'It had to have been a huge relief when Alun contacted you after your release – you must have been worried about your employability with a record for fraud. Carolyn mentioned you even considered other lines of work?'

'Only briefly.'

287

'You still wanted to work in accountancy, then?'

'It's the profession I'm trained in.'

'You don't enjoy it, sir?' Jo asked.

A small shrug. 'It's what I've always done.'

'If you don't like it, why *not* do something else?' Robin asked. 'Especially after a break? When you were released, that could have been an opportunity, couldn't it, to try something different?'

'It's difficult to find a job in your fifties, Chief Inspector,' he said, 'even without entanglements with the law. Where would I suddenly rustle up a second career that earned anywhere near as much?'

'Money's important to you?'

'It's important to everyone. Anyone who says otherwise is delusional.'

'Well, everyone *needs* money, but there are gradations to how much value people assign to it.'

His expression told her she was woefully naïve.

'From what Carolyn said, it was important to you to keep Theo at Summerfield?'

'That was our top priority, she and I agreed. Why? Is it somehow . . . *problematic* for you, private school?'

'No,' Robin said honestly. When they'd lived in London – not that she was going to tell Eddie Gillespie – Lennie had gone to Ravenscourt Palace Girls, a private day school where the bright kids on scholarships were the only ones whose parents earned less than a couple of hundred thousand a year. One of the most painful things about leaving London had been having to take Lennie out of RPG; she'd loved it there and cried when Robin told her. It made sense that the Gillespies wouldn't want Theo to have that disruption, especially when there was already major upheaval at home. And yet, Robin thought, he was a popular boy, he would have adjusted quickly and, being academic, he could certainly have applied for the grammar school like Molly had last year.

'It was also important to *me* not to cause my wife the upset of losing her home. She's poured a lot of effort into this house, and she loves it.'

Robin nodded. Again, perfectly reasonable.

'People like us have standards, Chief Inspector.'

People like us? Bloody hell. 'Standards?' she asked coolly.

'Of living. Of how things are done. Yes, we hit rough patches sometimes, but we don't just admit defeat and . . . move to a caravan park. We soldier on. I might not love being an accountant, but it's a job that affords me and my family the standard of living that we . . .' He stopped, and Robin had the feeling he'd only just stopped himself saying 'deserve'. 'That we're used to.'

'That's why you submitted the fraudulent tax return?'

He gave her a hard look. 'My cousin's business was struggling – he was about to go under. He had a wife and three children. I had a responsibility to try to support him.'

'By breaking the law?'

'By trying to keep things going until they could get better.'

'With the Inland Revenue as the faceless, impersonal victim?'

'I didn't *say* that.' The words were almost a growl.

'No,' she conceded. 'Purely out of interest, would you feel sympathetic to someone who *did* live in a caravan park and defrauded the state? Benefit fraud, for example?'

'Oh, for crying out loud.' He shook his head, eyes pressed shut, as if her false equivalencies were beneath him, and someone like her couldn't possibly understand. She longed to tell him her dad was an accountant, too, but again, the less Eddie Gillespie knew about her, she realised, the happier she'd be.

'Did you accrue any debt, Mr Gillespie, you and your wife, while you were away?' Jo asked, pen poised above her notebook.

'Some.'

'How much, roughly?'

'Enough.'

Jo raised her eyebrows.

'Forty thousand,' Gillespie admitted, grudging.

'So I'd say you'd be grateful for a decently paying job again,' Robin said, 'and yet, when I was here on Sunday and he came to the door, I didn't get the impression you like Alun very much. I found it a little surprising, to be honest, especially when he's been so supportive of a friend in need.'

'It's not a question of *gratitude*,' he said. 'I'm good at what I do. He's getting a bargain.'

'Is that why he hired you?' She remembered Carolyn's phrase. 'Your stock is down?'

'Probably.'

'So *not* because you're friends then?'

He narrowed his eyes – *I see what you're doing, trying to trap me with your sophistry* – and said nothing.

'If you don't mind me saying so, sir, your wife *does* seem grateful to Mr Morgan.'

His hostility turned to scorn. 'Oh, *she* thinks he's wonderful. She's completely taken in by him.'

'In what way?'

'*Oh, Alun, thank you for everything, thank you.* As if we were on our knees and he came round dispensing *alms* or something.'

'Which part of that bothers you most?' Robin asked, watching him carefully. 'That he makes you feel like a charity case or that she's appreciative? I can see how someone like him might be appealing after major financial insecurity, and physically, he's attractive.'

Eddie Gillespie muttered something under his breath.

'I'm sorry, sir, I didn't catch that.'

'I said, he is *now*. It's amazing what money can do.'

'He wasn't good-looking back then, you're saying, at school?'

'No.'

'Do you have any photographs of him from those days?'

'No. Why would I?'

'Well, if you were friends . . .'

'It was the eighties, Chief Inspector,' he said, playing a card he was pleased with. 'People didn't have cameras then like they do now, pulling them out every few seconds.'

'No, you're right,' she agreed. 'Though *I* had a camera in my teens, a little one from Dixons – it took terrible pictures – and I wasn't *so* many years behind you.'

'Look, with respect,' he said, frustration boiling over, 'while we sit here reminiscing about your substandard tech of old, my son has been missing more than twenty-four hours and you've got sweet FA. Ben's been dead for ten *days* – when are you people going to get off your arses and *do* something?'

'Mr Gillespie, were you friends with Stefano Fiore?'

He startled – there was no mistaking it. 'Fiore,' he said. 'You mean at Clarendon? The Italian? Who died?'

'Yes.'

'No, I wasn't. We weren't friends. I never understood him, honestly – he was rich and good-looking, but he chose to hang around with the crew most of us called the Untouchables. And yes, I can see now the name was cruel, but teenage boys are, aren't they?'

'Some are,' said Jo. 'My little brother's a total softie.'

'Was Alun Morgan one of these "Untouchables", Mr Gillespie?' Robin asked.

He looked her in the eye and she saw it again: *I see what you're doing.* 'No,' he said. 'Awful as it sounds, I doubt I would have been friends with him if he had been. I was a spoiled little sod back then, I'm afraid to say.'

But so much better now, eh? Robin thought.

With the journalists, it was impossible to talk in the street, so she and Jo started back to the station in their cars and spoke on the phone. 'He's lying,' Robin said. 'No doubt about it. He and Morgan weren't friends at school.'

'Yes, and Morgan *was* one of these so-called Untouchables,' Jo said. 'All the other people I've spoken to have said so. So why the job offer?'

'An opportunity for Morgan to stick it to Eddie? *Look at me, Golden Boy! Remember how pathetic you thought I was? I'm the boss of you now! And I'll come round your house and flirt with your wife, too!*'

'Maybe, or the other idea – Morgan's got something shady going on business-wise and he wanted Eddie to handle it for him with his fraud expertise.'

'The problem I have with that idea,' said Robin, braking to avoid a fox darting out between parked cars, 'is that Morgan must be very astute to have built a business the size of Myrmidon, and let's face it, Eddie got caught. If you were him and you had something shady in mind, wouldn't you hire someone who *hadn't* been caught?'

Jo laughed.

'Also,' said Robin, 'has any of our digging into the business found any irregularities?'

'No,' admitted Jo. 'Not as far as I've heard. Not even the suggestion of any.'

*

Knowing she'd still be at the station, Samir called Robin there just before ten o'clock. 'What news?'

'None,' she said, frustrated. 'No credible sightings, no calls on the hotlines, no CCTV that we've seen so far. At this point, for all we know, Theo walked down Norfolk Road yesterday afternoon and disappeared in a puff of smoke.'

Chapter Forty-Four

Robin lay on her back, eyes open. In the tiny room, the strip of light under the door was enough to pick out the curling edges of the thirty-year-old glow-in-the-dark stickers on the narrow slats of wood two feet above her face. From another foot above those came the soft sound of Len breathing, asleep at last.

Jeremy Handley – how *dare* he phone Lennie? She felt the outrage flare again. Fuck him and his naked ambition, trampling children underfoot in his scramble for self-advancement.

She pushed the sheet down again and willed the whisper of breeze from the window to find a bit of exposed skin. Her parents kept their house so hot, she didn't understand how they weren't completely desiccated. Between the size of the room, the bunk beds and the temperature, it was like trying to get to sleep inside her mother's hostess trolley.

She was slipping backwards again. She'd thought she was done with the bunk beds – she'd thought that twice now – and yet here she was, again. As a child, she'd slept here for fifteen years, with Luke snoring and moaning and farting overhead, and she still wasn't out from under. Far from it: now the fate of her child was in his hands while he doubtless lay snoring and farting on a different set of bunk beds a few miles away across town.

How had it happened? How had they started in the same beds with the same parents, the same house, the same chances – at least on the face of it – and ended up in two such completely different positions?

Was it school? Apart from their mother's attitude towards them – Luke her favourite, Robin regarded as his perpetual tormentor – school had been the big difference. Though she had gone to the grammar, Luke had gone to private school, too. Like Ben, as they'd learned from the Renshaws, he'd failed his eleven-plus and her parents had pulled out the financial stops to give him a shot at a better education than they thought he'd have at St Saviour's, the local comprehensive where he'd have ended up otherwise (and where Lennie currently was).

She wondered now if her parents' decision had also been to do with the company he'd be surrounded by. As they'd always known – and as he'd proven definitively over the summer – Luke was highly susceptible to influence. She was sure her mother would have factored in a potentially better – or at least better-to-do – class of influence when she'd done her cost/benefit analysis.

And yet somehow, despite seven years there, aged eleven to eighteen, Luke *hadn't* come out of it with well-to-do friends. They themselves, the Lyonses, were middle-middle-class all the way through, Dennis was an accountant, too, but Luke had always had a chip on his shoulder about 'posh bastards'. In the past, she'd suspected that part of his problem with Samir – apart, of course, from his skin colour – had been that with two doctors for parents and Aisha, his older sister, doing medicine at Cambridge at the time, Luke perceived him as posher than him.

As soon as he'd left school, Luke had gravitated towards his local friends, an odd collection of people with no obvious common ground other than being roughly the same age and a bit bitter. One of them had been 'Hideous' Billy, as she and

Corinna had used to call him, Billy Torrence. He was a little
creep, always had been – Natalie, Luke's wife, loathed him and
banned Luke from having anything to do with him.

It had been Billy who'd swooped in when Luke was at his
most vulnerable, separated from Natalie and worried sick about
their mother in hospital after her stroke. Billy had taken Luke
to the riot at Rose Road.

Needless to say, he would not be there to give her brother
a job when he'd served his sentence – at least, not a legal
one. But then, what would Luke have to offer an employer
anyway? At least Eddie Gillespie was professionally qualified;
her brother had scraped five GCSEs with grades that hadn't
been mentioned since he'd opened the envelope, a single A
level (Business Studies, with a D), and 'uninspiring' would be
a generous description of his work history.

The other difference was that Eddie Gillespie's crime was
white-collar. Luke had confessed to charges of violent disorder,
which also determined *where* he would do his time. Gillespie
had served his in an open prison; there'd be none of that for
Luke. Anne Heywood had complained that the police treated
her family like Fred West, but Luke was currently *in* the prison
where West had hanged himself to avoid standing trial.

Good influences would be thin on the ground in HMP Winson
Green, let alone useful contacts. What would Luke *do* when he
got out, in however many years the judge decreed on Monday?
No job, no wife, a record of violent crime. He'd be shafted.

Unless someone helped him out. But who would that be?
Luke wasn't Alistair Heywood, with a family business waiting to
catch him. Who'd be *his* Alun Morgan? Who could he be useful
to? Who'd pay him for anything, apart from Jeremy sodding
Handley, hungry for information that would ruin their lives?

For all the heat of the room, Robin's skin went cold.

'*But* this – *my mother* – this *is on you.*' Dominic Heywood.

She remembered the way he'd fallen to his knees on the grass as his mother's body came out on the gurney, his fury outside the door of his flat. Kilmartin had taken it on himself to tell the Heywoods the news about Amy – for once, Robin had been glad he'd stolen her thunder – but apparently, while they'd been gratified their case had been dealt with, and dealt with *first*, if she'd hoped that Dominic's rage had been calmed, she'd hoped in vain.

'*Let me tell you this, DCI Lyons: my sons loved their mother –* loved *her – and they're angry.*'

She'd written off the idea of Handley having reached Luke inside the prison because he was young and not local – though in the dark in the small hours, that seemed like wishful thinking. But Dominic *was* local. The Heywoods had the ACC at their beck and call, for heaven's sake; by comparison, the other end of the spectrum would be the very lowest-hanging fruit.

Cheap fruit, too. If Luke helped the Heywoods out now with some damaging information, maybe they'd promise him a job when he got out. Or maybe they'd just straight up offer him money. He couldn't use it himself, but if it went to Natalie and Jack . . . It would be something to give them, a way to say sorry to Nat, to be some sort of father to Jack while he was inside, at least help buy him the things he needed when he'd failed him so dismally in every way apart from loving him. Because Luke did love his son – deeply.

'*We know who you are.*'

And what if Jeremy Handley was in touch with Dominic? Would he have called him for his article – was that possible? Yes, infinitely possible – *likely*. Even if they'd done nothing wrong, with Anne's death, the Heywoods had become key players and she, Robin, was the focus of their rage.

'*This is on you.*'

But Handley had called her *before* Anne died, hadn't he? Yes, she remembered: he'd called that first evening, within hours of their releasing Ben's identity, she'd been waiting for Lennie at Austin's house, outside in the car. She'd wondered how he'd got her number.

Could Handley and Heywood know one another anyway?

Putting her hand down, Robin patted the carpet until she found her phone. Its rectangle of light was so bright, it illuminated the whole room. Quickly, so as not to wake Lennie, she adjusted the brightness, then pulled herself up in the bed, opened Facebook and searched for Jeremy Handley. Age twenty-seven – Dominic was twenty-seven, too.

She went to his 'friends' and hit 'See all'.

Shit, Zuckerberg, what's wrong with alphabetical order? Her eyes slid over the names at first, barely registering either words or pictures until she stopped, took a deep breath and made herself work through them methodically, one little screen by one.

After about twenty, she stopped. There he was: Dominic Heywood, Property Developer at Heywood Properties Ltd. Lives in: Birmingham. From: Birmingham. Studied Business at Newcastle University.

She checked Handley's profile, but she already knew: he had studied at Newcastle, too.

Robin let the phone drop face down on the sheet. Connections, networks – was there anywhere these people's tentacles didn't reach? Problems getting a job after a criminal conviction? Rely on the old school tie. Need a friendly journo to pressure a detective? Just call up your old university drinking buddy.

God almighty.

Chapter Forty-Five

Robin felt as if she'd barely been asleep at all when she woke to the sound of her mother drawing her bedroom curtains. The past twenty years vanished, her adult life reduced to a figment of her imagination.

'Thursday, love,' Christine said.

Four days to go.

Her mother stood for a moment, her dressing gown lashed around a middle slimmer than Robin ever remembered it, and looked across the garden. 'Bitter cold out.'

As soon as her eyes were properly open, Robin reached for her phone and scanned her messages. Nothing.

'He hasn't turned up then?' asked Christine.

'No.'

'Do you think he's all right, Mum?' asked a small voice from overhead.

'I hope so, lovely. But honestly, I don't know.'

Robin showered then had breakfast at a laid table for the first time since they'd moved out to Mary Street, her mother leaping up to refill the toast rack as her father ploughed through his usual three slices. 'Stay here again tonight,' he said as Robin drained her orange juice. 'It's nice to have you, whatever the circumstances.'

Robin was touched. 'Thank you, Dad. It's nice to be here.'

She dropped Lennie at school in time for her to meet Austin for early-bird library hours and was at the station by eight. She'd just finished hearing the handover from the overnight team when Malia signalled to get her attention. She was on the phone.

'Guv, I've got a PC Ainslie from the neighbourhood team in Brierley Hill. They had a call about half an hour ago from a man called Ron Jackson whose bins were turned over by animals last night. When he went out to clean up, he found a new Samsung Galaxy.'

'In a case?'

Malia nodded. 'Pale green with little flying saucers.'

A development at last, but far from the one they wanted. As the news travelled the room, Robin could see the energy level dropping again. After a quick chat with Malia, she called the team together for a two-minute meeting.

'The last thing we can afford is to lose a sense of urgency, either our own, or the public's,' she told them. 'So, for that reason, we're not going to release this. We've asked this Ron Jackson who found the phone to keep the news to himself and we'll do the same.'

'It doesn't look good, though, guv, does it?' said Hanratty.

Several people agreed. Theo wouldn't have dumped his phone, they were thinking. He could just change the SIM to stop anyone tracking him and the handset was only a couple of months old, it was valuable. If he needed money, he could sell it.

'Until we have concrete evidence otherwise,' she said, 'he's alive and well.' She wondered if anyone believed it. Even her.

*

After the meeting, she spent fifteen minutes answering the numerous flagged emails in her inbox then told Malia she was going out for an hour or so, but to call if she needed her.

'*My sons loved their mother* – loved *her* – and they're angry.'

As she drove to the Mailbox, Bill Heywood's words replayed themselves. Robin remembered Dominic's rage again and wished Varan was with her now. It wasn't possible, though; she'd had to come alone.

She hadn't phoned ahead, so when she rang the bell, she wasn't surprised by the delay that followed the approach of heavy footsteps on the other side of the wall. Two locks clunked back before the door opened on Dominic himself in jeans, a shirt, and weird tan soft-leather shoes – not quite slippers: too *déclassé* for him. He looked at her – *What the fuck now?* – then turned and stalked away, leaving the door open behind him.

Robin followed him to the main room, which was showing the effects of having three times its regular number of occupants. A pile of clothes was slung over the back of the sofa and two pairs of trainers had been kicked into a corner and left there. No one had loaded the dishwasher for a while, leaving stacks of bowls and plates to accrue on the counter, along with maybe twenty cups and glasses. They'd had a takeaway last night; the containers were there, too, the scent of fried noodles still on the air.

No suggestion that she take a seat. Instead, Dominic stood with his feet planted, arms crossed, letting Robin see how much bigger he was.

'Are Marcus and your father here?'

'No. They've gone to the gym. It's in the building, if you need to account for their whereabouts.'

'No, no problem,' she said, 'it's you I need to talk to. Two things. First, did you set your university buddy on me, Dominic?'

She'd surprised him, but he hid it quickly under a sneer. 'What are you talking about?'

'Jeremy Handley of the *Daily Record*. You were at Newcastle together, you shared a house, and now here he is phoning and digging for embarrassing dirt on me.'

'Is he?' He couldn't keep the smirk out of his voice.

She looked at him. 'Distracting me from trying to catch Ben Renshaw's killer. Maybe I'll take a leaf from your book and talk to ACC Kilmartin about it, see if there's anything he can do.'

He looked at her, eyes glittering. 'Funny. You know, I don't know if you've ever thought of it like this,' he said, 'but we've got something in common, you and me: we've both got a brother locked up. What I didn't know until yesterday is that your *daughter* was at the protest, too.'

Robin felt the floor shift under her feet, as if Dominic's comfortless marble was attempting to tip her off. 'Yes, she was – to *counter*-protest. She was the only person who stayed with the officer who was injured.'

He lifted the corners of his mouth, but it wasn't a smile. 'You must be ever so proud.'

'I am.' She made eye contact and held it. 'Always. The second thing I wanted to ask you about, Dominic, is Alun Morgan.'

'Morgan? What, the Myrmidon guy? Why?'

'So you know him?'

'Yeah, we've met a few times.'

'In what context?' *Socially, perhaps?*

'In the *context* of a project we were developing. We've done business with a friend of his in the past and he told us Morgan was interested in investing. We had meetings, but in the end it fell through, didn't come to anything. End of.'

'Why did it fall through?'

'The vendor of the land decided he wasn't selling after all. The project was site-specific.'

The speed with which he produced the information suggested either that it was true or that he'd had the answer prepared. Which, was impossible to say. 'Have you had contact with Mr Morgan since?'

'Apart from bumping into each other now and again at events, no.'

'Any ill feeling between you?'

'No. Why would there be? It was just one of those things, a project that didn't come off.'

'When was this?'

He shrugged. 'I don't know – about three years ago?'

'So before what Alistair did?'

'Before what you keep *telling* us Alistair did.'

'Dominic, do you have records relating to this project?'

He frowned. 'Some, of course. I don't know what exactly, or how many.'

'Who's going in to the office at the moment?'

'Everyone, apart from us. Claire's keeping an eye on things, Dad's assistant.'

'Call and ask her to put the records together, please. Now. Ask her to have them ready in an hour – I'll send someone to pick them up.'

Back in the car, Robin got out her notebook and wrote down her thoughts as quickly as possible. Her hands were still shaking, but she was excited, too, because she'd discovered a connection between the Heywood and the Gillespie families that Peter Hailey's inquiry had missed.

Alun Morgan – he had links to them both.

She warned herself not to race ahead: they were far from

having enough to be sure he was involved, let alone the key to it all. And yet, there was something here, she could feel it. Morgan had hired a convicted fraudster; Eddie Gillespie had lied about their friendship. And what, if anything, had been Stefano Fiore's role? She remembered Eddie's start of surprise. *'The Italian? Who died?'*

Chapter Forty-Six

The afternoon was almost gone by the time they reached Myrmidon Logistics. Robin and Jo had driven west from Rose Road, so the sun had set in front of them, draining the light from the sky. As they pulled on to the premises and parked outside the offices, just a band of turquoise remained, stained virulent orange at the horizon.

She'd already known the business was huge, but seeing it gave her a proper appreciation of the scale. They'd driven the edge of the lot to reach the gate and passed forty or fifty HGVs, their gargantuan cabs dwarfing the chain-link face. On the other side of the property were high-sided white transit vans – forty or fifty of those, too – all bearing the Myrmidon logo of a gold-winged sandal.

Before seeing Dominic this morning, Robin's plan had been to pay Morgan a visit directly afterwards. After learning about his connection to the Heywoods, however, she'd wanted all the available facts before talking to him, including whatever – if anything – they could glean from the paperwork they'd collected from Claire Philips.

There'd also been another deeply worrying development as far as Theo was concerned. When she'd arrived at work, Malia had been waiting for her. 'I was about to ring you,' she'd said. 'What's going on?'

'I've just spoken to Forensics. They've charged the phone and it's definitely Theo's.'

'Any prints?'

'Not even a partial: both the phone and case were thoroughly wiped.'

No surprise there. What self-respecting criminal left prints these days?

'But, guv, it looks like it might have been so *thoroughly* wiped in order to get blood off.'

Robin's heart had sunk. 'By which you mean, they didn't get it *all* off?'

'Apparently there was still a tiny bit left round an inside seam in a corner of the case.'

'Enough for profiling?'

Malia had nodded. 'Just about. It's gone to the lab already, top priority.'

'Right.' Robin had thought. 'His parents know the phone was found, don't they? Did they have any idea why Theo might be in Brierley Hill – friends there, contacts?' It was a patch way out on the furthest edge of the urban sprawl of Birmingham and its satellites, about twenty miles down the M6. When people thought of it, it was largely for its shopping centre but even that was old news since Grand Central and the new Bull Ring.

'No,' Malia said. 'He doesn't know it at all, apparently.'

It'd be twenty-four hours before they got results from the lab, even top priority, so Robin had made the decision not to tell the Gillespies about the blood for now. Until they knew for sure, there'd be no point in adding to their torment. If the blood was his, there'd be plenty of time for pain. *More* pain.

That was the last development of any significance. For all their efforts, they were drawing blanks left and right. So far, the house-to-house in Brierley Hill had proved about as fruitful as the ones around Moseley Bog and the Heywoods' house. The police presence had attracted notice, though, and Sara Kettleborough at the *Post* had texted asking for confirmation that Theo's phone had been found. Robin had considered asking her not to run it, but there was always the possibility that someone who'd been in Brierley Hill at the time might see the news and remember something.

The downside was that the national media had picked up on the mini-scoop. Heart in her mouth after the exchange with Dominic, Robin had checked the *Record*'s website. Nothing about her, thank God, but she prayed the Gillespies didn't see the headline: *Mounting Fears for Missing Theo*. Fears *were* mounting, though, not least her own. She was fighting them, correcting her mental narrative whenever she caught herself thinking it, but she was less and less convinced now that they'd find Theo alive. The spilled ink spread ever outward; most likely, it had surrounded him.

When they pulled into the Myrmidon car park, Robin was relieved to see a Jaguar parked directly outside the office-building door. She'd considered calling ahead to avoid a wasted trip but the element of surprise had value enough to make it worth the risk. She parked a few spots down, and they got out of the car and went inside.

When she'd finished looking at their ID, the receptionist told them she'd see if Morgan was available.

'If he's here, he's available,' Robin said. 'We're police.'

'Of course,' the woman said, looking embarrassed. 'Sorry.' She hesitated, then took the risk. 'Is this about Eddie Gillespie's son? We're all so worried. Is there news?'

'I'm sorry, I'm afraid I can't say.'

The woman stood and disappeared through the door behind her and when, two or three minutes later, it opened again, the man Robin had seen online was with her.

It was hard to imagine he'd ever belonged to a group called the Untouchables. In person, he was better-looking than in the photographs she'd seen – and he hadn't been at all bad in those. His eyes were intelligent, his mouth generous, as she remembered, and his hair was an appealing colour somewhere between red and brown. Robin tried to find the right word. Russet? Fox? The pale blue shirt under his grey jacket was unbuttoned at the collar.

'Chief Inspector? Alun Morgan.' He shook hands with Jo, too, then held the door open for them. 'Please.'

They followed him down a corridor lined with glass-fronted offices, almost all of them occupied by people either on the phone or working at computers. Robin wondered if one of the unoccupied ones belonged to Eddie, then remembered the three people whose titles, at least, seemed senior to his. This had a 'corridor of power' feel, but the building had two floors; presumably there were more offices upstairs.

'Sizeable operation,' Robin said. 'It's impressive.'

'Thank you,' Morgan replied, 'I've been lucky, worked hard.'

His office was at the end of the corridor. It was three times the size of the ones they'd passed and while all of those had been modern, well-outfitted – no crumbling foam on *their* chairs – his looked actively chic. There was a European designer vibe about both the desk and the long tan-leather sofa, and a number of glossy plants lined the windowsill and grew from planters on the floor. Hard to believe it was on a trading estate minutes from the M5.

He closed the door, then gestured at two tan-leather chairs before sitting down at the desk. 'How can I help? Priti says it's about Theo Gillespie, the poor lad.' He looked grave.

'You know him, sir, obviously?'

'The whole family, yes. Eddie and I were at school together and though we dropped out of touch for a while, he works for me now, which I'm guessing is why you're here.'

'Yes. When you say "a while" – we heard from the Gillespies that, actually, it was more than thirty years. Is that right?'

'Yes, about that, it must have been. We're getting on – getting old.' A small huff, *Time, eh?* 'Eddie's been here for nearly two years already.'

'But you got back in touch after that long to offer him a job?'

He nodded. 'I'd heard he was in a tight spot.'

'Mightily strong old school tie.'

'What?'

'You offered him a job thirty years later on the basis of having been at school together?'

'Eddie's clever, always was – we used to be competitive, especially in maths.' He sighed. 'It sounds old-fashioned, but I think your past is important. Especially the significant times in your lives. When you've been close to someone, then you're always tied.'

Jo made a note and Robin guessed it was along the same lines as the thought she'd just had: so Alun also said they'd been friends at school, then.

'What about his fraud conviction?' Robin asked.

'I presume you know the history there?' He met her eye and held it. 'Sometimes people do the wrong thing for the best of reasons.'

She felt a flush of alarm: did he know? No, of course not, how could he? *Why* would he? Bloody hell, she had to get her paranoia under control.

'Going back to your school days for a moment, sir,' Jo said, unwittingly coming to her rescue, 'were you close to a boy called Stefano Fiore?'

Morgan jumped as if she'd given him an electric shock, then put a hand on his chest. 'Sorry, that caught me off balance. You know, I think about Stefano every day, but I haven't heard anyone else say his name for years. Yes, yes, we were close.'

'But he died?'

He nodded. 'It was . . . terrible. One of the worst times of my life, honestly. He was my best friend, incredibly important to me. The first person, I think, who saw a version of me I actually liked, if that makes sense.'

Robin thought of Samir. 'It does,' she said. 'We're sorry to bring it up again.'

'No, it's all right, it's a long time ago now. It's *nice* to hear his name. To know he hasn't been completely forgotten.'

'Can you tell us about him?'

'Of course. And, in fact, I can show you a picture.' He picked up one of the frames on his desk and passed it to her.

Robin held it so Jo could see, too, and they looked at a boy of seventeen or eighteen in khaki shorts, a white shirt and plimsolls standing on a worn stone step, an intricately carved wooden door behind him. He was dark-haired and deeply tanned, teeth very white as he smiled at the camera.

'I took that in Florence,' said Morgan. 'The summer before he died. His parents had a holiday place in Tuscany and they invited me out there for a whole month. We had the time of our lives.'

'Excuse me asking, sir,' said Robin, 'but were the two of you just friends?'

'Yes, just friends, but Stefano *was* gay – he came out to me that month in Italy.'

'Was he attracted to you?'

'I don't know. I never got that impression, honestly. I wasn't an early bloomer, put it that way.' He huffed again, half-smiled. '*He* was good-looking, though, as you can see.'

'Was it a problem, when he came out?'

'To me? No. I'm not homophobic. Probably why he felt able to tell me.'

'How about to other people?'

'He wasn't out to other people.'

'Really?'

'No. The idea terrified him. His family were Italian, old-school Catholic, extremely conservative – his father, Paolo, *was* a homophobe. There were some awful comments that month – damaging, I'd say. With the benefits of age and hindsight now, I think Paolo was hoping that if he could impress on Stefano how absolutely unacceptable it would be to him, he could somehow make it not so. Or at least force him into some sort of double life, cover-story marriage and children. Save the family reputation. At school, there was none of the eternal damnation Sodom and Gomorrah stuff, but there was plenty of scorn and disgust from some parties.'

'Poor boy.'

'Yes,' he nodded slowly, 'poor boy. For all his advantages.'

'What happened the day he died? We know the inquest found misadventure, but that's really all we've been able to discover. Was there ever any suggestion of foul play?'

'No. His body wasn't in great condition when it was found, he'd been bumped around as the river carried him, but nothing that was obviously suspicious.'

'It sounds like he confided in you. Had anything been going on in his life that you knew of? Apart from the situation with his father.'

'I don't know,' he said. 'Only what was released at the time. I was on exeat that weekend, I'd gone home for my aunt's wedding. I've always kicked myself, thought if I'd been with him, I'd have been there when he went into the water – or told him not to go into the water in the first place.'

'He'd drunk a lot?'

'I wondered if he'd gone swimming to try to sober up before coming back to school. They'd have given him hell for being drunk.'

'Why *would* he have drunk so much? Especially if he was alone? Drinking with your friends, egging each other on – things get out of hand. But drinking alone, ploughing through a bottle of vodka . . . Was he depressed? It sounds as if he was living under a lot of pressure.'

'Yes.'

'This must have come up at the time, but do you think it might have been suicide?'

'That,' he said, 'is a question I'd still like someone to answer.'

'It was investigated, though?'

His expression darkened. 'As far as I saw, not very thoroughly. The whole affair was glossed over: *what a shame, he got drunk and drowned. Now move on, everyone – no distraction from what's really important here: A levels just a month away, the school's got a reputation to uphold.* I lost my best friend and no one even bothered to find out what really happened.'

'That must have been very hard.'

'Well,' he said, 'it's old history now.'

'But your past is important. Especially the significant times in your life.'

He tipped his head. 'Touché.'

'Mr Morgan, on a different note, what's your relationship with the Heywood family?'

The change of direction surprised him. 'The Heywoods? Bill and sons? Well, I wouldn't go as far as saying we have an actual *relationship*, as such. We know each other a little, we've run across each other in business a few times and we've a couple of mutual friends. A few years back, I was going to invest in a project of theirs, a redevelopment of an old warehouse on one of the canals, but the guy who owned it changed his mind last minute and that was the end of it.'

'How much were you going to invest?'

'Two and a half million.'

'Lot of money. Did you pay any of that upfront?'

'I did, yes, but I got it back when the deal collapsed. I didn't lose anything.'

'All right, good.' It was what they'd seen from the Heywoods' paperwork, too, no obvious irregularities, but Robin had hoped nevertheless. 'So there's no bad blood between you?'

He shook his head. 'Not personally. I know the poor Gillespie family have had a hell of a time with them – that car accident, bloody hell – and I'd certainly never do any sort of business with them again for that reason, but myself, no.'

Chapter Forty-Seven

The third week of November now, and as she waited for the lights on Stratford Road, Robin looked at a trio of cardboard elves in candy-cane tights dancing in the window of the off-licence where her dad bought his biannual bottles of Scotch, vaunting their season's specials on handwritten envelopes carried by a curl of painted breeze towards a postbox labelled 'North Pole'. *Litre Tia Maria £19.99! Litre Baileys £19.99!*

What would Christmas be like this year at Dunnington Road? Miserable for her parents whatever happened on Monday, because, for the first time in almost forty years, Luke wouldn't be there for any of it. Even if the worst happened and he withdrew his confession for the stone, he'd get time for his own crime that would cover at least the next two or three Christmases inside. Would Natalie bring Jack over to see his Lyons grandparents or just spend the whole day with her own family rather than split it like they normally had? No, she'd come, Robin thought; she knew how important Jack was to them.

But if the worst happens, Lennie might not be there. She shook herself physically, to try and get the thought off her – away.

A man stepped out of the shop, tucked a bottle under his arm and zipped up his jacket. The temperature had dropped sharply since the sun had gone down; if Theo was alive, she hoped he was somewhere warm.

When she'd got in the car at the station, she'd felt the old feeling again, the physical yearning to see Lennie, but when she was two turns away from her parents', barely having thought it through, she glanced at the clock, then indicated in the opposite direction.

Robin had never liked Natalie, but she respected her. Her work ethic was undeniable and she set goals and achieved them – she'd bought a house (which was more than Robin had done, despite earning more money); she'd wanted a promotion, so she went to evening classes and got the certificate that qualified her for it. Christine – to Robin's irritation – had always loved her (it wouldn't have bothered her so much if she'd been sure at the time that her mother loved *her*), and over the summer Robin had come to understand why: Natalie helped keep Luke together; she shared the work of him.

Of the pair of them, it was Natalie who had the exam results, Natalie who was the breadwinner, Natalie who made things happen. She and Luke had been together since they were sixteen, but what did *she* get out of their relationship, Robin had often wondered. He must be bloody magic between the sheets to compensate for all his other deficiencies. She shook herself again, *ugh*.

'They just love each other, Robin,' Christine said. 'They're woven into each other's lives and they love each other.' She'd said it as if she were explaining a concept that would be alien to her, hard, loveless woman that she was – or at least that was how Robin had interpreted it.

Nat still loved Luke, Robin knew, even now. She'd been appalled by his presence at the riot, let alone what he'd done, and she was visibly suffering because of their break-up, even though she'd instigated it. They'd been fighting beforehand, in the spring – Luke had been fired from his job at the phone shop and suddenly it had been up to Natalie to earn *all* their money, not just the lion's share, as well as being the principal parent to their little boy, Jack, who'd been only six months old at the time.

Their house was a neat two-bedroom new-build on a quiet street about ten minutes' drive from Dunnington Road – as far as Luke could go from his mother, Robin had thought in the past, without the apron strings getting too tight. Natalie's little Renault was parked on the concrete patch outside.

Lights were on both upstairs and down. Robin considered. Ringing the bell might wake up Jack, so instead she knocked very gently on the sitting-room window and heard a cry of alarm inside that immediately made her wonder what she'd been thinking.

'I'm so sorry,' she said when the front door opened. 'I didn't mean to scare you.'

'It's OK – you were trying not to disturb this one, which I appreciate. Though, as you see, you needn't have worried.'

Jack, in a striped onesie, bottom padded by a nappy, looked at Robin balefully from his mother's arms. His fat little cheeks were crimson, his hair damp at the nape.

'Teething?'

'Big time. Thank the Lord for Calpol, eh, little man?'

Robin followed her into the sitting room, which to her surprise was quite untidy, at least by Nat's standards. The carpet could do with a hoover and there was a stale coffee cup on the table, as well as the wine glass that was in current use. Natalie herself looked as if she could do with a bit of an overhaul: her hair was stringy and in need of a wash, and some hours ago now, she'd covered a spot on her chin with an attention-seeking glob of concealer that had caked and was starting to crack. Robin had a flashback so vivid, it felt physical – she was back in London, so tired that, when she came home to a crying Lennie after a twelve-hour shift in which she'd attended an RTA with multiple fatalities, she'd sunk to her knees, Len in her arms like Jack was in Nat's now, and cried her heart out.

Natalie had caught her looking at the wine glass. 'Do you want one?'

'Love one, but I'd better not,' she said. 'Still got to drive home and I'd really like to get called into the station tonight.'

'The Gillespie boy? Still no sign?' She knew, of course, Robin realised, everyone did. The story was everywhere.

'No. But how are you getting on, Nat? You all right?'

Natalie lowered herself onto the sofa slowly, being careful not to bend Jack's legs awkwardly as she sat. When she was settled, he put a wet thumb back in his mouth and nestled his face against the side of her neck.

'All right,' she said, stroking his head, 'but no more than that. Honestly, I'm knackered and I'm sad, Robin. So *sad*.'

Despite herself, Robin was shocked. Natalie admitting weakness – to her? They had never in their lives – in the twenty years they'd known each other – had a conversation where they related to each other as individuals, rather than as adjuncts, one way or another, to Luke.

'How did it all happen?' Nat went on. 'How did everything go so wrong? I tried so hard to get things right and now my little boy's going to grow up with a dad who's in prison.'

Robin thought of Kevin Young, the mark on him from his father's jail term even now. And Morris' crime had just been selling on scrap metal that someone else had stolen, not nearly putting a man's eye out. 'I know,' she said. 'What can I do? Maybe when this case is finished Lennie and I could take Jack for the day, give you a day off? Or—'

'Don't worry. Your mum's brilliant, and so are my lot. It's just the sadness. This life that I had all planned out and now look – shot to hell. And it's my fault – if I hadn't told Luke I wanted a separation . . . It was supposed to be a kick in the pants – *Come on, man, get your act together* – but—'

'No,' Robin said, emphatic. 'No, Nat. None of this is your fault. You're not his keeper. He's a grown man, an adult, and let's face it, he bloody *needed* a kick in the pants. What he did is his responsibility, not yours.' Though Nat would bear a lot of the fall-out.

Nat snorted gently. 'Maybe if I say that often enough, I'll believe it one day.'

Jack stirred on her shoulder, his eyelids beginning to droop.

'Anyway, it is what it is and I should have another go at getting this one tucked in. Was there something specific?' In other words, thought Robin, ashamed of herself, What is it? Because unless there *was* something, you wouldn't be here.

'Nat, I need to talk to my brother. Urgently. Could you call the prison and get them to tell him you need to talk to him? If he thought something was up with you or Jack . . . And then, if he called you, you could ask him to call me . . .'

Natalie looked at her. 'You're not one of his numbers.' Prisoners had a very limited group of people they were allowed to call. Needless to say, Robin was not one of Luke's.

'But our parents are – if he called me there . . . Please, Nat. Will you try? Tomorrow?'

Lennie was in bed by the time Robin got to Dunnington Road. 'I'm sorry, love,' said her mother, seeing her disappointment. 'She wanted to see you, but she was absolutely shattered, couldn't keep her eyes open. It was one of the rougher days – very rough.'

At least, Robin thought, Len would be getting some rest, but as she crept in from the landing and slid as noiselessly as possible into the bottom bunk, she heard movement overhead. 'Mum?' came a whisper.

'Hi, lovely,' she whispered back, then stupidly. 'You're awake.'

'Of course – it's not like I can *sleep*.' As if it were her fault – which, ultimately, Robin thought, it was. 'Mum, I can't go through with it – I can't let Uncle Luke do it.' She paused. 'We have to stop him. I can't live the rest of my life knowing that I didn't.'

Chapter Forty-Eight

Lennie insisted on going to school, reminding Robin of Theo on the morning he'd heard the news about Amy, how he'd told his mother he was *'clinging on to what's left of normality'*. As a distraction, school probably *was* the best option; sitting at her grandparents' table, pushing mini Shreddies around a bowl of warming milk, Len looked tortured.

Robin waited until her mother took her boiled-egg shells out to the compost bin by the shed. She'd managed – finally – to calm Lennie down enough to sleep last night but then she'd lain awake herself for a further hour and a half, her head wrecked. 'I'll drive you to school,' she told her now.

Lennie looked up.

'We can talk in the car.'

By the time Robin reached the station, the rest of the team were already there. She sat on the edge of the spare desk and joined the others watching Tark as he inched his way across the room with a brimming mug of coffee. 'The suspense,' she said *sotto voce*. Tark's eyes were laser-focused on it, his tongue protruding with concentration.

'Edge-of-your-seat stuff,' said Varan. 'Entertainment money can't buy.'

'And wouldn't if it could,' Jo said.

'Oh, I don't know. There's probably a whole channel devoted to this kind of thing somewhere down the cable guide. Our boy could be a star.'

Tark lowered the mug onto his desk, then raised his arms in the air, triumphant. 'Behold the glorious victory.'

If she wanted to behold a victory at all, Robin thought, she'd have to: it was the only one they had. 'Tark, how much tape have we had in from Brierley Hill?' she asked.

He indicated a box on Hanratty's desk directly behind his own, two thirds full. 'From the point of view of watching it all, plenty. For seeing what we need, not a ton. Brierley Hill's not Moseley. If people have spare cash to hand, they're not spending it on security cameras.'

'Let's get everyone watching it this morning, top priority.'

'Righto.'

'Because even if we'd had a camera trained on Ron Jackson's bin the whole time, I don't think we'd be seeing any animals.' The realisation had come to her just now while she'd been coming up the stairs and she'd immediately kicked herself for not thinking it earlier. *Of course.* 'What are the odds, do you reckon, that of all the bins in Birmingham, animals would get into the very one the phone was dumped in?'

'Well, they have *got* a fox problem over there, according to the neighbourhood team,' said Malia.

'I believe it, they're everywhere, you can't drive the streets at night without seeing one. But if it was just a dump, pure and simple, what a crappy, *crappy* piece of luck for his killer.'

'Someone wanted to make sure the phone was found, you're thinking?'

'I am. People don't linger round their bins. Ron Jackson puts his rubbish out after dinner, you said, in the dark – takes it round the back, lifts the lid, chucks it in – and the bin men just pick the bins up and empty them straight into the lorry. The only way you'd look at your rubbish was if it was strewn all over the place and you had to pick it up by hand. And if you were doing *that*, you wouldn't miss a brand-new phone.'

Tark was nodding slowly. 'It was left in the case, too. If you wanted to hide that it was Theo Gillespie's, you'd take the case off, wouldn't you? Dispose of the two separately? There's been pictures of it everywhere – the *Post*, online.'

'*I* would, unless I was panicked and rushing, which the cleaning argues against.'

'So someone wants us to know he's dead?'

'Or someone wants us to *think* he is,' said Malia.

'Then why do such a thorough job of getting the blood *off* it?'

'To make it look plausible,' Robin said. 'No decent killer would dump a blood-covered phone unless they had to. If someone wanted to make us think someone *else* had done this . . .'

'Like the person or people who did all the witness intimidation?' said Malia.

Robin nodded. 'Maybe.'

'Or do you think it could be Theo himself?'

'I think that's a possibility, yes.'

'But why?'

'Million-dollar question. What interests me is the timing. He vanished the day he found out Amy had burned down the Heywoods' house, didn't he? I don't know what that means, but it feels significant.'

Malia and Varan nodded.

'So CCTV from Brierley Hill, plus whatever we got in from that last round at Moseley Bog, if anything.'

'A few bits,' Tark said, 'four or five tapes. We've done a couple.'

'So let's do the rest. Jo, how are you getting on with tracking down staff from Clarendon back in the day – any luck?'

'Well, the Head died five years ago – stroke, he was eighty-one – but the man who taught them maths just called me back and left a message.'

'Awarder of the much-coveted prize?'

'Ha, maybe. He's still local-ish, out near Hockley Heath. Shall I go and talk to him?'

'Definitely.' Robin picked up a Biro and tapped the end against her palm. 'Malia, I think we should get Claire Philips in, too, Bill Heywood's right-hand woman.'

'The Heywoods are back in the picture, then? For Theo now?'

'If something *has* happened to him, yes. But I want to put some pressure on her about their relationship with Alun Morgan, see if there's anything that neither he nor their paper-work is telling us, if there's something there. I also really don't like Theo's father. Eddie.'

She'd said it before she realised how true it was.

'I think something went on between those two – Morgan and Eddie Gillespie. I think it related to Stefano Fiore somehow, and I *don't* think Alun was the guilty party.'

The group was silent for a moment.

'Guv,' asked Malia carefully, 'do you really think whatever happened back then, thirty-odd years ago, has to do with everything now – with Ben's death?'

Fingers pressed to her lips, Robin thought. Did she? Really?

Samir's voice: *'If your antennae are up, then go for it. I trust you.'*

She remembered talking to Varan after he'd visited the Worcester school. What the hell could it be, she'd thought, this thing Ben and Theo were talking about, if even after Ben was killed, Theo couldn't tell anyone?

'Oh, God,' she said.

'What?' Malia looked alarmed.

'What if that's right?'

'If what is?' asked Tark, confused. 'Have I missed something?'

'Sorry – no. It's just occurred to me: what if Eddie was involved in Stefano Fiore's death and, somehow, Theo found out?'

The thinking was too provisional for the main whiteboard, so Varan wheeled out the mobile one.

Robin paced the carpet in front of it, marker in hand. 'How would it work, this theory – if it does?'

'Well, if you're right,' said Varan, 'and Theo did find out, then yes, it makes sense that he told Ben after the Worcester event. They caught a late train back, after the last StrengthInNumbers event they were going to do for a long time, they'd just been talking all evening about telling the truth? Imagine the burden he'd have been carrying, knowing something like that about his own dad?'

Robin remembered him in the family kitchen, his eyes swollen with crying. *'With me – especially after all this – we could talk to each other about anything.'*

She uncapped the pen and scrawled on the board:

Eddie involved in Stefano Fiore's death?
Did Theo find out?
Did Theo tell Ben?

'You think that's what got Ben killed?' said Tark. 'Knowing?'

'Not *knowing* per se,' replied Robin. 'Someone would have to *know* he knew. If he was threatening to *say* something, report it . . .?'

'But would he? If Theo had told him in confidence?'

'Well, if he knew Eddie had killed someone, then he'd feel

pressure to tell the police, don't you think?' Malia said.

'His best friend's dad?'

'*Murder?*'

'The teacher in Worcester said he thought Ben liked the attention,' remembered Varan.

'"*Justice campaigner as rock star*"?' said Robin.

'A rock star who was about to have his limelight switched off?'

They looked around at each other queasily.

'How would *Theo* have found out, though?' asked Malia. 'How would he know in the first place?'

'Maybe,' said Robin, 'Alun Morgan told him.'

Chapter Forty-Nine

Eddie Gillespie was outraged. 'What the hell's going on? Why am *I* in an interview room? With a bloody *tape* running? My son's the one missing – he's the *victim!*'

Robin had requested the same room in which she'd kept Marcus and his solicitor stewing, but Eddie Gillespie was alone and would apparently stay that way. 'Why the hell would I need a solicitor?' had been his initial response. They'd reiterated the suggestion in stronger terms, but he wouldn't hear any of it. When Varan started the tape, he informed it of Gillespie's decision.

'Mr Gillespie,' Robin said, 'please, come and sit down.'

'If you even *suggest* I've got anything to do with my son's disappearance . . .'

'I'm not going to suggest that.'

'Then why the hell am I—'

'We want to talk to you about Alun Morgan.'

'Oh, for *pity's sake*! You – how did you even *get* this job, Chief Inspector? Who do you know? Because I am having a hard time seeing how you hold on to it.'

Robin looked at him and said nothing. She and Varan waited in silence until, about a minute and a half later, Eddie conceded defeat, stopped pacing and threw himself into one of the chairs across the table from them like a petulant teenager.

'Why did Alun Morgan give you *your* job, Mr Gillespie?'

'Haven't we been through this?'

'Not to our satisfaction.'

'Because we were friends at school.' He said the words slowly, as if he were trying to teach them a sentence in a foreign language.

'But you weren't friends.'

He looked at them, *What are you talking about?* but Robin saw movement in his eyes, the faintest hint of alarm. 'Yes, we were.'

'Mr Gillespie, when we spoke at your home the other day, you told me that "awful as it sounds", you doubted you'd have been friends with Morgan if he'd been one of these so-called "Untouchables".'

'And?'

'We've heard from six sources now that he *was* one of them.'

'Well, I must not have *thought* he was one, then.'

'I find that hard to believe when, by all accounts, it seems you were – and are – quite aware of social hierarchies.'

'This is total crap,' Gillespie muttered. 'No wonder you lot weren't able to catch anyone last year – no bloody wonder. Useless, the whole lot of you.'

'What was your relationship with Stefano Fiore, sir?'

Caught unawares, he startled a little. 'I didn't have one. As I told you.'

'That's right. Because – for reasons you didn't understand – despite being rich and good-looking, he hung out with the Untouchables.'

He shrugged.

'For the tape, please, Mr Gillespie.'

'Yes.'

'Would you have liked to have been friends with him, if he hadn't been one of that group?'

'No strong feelings either way.'

327

'His father was very successful, very rich: houses in Milan and Tuscany, big yacht. Sounds socially acceptable to me.'

'There were a lot of people in the year. Of all the people there, I don't know why you're fixated on Fiore.'

'Because he died.'

'Also,' Varan added, 'it *wasn't* that big a year. According to the school records we've seen, there were only thirty-two of you.'

'You can't be close to thirty-two people. There are always groups – cliques.'

'Of course,' Robin said. 'But it does lead us back to the question of why Mr Morgan gave you a job, especially when, by some accounts, you were cruel to the Untouchables. Even if he wasn't one himself according to you, they were his friends.'

'I wasn't crueller than anyone else.' He took an audible breath, long in, long out. 'Honestly? If you want the truth, I think the job was an act of revenge. He wanted to rub it in my face, Myrmidon, his success. He wanted me to stick it in my pipe and smoke it because he was jealous of me at school and he wanted my approval then and he didn't have it. It's the loser's revenge: *Look at me now.*'

'So you definitely *weren't* friends.' Varan angled his face down, trying to hide a smile.

'Which then takes us in a different direction, I think,' Robin said. 'First: why would you take a job with someone you thought disliked you so much?'

'Because I'd just got out of *prison*, Chief Inspector. Come on,' he encouraged, 'you can do it, it's not rocket science. Because I needed a salary I could keep my wife and son on in an acceptable way.'

'I'm not sure I would have gone for it myself.'

'Sometimes, for the sake of your family, you just have to lump things, don't you? Do what you have to do – suck it up, as Theo and his friends say. And as you told me the other day, people value money differently.'

'You obviously value it very highly, Mr Gillespie.'

'So what if I do?'

'Looking at it from the other side for a moment, if I were Alun Morgan with this multimillion-pound business, international clients, a ton on my plate, frankly, I'm not sure I'd have bothered with you unless it was important, especially when you weren't friends.'

Gillespie was getting angry now. 'I've just *told* you: he was making a point, getting revenge.'

'You really think you meant so much to him, thirty-odd years later? I don't buy it. I *do* think he had an agenda when he hired you, yes, but I think the stakes were much higher than that. Which is why I'm going to ask again: what was your relationship with Stefano Fiore?'

'And I'll tell you again, I didn't have one.'

'Were you with him the night he died, Mr Gillespie?'

'What? No, of course not – I was at school, I didn't go out that day.'

'You remember where you were, just like that?' asked Varan. 'On a night thirty-something years ago?'

'I do,' said Gillespie, looking him straight in the eye. 'Of course I bloody do. Someone *died* – someone we'd been in class with every day! Things like that stay with you, every detail, especially at that age. I'd stayed in to revise, I worked late in my study, then, when I got back to the dorm, the house-master was freaking out because Fiore wasn't back. Of course I bloody remember!'

Robin glanced at Varan and saw her thought reflected back at her: he was telling the truth.

Shit.

*

Upstairs, they went back to the board, she and Varan, Tark and Malia. Jo had left over an hour ago to track down the maths teacher, obviously disappointed at being dispatched away from the action.

They'd been back up for a couple of minutes when Samir came through the door, face expectant. When he saw Robin's, he frowned. 'Not it, then.'

'No, but *something* happened, I know it. Gillespie himself brought up the idea of payback, though in his mind – if he's to be believed, which, NB, I highly doubt – it's some kind of revenge for him having been the golden boy in their schooldays and a bit mean.'

'Could he have *driven* Fiore to suicide? If he'd been bullying him and Fiore was under psychological strain anyway?'

'I don't know. Incredibly difficult to prove, either way, especially three decades after the fact.'

'The bit that wasn't working for me in the whole theory, though,' Samir said, 'was why, if Morgan knew or suspected Eddie had killed Fiore or been instrumental like that, he wouldn't have said something at the time? Why not just shop the guy?'

Robin nodded. 'I know, it was a weakness. Because he was afraid of him? That was what I was hoping, honestly. If he'd killed once, he could do it again?'

'Except he *hadn't* killed.'

'Well, yes, there is that . . .'

'Also, for thirty years? Even when Eddie was in prison for something else? When he, Morgan, had made this big success of his life and must have felt secure?'

She gave him a look: *OK, yes, thank you, you can stop now,* but then she remembered Morgan behind his long modern desk.

'He wasn't out to other people. The idea out terrified him. His family were Italian, old-school Catholic, extremely conservative – his father, Paolo was a homophobe.'

Was *that* why Morgan kept Fiore's secret? For his family's sake?

Downstairs again, Varan restarted the tape.

'Mr Gillespie,' Robin said, watching him carefully, 'you've told us that you and Mr Fiore weren't friends, we've got that, but were you in a sexual relationship with him?'

Eddie Gillespie looked first confused, then utterly repulsed. 'A *relationship*? With Stefano Fiore? Jesus *wept*.'

Chapter Fifty

After they let him go, Robin stayed at her desk for the rest of the afternoon and fought the temptation to bang her head on it. She had the feeling there was one connection they hadn't made and if she could just make it, everything would come into focus. What the hell was she missing?

It wasn't only frustration that was bothering her, though, but another growing awareness.

How did you even get this job, Chief Inspector?

She didn't think Eddie Gillespie had been hinting at dark knowledge of her secrets – though so many other people were doing it at the moment, why not him, too? But no, he'd just been grabbing at the jobs-for-the-boys idea, clearly familiar in his circles, in an attempt to undermine her.

He didn't know how close to the bone he'd cut.

She had her job at West Midlands because of Samir. When she'd been on the outs with the Met and the DCI spot here had opened up, she'd applied because he'd asked her to. She reminded herself that she'd been vindicated at the Met, that she'd been offered her old job back, she'd had a choice between them, and yet . . . And it was beyond question that Samir helped her in the role, too. How many times had he fought her corner against Kilmartin? How many times had he defended her, backed her judgement? Why? Because they were friends, because they went 'back and back', not quite old school tie, they hadn't been at school together, but old school-era tie, absolutely. What right, then, did she have to judge the Heywoods and Eddie Gillespie and Alun Morgan for their cosy connections?

More than that – the idea was sickening – Samir was now helping her to pervert the course of justice. In protecting Lennie, they were breaking the law, and for that, they were worse than Bill Heywood and his whispers in Kilmartin's ear because she and Samir were *officers* of the law – it was their job to uphold it. They weren't just breaking the law, they were taking a sledgehammer to their own integrity.

All this in mind, her heart sank when her mother called her mobile just after four o'clock. 'Robin, love?'

Handley, Robin thought. 'Just a sec.' She stood up, rounded the desk and closed her office door. 'What is it?'

'Natalie's just rung.'

Robin tensed. 'Has she?'

'She said Luke's going to call us this evening, at the house. Nine o'clock. She said to tell you.'

Natalie. Robin felt a flood of gratitude. Whatever Luke actually said, Natalie had made it happen, she'd come through for her. As soon as she hung up with her mother, she texted her. *Thank you, Nat. So much. X*

Then, back in her mental quagmire, she asked herself what *she'd* ever done for Natalie.

At quarter to six, Tark appeared in her doorway. 'Guv?'

With yet another sinking feeling, Robin followed him back to his desk, where he pulled up a chair for her next to his own. Malia and Varan gathered behind them.

The clock at the bottom right of the picture on-screen read 20.52. 'Last Sunday night,' he said.

Moseley Bog.

'Literally the second-to-last tape we had from there.'

The small house-to-house team who'd visited the handful of addresses that hadn't answered the door in the first rounds had got it from a house on Pensby Close, a quiet cul-de-sac of bungalows and modest but proudly maintained terraced houses on the short south-east facet of the park.

'The owners were on holiday in Florida last week, they said.'

The camera had been installed to keep an eye on the front of the house, which, judging by the view, was at the end of the terrace facing the area of grass from which a footpath led into the woods. Someone walking from here to meet Ben at the clearing would be coming in at a right angle to the path he'd most likely taken from the Yardley Wood Road entrance.

With key pieces of footage, Tark had a habit of starting the playback early to build suspense – after hours of tedium, these were his moments – and for a few seconds nothing happened. They waited, eyes trained on the well-kept front garden and a slice of the tarmac bulb beyond.

'There,' he said suddenly, pointing a finger at the top right-hand corner of the screen, where a figure had arrived. White trainers, dark trousers. Until he was halfway across, they only had the lower half of him, they couldn't see his shoulders, let alone his face, but they didn't need to. It took the boy eight or nine seconds to cross the screen, his right leg taking more or less normal steps forward, his left following gingerly, touching the ground with half the pressure.

*

Usually after such a major development, a team would be jubilant, but with this case, every step forward seemed to come with a punch to the gut.

'It doesn't have to mean he killed Ben, does it?' said Varan. 'There could still be a different explanation.'

'He lied to us,' said Malia. 'We spoke to him on Monday, the very next day. He didn't forget where he'd been in that time or get his evenings mixed up – he lied.'

When Robin and Varan arrived at the Gillespies', the same two journalists as last time jumped out of their car but again got nothing for their efforts.

Eddie opened the front door and Varan moved him quickly backwards out of sight.

On seeing their faces, his *Now what?* hostility dissolved instantly. 'Have you found him?'

'Eddie?' Carolyn appeared at the top of the stairs. 'What's going on?'

'We haven't found him,' Robin told them. 'No. But we need to talk to you both. Could we sit, please?'

In the sitting room, as Varan's glance told Robin he'd noticed, too, Eddie took his familiar chair rather than sitting with his wife. His hands gripped the arms, fingertips making deep dents in the upholstery. Robin wondered if he'd told Carolyn what they'd asked him at the station or if he'd made up a story of some sort.

She took a mental breath. 'As part of the larger enquiry,' she began, 'our CCTV team's looking at footage from a number of different areas, including, of course, the streets around Moseley Bog on Sunday evening. This evening, I'm afraid to tell you, we've seen CCTV footage that shows Theo heading into the woods just before 9 p.m. that night. We believe that's shortly before Ben was killed.'

Silence for several seconds, but then Eddie erupted.

'What are you trying to say?' he demanded. 'That *Theo* killed Ben? Don't be ridiculous.'

'We don't know what it means yet, except that Theo lied to us, which is very troubling. As you know, he said he'd been here all evening on Sunday, up in his room.'

Carolyn put her hands to her mouth.

'There's no way it's a mistake?' asked Eddie, less certain now. 'That it's not him on the tape?'

'No. His gait is very distinctive.' She gave them a moment to absorb what she was saying, then asked, 'Mr and Mrs Gillespie, were you aware that he left the house on Sunday evening?'

'No,' said Carolyn. 'We thought he was doing his homework. We lit the fire because it was cold and we were watching a film, like I told you.' She turned to her husband as she remembered, her eyes widening with realisation. 'We closed the door, didn't we? And drew the curtains to keep the heat in.' He could have slipped out without or knowing.

Eyes flicking to the dashboard clock every couple of minutes, Robin drove back to the station to drop Varan off. As if he'd been worried the journalists would read his lips in the rear-view mirror, he waited until they rounded the corner of the Gillespies' street before speaking. 'Theo wasn't abducted, was he, he vanished under his own steam?'

'That's what I think.'

A small part of her clung to the hope of a different explanation, but as the evidence mounted, it was harder and harder to avoid the conclusion that in looking for Theo, they were also looking for Ben's killer.

Immediately after seeing the footage, they'd done a huge new social-media push, no holds barred. Twitter, Facebook,

Instagram, Snapchat – blanket coverage. If Theo was hiding, there was a good chance he'd have left Birmingham, where people would be looking for him and were more likely to recognise him. He could well have gone to London, or somewhere further afield, less obvious.

To really get the word out, they needed to get the search trending and so, casting aside any notion of 'treading carefully' as far as the Heywood family were concerned or Jeremy Handley, she'd asked that everything be plastered with the StrengthInNumbers hashtag.

'Do you think it's why he disappeared after he heard what Amy did?' Varan said as they came down Harborne High Street.

'What's your thinking?'

'He knew that by doing what he'd done and lying about it, letting suspicion stay on the Heywoods, he'd caused Amy to do what *she* did. Anne's death is terrible, of course, but Amy – until then, she'd been a totally innocent party, his friend's little sister. She's fifteen, and her life's ruined.'

Chapter Fifty-One

Robin reached Dunnington Road with seven minutes to spare, just enough time to take some steadying breaths in the bathroom, out of sight, and then, in their bedroom, to check with Lennie. Len had changed out of her school uniform into her black jeans and an olive-green vest top. With her hair tied in a knot, no make-up, she looked simultaneously ready to go into battle and so young that Robin remembered her as she'd been at eight and nine. It made her heart hurt.

'You're totally sure, Len?' she asked. 'You can still change your mind.'

But Lennie shook her head. 'No, Mum. Nothing's changed since we talked this morning – it hasn't changed for weeks. I'm sure.'

They gathered around the table, the two of them and her parents, the landline handset lying between them like a grenade. Before they came to sit down, Robin had seen Christine quickly brush her hair in the hall mirror. Ridiculous, of course – who could see them? – but for her mother, she understood now, looking impeccable had always been self-fortification. Dennis reached out and laid his hand on her arm. Robin took Lennie's hand as much for her own benefit, she suspected, as her daughter's.

The minutes began to stretch – four minutes past, five, six. When the phone finally rang, Christine flinched. Robin was briefly afraid it'd be one of her mother's friends calling for a State of the Nation catch-up, that Luke would ring in the time it took Christine politely to get whoever it was off the line and then, taking umbrage, he wouldn't try again.

Her mother breathed deeply then answered. 'Luke? Oh love, it's good to hear your voice. I've been so worried. We're all here – me and Dad, Robin and Lennie.'

'Hello, son,' her father called. As if he were at a séance, Robin thought, contacting someone on the other side.

Her mother started peering at the buttons on the phone, by which Robin guessed Luke had asked her to put him on speaker. 'Here, Mum.' She took it from her, hit the button, then rested it back on the table.

'Have you been all right, Luke, love? Like I said, we've been so worried, Dad and I.'

Lennie, kept completely in the dark about his radio silence, looked at Robin: *Why? What were they worried about?*

'I'm all right.' He was aiming for gruff, Robin thought, but anyone who knew him like she and her parents did would hear the effort. 'I just needed to do some thinking, on my own. Get my head straight. I'm OK.'

'Luke,' Robin said, 'thank you for ringing. Really.' He said nothing, so she ploughed on. 'Lennie and I need to talk to you.'

'Yeah?' Attempted nonchalance this time, but another fail. In the background of the call, she could hear two male voices, distant but raised. 'Why's that then?'

Lennie gestured that she wanted to talk. 'Uncle Luke? It's me.'

'Hiya.' Softer.

'I've been thinking, too. Look, at the time, in the summer, I was so scared, I just went along with it, but I don't think you should do it – I don't want you to. Before Monday, say you didn't. Please.'

Silence from the other end, then, 'What's going on?'

'Nothing,' said Lennie. 'It's just the wrong thing to do and I don't want you to do it and I don't want to be *responsible* for you doing it.'

'But if I don't,' he said, 'then there'll be a trial, won't there?'

'Maybe,' said Robin. 'But if there is, there's no evidence. But, Luke, I think Lennie's old enough to make the decision and she's made up her mind.' Beneath the abject terror, she felt a swell of pride. Lennie, her daughter – twice the woman she'd ever be.

A pause and then, utterly Luke-like, he said, 'What do you think, Mum?'

'When Robin rang me earlier,' she said, 'honestly, I was shocked. But now I'm proud of Lennie for it, just like I'm proud of you for taking it on in the first place.'

'Yes,' Robin said. 'Thank you, Luke. You'll never know how grateful I am to you. Never.'

Another pause. Then, 'No.'

For a moment, Robin thought he was agreeing with her – no, he never *would* know. Typical, always the hard edge with her, even when she was trying to thank him.

But Lennie had read him faster: No, he wouldn't do it. She turned to her, stricken. 'Mum?

'No,' Luke said, more forceful now. 'I'm not going to with-draw the confession, so don't bother trying to persuade me, all right? I'm not going to change my mind.'

'But why?' Christine pleaded. 'If there's a chance the danger's over now and Lennie says she doesn't want you to—'

'It's not right, Uncle Luke. *Please.*'

'I'm sorry, Len, but I've decided. We don't know what the

sentence'll be for it, anyway. Relative to the other thing, maybe it won't be much.'

'Luke, son,' said their father, 'think carefully. Lennie and Robin are giving you the chance to—'

'For fuck's *sake*, Dad,' he spat, 'do you have any idea how *sick* I am of hearing what Robin's doing, what Robin's "giving me". This is mine – my turn. She can't come in at the eleventh hour trying to be the good guy. No.'

In the shocked silence that followed, Robin had a thought that chilled her.

'Luke,' she said, 'have you seen the local news these past two weeks? Ben Renshaw and Anne Heywood.' Amy Renshaw and one way or another, Theo Gillespie, too, in the relentless seep of this appalling case.

'Yeah, I've seen.'

'There's a journalist digging around us. You and me.'

'Yeah, from *The Record.*'

Her mother gave a small cry of alarm. Robin immediately thought of her stroke – she shouldn't be dealing with stress like this.

Lennie was looking at *her*: journalist? What the *hell*?

'Did he get hold of you, Luke?' Robin asked.

To her surprise, he laughed. 'Get hold of me? What, like, phoned for a *chat*?'

'Lukey . . .' said their father.

'But yeah, he "got hold of me". Someone in here came to talk to me. He offered me money.'

'For what?' said Christine.

'Dirt on Robin, Mum. Her relationship with Samir, what happened at the riot – why her daughter ended up with that officer. Bent copper stuff.'

The sharp in-breath was Lennie's this time.

'What did you say?' Robin could feel her own heartbeat.

'What do you think I said?'

'I don't know.'

'Yeah, you do. You think I took it because that's what I'd do, isn't it? Sell you out?'

Of course she did, because he'd done it before. She said nothing.

'I said, Robin, that there was nothing *to* say, nothing *to* sell: the truth was already out there.'

A wave of relief broke over her, so intense she felt dizzy. But the moment it began to recede, she thought of Jack and his ruddy cheeks, how he'd pressed his face against Natalie's neck seeking comfort, thumb in. And Nat, exhausted, working and bringing him up on her own. *Firefighting all the time.*

Her child over his.

'What about Jack?' she said. 'You'll be away longer. You'll miss more.' Unless he let him visit, by the time he got out, most likely, his son wouldn't know him at all.

'But when I'm out, I'll be able to look him in the eye. I hurt someone – even if it was on the spur of the moment, I still did it. But if I do *this*, I did a good thing, too. Jack'll never know it, but *I* do: I'll know I did what I could to make things right and, sorry, Robin, but no, I'm not going to let you take that from me.'

Next to her, Lennie gave a wrenching sob.

'Luke, please,' Robin begged, 'just—'

But it was too late: he'd ended the call. He was gone.

Chapter Fifty-Two

Before they started the interview, Robin and Varan spent a few minutes watching Alun Morgan through the one-way mirror. He was up from the table and walking about, which was perfectly reasonable: the chairs in there wreaked havoc on your spine. At the same time, however, something about his pace and apparent concentration reminded Robin of an actor about to go on stage.

'What do you think?' she said. 'Nervous?'

Varan kept watching. 'It's like he's psyching himself up, isn't it? As if he's about to go into the ring.'

Morgan's solicitor, a dark-haired man in his forties whom neither of them had met before, was sitting at the table, calmly consulting his notes, occasionally asking a question and writing more with a smart ballpoint pen that he'd taken from a pencil box the size of a cigar case.

'Ready?' Robin asked Varan. 'Let's do it.'

When they entered, Morgan greeted them warmly. He moved back to the table, putting it between them before shaking hands. 'Good to meet you,' he said to Varan, 'and to see you again, Chief Inspector. Though, honestly, I preferred yesterday's venue. These chairs are no joke.'

'I know. If it helps at all, we have the same ones on this side of the table.' She offered her hand to his solicitor. 'DCI Robin Lyons.'

'Charles Colton.'

'Mr Morgan, uncomfortable as it is,' Robin began, pulling up to the table, 'I'm afraid we need to interview you here because of the gravity of some of the questions we're about to ask.'

'I understand.'

'Good. So we'll get started. DC Patel, could you do the honours?'

Once the tape was rolling, she went on. 'As you know, we're currently investigating a situation in which at least two people have died, Ben Renshaw on the night of Sunday the eleventh of November at Moseley Bog and Anne Heywood at her home on Salisbury Road, Moseley, in the early hours of Wednesday, the fourteenth. We also have an active missing-persons case with Theo Gillespie.'

Morgan nodded, then remembered he was supposed to be audible. 'Yes.'

'For our records, I'd like to start by asking where you were on Tuesday afternoon *this* week, the twentieth.'

'That's when Theo was last seen? Of course. I was in Derby for lunch and a meeting with a potential new client.'

'What time did you finish there?'

'Just before five, I think, though I can check to see if anyone can be more specific.'

'Thank you, but we can do that if we need to. How many people were at the meeting?'

'Well, me and Jasmine, my Chief Account Manager, then four people from Langden – the firm we were talking to.'

Robin waited for Varan to finish writing before moving on. 'How about the evening of Sunday the eleventh?'

He thought. 'I was at home.'

'Anyone with you?'

'My wife, our two boys and my parents-in-law who were staying with us for a few days.'

'What time did you have dinner?'

He frowned slightly. 'I couldn't say exactly, but about the same time we usually do on a Sunday, around six thirty, seven o'clock.'

'And after dinner?'

'We washed up, then watched some television, tucked the boys in and went to bed on the early side ourselves, I think, ten or half past.'

'Did you leave the house at all that evening?'

'No.'

'OK, thank you. Mr Morgan, can you tell us a bit about your business?'

'My business?' He was surprised. 'Well, I'm in logistics, national and international. We handle freight for all sorts of customers – high-street retailers, drinks companies, furniture makers. We're pretty sizeable now – we employ over five hundred people, and we've got a European depot in France and plans for another in Germany.'

'You say "we", but you're the sole proprietor, is that right?'

'Yes, but I've worked with my core team for years, in two cases from the very beginning.'

'Your father also owned his own haulage firm?'

He nodded, but at the same time Robin saw a trace of unease: why did she know all this? 'Yes,' he said.

'Given you were in the same field, you weren't tempted to join his business rather than start up on your own?'

'It's always been important to me to be independent. I'll admit, I was worried if I worked for my dad, I'd be stuck in a father-son dynamic that would have driven me nuts. Also, if I managed to make a go of it, I didn't want anyone saying I'd had it handed to me.'

'You didn't think about going into a different kind of business, though?'

'I grew up around it – it was what I knew.'

'Right. Were you close to your father?'

'Not really, but I respected him. He was a self-made man, he hadn't had anything handed to *him*. And he lost my mother far too early.'

Robin made a note then changed tack slightly. 'You were a talented mathematician, we've heard.'

He smiled. 'Are you thinking of that bloody maths prize? Gillespie won it twice and he never lets me forget. Amazing what people remember, isn't it?' His eyebrows flicked up.

'Well, the prize, yes, but we've also spoken to your old maths master.' She turned to the page of notes Jo had given her after her trip to Hockley Heath. 'Mr Leigh.'

Morgan smiled. 'He's still around?'

'Yes. He spoke very highly of you, apparently, and said he's followed your progress. The DC who spoke to him said she thought he was proud of you.'

'Really?' The information seemed genuinely to touch him. 'That's nice to hear,' he said after a few seconds.

'It sounds as if he cared about you quite a bit. He said he worried about you back then. You were five when your mother died?' Robin saw unease again: why did they have so much detail about *his* life? Why did they need it?

'Yes,' he said, though, 'that's right.'

'And, as his understanding went, your father was hard on you. Very hard.'

Morgan looked at her, taken aback. 'How did he come to that conclusion?'

'From observing you, and then he asked Stefano Fiore.'

Morgan said nothing, but Robin saw conflicting emotions move across his face – anger, defensiveness. Shame. They passed, though, and she saw that, again, he looked moved.

'He cared enough to do that?'

'Mr Leigh? He did. You confided in him?' she asked. 'Stefano, I mean.'

'Until I met my wife, he was the only person I ever told. I swore him to secrecy – bloody Stef.' He tried a smile but couldn't manage it.

'Did your father abuse you, Alun?'

'Sexually, you mean?' He recoiled. 'No – no. Of course not.'

'But he beat you?'

Silence for perhaps thirty seconds. Morgan was looking down again and Varan took the opportunity to catch her eye.

'Yes, he did,' he said finally.

'Badly?'

More silence. 'Sometimes. During the holidays, when no one would see the evidence – it was always a happy time when we got too close to the start of term and he had to stop. One of the many great things about that month in Italy, by the way – four whole weeks of a summer without having to wonder when he was going to beat seven bells out of me.'

'Why did he do it?'

Morgan sighed. 'I think you can guess the answer to that, DCI Lyons.'

'He thought you were gay?'

'He did.'

'But you're married to a woman?'

'Yes, and I love her.'

'Sexuality doesn't have to be binary,' said Varan earnestly.

Morgan looked amused. 'So I hear.'

'Did anything ever happen between you and Stefano?' Robin asked.

He shook his head. 'As I said before, that wasn't our relationship. We were just friends.'

347

'You told us yesterday he was the first person who saw a version of you you actually liked.'

'Yes, and you know, I said it without thinking, but I've been thinking about it ever since and it's true. I walked around in a cloud of self-disgust back then and Stef made me feel like maybe I didn't have to. After seeing *his* father, I felt so angry for him – that someone like Paolo, who wasn't worth a hair on his head, could make him feel dirty and small.'

'You never felt angry for yourself?' Varan asked.

'What?' Morgan looked surprised. 'No.'

'When you were getting beaten?'

He shrugged. 'When you grow up with something from when you're very small, it's what you expect, you think it's normal. It wasn't until later that I realised it wasn't.'

'Alun, is Eddie Gillespie bisexual or gay, that you know of? Closeted?'

Morgan looked at her, full beam. His pupils were huge suddenly, despite the brightness of the room. 'No,' he said. 'Not that I know of. Why do you ask?'

'Mr Leigh said he'd thought at the time that Eddie had a fixation on Stefano.' She consulted Jo's notes. 'He remembered because he'd "been actually relieved when he heard Eddie had a cast-iron alibi for the day Stefano went missing".'

'I remember the police talking to Eddie at the time. Briefly.' The word had a definite edge.

'This fixation – if it wasn't sexual or romantic, then what was it?'

Morgan met her eye again and Robin had the idea that he was weighing her up, deciding whether or not she could be trusted.

'It wasn't that Eddie wanted to have a relationship with Stefano, Chief Inspector.' He put his hands on the table, palms down. 'Of any kind. He wanted to *be* him. Stef was good-looking, he was clever, popular, he'd have inherited a fortune. He had the confidence to be friends with whoever the hell he liked, cool or not, Untouchable or not. And on top of it all, he was kind – that was what Eddie really couldn't get his head around. When you had all that, why the hell would you *need* to be kind? Couldn't you just do whatever you wanted, sod everyone else?'

Robin let the statement breathe for a moment.

'Alun,' she said, 'what happened to Stefano? The day he died. I think you know more than you told us yesterday.'

For the first time, Charles Colton looked up from his note-making and put out a cautioning hand.

'It's OK, Charles,' Morgan told him. 'Honestly, the day he died? I don't know. If he'd even *hinted* to me he was thinking about suicide, I would never have gone away for the exeat – never. I don't know if he was planning suicide and didn't tell me because he knew I'd stop him or if it really was an accident.' He paused, seeming to weigh something up. 'Either way, DCI Lyons, when he went down to the river with a bottle of vodka, I think it's clear he was looking for *some* kind of oblivion. Whether temporary or permanent, we won't ever know.'

'What was he trying to forget, Alun?'

Morgan opened his mouth as if to speak but stopped. His eyes were shining with tears.

Robin waited.

'That Eddie Gillespie raped him,' he said.

Silence apart from the whirr of the tape and the sound of a door shutting at the other end of the corridor.

After what felt like a long time, Varan said, 'I'm sorry, sir, I'm confused – I thought you said Eddie *wasn't* attracted to men.'

'For all my naïvety, DC Patel, one thing I do know is that rape isn't about attraction. It isn't even about sex. It's about

349

power. Anger and power.' He closed his eyes, looking sick. 'Eddie hated Stefano's power, he was jealous of it, he wanted it. So, one night, when he'd been drinking, he went to Stef's study and he took it.'

Shortly afterwards, Robin suggested a break and she went to Samir's office. When she told him what Morgan had said, Samir closed his eyes briefly, hand over his mouth. For a minute, they sat in silence together. For all the pressure she'd felt since the morning Ben's body had been discovered, her keenness to know the truth was tempered with reluctance. What chain of horrors had Eddie Gillespie set in motion thirty-odd years ago? How many people had been dragged in?

'Could we ever charge him?' she said. 'Eddie.'

'Well, there's no statute of limitations on rape, as you know.'

'Yes, but unless there are some miraculous, previously unmentioned forensics, there's no evidence, either, just Morgan's word against his.'

He nodded, looking at her over steepled fingers. 'What I don't understand is why Morgan didn't say something at the time. Why not tell the police? They must have spoken to him, if he was Stefano's closest friend.'

'Because Stefano made him swear not to.'

'What, even after he was *dead*?'

'"Whatever happens", apparently – Stefano's words. "Whatever happens, no matter what, while my father is alive, you swear."'

'So why's he telling us now, then? What changed?'

'The father died.'

Samir stared at her. 'You're kidding me.'

'Two years ago, in Milan.'

Chapter Fifty-Three

'Mr Morgan,' Robin said when they resumed, 'at your office yesterday, you told us you got in touch with Eddie Gillespie after hearing he was "in a tight spot". Do you remember who you heard that from?'

He frowned. 'No, actually, I'm not sure I do.'

'Someone from school? A mutual friend?'

'Yes, it must have been.'

Robin saw Charles Colton straighten slightly, his attention sharpening.

'You keep in touch with people from Clarendon, then, despite what sounds like quite a difficult time there? Apart from what happened to Stefano, and the situation with your father, you were one of these so-called Untouchables. Who do you still talk to?'

Silence.

Colton put a hand on Morgan's forearm. 'If there's anything you don't want to answer, Alun, you can decline to comment.'

'Thank you, Charles,' Morgan said, the edge on his voice again, 'I'll do that.'

'Were you still in touch with the Fiore family?' Robin asked.

'No.'

'How did you find out that Paolo had died?'

'I looked him up. Online.'

'Right. Would it be accurate to say that when you heard that piece of news, instead of hearing about Eddie's situation "on the vine", you looked him up, too? You went looking to see what he was up to and discovered he'd played straight into your hands?'

'No comment.'

'Or perhaps you'd always kept tabs on him?'

'No comment.'

'Either way, when Eddie Gillespie was released from prison, you offered him a job in your company, the man you claim raped your best friend and likely contributed in some way to his death.'

'That I can't deny.'

'Putting aside for a moment why on earth *you* did it, why the hell did *he* accept, that's what I don't understand. All this rubbish about schools and houses and social standing, even his debts, but, really, could he, in good—'

Morgan cut her off. 'He accepted the job, Chief Inspector, because he doesn't know I know – he has no idea. He's clueless – in fact, he's completely oblivious. In *fact*, I don't think *he* even remembers what he did – I think he's just wiped it from his mind: unimportant, why waste the disc space?'

He was losing his temper. His colour was rising, his hands moving more, and faster.

Colton saw it, too, and put out the warning hand again. 'Alun, take a moment.'

But Morgan brushed him off. 'Eddie Gillespie is a monster – an amoral, oblivious *monster*. Twice winner of the Clarendon School maths prize circa 1985, yes, let us not forget *that* – pathetic – and a monster who killed Stefano as directly as if he'd held his head under the water himself, then dried off and gone back to his physics revision.'

'So what *was* your goal in offering him a job?' Robin pressed. 'You *helped* this man – this monster – whom you say essentially killed your friend?'

'I don't say it, he *did* kill him. And only someone as fucking oblivious as *Eddie*,' he laced the name with scorn, 'would not only fail to smell a rat but act as if it were only right and proper that I *should* offer him a job when he got out of jail. Of course: Alun Morgan, Untouchable, still clamouring to touch the hem of Eddie Gillespie's garment after all these years.'

'Chief Inspector, can we take a break?' said Colton.

'I'm fine,' snapped Morgan. 'They need to know who Eddie is. *What* he is.'

'Why the job offer, Alun?'

He met her eye and held it. 'Access.'

'I'm sorry?'

'That's what I wanted. That's what I've been paying for. Access.'

Robin felt a shift in the air as if a window had opened. Varan felt it, too; subtly, subconsciously, she thought, he moved his torso away from the table. From Morgan.

'Access to what?' she asked.

'Eddie's life. He stole Stefano's, destroyed it, so I wanted to mess around with his a bit.'

The hairs came up on Robin's arms. 'Mess around how?'

'Make a nuisance of myself, turn up unannounced at their house, flirt with Carolyn just enough to ruffle his feathers. More than anything, I wanted to humble him – he's fifty-one, the same age as me, but he's the most junior member of the accounts team, earns peanuts and we work him like a dog.'

Robin considered him, his high colour and blazing eyes. 'It's not enough,' she said.

'What do you mean?'

'You're angrier than that, Mr Morgan. Much angrier. I'm not saying I blame you – far from it – but I think you're so angry, you'd need more. Stefano was the first person who really saw you, his picture is on your desk more than thirty years after he died – why put yourself through having to see Eddie Gillespie at work – in *your* business – every single day?'

'Chief Inspector, might I *please* be allowed to talk to my client?'

'I'm fine, Charles,' he barked.

'Really, I—'

'I *said*, I'm fine.'

Robin went on, afraid to lose momentum. They were close, so close – she could feel it. 'Mr Morgan, at your office, you told us you knew the Heywood family and that, through a friend, you'd been going to invest in a development project of theirs.'

'Yes.'

'You said that when the project fell through, the money you'd advanced was returned, correct?'

'Yes.'

Robin paused for effect. 'Since speaking to you about it, we've looked at the Heywoods' records for the venture, which confirm that.'

He was watching her carefully. 'So . . .?'

'But we've also spoken to someone who told us that while it looked as if things were going ahead, there was a dinner for the investors' – she consulted Malia's notes – 'at a private dining room and a fight broke out. Is that correct?'

'Yes, it is.'

'Can you confirm who was fighting and what it was about?'

'*I* was fighting. I punched Heywood in the face.'

'Bill Heywood?'

354

'My wife came back from the ladies and told me he'd followed her in there. He'd pushed her into a cubicle and tried to kiss her, then stuck his hand up her dress. When she slapped him and shoved him off, he called her a frigid bitch. So yes, I lamped him.'

'And what was your reaction when you heard that Alistair Heywood, Bill's youngest son, had raped Molly Zajac?'

'I thought, like father, like son. I was disgusted, of course, but not surprised. I've seen it over and over again, at school, at university, in business – the sheer *entitlement*. It makes me sick. The boy was brought up in an environment where that was acceptable: his father assaults women. Is it any wonder he'd go out and do the same himself? See something you want? Just take it. Even if it's another human being.'

She locked eyes with him. 'Did *you* see something you wanted?'

'What?' Morgan's solicitor jumped in his seat. 'Alun, don't say another word.'

Suddenly, Morgan looked uncertain. 'What are you talking about?'

'I meant, when you heard what Alistair did, did you see an opportunity?'

A big boy did it and ran away.

The Heywoods' explanation for why the very people *they* might want to harass were conveniently being harassed by someone else: someone else had wanted to hurt Ben and Theo – or perhaps only Theo; maybe Ben was just necessary collateral damage – and to use *them* as the fall guys.

Ridiculous, she'd agreed with Peter Hailey.

'Chief Inspector,' said Colton, voice loud, 'this has gone far enough. I—'

Robin ignored him. 'Mr Morgan, when you heard what Alistair Heywood had done, and that Ben Renshaw and Theo

Gillespie were going to testify for Molly, did you see an opportunity to kill two birds with one stone? If you could get the police to believe the Heywood family were intimidating those boys, you could incur serious legal consequences for them while at the same time avenging Stefano by hurting Eddie Gillespie's boy.'

Alun Morgan looked at her, eyes glittering.

All those different acts of intimidation, the risk of being caught every time. They'd talked about the Heywoods being able to afford to outsource the work – and pay for silence afterwards – but Alun Morgan was a rich man, too. A rich man, it occurred to Robin suddenly, with unrestricted access to a size of lorry that could easily transport a car that had been involved in an 'accident' over the Channel into Europe, never to be seen again.

'Throughout our investigation,' she said, 'one of the questions my team and I have asked ourselves numerous times is why – apart from the initial attack – nothing happened to Molly, either last year or this. It's because she was a victim, isn't it? Like Stefano.'

Silence.

Robin was about to ask her next question when there was a knock on the door. *For Christ's sake, really? Now?*

Jo stuck her head in. Varan told the tape that they were pausing the interview at 3.24 p.m. and Robin stepped out into the corridor, pulling the door closed behind her.

'This had better be good.'

'I know, I'm sorry, guv, but it *is*. We've got Theo.'

Chapter Fifty-Four

In the end, for all the social media, it was the local newspaper that had done the trick. Trevor Billings, a retired postmaster in Halesowen, had been following the story via Sara Kettleborough's pieces in the *Post* and when he'd opened the door to the shed on his allotment and disturbed a young man with shaggy blond hair curled up on the cushions from his fold-out lounge chair, he'd recognised him. Theo had grabbed his backpack and made a run for it, but Billings had called the police on his mobile and by a stroke of luck, a Response car was in the area. They'd intercepted Theo three streets away and brought him directly to Rose Road.

It was seven o'clock when Varan came to let Robin know that the duty solicitor had arrived. 'It's Patricia Millard, guv,' he said.

'Good.' Theo had refused to let his mother find him representation, and whatever he'd done, whatever the truth of the situation turned out to be, Robin was glad he had someone decent on his side, given the legal fire power all the other players had brought to the table. In her fifties, Millard was a partner in a small local firm that specialised in campaigning cases and she did more than her share of *pro bono* work.

Robin finished putting her notes together and they went downstairs to start the interview.

Theo was sitting next to Millard at the table, his head down. He'd washed his hands when he'd used the loo and, by contrast to the rest of him – clothes, face and hair – they looked very clean. All Robin could see of the hair was what stuck out around the edges of a black beanie, which, despite the heat in the room, he'd declined to take off. Given his apparent mental state, she could imagine him believing it was the only thing holding his head together. When he'd been booked, his backpack had contained thirteen packs of painkillers and two-thirds of a bottle of vodka.

'How are you, Theo?' she asked, making her voice gentle.

Eyes down, he shook his head.

'You look tired. Did you sleep at the allotment every night?'

'Not the first.' His throat was thick; he cleared it. 'I slept in a library doorway to try to keep warm, but I was scared someone would see me.'

'Did you walk to Halesowen?'

A small nod.

'Via Brierley Hill?'

At that, he looked up.

'Yes, your phone was found. You wanted us to think you'd been killed, was that the idea?'

Head down again. 'Thought it would be easier for Mum.'

'Than thinking you'd done away with yourself?'

A small grunt.

'Were you really going to do it? The pills?'

'I tried. Twice. Bottled it.' He started to cry now. 'Then I realised, if I did it like that, when my body was found, they'd do an autopsy and it *wouldn't* be easier for her.' He swallowed hard, as if he had a lump of something jagged and dry stuck in his throat. 'I needed to find a different way – something that looked . . . I don't *want* to die.'

Robin shook her head. 'No.'

In a second, his expression turned fierce, defiant, as if she'd just denied him the option. 'But I don't want to be alive, either, not now.' A tear fell from the side of his nose and landed on the table.

Varan slid a box of tissues across. Theo pulled out two and immediately crushed them in his fist, as if holding on to them for dear life.

'What happened?' Robin asked.

He shook his head and sniffed. 'You know, don't you? Isn't that why I'm here?'

'I think I do but why don't you tell us?'

'Theo,' Patricia Millard cautioned. She looked to Robin. 'DCI Lyons . . .'

Robin gave her what she hoped was a vaguely reassuring look then ploughed ahead. 'You killed Ben, Theo, have I got that right?'

'I didn't *want* to, it was an accident!' he flared. 'A . . . mistake. I . . . Everything got . . . out of control. It all just got out of control.'

'How? Tell us how.'

'Because he wasn't *listening* – he wouldn't *listen* to me. And we've talked about it so much, *so many times.*' He sobbed. 'People can't be made to report if they don't *want* to. It *happened* to them, so it's *up* to them. It wasn't his right to decide to go to the police.'

Robin glanced at Varan and saw that he was frowning, too. 'Theo,' she said, 'so we're clear: Alun Morgan told you about your father and Stefano at school, what he says your father did?'

'*Yes.*'

'And you told Ben who then wanted to go to the police?'

'No, that's not *it*.' Frustration. 'I wouldn't have *cared* if he told you what my father did. I'm *glad* you know, you should. He *deserves* to pay. But it's different because the person *he* hurt is dead, he's beyond being savaged all over again in court, in the media. But *I've* seen it, I've seen what happens. Even if you win, even if you get a conviction . . .'

Robin put a hand across the table and laid it in front of him. 'Theo, I'm sorry, I don't understand. Are you saying *another* person was raped – not Stefano, someone else? You told Ben about another case, a different one, and he wanted to report it – that's what you were arguing about?'

'*Yes.*'

'I know this is very sensitive, that anything to do with StrengthInNumbers has to be confidential—'

'I can tell you,' he said. '*I* can. Because it's my story.'

Robin looked at Varan and then at Patricia Millard, whose face wore the same appalled expression.

'Theo,' Robin said, 'are you telling us *you* were raped?'

He leaned forward and put his face in his hands. 'Yes.'

The small word filled the room.

'And you confided in Ben.' The pieces of information they'd collected began to arrange themselves into a picture. She saw him next to his best friend in an empty carriage, the StrengthInNumbers event just finished, all the talk of community and support playing in his ears. 'On the train back from Worcester, your last talk.'

His surprise told her she was right.

'What happened?'

He swallowed and wiped a hand across his eyes, one then the other. 'He was great at first, that night. He was really affected – he cried. I was glad I'd told him. Just not feeling alone with it any more . . .'

Strength in numbers.

'Then two days later, he came to me and said I had to report it. If I didn't, I'd be undermining everything we'd done on the site, all our work – if it ever came out, we'd be branded as hypocrites. We needed to put our money where our mouth was, he said, but it wasn't his money, was it, it was *mine* – I was the one who'd be exposed; if the case went to court, *I'd* be the one who had to stand up and detail every little thing that happened to *me*.'

'And you told him this?'

'Over and over and over again, and he just wouldn't listen. If I wouldn't go to the police, he said, it was his responsibility: my attacker had to be brought to justice, I owed it to anyone he might attack in the future.'

'But when you'd told him you didn't want to,' said Varan, 'asked him—'

'I didn't ask – I *begged*.'

'Why couldn't he respect that?'

'Because he'd lost sight of what it was really about. For him, it wasn't about the individual cases any more or *people*, it was a mission – *his* mission. With school shutting us down, he was scared that it would all just go away. The profile it gave him, all the articles in the papers and talking on TV . . .'

Robin remembered Kaia Powell, the graduate student. *When the others got disheartened, he was the one who got them fired up again.*

'I asked him to meet me at Moseley Bog,' Theo sobbed, 'so that we could have a smoke and calm down, try and sort things out, but he just wouldn't let it go, he just wouldn't *stop*. When he got up to leave and told me again "for the final time" that if I wouldn't report it, he would, I . . . I didn't mean to do it – the thought never . . . But the idea that he would actually do that, take what had happened to me and . . . The *feeling* – I can't explain it. He was turning to go – a couple of feet away on the ground, there was a branch – I bent down and grabbed it. I just wanted him to *stop*.'

He put his arms on the table and buried his face in them. Maybe a minute passed before they heard him say, 'He was my best friend. My best friend.'

Chapter Fifty-Five

They'd been careful not to let the news of Theo's return reach Alun Morgan. When Robin and Varan re-entered his interview room at almost 10 p.m., they took their seats and Varan started the tape again without saying a word. Morgan's face told her that he'd registered the change in their demeanour and knew it boded ill.

'Mr Morgan, Mr Colton, since we last spoke, there have been two significant developments in the case.'

'Good,' said Colton decisively, as if it were a given they would be exonerating.

'One's good,' she said, letting her eyes flick onto Morgan's face. 'Theo Gillespie has been found alive and well – physically well, at least.'

'Really? Oh, that *is* good news – great news.' Colton seemed genuinely pleased.

'Perhaps not so good for your client, though, I'm afraid,' said Robin. 'Before he was found, we had reason to believe that Theo Gillespie was connected in some way to the death of Ben Renshaw. What we didn't know was what exactly had happened or why. We've spoken to Theo this evening and he was able to answer both those questions.'

He was trying, but Alun Morgan couldn't now hide his alarm.

Colton was watching Robin keenly. 'Would you care to enlighten us?'

'It seems Ben was killed because he was threatening to come to us – I mean West Midlands Police as a whole, not Homicide specifically – with information about a serious crime. Theo had given him the information in confidence and since Ben was his oldest friend, he didn't have any reason to believe he would break that trust. Unfortunately for them both, Ben surprised him.'

'What's going on here?' Colton demanded. 'What crime?'

'On their way home from their last StrengthInNumbers school visit about three weeks ago, sir, Theo Gillespie told Ben that he'd been raped by your client.'

'What?' Stunned, Colton looked at Morgan but Morgan refused to meet his eye.

'How did it happen, Alun?' Robin asked. 'We've heard it from Theo, but now we need to hear it from you.'

Nothing. Morgan had bowed his head so that his chin almost touched his chest. He was so quiet that only when a tear dropped onto his shirt front did they realise he was crying.

He sniffed and rubbed the back of his hand under his nose as if he was a child. 'It was like a nightmare,' he said. 'A nightmare. But I've never woken up.'

'What happened, Mr Morgan?'

He swallowed. 'The Gillespies had a party. Eddie would never have invited us, but Carolyn did. On the day, though, my wife wasn't well, so I ended up going on my own. Part of my plan to make Eddie's life fun,' he said bitterly, 'introduce myself to people as his boss in a loud voice so that he could hear me, nothing much worse than that. But the drinks went down too quickly and being there, in his house – I hated him. *Hated* him. To see him standing there laughing, having a good time – after what he'd done? It made me sick.'

'Why didn't you leave?'

'I was going to. I was actually in the hallway, my phone was in my hand to call a taxi when Carolyn saw me and told me I couldn't go before she'd had a chance to introduce me to these friends of hers she wanted me to meet. We went back into the kitchen, but they were deep in conversation with other people and I'd reached a point where I just couldn't stand another minute in a room with Eddie, so I told Carolyn I needed some fresh air. Their garden's large and when I got out there and walked across the lawn, I smelled weed from the far end. I went to investigate.'

'Did you know it would be Theo smoking?' asked Varan.

'I don't remember having the thought at the time,' he said, letting tears drop into his lap unobstructed, 'but afterwards I thought I must have – the party where Alistair raped Molly, Theo and Ben were outside smoking weed, weren't they? On some level, I must have known, because when I reached him, I already knew I was going to tell him what Eddie did. God, the irony,' he sniffed and rubbed his nose again, 'I remember thinking that, *The irony*, that one of the kids who set up StrengthInNumbers was the son of a rapist.'

'What happened?'

'We talked for a couple of minutes,' Morgan swallowed again. 'He was stoned, I was drunk – and I told him.'

'How did he react?'

'He didn't believe me, just wouldn't hear it. I brought up a photo of Stefano on my phone – a picture I took of the one on my desk, I don't have many – and he knocked the phone out of my hand. It was that gesture – that "get away from me", the utter lack of regard. It was horror, I know that now – he was horrified at what I was telling him – of course he was – but it didn't feel like that. In that moment, it felt like he was telling me Stefano was worth nothing.'

He looked at them and his expression was incredulous, as if he were recounting something he knew he'd seen but still couldn't make sense of. 'The anger,' he said. 'No, it was *rage*. I did what I did, they were my actions, I know that, I own them, but it was like madness – I was out of my mind, out of my *body*. Before I knew it, he was on the ground and I . . .'

With a terrible guttural cry more animal than human, he fell forward, forehead hitting the desk. He covered his head with his hands, back heaving.

Varan looked at Robin with the mix of horror and dismay she knew was on her own face, as if he, like her, could feel the sound of Morgan's weeping in his bones.

Chapter Fifty-Six

It was only five days before Christmas now, but the sky was high and sheer, blue as a day in May. Pitiless, was the word that came to Robin's mind as they walked up the road to the church through clouds of their own breath, a blithe preview of next summer and the one after that, summers Ben and Anne and Stefano would never see, in which they'd exist only as memories and photographs, stories that had ended far too soon and had begun the slow process of losing their detail and dissolving into history. *Life goes on – next!* The sharpness of the air made Robin's eyes smart.

Today, however, Ben was the focus, the reason for the thick column of people moving up the church path and those still waiting their turn in the road outside the lychgate. He was the reason for the press photographers, too, though the uniforms at the barriers held them away from the mourners, the majority of whom, Robin saw as they got nearer, were his own age, friends and classmates – she recognised Mo, and Lily with him. Perhaps, she thought, some were people helped by his work on StrengthInNumbers, come to say thank you.

Regardless of the sky, the churchyard was white over, frost glittering on the grass and headstones. Time on ice, suspended.

Amy would be here today. Given special dispensation to attend the funeral, though not the wake, she was being brought from the young offenders institute where she was waiting sentencing. She was probably in her seat already, Robin thought, brought early by her escort and tucked in at the front of the church with her family so she wouldn't have to – or couldn't – face anyone else. Her sentencing was scheduled for the beginning of February and they hoped that her age and grief would be given due weight in the decision. With the planning she'd done, however, and the use of petrol, it would be years, not months. Certainly, she would spend the rest of her teens imprisoned.

Robin had lost any faith she might have had by the time she started secondary school but the thought of Amy's situation made her want to offer prayers of gratitude anyway. *Thank you for keeping my child safe, for allowing the man she hit to make a full recovery, for the CCTV blind spot that kept what she did invisible.*

And for Luke. Yes, thank you, for Luke, who protected her.

At his sentencing, the judge had handed Luke a total of six years – four for his own crime, two for Lennie's. He wouldn't serve six – with good behaviour, it would come down substantially – but again, he'd be inside for years. They'd all known it was coming, they'd tried to prepare themselves, but the reality of it lay heavy on the whole family, Lennie especially.

Never one to miss an occasion where there might be a camera, Kilmartin made a show of spotting them across the crowd and began to weave his way over. 'Samir, Robin. Dreadful day, dreadful day.' He looked excited by it, the brass buttons on his dress uniform glinting in the hard light. As he moved to stand next to her, she wondered what he was doing, then followed his glance to one of the photographers, who, sure enough, was taking their picture. 'That's a beautiful coat, by the way,' he said out of the side of his mouth. 'You look terrific – very professional.'

She and Samir had timed their arrival so that they could slip in at the back without drawing attention to themselves, and inside the church, they took the last available half-pew at the back. Kilmartin sidled in next to them so that she was sandwiched between him and Samir, both their upper arms pressed against hers, their thighs touching if any of them moved. A tapestried hassock bumped her knees.

Two rows ahead, she spotted a dark head, and as if feeling the pressure of her eyes, Peter Hailey turned and gave her a small smile. On her left flank, she felt Samir shift slightly.

The expectant murmur of a large body of people laced with the sound of sobbing from the front was eclipsed suddenly by a booming chord from the organ and, over her shoulder, Robin first sensed rather than saw the coffin, glossy and ink black, carried high on the shoulders of six young men, Mo and Pierre, then others, cousins, she guessed, or family friends. On her right, Kilmartin shuddered theatrically at the memento mori.

Just as the doors were closed, Robin saw movement in the shadows at the back of the church on the other side: a tall woman, fair, very thin, in a black coat and hat. Robin leaned back so that she could see around Kilmartin. Yes, she'd been right: it was Carolyn Gillespie.

The coffin was laid on its trestle at the front and the vicar welcomed them to the church and told them that they were gathered today to celebrate the life of Benjamin George Renshaw. A life that, although short, he said, had been lived to the fullest and dedicated to God's truth, 'even when that brought him into jeopardy, even when, finally, it cost him his life'. At that, she looked at Samir and saw her own misgivings reflected in his eyes. They'd wondered if, as time started to pass, the Renshaws would begin to see the nuance of the situation, but no, or at least not yet. For now, to make sense of it all, give them something to cling on to, Ben would remain the valiant campaigner, the one who turned the torch on those things that others would try – even kill – to keep secret.

'My son,' began Roger Renshaw's eulogy over a gulping sob from the first pew, 'my shining sun.'

Afterwards, they made their way out and into the hard light of the churchyard again, where Robin and Samir moved to the fringes and waited to see if they would be allowed to pay their respects to the Renshaws. Kilmartin spotted a smartly dressed couple, thankfully, and darted off at unseemly speed to talk to them. As she watched his departing back, Robin caught sight of Marni Weston.

Feeling a hand on her arm, she turned to see Molly Zajac. In black coat, black tights and lace-up shoes, the gate and the old stone church behind her, she looked like a Victorian orphan. Her skin was so pale, Robin could see the blue of a vein in her temple.

'I'm so sorry, Molly.' Robin met her swollen eyes and hoped she would know she meant not for Ben – though that, too – but for Theo: he was also in custody, also waiting to hear how many of the next years of his life would be spent there. Unlike Amy, at least what he'd done had been impulsive, the act of a moment. That would weigh heavily in his favour.

'I still think it's my fault,' Molly said, barely audible over the low rumble of people beginning to make moves towards their cars and the reception at Emma's mother's house in Solihull. 'If I hadn't reported and pressed charges, none of this would have happened. Ben, Amy, Theo . . .'

'No,' said Samir, reaching out to grip the top of her arm. 'You did the right thing – absolutely the right thing. You brought Alistair Heywood to account and you stopped him doing it again, to someone else. You did what you *had* to do.'

'This started long before you – long,' Robin told her. 'What

Alistair did to you wasn't the beginning, it was part of a cycle and *you* ended it. Please believe that – hold on to it.'

'Thank you.' She looked down. 'I will.'

'I'm sorry about you and Theo. You loved each other, it was so obvious. What happened to you both was . . .'

Molly tipped her head to the side, birdlike. When she looked up again, her eyes were bright. 'We still do,' she said very quietly. She glanced around as if she were afraid that if anyone heard, they might set about her. 'If anyone can understand what he did, how he felt, it's me. I don't know what'll happen, obviously, but his lawyer thinks they might take what happened to him into consideration when it comes to sentencing.'

'Yes,' Samir said. 'I think so, too.'

Molly nodded quickly. 'Well, I'd better . . .' She turned to look at the crowd behind her, briefly back at them again, then was gone.

They were not going to be allowed to give the family their condolences. As if shielding them from her and Samir, their inner circle formed a group around Roger and Emma Renshaw and rushed them past to a waiting black car. From the safety of the back seat, Roger Renshaw met her eye, held the stare, then turned his head away.

Samir saw it. 'OK?' he said quietly.

'Yes.'

The Renshaws' car started to move off, but it had only gone about ten feet when it stopped again. The back door on the opposite side cranked open and they watched Emma Renshaw get out and start weaving through the mourners still gathered outside the gate. Robin shifted to see who she was looking for and caught sight of Carolyn Gillespie walking quickly away down the walled lane opposite.

Emma was walking so fast, she was almost running. 'Carolyn.'

Carolyn stopped but didn't turn.

Robin saw unease ripple through the crowd – was there going to be a scene? Should they do something – step in? A couple of men in their forties separated themselves from the edge of the group and started in their direction as quickly as they decently could, but Emma had built up enough of a lead that they couldn't intercept her in time.

As the sound of her footsteps grew closer, Carolyn turned and the women faced off, three or four feet of road between them. They looked at one another and then – impossible to say who moved first – they came together.

They held each other tightly for at least a minute, then pulled away. Emma appeared to say something, then, with a nod, she turned, walked back towards the car and got in. Almost immediately, it pulled off again and drove away.

Robin turned to Samir to find that he'd been watching her.

'Straight back to the ranch now,' he said, 'or do you need a drink first?'

'Drink.'

'Correct answer.'

As they walked back down the street to his car, he reached out and put his arm through hers.

Acknowledgements

Thank you first to my fantastic agent, Victoria Hobbs at A.M. Heath, for whose support and wisdom I am so grateful.

With this book, Robin and I have joined the remarkable team at Orion, where I am lucky enough to work with the excellent Sam Eades, Lindsay Sutherland, Ellen Turner, Ellie Nightingale and Snigdha Koirala. Thank you all, and thank you Katie Espiner, for your faith and match-making skills! I'm grateful, too, to Francesca Pathak and Sarah Benton for all they contributed to this book.

Thank you to Colin Scott, to John Sutherland for his very helpful police notes, and to Sarah Heller, for kinds words just when I needed them.

Polly Whitehouse and Guy Meacock, without you my UK visits wouldn't be possible. Suzy and Paul Rosen, without the at-home writing retreats, this book would never have been finished. Thank you all – I appreciate you more than you know.

Finally, again – and always – the biggest of thanks to Joe and the Bridge for the love, the ridiculousness and the enduring tolerance.

Credits

Lucie Whitehouse and Orion Fiction would like to thank everyone at Orion who worked on the publication of *Last Witness* in the UK.

Editorial
Sam Eades
Snigdha Koirala

Copy editor
Jade Craddock

Proof reader
Laetitia Grant

Audio
Paul Stark
Jake Alderson

Contracts
Dan Herron
Ellie Bowker

Design
Tomás Almeida
Joanna Ridley

Editorial Management
Charlie Panayiotou
Jane Hughes
Bartley Shaw

Finance
Jasdip Nandra
Nick Gibson
Sue Baker

Marketing
Lynsey Sutherland

CREDITS

Production
Ruth Sharvell

Publicity
Ellen Turner

Sales
Jen Wilson
Esther Waters
Victoria Laws

Toluwalope Ayo-Ajala
Rachael Hum
Ellie Kyrke-Smith
Georgina Cutler

Operations
Jo Jacobs

376